*Other Books*
*by*

# *M. A. Farrell*

## *Fiction:*

### *STATE OF MINE - Volume I*

### *STATE OF MINE - ReWrite - Volume III*

## *Fact – Political:*

**The Cloud and The Rose Garden**
**(How Wall Street & Washington Broke Capitalism)**

F I R S T E D I T I O N
Printed on acid-free paper
Library of Congress Cataloging-in-Publication data has been applied for

ISBN 9780984696604

# IN GOLD WE TRUST

*A peoples' money is their reflection. If it is strong and respected, so too are they. If it be weak and debased, so too are the makers.*

- Milton Bern

Professor of Economics

Secretary of the Treasury, Wyoming


*The problem is not the Federal government. The problem is Federalism!*

- Joseph Bascomb

Resistance Radio Spokesperson

Somewhere-in-hiding, USA

# CHAPTERS

# Prologue

America is mired in an endless depression brought on by the Federal government's debasement of the dollar and uncontrolled spending. Second term President Rivera has declared the situation a national emergency, granting himself wartime powers and ever-increasing autocracy. To ensure the President's hold on power, a domestic agency reporting to Homeland Security has been in existence for nearly ten years. The purpose of the Department for Domestic Disturbances (DDD) is to crush dissent against the Administration's mounting failures.

An agent of the DDD, Joshua Stillwater, has been ordered to infiltrate the tight-knit society of Wyoming. With most States dependent upon Federal bail-outs to stave off bankruptcy, they have ceded their waning power to Federalism expanding within Washington D.C. Yet Wyoming, a State that has chosen open opposition to Federal dictates, is thriving, enjoying a renaissance of technology, innovation and prosperity. And they base it all upon mountains of gold acquired as backing for their every-strengthening currency, the Wyoming Credits, or WC. The first of Stillwater's mission parameters is to find the gold. The second is to understand from where Wyoming's success derives.

And the third is to apprehend or terminate a former, number-one radio-talk-show host that is relentless against the excesses of the Federal government; the President and the DDD being a favorite target. Joseph Bascomb's clandestine broadcasts heap the greatest praise upon the economic miracle blossoming within Wyoming. Banned from the airwaves by Federal law, Bascomb has gone *underground* and there have been sightings of him within Wyoming.

Joshua Stillwater faces a dilemma of duality. Being born and raised in Wyoming, he is torn between loyalty to old friends and his requirement to satisfy the demands of his boss and head of the DDD, Robert Maxton. For fifteen years Stillwater has been away from the State, self-exiled after a broil with one of the Wyoming's most powerful men, Charles Warner. The fight left Stillwater emotionally scarred, for he had revered Warner since Josh was a boy. He was raised on Warner's ranch which led, as circumstance can, to a passionate love for Sam, Samantha. The problem: she is Warner's daughter, and one of only two children, along with brother Ben Warner. Stillwater, half American-Indian and half White, is seen by the powerful rancher as below his daughter's social station. Charlie Warner has big plans for daughter and son. Joshua Stillwater is a fly-in-the-ointment that could ruin those plans. With Joshua returned, Warner is not a happy man.

1

Stillwater has one homecoming that is warm and stirring, this with the Dillons. Jake Dillon, his wife Louise and their two sons, Jeff and Jimmy, are the ones that have always accepted Joshua; treating him as family. Although Jake and Jeff haven't changed in Stillwater's eyes, he is surprised that the now-dynamo inventor and entrepreneur, Jimmy, is gay. Jimmy and his life-partner William are MIT alum, inventing futuristic products that contribute to the State's thriving economy and, with their combined super-IQ's, have produced a surrogate son of equal intellect: Bernard.

During a hunting trip with Ben on Dillon's land, Joshua reacts quickly against an assassination attempt upon his once-best friend. The aftermath is Ben's appreciation of Stillwater's military background and an offer to join the State's efforts to fend off the Federal government's ceaseless pressure for Wyoming to conform to Federal law. Joshua tries to understand if Ben has knowledge, or at least suspicion, of Stillwater's real purpose in Wyoming. *If he knew, would he be making the offer, and why?* It appears an impossible scenario for Joshua. If he *defected* to Wyoming's cause, it would be he, not Bascomb, heading the list of the government's *Most Wanted*. He declines Ben's offer for the moment. But it continues to pick at the back of his brain.

Could he really *come home?*

His scales could tip either way. And he knows a major influence to be the person he is now on the way to visit, Sam. Does she still carry the torch that now has rekindled a flame within him?

There's only one way to find out.

# Chapter 1

## Smooth Ride

### Casper to Cheyenne

Josh stood on the platform of the Casper-to-Cheyenne high speed train. It had been one of his stranger mornings. It only dawned on him now that Ben Warner, Charlie Warner's son and once-best-friend of Joshua, had been hunting more than antelope back on Dillon's ranch. Josh's services had been his target. It was unsettling. Was he supposed to be flattered by Ben or fear him? It was now obvious that Ben's role in this State's actions against the Federal government was not passive. But what was he, Josh, supposed to do? To whom was his loyalty?

He now thought back to how the morning had ended. After the assassination attempt on Ben by a ghillie-suited sniper, Ben and he galloped the horses back to Ben's truck, without talking. They had driven to the ranch house, without talking. They had hung from a tree the antelope Josh nailed earlier that morning with a three-hundred-plus meter shot. Still no words between them. They had circled the legs with Ben's knife, and split the skin downward, without talking. Then they tugged the skin, undressing the animal, until the outer pelt reached its head. Ben had grabbed a battery-operated sawsall, removed the head and skin and then split the carcass in half, all in silence. They took a canvas bag Louise had provided, pulled it up over the meat and tied the string ends. Ben had gone inside, said his goodbyes, and reemerged outside. Stepping into his pickup, he leaned out the opened window, face turned to Josh. He opened his mouth to say something, but then turned his head back and gave a wave. Josh waved back, noting Ben's focus on the side-view mirror. Josh kept his gaze until the eyes disappeared within the roiling dust cloud of Ben's departure.

William and Jimmy had long since departed for their Guardsmen duties. Jake was prepping the futuristic *LectricAire*, an all-electric plane designed and built by his brilliant son Jimmy. Jake was preparing to shuttle Josh the short distance to Casper, where the former Army Captain – now DDD agent – would pick up his investigation of the recalcitrant State.

While Jake walked the perimeter of the plane, Josh went into the house and changed from his hunting clothes of the morning. As he packed his few belongings, Josh nodded towards the entrance of his room at the

3

appearance of Louise, Jake's wife. Ten-year-old Bernard, Jimmy and William's surrogate son, stood next to Louise. After Josh collected his carryall the threesome made their way out onto the front stoop. Louise pulled him down and threw her arms around his neck. She hugged him hard, hesitating to release her grip. When she finally released, she was staring into Josh with unflinching eyes. Her voice was low, but her words were strong, "Joshua Stillwater, for once in your life, think before you start running away."

***

Emotion flooded him as he now recalled the words. Trying to clear his vision, he looked around the modern train terminal in which he was ensconced. It was in the middle of Casper, underground. Jake had landed the **LectricAire** at the old Natrona County Airport, where Josh had grabbed a CityCar for the station.

The rail terminal was ultra-modern. A thick, glass ceiling overhead doubled as the floor level of an atrium-centered, downtown mall. Below, train platforms were numbered one through twelve. Moving walkways arched overhead, allowing ease of transit from one platform to the next. The train Josh now stood before had originated in Portland. Soon it would be on its way to Cheyenne. But there were short-haul trains running exclusively between Casper-Cheyenne and Casper-Gillette. These were more frequent than trains arriving from out-of-State.

As the rails of each train platform dead-ended within the terminal, attendants entered each car and flipped rows of seats up and over, facing them in the opposite direction. This design Wyoming had borrowed from Asia. But it was one of the thousand little things Josh had seen in Wyoming that made so much sense. A stark comparison to the hopelessness, grayness and idleness of the surrounding bankrupt nation, this vibrant State was growing on him.

A soft chime sounded and a woman's voice announced that the Cheyenne train was ready for boarding at the platform where Josh now stood. The doors opened and people milling nearby entered. The train would be nearly full, but no one pushed or elbowed. There was no reason as seats were pre-assigned. He carried on his duffel and garment bag. A large, open bull-pen for luggage was just inside the door. Rods for hanging bags ran above the bin. Additionally, metal shelving ran, both sides of the aisle, the length of the car. Josh stowed his luggage, checked his seat number, walked down the aisle and took the seat nearest the window. It was as wide as a first class airline seat, had a foot rest that extended forward at a forty-five degree angle and a back that reclined nearly the same degree. The combination was comfortable, even for Josh's six-foot-four frame.

In another ten minutes a voice announced the train's departure in five minutes. He looked at his watch and noted the time. When the mag-lev, superconducting train pulled away from the station, it was at the scheduled departure time to the minute. Speed built with ease and quietness. The only sensation of acceleration was a slight pressure pushing him into his seat. Within minutes they were in open prairie and doing over five hundred kilometers per hour. The sensation was eerie as the train rode on a cushion of air that was actually a magnetic field. There were no clickity-clack sounds of the rail or jarring of cars as they rounded a bend. It was actually smoother than an airplane. No screaming engines, angles of climb or descent, air turbulence, or hard landings. With the speedy delivery to the terminal by CityCar - the electric, individually-navigated transit car system that reigned exclusively within Wyoming's major cities - the short walk to the train and the ease of boarding, Josh found no flaws in Jimmy's prior adulations of the State's emphasis upon technological leaps in transportation. The best part would be the lack of waiting for luggage at the other end.

The window view took some getting used to. Fortunately the rail bed perched the train several meters above the electrified, three-meter high fencing that demarked the right of way on both sides. This gave an obstruction-free view of the expansive prairie and the beginning of Colorado's Rocky Mountains to the south. There were no electric poles flashing by as the train sat upon a magnetic field created by the Meissner effect within a large, superconducting cable buried between rails. Jimmy Dillon had explained this to Josh during his visit to *Dillon & Dillon Industries*, the amazing conglomerate of futuristic-tech manufacturing that Jimmy and his partner William Dillon had birthed outside Gillette.

Due to the train's incredible land speed, anything closer than a couple of miles was a blur, potentially upsetting to a stomach. But, as with Josh's earlier ride in the **Thompson**, a bullet-shaped, hydrogen-fueled car given to Jimmy by a customer of the same name, Josh had learned to focus on objects far away.

He rose and made his way from his seat to the club car. The latter was about half full. People were sitting at tables either talking with one another or staring into space. Joshua was now familiar with the small black disc affixed atop some heads. The eyes of these passengers showed the fixed gaze of **Neu-Net**, the neural-implant communications network growing in popularity within the State. It was another of the State's incredible technologies, whereby a bio-electric connection with an individual's brain neurons could broadcast voice and sight between users that had been implanted. And, as with most accepted technologies, the slang *Netting* had emerged. The site of someone with a disc upon their head, combined with the thousand-yard stare meant one was communicating with another party. Josh had originally thought the technology creepy, an unacceptable invasion of the body. But as his knowledge and familiarity with the system grew, he had softened his predjudice of **Neu-Net** as some *Cyborg* takeover of humanity.

His view swung away from the *Netters* to an automated bar at one end of the club car. It dispensed beer and wine for a charge. A soft-drink and assorted water dispenser was at the car's other end. He didn't need a beer this early in the morning, but wanted to see how well an automated beer dispenser worked. He pulled out his plastic WC's card, the coin of realm within Wyoming, pressed the backing magnetic strip and thumb protruding through a hole in the card, upon a screen and then followed the digital instructions. A large plastic cup dropped beneath a liquid dispenser. He chose his desired brand of beer from six names displayed. The cup began filling until, halfway, the dispenser stopped and waited as the foamy head dissipated. After this brief interlude it continued to fill, but at a slower rate until the amber fluid was nearly to the top. *A perfect pour*, Josh thought, smiling.

After taking a long tug and licking foam from upper lip, he continued his survey of the club car. There were four glass booths along one side. They were privacy booths for phone calls. Two of the booths were of frosted glass, the other two clear. The frosting indicated they were occupied. When a user departed, the glass frosting cleared. It worked via an electrical charge exciting a gas within panes. Josh had seen this same concept used for offices and conference rooms at Jake's and his oldest son's downtown Casper office building for *Dillon Enterprises*.

Joshua thought about his obligation to check in with Tex, another DDD agent paralleling Josh's efforts, and his inept and surly boss, Robert Maxton. It depressed him. *What am I supposed to tell them? Do they want to hear how squared away these people are? How their economy is booming while the rest of the country is sucking wind? How they tried to recruit me?* He knew the first two items neither Tex nor Maxton would care. But the third, Ben's attempt at recruitment, would be appealing to their devious minds. Recruitment would put Josh behind the curtain, privy to Wyoming's secrets. Could he be that duplicitous to people who placed trust in him?

Right now he was merely a spy. Entering their camp under a false flag, he became a potential traitor.

He mentally scraped together details he had learned or seen. If he could tell Maxton one compelling fact, he could skip the recruiting angle. But items of great import were slim: their currency wasn't really a currency. It was credits and debits on a State computerized ledger. But it was backed by, and convertible to gold. The State had a wealth of energy resources: coal, natural gas, hydroelectric, wind, geothermal, and, apparently confirmed by Jake Dillon, nuclear. Nearly all of natural resources were used for generation of electricity, powering an all-electric society. Ten year-old Bernard had slipped by mentioning the name **WyStar**, and this had tightened everyone's sphincters. Ben had stopped just short of confirming Joseph Bascomb's presence with the State.

Before the Federal *Sedition Act* and before accompanying FCC rulings to muzzle dissent upon the airwaves, Bascomb had been the nation's number-one talk-radio commentator. His vociferous attacks exposed the human cost and the economy's loss through increasing centralization of Federal power, the increasing autocracy of President Rivera, and the unconstitutional threat of Rivera's secret police; Josh's employer, the DDD. Refusing to cede to the FCC clamp down, Bascomb continued his jibes, barbs and exposés. This brought him imprisonment. Yet his dedicated followers affected his escaped, whisking him away to a protective sanctuary. He continued broadcasting clandestinely, becoming the voice of growing resistance to the expansion and centralization of Federalism. Bascomb became an icon to those that resisted and anathema to those he verbally assailed. He ranked Number One on the DDD's Enemies List. Catching or killing this agitator and muckraker would pull a major thorn from the Administration's side as well as raising Robert Maxton's star within the Department of Homeland Security's bureaucracy.

Was a strong suspicion of Bascomb's whereabouts sufficient for reporting? Josh shrugged. He knew Maxton would go into a rant of how worthless Josh was, but so be it. He looked at his watch. With the time difference between here and D.C., he hoped Maxton was out to lunch.

Josh ducked his head as he entered one of the clear booths. He sat on a leather upholstered bench. Apparently weight upon the seat activated the glass frosting as the panes clouded for his privacy. Joshua pulled out his cell phone and punched Maxton's speed dial number. The phone barely had time to ring before his boss's shrill voice answered, "Where the hell you been? I haven't heard anything for nearly three days. I didn't send you out there on vacation! You better have something damn important to report."

"Nice to talk to you too, boss," Josh wanted to tell him to go to hell, but this was as frosty as he thought it prudent.

"Don't give me your wiseass crap, Stillwater. Tell me what you've found out, and it better be good."

"Well, I've got a pretty strong confirmation that Bascomb is here."

Josh could envision Maxton gripping the phone tightly. His voice dropped a few decibels, "Where? You got his location? Tell me now and we can assemble a team and have them on the way in two hours."

"Hold yer horses. I said I pretty-well confirmed he's here, in the State. I didn't say I had him located."

"That's it? Hell we already knew that! What smoke are you trying to blow up my ass?"

"Before I left, you said it was *thought* he was here." Josh knew he was going to have to say something stronger than pretty sure. "So I'm telling you I'm confirming that. It's a confirmation you didn't have forty-eight hours ago."

Maxton was grumbling something unintelligible. Josh fell silent, allowing Maxton restart the conversation.

"Ok, you got a confirmation. Now get me a location. Hell, better than that, kill the sonofabitch. You've killed people before. Earn your pay, Mr. Special Forces."

Josh thought he earned his pay just having to listen to Maxton. This he didn't say.

"I got something else."

"What?"

"The word, or name or acronym **WyStar**, mean anything to you?"

"No, what the hell is it?"

"I don't know, but it sure gets people here uptight."

"How was it used? Who said it?"

"It was accidentally dropped in conversation by a..er....friend," Remembering it was the child Bernie's misspeak before adults, Josh wanted to say 'kid' just to hear Maxton's reaction, but thought better. "Everyone got all tight jawed at the slip and the friend got stink-eye from the crowd. Just thought it might be important."

Maxton was quiet on the other end for a few moments. Then he said, "Sounds like crap to me, but I'll run it by some people. That all you got?"

"Yeah, right now."

"Where are you?"

"I'm on a train heading to Cheyenne."

"Train? Sounds too quiet to be a train. You shacked up with some pro in a motel?"

"No, I'm on a train. And if you don't believe me, tough shit."

"Watch your mouth, Indian boy. What's in Cheyenne?"

"An old girlfriend." Joshua was referring to Samantha, Sam. Ben and Samantha Warner were siblings, the two children of Charlie Warner. Joshua had grown up on the same ranch with the two, as his Anglo mother had been cook and maid for the ranch hands. It was an affair between his mother and a Shoshoni ranch hand that had spawned Josh. When Josh was two his Dad headed for the mountains of Montana, deserting Josh's mother. This left her to eke out a living on Charlie Warner's five-hundred thousand acre ranch - *Five Fingers*. Charlie had been nice enough to build a small, clapboard house for Josh and his mother.

Josh's life had been intertwined with *Five Fingers* and the Warners until he left as a teenager. Returning when he was twenty-five and on leave from the Army, Josh and Sam secretly began a torrid romance. But, by Charlie Warner's script, Sam was destined for greater things than a half-breed Indian boy whose greatest aim in life was to kill for his country. Sniffing out the affair, Charlie confronted them in a barn, and in the throes of passion. The ensuing, one-sided battle left Josh battered, embarrassed and ashamed. He could never openly assault the man that was his ideal as a surrogate father. Instead, he endured the beating as just punishment.

Warner banished him from *Five Fingers* and Josh began a fifteen-year self-exile from his friends and family in Wyoming.

Maxton jumped on the mention of a girlfriend, "Shit, I knew you were just there to bang some broad. I'm telling you Stillwater, if…"

"Just shut up for once, Maxton, or I'm going to hang up."

The line was silent again. Josh finally spoke, "She works for the Governor of the State. With a little luck and a little prodding, I may be able to find out what's going on around here."

"I would have expected you to burrow in deeper with your connections. I don't know if you're even worth the time and expense. If I was smart, I'd tell you to pack it in and get back here. Hell, *Canary* has more going on than you, and he's never even been there before?"

Josh tensed, "Like what?" *Canary* was the code name for another DDD agent that Maxton had sent into Wyoming. Josh and he had communicated by phone. Stillwater didn't know who the agent was, didn't even know what he looked like. Only *Canary*'s southern drawl had given Josh a clue from where the man hailed. He was a Texan, leading Josh to call him 'Tex.'

"What do you mean, 'like what'?"

"You said *Canary* has something going. What is it?"

"Ask him yourself. You guys are supposed to be communicating. You've got twenty-four hours to get something good or I'm pulling your plug. Got it?"

Josh understood the *pulling-plug* reference and all its ramifications. Successful in his career as Captain in Army Special Forces, Stillwater had been served up to a general court martial for cowardice. It was a ludicrous and egregious lie. Stillwater's record in the Army was one of courage and valor, mission after mission. He had won a slew of medals as proof. Yet one mission, his final, became a disaster resulting in several wounded men under Stillwater's command. The cause was cowardice of newbie officer. It was Joshua's bad luck that the newbie was also the son of a U.S. Senator. It was even worse luck the Senator was Chairman of the Armed Services Committee. The facts were seriously skewed and skewered until *Stillwater*, not the Senator's son, became the perpetrator of cowardice. He was convicted, dishonorably discharged and given seven years at the United States Disciplinary Barracks, Fort Leavenworth,

Leavenworth, Kansas. In a weird twist of events, Robert Maxom of the DDD entered into Stillwater's life. Literally a back-room deal allowed Joshua to escape prison time if he joined the DDD. The catch was, he would have to serve seven years with the DDD. At any time, for any reason during this period, Maxton could fire him, which meant a direct trip for Stillwater to Leavenworth to serve the full seven, no time off for DDD service. Pulling Josh's plug was a reminder of Maxton's constant power over Josh's life, at least for a few more years.

Twenty-four hours left Stillwater no time. He had to play out some line to Maxton. Keep him on the hook. The guy had to think Josh was valuable and, therefore, allowed to continue his mission. There was only one interesting piece of the puzzle he had found. He was mulling over potential harm to Wyoming versus potential interest to Maxton.

"Stillwater, you still there?"

"Yeah, yeah. Now listen. This could be important to your people. This State is exporting energy, and a lot of it. It is the main money source that got all this economic activity rolling. I don't know how they're getting it out, but they are."

"You mean they're sending energy to other States?" Maxton had firmly bit.

"More than other States, other Countries. They're moving electricity internationally."

"Now that is something! The President would love grabbing that energy and redistributing it to those in need. It would sure boost his popularity, and cut down our oil imports." Maxton paused a moment. "Forget the twenty-four hours, Stillwater. You find out how they generate it and how they ship it, or transport, or send, or whatever in the hell they call it."

Josh smiled. The hook was firmly set. He just hoped it wouldn't prove too valuable, that any harm to Wyoming's efforts would come from the knowledge. Another point hit him.

"And by the way, if anyone's interested, tell them this entire State is mobilized. You should already know this from birds overhead. Every able bodied man and woman is in a Wyoming State Army unit and uniform. Not a National Guard uniform, a State Army uniform. And they're having military maneuvers all this week. This whole State is a bee hive. I just hope they aren't in possession of any stingers."

Maxton ruminated, "Yea, makes sense, the mobilization thing. That's probably why the White House ordered the U.S. Army to take up residence on Wyoming's border."

"What?" Stillwater was taken with surprise by this revelation.

Maxton nervously snapped a reply, "I probably wasn't supposed to let that out of the bag. So you keep your mouth shut. The military isn't there yet, but I understand it's on the way. It'll be pretty public in a few days. So just button it till then. Got me!"

"Whatever," Josh responded. He tapped the phone off and sat in silence. With that last point, he knew Wyoming's mobilization wasn't an exercise. They had to know what the Feds were up to. In part, Jimmy and William's inclusion as officers demonstrated the State's resolve. It had even slipped that Ben was a General, but he denigrated the title by saying it was only honorary. *Bullshit*, thought Josh. *These people are up in arms, literally. But for what? How can they hold off the Federal government? What kind of materiel could they have? The National Guard is always given the cast off, worn out and obsolete materiel from the regular Army. What are these people up to? They all act as if they're holding four aces when all they probably have is a pair of deuces.* Ben was serious when he asked Josh to come over to Wyoming's side. Josh had known Ben his entire life. The man was not stupid, and he definitely wasn't suicidal. So what did he know that he hadn't told Josh?

And what had Tex found out?

Josh tapped his phone back to life, scrolled down previously received calls and hit the only 713 listing. It went directly to a standard company recording for voicemail. He left no message. Someone in his line of work never allowed their voice to be recorded, unless you went through Wyoming immigration. His caller ID would be notice enough. He tapped the phone off, pocketed it and left the booth.

The announcement came through hidden speakers. They were arriving at Cheyenne in seven minutes, exactly on time. Josh walked back to his car and seat, flopped down his tall frame, and began sorting through thoughts. Those concerning Ben most troubled him. *Why would Ben leave the State right now, right when things seemed to be heating up? Where is he going?* Josh ran through the morning's conversation. *Texas, that's it. But what the heck is so important in Texas?*

He felt the train decelerating. His thoughts turned from Ben to another Warner, Samantha.

## Chapter 2

### Visitor's Surprise

### Cheyenne, Wyoming

As the train approached the outskirts of Cheyenne, it gradually descended underground. When it came to a stop, Josh looked out at a cavernous station lit up brighter than the overcast sky somewhere above. There was the same multitude of platforms and overhead moving walkways as in Casper. To Josh, the forty-five minute ride had passed in a blink. He grabbed his luggage and departed. Overhead, signs provided directions to the nearest CityCar. The city commuter system came directly down into the rail terminal. It arrived at the same level as the train platforms. Josh walked over to the CityCar line of waiting patrons. It moved quickly and he was in front of a car in less than two minutes. Now an experienced commuter, he tapped DESTINATION on the Car's screen. Looking down at the address Jake had provided, he typed it in. The screen displayed GOVERNOR'S MANSION and asked for confirmation. Josh was more than surprised. After the whirring of his mental gears, it made sense that if Sam worked for the Governor then she worked out of the Mansion. Everyone said she had an important job. *Probably an aide or executive assistant*, he thought. Selecting YES and paying with his WC card, he entered the vehicle.

CityCars were electric cars that derived their power and navigation from round discs space about meter intervals and embedded within the roadway. The discs delivered power to the Car's motors via electro-magnetism. The Cars were the only method of transport within Wyoming's major cities. All other vehicles were restricted to outside a loop that encircled each city. The Cars were a perfect ballet of synchronization. Governed by a central computer that was continuously 'learning' traffic and demand patterns, a CityCar was guaranteed to respond to an individual's summons within a three minute window.

The Car powered up and out of the underground station, ran north on Highway 85, Central Avenue, away from the downtown and towards the intersection with I 25. Near the junction, the car veered off an exit and turned left. In a moment they were heading up a circular drive, a marble sundial standing in the middle of the circle. Josh had never seen the mansion before. He thought the term *mansion* overstatement. By other States' standards, this mansion was modest. No Victorian three-story, no columns, no grand entry steps, no acreage of gardens, just two mullioned glass doors at the end of a tree shaded sidewalk. The single story rambler was sheathed in cedar siding meeting large moss rocks.

As he exited the Car, Joshua caught his reflection in the window. He ran his fingers through mussed hair, trying to pull it back. During the visit at Dillon's ranch, William had, in front of his partner, Jimmy, swooned over Josh's incredibly black hair. Maybe if his hair was such an asset, Josh should pay more attention, for Sam. He felt foolish when he saw his audience of one, watching his preening with a raised eyebrow. Joshua quickly withdrew his hand from hair and walked towards the man dressed in jeans, cowboy boots and sheepskin lined denim jacket. Joshua assumed he was security personnel. He recognized the NEU-Net disc atop his head. Joshua cleared his throat and announced, "I am here to see Samantha Warner."

The guard asked, "Your name, Sir."

"Josh, eh, Joshua Stillwater." He replied.

The guard stared at Joshua's face a moment, capturing and sending his image to a remote computer. He apparently received confirmation of Josh's facial ID as he nodded. He asked Josh for his visa. One of the items most troubling to Joshua since returning to Wyoming after fifteen years was the Customs and Immigration all persons endured at entry points into the State. After all, he had thought, he was born here. Yet he was not considered a Citizen of the State. As an ALIEN, he had to carry and present upon demand an identification card that also encoded the terms of his visa.

Josh offered it up to the security guard who zipped it through an upper attachment to his touch-screen phone. The guard held up the phone displaying a phrase. He instructed Josh to read the phrase towards the phone's. The word MATCH appeared. Obviously the guard's phone incorporated some app matching Josh's voice to the voice file encoded within the visa card. He knew his voice, finger prints and face had been registered when he initially entered the State. This had not pleased him at the time. It pleased him less now. After the phone chimed acceptance, the guard held out the card. He said with a wry smile, "I think your hair looks much better in your entry picture." Josh snatched the card from his fingers.

The entry doors gave an audible, electronic buzz. The guard grabbed one door handle and held it open. Josh entered and walked along a tiled foyer.

It was only two or two-and-a-half meters wide and ran the width of the house to a back patio. Joshua could see the park-like setting of the back area through wood and glass doors duplicating the front entry. A few steps down the hall, to the left, a stone-framed entry containing two tall doors was apparently his destination. A young lady signaled for Joshua to follow. Both sides of the door sported Wyoming State flags. Joshua noted it was proper protocol for a State to display the Nation's flag opposite the State flag. He stepped through into a large great-room. In the center was a setting of two chairs with an end table between. Behind was a large, free-standing, floor-to-ceiling column of mortared sones providing a chimney to the fireplace now filled with crackling logs. The young lady escorted Joshua away from the fireplace to another setting near the window, this one consisting of a long couch with a modest wooden tea table in front, a leather chair at one end and a Chippendale chair at the other. The oddity was that the formal Chippendale was upholstered in sheepskin and the leather chair was actually furry, black cow hide. Josh was directed to the couch and told the Governor would be with him shortly. Would he like tea or coffee, she asked.

His answer was delayed. He declined both, thinking, *Why would the Governor be coming out? Is Sam trying to impress me?* The aide nodded and exited the room.

Joshua scanned the open area. It was a demur setting. It certainly wasn't a mansion. *Not real fancy*, he thought. *Certainly nothing to measure up to a Federal building.* A wing of the great room jutting outward between the trees held a wide, long dining table and chairs. It was in the shape on 'U' with the bottom much shorter than the runs beyond.

Next to the seating area, there were photographs, all portrait shots. A first grouping was in black and white while the majority was in color. Josh recognized the last photo as Sam. There were brass plaques underneath each photo with writing he could not make out from the couch. He surmised it must be the name and title of each person. He was curious to know what job Sam held. He rose from the couch and walked closer to the framed photo. He read the plaque and was stunned. Samantha E. Warner was the current Governor of Wyoming! The other photos were past governors, arranged by dates of succession. Was this some trick they were all playing on him? Why hadn't anyone told him? His mind was in turmoil. If Sam was the Governor, then she was also the leader of this revolt, or mutiny, or rebellion, whatever in hell you called it. That also meant she was in the cross-hairs of the Federal Government. How could this have happened? When he left, she was no politician. She never talked about what was going on in Cheyenne. When and where did this metamorphosis take place?

He heard voices approaching. Two dark, wooden doors across the room flew open. Sam was leading a group. There were three men and one woman. All were dressed immaculately and all spoke among themselves as equals. Sam and the entourage rounded the stone fireplace column and headed his way. Josh was uncomfortable in formal settings. He was trying to figure out how to stand and where to park his hands as they approached.

She looked stunning, a thin, wool dress-suit tailored to her tall, athletic body. Long, blonde hair flowed downward past her shoulders. Her legs were firm and long, jutting her derrière upward upon high heeled shoes. Her face had changed some. It had lost the child-like innocence he had known. It was still beautiful, but now had the maturity of a strong woman. Her green eyes still captivated him. Her smile was relaxed and genuine. His unease changed into anticipation as she approached. His heart beat rapidly in expectation of their bodies meeting in a tight hug.

But this was not to be. Instead, Sam offered both hands, held forward, palms down. Joshua picked up the clue and lightly held each hand in his.

"Joshua Stillwater, I am so happy to see you again. We all thought you had disappeared forever. Where have you been keeping yourself? Let me look at you." Sam leaned back slightly, pulling both their arms straight out as those luscious eyes scanned his entire body. The greeting was friendly, but Joshua thought she had said it in the same manner a thousand times to a thousand visitors. There was no deep passion burning here, at least none Joshua could see. It saddened him but he tried to keep it light when responding, "Sam, you look great. And all of this…" They had dropped hands and Joshua used his right to panorama the entire building, "You must be very proud with what you've achieved."

Sam held up her hand in protest, "Not me, Josh, it's what the people of this State have achieved. That's what I am proud of, this State of Mine. The rest is mere trappings."

"Well, we're not trappings, Sam." The lone woman among the three men stepped forward. "Please, introduce us to this gorgeous man."

Sam chuckled, "I am sorry Liz. Joshua Stillwater, this is Elizabeth Brigham, Governor of Utah. And behind her is Mario Almondo, Governor of California, John Hughes, Governor of Nevada, and Scott

Fodor, Governor of Colorado." Josh was more than overwhelmed as he shook each hand. It was more than their titles, it was their casualness.

Sam continued, "Joshua is a dear friend, practically a brother. We grew up together on the same ranch. He took off for the big city about fifteen years ago and we haven't seen him back until today."

"Ooooh, a man of mystery. Tell us Josh, where have you been all this time?" The Governor of Utah was almost swooning.

Josh felt as if he'd been doused with cold water. Not only could he not be alone with Sam, but he felt defensive right out of the shoot. A touch of anger flared within, so his answer was meant to startle, "Uzbekistan, Afghanistan, Georgia, Armenia and a few other places I'm not at liberty to discuss."

The eyes of all the governors widened. "Those are dangerous places, Mr. Stillwater. Mind if I ask what you were doing there?" It was Governor Hughes asking.

Josh shrugged, "Naw, I don't mind. I was killing people."

The four visiting Governors looked at each other with raised brows. Sam's eyes scolded Joshua as if he were ten years old and had just let off a stink bomb.

Josh held bent arms out in front of him, "What? They asked."

Sam shook her head and turned round to her guests. "Well, I guess on that high note, we can all begin today's tour." She stared beyond Josh for a moment. He noticed the black disc between threads of her golden hair. A moment later appeared the younger lady that initially greeted Josh. She held a heavy wool coat over one arm. "Yes, Ms. Governor." Josh noticed the disc upon her head as well. Obviously the two were in communication. *That NEU-Net still creeps me out*, he thought.

Caroline, Sam's EA – executive assistant - draped the coat over Sam's shoulders. Joshua and she headed out the door held open by the security guard. Joshua noticed that, when the guard's arm was extended with the door, a shoulder holster appeared under his left arm. It held a heavy piece of armament.

Outside a bus/motor home awaited. It was painted in Wyoming's colors, blue and white. But there were no markings, no signage. Even the manufacturer's name was nowhere evident. The windows were tinted beyond dark. They appeared completely blacked out. Sam swept her hand towards the open doors and the Governors began filing inside, past a driver.

Josh turned to Sam, "Where you going?"

"*We*, meaning all of us, are going on a tour. And you shall find it most interesting."

"Tour? We? I, ah, well, I thought we might have some time together, you and me, ah, alone." He looked into her eyes hoping for a glimmer of warmth. Only business stared back, so Josh hurriedly added, "You know, just to sit and talk, catch up."

Sam patted his hand, "We will have ample opportunity for that, Josh. The bus ride is two hours one-way. We can talk till our jaws are sore. Now let's board as we have a tight schedule."

It wasn't exactly what he had in mind, "Naw, you go on ahead with your other Governors. I'll catch up with you later. 'Sides, I don't fit in with this crowd."

Sam shook her head, "Nonsense. You *are* the people Josh. And we Governors are merely elected officials of the people, not royalty. Now, please, let's board. I am very anxious for you to see what we have accomplished."

She reached out and gently took his elbow, steering him towards the vehicle. Her touch instantly melted his defenses. He boarded.

The interior appeared as someone's comfortable living room. There were couches and reclining chairs, end tables, reading lamps, a bar in the rear, a small bookshelf filled with selections, work tables with folded down leafs. Indirect lighting traced the perimeter of the ceiling, giving a warm, yet substantial light to the room.

Sam entered last and slid a door closed. The room was now completely isolated, cut off from the driver and any view out front, sides or back. She remained standing in order to address the group.

"Gentlemen, and Lady, we are about to take a drive of some distance. Unfortunately for our State, we have jealous and zealous suitors that wish to steal our maidenhood."

Everyone snickered, even Josh.

"Therefore we require a level of security to protect our, ah, assets. Think of this vehicle as our chastity belt."

Elizabeth Brigham giggled while the men openly laughed.

"You will really have no idea where we are going, even in which direction we proceed. Normally, we allow no cell phones or personal electronics. Additionally you would all be subject to a personal search for tracking devices. However, today we are extending the courtesy of trust. The bar is open at any time. There are snacks and cold drinks in the refrigerator underneath. Please, do not get liquored-up as we will be sharing a great deal of technical information later and wish for you to be sober."

More snickering.

"Additionally, there are wash-rooms at the back. Any questions?" No one spoke. "Fine, let's get underway." With that she stared for a moment and the mobile living room quietly and smoothly slid away from the Governor's house.

Sam settled in a chair near Josh. He asked, "This use the same power as the CityCars?"

"No," she responded. "It's hydrogen-fueled electric. We are hitting the open road, where CityCars do not roam."

"You use this for all your tours? Keeping the visitors in the dark, literally."

"Actually, we developed this for the gold inspection teams."

Josh's interest ramped up, "Gold inspection?"

"Yes. I will give you more details later. The overview is this: gold backs our WC. For the world to accept the WC, they have to know we actually have the gold. So an international team of inspectors come and inspect. We use this coach to transport them to the gold reserves. We make sure they are not electronically tracked or followed, even from the air. We also know when and where satellites are keeping an eye on our State. We schedule departures to miss the over-flights." That was all she offered.

Josh asked as casually as possible, "So, we visiting all that gold today?"

Sam shook her head, "No. That is only for the inspectors. The Governors have already been briefed on today's agenda. That's why I'm only addressing you. We are going to our Energy Development Facility."

"Like a research lab?"

"Originally," offered Sam. "Now we are in full production."

"Production of what?"

"Limitless energy," her response was nonchalant.

"Limitless?" Josh raised one eyebrow. "Ahh, come on."

"It is virtually unlimited, Joshua. It is one of our major products. The States represented by two of these Governors are already our customer. The other two are considering it."

"So we gonna sit through a sales pitch, for the other two?"

"That and so much more. Now, be nice and go get me an orange juice."

***

The two hours seemed to fly by. Josh could tell when they left the interstate. They had to have been on I-80, for the trip had been nearly a straight line with no sharp turns. Whether they had headed east or west, he couldn't be certain. But a two-hour trip east from Cheyenne would have put them an hour into Nebraska. They might have built a facility in Nebraska to avoid Federal scrutiny, but he doubted it. His guess was west.

They now pulled off the interstate, Josh knew, because curves were often and tires sounded as if speed had decreased. Eventually they decelerated to almost a stop, made a sharp right turn and then a complete stop. The bus then accelerated. *Probably a guard gate*, Josh thought. Then they proceeded down a steep incline, leveled off and continued another minute before coming to a complete stop. *A tunnel or underground parking.*

Sam stood up signaling their trip had come to an end. She slid open the door to the driver compartment and exit. "I told you the time would pass quickly. Let's all proceed to our briefing." She exited the coach and the others followed.

***

They sat on tiered, cushioned seats, looking out through panels of glass soaring three stories, slanting from the bottom outward as the panels rose. Flat metal slats spaced every two meters upwards on each panel jutted straight out the same distance. The glass started at a meter off the auditorium floor and slanted outward to its terminus at a downward-slanted roof, hanging outward, far beyond the glass. The metal/cement/water-proofed ply-roof was topped with soil and natural foliage. Joshua thought the design no accident as it would be impossible to know these buildings even existed from the air, especially from an eye-in-the-sky

The small clutch of dignitaries, sitting half-way up and in the middle of the amphitheater, was dwarfed by the twelve-hundred seat room. The guests had a panoramic view across to an opposite mountain containing a twin to the building in which they now sat. Between the two structures nearly a kilometer apart was a meadow containing an enormous lake. The lake was raised ten meters in the air with a twenty-meter wide column of concrete supporting the middle and a steel columned superstructure surrounding the perimeter. Beyond this, sides angled downward, adding to the illusion by softening any shadows that could reveal the raised characteristics. The bottom of the lake appeared to be formed by numerous and enormous round pipes that were painted in varying degrees of blue, darkening towards the center. Re-circulating water kept the artificial reservoir filled to a depth Josh estimated around thirty meters above the pipes. A mist clung to the top of the water, constantly fed by evaporation off the top of the lake. At one end, a waterfall cascaded down a mountain side where the lake began and then spilled over the other end, sieving through large boulders and disappearing underground. Underneath the lake, personnel in blue and white lab coats walked among a park of shrubs, short trees and benches. Some were sitting, eating. Others were apace, scurrying to their destination. Light filtered through the lake bottom above and, passing through the spacing of pipes, lit this under-umbrella green. Joshua understood the design: the slanted glass, the covered commons and the mountain-recessed buildings, were designed to keep out prying eyes. But the raised lake, the pipes, the waterfalls did not so easily succumb to an answer.

21

Then another thought struck him.

*This is that lake within the valley shown in the satellite photo Maxton gave me! This is what Jake and I flew over when he got upset at my questions,* Josh thought. *Washington would give a ton of gold to know what's going on here.*

Joshua was impressed by the facilities but didn't really see how an office structure could be dedicated to energy production. With their other plants out in the open, why hide this one? The place, in his mind, appeared more a software research campus.

He saw Sam step onto a small platform. Side, handrails emerged and rose around the circular perimeter. The platform rose nearly to the eye level of Josh and the other visitors. Sam pinned a small microphone to her lapel, looked up and smiled.

"Good afternoon. I know we all had a long drive getting here. However, I hope the accommodations and camaraderie made the time pass easy."

All smiled and nodded approval.

"Good. First, let me introduce you to **WyStar**. Today you are going to see the future of energy production. This site contains nearly two hundred researchers and their assistants, all experts in their fields."

Joshua's interest immediately perked up at the mention of **WyStar**.

"Which fields?" interjected Governor Fodor.

"Well, there is a variety. But all are aimed at the same results. We have specialists in applied physics, theoretical physics, mathematicians, a broad spectrum of engineers, machinists, metallurgists, and many techs."

"And all to what aim?" again Governor Fodor.

"To produce energy, Governor. Clean, cheap, renewable and self-sustaining energy."

"That's a pipe dream." The same voice searched his peers for support, but was met only by looks of annoyance.

"Well, Governor, at one time it *was* a dream. But as you will witness today, the pipe part will be left for others to smoke."

Everyone laughed, even Governor Fodor. Stillwater was impressed with Sam's cool-under-fire manners and her ability to disarm an opponent.

"So, if I may hurry us on a bit, I would like to introduce Dr. Wai-Lin Zhou of China. Dr. Zhou is our Director of Implementation for Project **WyStar**. Dr. Zhou."

The thin, Chinese physicist entered from the left stepped upon another platform that rose to an equal height of Sam's. He was dressed in black pants, a pale blue shirt and dark blue tie, topped by a white, knee length lab coat. A large number 1 was embroidered upon the coat's front panel, just above the left pocket. His expression was jubilant, enthusiastic. His first greeting was in Chinese.

"'下午好!' This means good mid-morning in Simple Mandarin. Welcome to all. I wish to postpone questions as we proceed until we reach the end of the presentation. Before we enter the world of **WyStar**, I wish to cover some basic materials on our area of focus. Every researcher at this facility has spent part of their career at a Fusion research facility. We have researchers and engineers from many differing stages of Fusion's development. They have come from Cadaracher, Cern, Lawrence Livermore, the National Ignition Facility, Ferme Lab, Princeton, the Chinese National Fusion Research Center, Italy's Ricerca Nazionale di Istituto di Fusione and many other esteemed labs. There are over sixteen nationalities represented in our researchers. And we have four primary sponsoring countries. In order of financial commitment, they are: Wyoming, China, Japan, and Israel. We have conquered issues that....."

Governor Fodor was waving his hand like a school child. Dr. Zhou wagged his finger, "Rule one, Governor. Questions at the end, remember?"

Governor Fodor whined, "Just one quickie, please. It's not technical."

Zhou sighed, "Since you insist."

Scott Fodor dropped his hand and smiled in triumph. "Why Wyoming? Why here? Why did you come here?"

Zhou frowned," That's three questions." He held up his hand to stave off Governor's objection. "However, I will answer them in order: commitment, commitment, commitment."

"Aw, come on Doctor. A little more detail, please."

Zhou looked at Sam and received a nod. He shrugged, "Alright. Why Wyoming; because it demonstrated the commitment to solving the unsolved of Fusion. It provided the initial seed money, a lot of money. It built these beautiful facilities. It took a three-pronged approach at finding answers. And what I mean by three-pronged will be explained shortly, so I will not expand here. And finally it invited a lineup of the most distinguished researchers in the world. I wanted to be part of it. China wanted to be a part. From day-one there was a strategic vision created by Wyoming. They weren't doing all this to prove they could or to save mankind. They were doing it to enrich their Citizens, their State, to make money from energy production. When I saw what they already had in place, I could not refuse. There was a fever to succeed. There was electricity in the air, and all of us wanted to make it flow down wires. As the saying goes, failure was not an option. And success followed. Once we were assembled and understood the guidelines, strategies were based on business models, not research models. The four sponsors wanted a return on their investment. After all, combined they would invest more of their Citizen's money, in relative dollars of the time, than was spent on the Apollo Space Program or the Manhattan Project.

*There's the Manhattan Project*, thought Josh. *This is what Jake was talking about. I guess they were able to do it without the Federal Government.*

Dr. Zhou continued, "This wasn't a philanthropic activity. This was business. That's why we have a Board of Directors consisting of researchers and, from our four sponsors, business advisors with no technical background in fusion. That's why we succeeded. Why the program is in Wyoming and why all of us are here. And now, as they used to say on television, we return to our regularly scheduled program."

Chuckles all around.

"We have put together a presentation that can explain many points graphically as well as verbally. I ask all of you to reach in front and remove the pair of glasses from its pouch.

Stillwater followed instructions with the rest and was surprised to see the same type of glasses Jimmy had introduced at his factory. He smiled and looked wryly at the other guests.

"This is gonna blow your mind," he said for all to hear as he donned the eyewear. Governor Brigham looked at him, then to the glasses. Noticing Stillwater's self-satisfied grin, she put the glasses on and saw only black. She shrugged, leaned back and wondered at Josh's attitude.

They were all surprised as Dr. Zhou's voice resonated within their heads. It was beyond 'hearing' him. His words felt as if they were being thought rather than heard.

"The sound for our presentation is transmitted to micro receivers within your glasses. These inputs are then converted into vibration patterns along the stems of the glasses. As the stems touch your cranium, the vibrations are transferred through the bone of your skull and sound as if emanating as thought. The first time to hear such clarity, such tonality is startling. I understand this. The old phrase, 'I just can't get it out of my mind' seems to take on new meaning.

The select audience slowly nodded in agreement. Zhou continued.

"It might interest some of you that the media you will be watching is a new form, developed here. We call it Float Screen. There are no pixels. It is made from particles suspended within a minute magnetic field. The electricity that powers your glasses is delivered through E-Pho. This is a system developed by Wyoming's home-grown tech company, Dillon & Dillon."

Josh smiled at the reference and felt honored to personally know Jimmy....and, yeah, okay, his partner, the flamboyant William."

"E-Pho is a system that delivers electricity in the form of photons, or light, instead of its normal delivery via particles. Your glasses contain no batteries. That is why they are so light. They are receiving their power literally out of thin air."

Governor Fodor had removed his glasses for an inspection that included the interior of the amphitheater, trying unsuccessfully to see rays of light beaming towards him. None were visible.

Zhou continued his explanation of the particles restrained within the lenses, "Color is emitted via excitation of the particles at various cycles. Additionally, we can stack these particles upon one another to give a sense of depth perspective. We even allow some of the particles to escape and shoot towards you. This heightens a 3D effect. There is no projection system as the particles are manipulated by software. There is a very small but powerful chip built into your glasses."

"As for sound, we have taken a rather unconventional approach. Because we knew most of our visitors would not come equipped with NEU-Net, we designed a sound system to simulate, or nearly approach what we Citizens receive up here."

He pointed to the black disc upon his head.

"Now, on with the show!"

He pressed a button on the podium and both he and Samantha's platforms descended to the floor. The metal slats covering the outside of the glass panels closed, darkening the room as interior lights dimmed.

This motivated another thought in Joshua, *Those slats can keep light from leaking out, as well as in. I bet they close them at night to keep the place blacked-out.* This lead to a further thought, *And they slant the glass inward toward the bottom so it won't reflect sunlight during the day. Pretty smart design.*

Glass-wearing heads jerked as piercing lights emitting from the lenses produced a brilliant white blanket within the frame. The white emptiness morphed into colors. A subtle, undulating effect grew until the screen looked a shimmering white-colored cloth, rolling in waves. Centered was a blue and black bison within a seal. It was the State flag of Wyoming waving in a strong breeze. The flag ripples ebbed and flowed from in front of the viewers with such depth of dimension that several hands reached in front straining for a touch of the silky material. Their attempts were in vain.

As suddenly as it had appeared, the screen went black, and a voice emerged. It was the deep-baritone, succinctly enunciated voice of a once-famous actor that had made his mark in epic Bible and historical films. Joshua couldn't remember the name. The rich voice provided the sensation that it was directly within each person's head, as if God Himself were speaking. A bit eerie, thought Stillwater.

The voice began, "In the beginning, there was nothing, except blackness. Then an event occurred." A tiny dot of light grew in the middle of their vision. It began to vibrate. "And from the event, a universe was born." The center light exploded into millions of other lights, streaking outward randomly from the screen. Josh could only compare it to a movie of a commander standing on the bridge of a starship, accelerating to light-speed. The streaks of light flew directly at him. He unconsciously moved his head from side to side to evade the tiny missiles. But they disappeared as fast as they arrived. It was well beyond 3D.

The light show went black again. Then a whirlpool of colors and undulating swirls slowly illuminated the lenses.

"Great amounts of gas and dust coalesced to form an interstellar medium containing approximately seventy percent hydrogen with the remaining gas consisting of Helium. From this medium arose clouds, molecular clouds in that they contained $H_2$. These clouds extended over one-hundred light years in length."

Computer generated graphics had the viewer flying through clouds and then soaring into the blackness with a rear view of the cloud layer growing smaller and smaller, yet still extending into the infinity of the viewer's world.

"When the cloud's mass could no longer overcome its gravity, it began to collapse. The molecular cloud broke into smaller pieces until fragments reached stellar mass. Density increased. The fragments were less and less able to lose their energy. The temperature rise slowed the energy loss even more. Fragments then condensed into rotating balls of gas. The result, a Stellar Embryo. The collapse continued until the center, the core, developed enough pressure and temperature that energy began to diffuse outward. Through this convection and external radiation, the mass reached equilibrium and the collapse slowed. This was the Protostar phase. When the pressure and density built sufficiently, deuterium Fusion began. But this was not the fusion that would drive a completed star."

The screen brought the viewer down into the core and then radiated outwards in rippling distortions of heat.

"Material existing in the remaining cloud continued to fall into the Protostar until only a small percentage remained on the perimeter. This finally dissipated. Now existed a Pre-Main Sequence star. The source of energy at this stage was still from gravitational contraction. The contraction proceeds until sufficient temperature and pressure allow Hydrogen to fuse."

All of this was being graphically detailed in timing to the narration.

"We now have a Main Star. We now have Fusion: hydrogen fusing with hydrogen and producing the energy to run a solar system, self-sustaining and, by mathematical calculations, powering our solar system for another ten billion years."

The sun blazed within the entire screen, then slowly shrank as the recognizable planets of the solar system filled the screen and quickly minimized to relative size vis-à-vis the Sun, following their elliptical orbits.

"It has been the goal of science to harness for our civilizations this same source of power. Efforts have been made since the nineteen-seventies to achieve the dream of Fusion......however; it has been an elusive dream.

Nature is not bound to give up her secrets easily. There has been a trail of Fusion attempts. Lawrence Livermore's two-laser attempt was first, with follow-on of tandem mirror designs. Then Shiva, Tokamak and Nova. The Europeans were not idle. From the nineteen-eighties onward they have made several attempts and pinned enormous hopes on the doomed ITER, the advanced fusion research facility that was destroyed in a massive explosion. Since the World's economic collapse, Fusion research in the United States and Europe dwindled to nearly zero, due to lack of government funding."

"What is Fusion? What does Fusion actually entail? How do we measure success in achieving Fusion and what are the rewards if we succeed? What are the remaining problems and how do we overcome them?"

"The first question, the definition of Fusion and our desire to obtain it, is the most fundamental. The meaning of Fusion is in its name. It is the fusing of two molecules into one. It is how stars work. And, as in the stars, here on Earth, these molecules are hydrogen. When the two molecules fuse, they become slightly lighter. The missing component? Expelled energy in the form of heat. Heat that we on Earth can use to drive electrical turbines."

"But what of by-products or waste? Nuclear fission, in the United States, has created such toxic waste that the entire industry has been brought to a halt. Actually, even the waste of fission is a manageable problem if the Federal Government had, years ago, properly addressed it. But now, it has created such scale of fear that any favorable public attitude towards fission has, sadly, evaporated. Contrary to this, Fusion's by-product is a minute amount of helium, the gas with which we inflate children's balloons."

"As said earlier, Fusion uses hydrogen. But it must be in a form we can suspend, or hold until the process is underway. For Fusion here on Earth, we use isotopes of hydrogen: deuterium and tritium. When they are in close proximity to one another, heat and pressure can force them to overcome their natural repulsion and fuse into a helium molecule. Helium consists of two protons, and two neutrons. Additionally we are given a, single neutron and a burst of energy. And the good news, Deuterium is readily available from seawater, while tritium is available as a fission by-product."

"The ingredients are available. We have successfully demonstrated fusion in many different venues. So where is the problem? Is it the heat and pressure? The answer is Yes.... and No. We can definitely generate both.

This has been done with multiple, extremely large and powerful lasers aimed upon a BB-sized pellet containing deuterium and tritium. And we have reaped energy via heat. The problem in the past was the length of this event."

CGI images of the molecules fusing and the residue heat and neutron demonstrated across the screen, producing a large, white implosion.

"We only accomplished it for less than a millisecond. And it took the power used to run the households of ten thousand homes. And the heat produced wouldn't begin to replace the energy used to produce the event."

People in dark homes displayed. Some were amid shower, others staring at a blank TV pantomiming 'Whahappend?'

"We are at the crux of our third question: how is success measured, and what are the rewards if we achieve this success. The answer to the first part is: when Fusion generates more energy than is put into it, and we can continue the process on-going, we have success. The reward is that the world will have sustainable, clean, cheap energy for as long as civilization survives. Definitely a noble goal. The first countries to make the investment will be the industrial leaders of the world, and the best place to live on the planet. Energy costs will drop back to levels not enjoyed in the United States since the nineteen-fifties and sixties. Energy will be abundant, so the countries with Fusion will become Meccas to business and individuals. As Fusion pumps no pollutants into the air, and the resultant energy produced, electricity, is clean and quiet, countries with Fusion will be also be clean and quiet. Nations like Israel, with much arid land yet bordering a massive sea, will have abundant energy to turn the dry soil of their homeland, through electrically intense desalination, into a virtual Garden of Babylon.

Due to disastrous U.S. monetary policies and the resulting inflation, it is difficult to understand the impact of energy policy upon the nation in just terms of money. The best marker is energy costs as a percent of GDP – Gross Domestic Product – or the total amount of all goods and services created by the nation. In 2011 total U.S. energy costs were approximately 8% of the nation's GDP. Today, it is nearly 20%. The reason for this 250% rise: increased dependency on ever-more-costly imports combined with falling domestic production and a falling GDP resulting from this intractable economic depression. Falling GDP and rising costs of imports are directly attributable to the destruction of the U.S. dollar by the Federal government. Falling domestic production can also be laid at the feet of

Federal policy: no more new off-shore drilling due to spill concerns; shut down of the nuclear industry caused by lack of a national hazardous waste site; shut down of the Alaskan pipeline due to age, no replacement and falling oil production; no drilling in the Alaskan National Wildlife Refuge; no new permits issued for natural gas pipelines due to environmental concerns. But one bright spot:: the U.S. now has more windmills than Europe! Of course Europe started building theirs nearly nine hundred years ago when such technology could be called 'state of art.'

The United States today has become a beggar nation when it comes to energy. Counterproductive energy and monetary policies are the reason the U.S. cannot extricate itself from its economic malaise. Wyoming, along with its international partners has opted for a new path: Fusion. That, combined with a strong, disciplined monetary policy has produced the economic miracle you see today.

We now must focus on the Gordian Knot, the last question: What problems are before us and how can we overcome them. For us, the answer is simple. There are no problems. Wyoming and its partners are underway with Fusion as a viable, self-sustaining energy source. Yes, we still have processes to refine. However, in the meantime we are producing energy to power our economic miracles."

During the narrator's pause, the Governors looked at each other with surprise and youthful exuberance.

"We know you might be skeptical, but let us tell you how this was accomplished. First, we needed to understand the problems faced. They included; sustaining the plasma produced by Fusion within suspension; mass producing the numerous pellets required to maintain contiguous ignitions; and developing a method to capture the heat produced along with that extra, pesky neutron produced during Fusion."

"This could be a three month discussion. As this is a non-technical presentation, we shall simplify our answers. Our tour will provide answers to your many questions.

To the questions: Point number one; sustaining plasma in suspension. Plasma is a material halfway between liquid and gas. It is amorphous, meaning it does not have a shape unless you give it one. All other attempts to contain it employed a static field. This means fixed, powerful, magnetic fields attempting to hold together this ball of molten gas, for a better term, in suspension. The problem: plasma is like liquid. Imagine holding a perfectly round ball of water in your hands. It wants to bulge, sieve and escape through the tiniest of openings. It's impossible to have it completely surrounded, so some part turns rogue and your round ball isn't anymore. **WyStar** solved this by adding to the conventional theory of a fixed magnetic field, an additional, rotating field of particles. Through a continuous, bombardment of ions at the magnetic field, we keep it intact. Ions are charged particles. If we employ particles oppositely charged from the magnetic field, there is not only a repulsion of the particles, but an exertion of force upon the magnetic field within. This maintains the plasmatic core within sustainability. We can now sustain plasma for nearly six minutes! I emphasize this number by informing you that the original Fusion experiment achieved less than a tenth of a second. And the destroyed ITER, on its first and only run, achieved six seconds."

"You may ask, what happens after six minutes? This leads to the second point, more fuel. Every five-plus minutes a new fuel pellet must be injected. These pellets must be perfectly round, machined to a precision beyond any NASA specification. Under prior-known manufacturing methods, these pellets would cost a hundred-thousand Old US dollars. Pumping one of these nuggets into a chamber every five minutes would destroy the concept of return-on-investment. What to do? For an answer, we adapted what we already knew about electromagnetic fields. In similar ways as plasma, we pass a continuous mold through a chamber. Each mold contains a precisely measured amount of powered metal. The chamber is continuously pressurized with deuterium and trintium particles. Through a process we call **MagSynergy**, lasers focused on the molds create very high heat. As in the plasma chamber, the mold is spun at high RPS, that's revolutions-per-second, within a powerful magnetic field generated through the mold material. As the material from which the pellet will be formed and the mold are of opposing charges, the now-molten material forms a perfect ball without ever contacting the walls of the mold. The pellet has become the world's most perfect metal sphere, even more precise than a machined part. An intermittent laser, timed to the mold's rotation, fires through a nano-sized hole, opening a momentary void within the forming ball. The hole is smaller than the molecular size of the ball's material, yet big enough to allow the hydrogen molecules to pass through. The hydrogen laden gas pressurizes the pellet's interior void. With the laser beam withdrawn, the microscopic hole fuses shut. The mold then progresses through a quick cooling cycle, opens, and provides a pellet ready for injection. The pellet production line is adjacent to the Fusion chamber. We produce pellets every five-plus minutes and deliver them at the same rate to the core for the Fusion process. Therefore the entire system is continuous. The only time the system is down is one hour within a twenty-day period, and this for maintenance."

"Now for the last point. It was the most difficult. What to do with that one pesky neutron. Remember we said a deuterium and trintium isotope fused gave us helium? Well helium consists of the two protons and two neutrons of the hydrogen. But there is a residue, the heat and one escaping neutron. That neutron is a problem for two reasons. First, it can be a magician and change materials. If it was one or two or even two thousand neutrons bouncing around, this would be of no concern. However, in a continuous plasmatic reaction, we are dealing with billions of reactions where those neutrons can perform destructive transformations. The carbon atoms within the steel of the chamber holding the Fusion process can succumb to this neutron bombardment over time, thereby becoming brittle. A weakened chamber is problematic when needed to restrain the power of the Sun. Additionally, there are materials that are very friendly and useful to us. But if we constantly bombard them with massive amounts of neutrons, they may turn radioactive. The problem of radioactive waste would reoccur."

"Our answer is to turn the sow's ear into a silk purse. We use that single neutron for two purposes: to generate a fission reaction for heat and to neutralize radioactive waste. A Fusion chamber is a marvel of research. But to be practical, it must have its energy captured and put to use in generating electricity. Until **WyStar**, this side of the equation, electricity production, had not been addressed to a major degree. This is the three-track approach we spoke of in the introduction. While development was underway on the Fusion chamber, we had separate teams on pellet development and electrical generation, or EG as it is now referenced. The main developmental task of EG was the creation of an energy absorbent blanket. It is one thing to create heat, but another to capture and put it to use. A 'blanket' is required to absorb the heat, transfer it to liquid-transporting pipes, and then generate steam. By focusing on the single neutron problem, opportunity was siezed upon. The blanket was formed from radioactive waste."

"In the United States, nuclear waste produced by fission plants has long been a problem. As there was no known way to neutralize the waste, long-term storage was the only viable alternative. A national depository was required. But the Federal government could not agree on where the depository would reside. So instead of making a difficult decision, as usual politicians took the easy path, by making no decision. Radioactive waste was left for the fission plants to handle. After their storage pools filled, and with no national storage site availble, there was only one

32

alternative: on-site storage, above ground in containers, or 'coffins' as they have become known. This could develop into a potential disaster of monumental consequences. When the stop-gap measure became a public relations bomb, the citizenry demanded the plants stop adding to the problem. The solution: all fission plants were ordered to cease operations. The United States lost twenty-percent of its electrical generation facilities overnight. And the coffins still remain at the plants, subject to nature's erosion."

"But in the first decade of this century, the leader of the National Ignition Laboratory, Director Moses, made a bold proposal. Why not use radioactive waste for the EG blanket? The free neutron could be used to bombard the waste products, causing a fission reaction. His proposal was revived by **WyStar** researchers and a test program initiated. It worked. The resulting reaction produced enormous quantities of heat. This heat is conducted to molten sodium and transferred to water-generating steam, driving electric-generating-turbines. And the great bonus is that the radio-active materials used in the blanket are transformed into lighter and less radioactive materials. **WyStar** not only met our needs of energy production, but will solve, over time, the disposal issue for the United States' remaining fission plants.

However, this is not our main goal. Rather, it is to produce cheap, renewable energy. And **WyStar** has achieved this bountifully. We now invite you to proceed with your tour. Welcome to the future. Welcome to **WyStar**."

The view within the glasses darkened as the amphitheater lights rose and the window shutters opened. While everyone took a moment to allow their eyes to adjust, they applauded enthusiastically. Dr. Zhou and Samantha were once again upon their raised platforms.

"Questions?" the Chinese Director asked.

As expected Governor Fodor spoke first, "The presentation said the blanket of nuclear waste was converted to less radioactive materials. But it's still radioactive, right? So what do you do with it? Sounds like you just transferred the problem to Wyoming. Aren't you concerned you're poisoning your own State?"

Zhou shook his head, "Not really. Fission plants in the U.S. use only about five percent of the energy available within a nuclear rod."

"Huh?! Five percent, that's all?"

"Yes. Europe and and Asia do not have anything close to the waste problem of the U.S. They use a different system, reprocessing. This process separates uranium and plutonium from the nuclear waste materials. Russia alone reprocesses nearly 5000 tons annually, followed by France's facilities in La Hague."

"Why don't we reprocess the waste?" It was Governor Brigham.

"We used too until President Carter banned it. President Reagan tried to restart the program but could not muster the support of Congress."

Elizabeth Brigham followed on, "Why did Carter ban it? I didn't personally care for the man, but I know he wasn't stupid. What was he worried about?"

"Plutonium," blurted Josh, surprised at his comment.

Dr. Zhou looked at him and nodded, "The gentleman is correct. One of the items extracted during reprocessing is plutonium?"

"Like they use in bombs?" asked Governor Fodor.

Josh nodded. But the doctor shook his head, disagreeing, "Ultimately the plutonium extracted *could* be used to make a nuclear weapon. However, it would have to be enriched. The product extracted is not weapons-grade quality. Originally it was thought we would be awash in plutonium if we reprocessed. However, this was unfounded. There are several plants throughout the world that mix the plutonium with enriched uranium achieving a mixed-oxide, referred to as MOX. This mixture is used in portions of twenty to fifty percent in existing nuclear facilities. Instead of tackling and solving the problem like other countries, the U.S. shied away and created a larger problem, nuclear waste storage."

"Well, weapons-grade or not, I wouldn't allow any reprocessing or use of plutonium in my State!" Governor Fodor folded his arms across his chest in punctuation to this declaration.

Zhou shook his head slowly. But it was Samantha who responded, "Scott, that is exactly the attitude that has this country in such dire straits. Anything ever applied to man's needs carried a danger. Kerosene replaced whale oil for lighting, but was more volatile. Natural gas in our homes allowed us to warm ourselves, cook our food and read at night. Yet it could also burn your house down. Steam boilers on trains were notorious for explosions and killing of humans. Cars gave us mobility, and the highest source of human death tolls. Every advance in

34

technology comes with a danger; the greater the advance, the greater the danger. Yet time and again we see those dangers handled in less dangerous ways or relegated to unconcern. You fill your autos with petrol without concern. Yet gasoline, pound for pound, is more explosive than TNT. Should we have stopped all automotive development? These dangers are dealt with. Many are replaced with newer technologies that have greater potential for danger. But that should not stop us from progressing. We reprocess here and produce plutonium. We also blend it into fuels that create electricity, cheap electricity. And I remind you, the main reason you are here is to purchase that electricity."

Governor Fodor dropped his arms but gave a harrumph as indication he wasn't completely won over.

Governor Brigham raised a finger. Sam responded, "Yes Liz?"

"Well, I was thinking. We have three nuclear plants in my State that have been shut down for nearly three years. You mean Wyoming could free them of their nuclear waste and allow them to resume generating electricity? That would be a huge boon for us."

"Unfortunately, the answer is No." Your State chose the path of obeying Federal mandates and refuses the transport of your waste. So you still have quite a mess on your hands. And even if we were allowed to remove it tomorrow, you still have your Rubicon to cross with the Feds. Do you ship, at your expense, the waste product here? Do you restart your plants in defiance of Federal law? Or let them sit idle?"

"That's a no-brainer, as far as I am concerned. They act as if they want to keep us dependent on foreign oil for our energy."

Sam half-smiled, "They do, don't they." She continued, "But Liz, remember one thing. As a Governor you have a lot of authority. It's amazing how much power you have in one little-ol' pen. Executive orders roll out of President Rivera's office like rain. You have the same right to make executive law to protect the interests of your State. Sign an executive order. Make sure it's an issue that your Citizens, in overwhelming numbers, support. If your legislature is too weak-kneed when it comes to bucking the Feds, ignore them. Try it and you'll find out one thing: your Citizens will rally around. The people of your State are hungry, thirsty for change. But change makes sense, benefits the vast majority of your Citizens and restores a Constitutional right of the States over a despotic ruling by the Federal government."

Governor Brigham nodded sharply one time. Through tight lips she said, "Sam, you and I need to talk after this tour is through."

"Be glad to, Liz." Sam scanned the audience, "Any other questions? If not, we'll have a brief refreshment service in the antechamber and then head on down. There we can get into deeper subjects." She smiled, broadly.

# Chapter 3

## Down Under

### The Energy Complex

After coffee, tea and juice offerings, Sam recommended a restroom break. When all reassembled, she and Dr. Zhou led the tour through a hallway that slanted downward and ended at a thick steel door. A Wyoming Army sergeant stood with automatic weapon at the ready. He nodded at Sam and took a step to the side, never taking his eyes off the rest of the group. *This guy looks serious*, thought Stillwater.

Sam and Dr. Zhou walked to opposite sides of a door wider than two arms' length apart. In front of separate scanners, each pressed a palm to their unit, held their faces close for identification and repeated a phrase printed on the screen. Then Sam turned to the group, "It requires two authorized persons simultaneously."

Josh was thinking of Maxton. This would be his Valhalla, right now, right here. To be the-fox-in-the-hen-house would be his crowning moment. But, looking around, Josh knew this facility would be a tough nut to crack.

The door opened into another antechamber. Josh followed the group down curving steps. He guessed it led to a tunnel. Down about five meters, the stairs ended and they were in another antechamber, concrete lined. Sam again turned towards them.

"We have another security check here, same as the first. As a security precaution, you can see that we will enter a concrete vault. There is a pipe that leads from here to our lake above. If the facilities were attacked, an automatic valve would open and this room would immediately be pressurized with ten thousand gallons of water. But don't be nervous, the valve has never malfunctioned, yet." She and Zhou then turned towards two more security panels.

A few faint-hearted attempts at laughter emerged. As Governor Hughes entered, he studied the ceiling, floor, confirming the emptiness of a vault-like structure. He pushed Governor Almondo gently in the back and towards the next door.

'Vault' seemed apropos to Joshua as the next door swung open for all of them to enter. The door was massive, nearly two meters thick. It looked like a bank vault door with the same rods recessed that would extend into the steel and concrete casing once closed. But it was far greater in size.

The rods appeared nearly twelve centimeters in diameter. The door swung open, allowing their passage and then closed, both effortlessly and noiselessly. As Josh passed by, he assessed the door from an assault basis. He mentally rolled through a list of explosives he had available when in Special Forces. He wasn't sure any would work on this door, not without bringing down the tunnel roof and, probably, the water stored above. *This may be a civilian operation*, he thought, *but they've paid attention to security.*

On the other side of the door was another tunnel. This one displayed a string of lights far into the distance. The floor slanted downward for the entire travel. They were going deeper and deeper. Stillwater noted the round, tube-like construction of the tunnel. Round tubes were the strongest for displacing pressure, including bomb percussion. A dark colored carpet floor runner ran before them. This was to give grip and resistance against sliding on a bare, concrete floor.

Josh knew they were nearing the tunnel's end as the floor began to level. Another vault door faced them. Sam and Zhou went through the ID verification once more. When the door opened, they passed into another chamber. It was more brightly lit with walls paneled in stained wood. It appeared as a lobby in a fancy hotel, complete with upholstered settees and sconces. Large, stainless steel doors set in a wood frame fronted them. The doors and a single large button to the left indicated an elevator. Sam pressed the button and a voice came from a speaker a few centimeters above.

"Yes?"

"Governor Samantha Warner, Dr. Wan-Li Zhou, and five guests."

The speaker replied, "Yes, Governor. We show you on the schedule. The elevator will be up in a few minutes."

Sam thanked the speaker and turned to the group and smiled, "We keep the elevator at the bottom unless requested. Any visitors have to be cleared prior, even myself. The vertical shaft is nearly seven-hundred and fifty meters deep."

"My God! That's almost twenty-five hundred feet down. How long for the elevator to get here?"

Sam answered, "About twenty-five minutes. It is quite fast."

"But why so deep?"

"To protect from internal and external threats. Internally, down at the bottom, we are dealing with some powerful processes and potentially dangerous materials. If anything goes wrong, we can seal it off from potential contamination leaking to the outside. We are well below any water tables, so we don't worry about contaminating that as well. And, geologically, the area has been without earthquakes for nearly 5 million years."

"What external threats are you speaking of?"

"Possibly a bomb, a bomb of significant power dropped from above."

"Are you talking about a military strike? You actually think the Federal government would attack a State?"

"If the foundation of power is rocked beneath Washington D.C.'s feet, Governor, I believe the Federal Government of the United States is capable of unspeakable retaliation. An attack upon a politician's power can produce a greater response than if our borders were under attack. I think that has already been proven."

Governor Almondo looked around the chamber with a hint of panic in his eyes.

"Don't worry, Governor. The round concrete base holding up the center of our lake is twenty meters wide and twenty meters thick. It is a dome, a cap over this shaft. And the perimeter of it is sitting directly above your head. Any bomb dropped would have to penetrate that mass of dense steel, aggregate and cement. Our engineers believe it to be quite impenetrable." Sam smiled.

This fact did not seem to placate the Governor as his eyes were even wider. Josh was rolling the U.S. military's arsenal of bunker buster bombs through his mind and couldn't think of one capable of penetrating that thickness. He was about to tell the nervous Governor, but thought better. The elevator light lit and a bell chimed.

The doors opened on a large elevator car, easily capable of handling three times the amount of their group. All entered except for Governor Almondo who hesitated and stopped in front of Josh. Stillwater said, "Can't let the girls show up the boys, Governor." He gently pushed the man into the elevator, grinning at Sam. She smiled back.

"As you can see, we all fit quite easily within this car, with room left over. It is three times the size of the largest, standard car and was specially built for our needs. Now, we will descend quickly, about thirty-five meters per minute. We pass through definite pressure gradients so you might want to clear your ears as we go. Also, you might feel a little light in the feet. It helps to hold on to the side railings. It's actually kind of fun. So here we go everyone." She pushed the down button, the doors closed and the bottom fell out from underneath them.

During the descent, Josh noted the back of the car. It incorporated another set of doors. "We exit out the back?" he asked. Dr. Zhou shook his head and answered, "No, those doors are for inspection. This elevator shares the shaft with large pipes transporting steam upward to our lake where it is cooled and then returns downward. Additionally, it holds the cables transporting the megawatts of electricity produced and ready to transport to our customers. The doors allow technicians to slowly rise up the shaft while checking that all systems are intact." Josh nodded his understanding. But it did not please him to be traveling downward thirty meters away from live steam and millions of electrical volts. He mused if one would die quicker being boiled or electrocuted.

The elevator slowed gradually until coming to a complete stop. The front doors opened upon an enormous, semi-oval cavern. It was nearly twenty meters high and a hundred meters in diameter at its longest point. Pipes and cables crisscrossed the ceiling, hanging from anchors, brackets and metal straps. At one end of the oval was built a three-story complex. The other end was two-storied.

Dr. Zhou stepped in front of the group, now exited from the car. He explained the view. "Welcome to the Wyoming International Energy Development Facility. This large open area we refer to as the transition mall. In the beginning, large pieces of equipment were lowered via the shaft now covered by the concrete dome you saw earlier. As you can see, the elevator mechanism only takes up a small part of the shaft. As I explained during the descent, the pipes entering the shaft from overhead transport steam that has already driven electrical turbines, up to the surface for cooling within our artificial lake. And those large cables entering the shaft from the opposite side are for transit of electricity produced here.

At that end of the chamber," he pointed to his left, "are offices, cafeteria and dormitories. When we originally lit the fires of our reactors, several of us were down here for over a month. Today, we have staff that work in shifts. Those on-shift, but not on-duty, can rest or catch up on paperwork or read, et cetera. At the other end," he pointed to his right, "is the maintenance area, including a complete machine shop and stores of parts. Next to it is the experimental lab. We found in the beginning it was easier to duplicate potential problems through small-scale experiments away from the reactors and study the results, rather than deciphering what was occurring within a given reactor.

Above those two areas is the main monitoring center. You can see we have several people on duty at any given time. Their task is to monitor the various reactors and reactions within. Each person you see through those glass windows has the right to declare an emergency. This would immediately notify me and other management personnel if we were topside. There are only two people down here that can shut down a reactor, and they must be green-lighted by a committee of four residing topside. I am one of the four. Each of us has a replacement if by chance we are away from the facilities. Nuclear reactions, either fisson or fusion can become uncontrollable if shut down improperly. This was one of the problems at Chernobyl and Three-Mile-Island; although the last example had far less serious consequences."

Dr. Zhou noticed someone heading into the experimental lab. "Here is someone I wish for you to meet." He cupped his hands around his mouth and shouted, "Alex, may we have a moment?"

A six-foot–two, lanky man in jeans, western shirt, and cowboy boots turned to locate his hailer. He had a large sack in his hand. It was a sausage-like roll. He held up one finger, indicating he needed a moment. Then he hurried inside the lab. He reemerged shortly thereafter, hands free of the sack, and strode in their direction. Josh noticed his hat. It wasn't the fact it was a cowboy hat, it was how dirty and mangled the straw was that surprised him.

"Doc, how ya doin'. What can I do for ya?" the man asked.

Josh immediately picked up the speech pattern of a Wyomingan.

Dr. Zhou made the introductions, "Everyone, this is Dr. Alex Sidney."

Josh raised an eyebrow. *This guy certainly doesn't look like a brainiac. But neither does Jimmy Dillon.*

"Just Alex, Doc. You know I don't mess with titles."

Dr. Zhou nodded, "Always with the modesty, Alex." He turned to the group, "Alex has been of great service to his State. His ability to translate theoretical models into actual machines is remarkable. I can say without reservation that we would still be jumping hurdles without Alex's contributions."

Alex said nothing.

"So what are you working on in the lab, Alex?"

"Just a small particle differentiator. We're trying to come up with a portable system that can externally measure particle waves and quantities remotely from outside their chambers."

"Why not show our guests?" Dr. Zhou urged.

Alex thought for a moment and then nodded, "Not much to see. But, sure, come on." He led the way and the group followed, towards the experimental lab. Alex picked up his pace and out distanced the others so that he was already in the lab moments before they arrived. As the group entered, he was shaking out a large thick blanket over a pile of sacks like the one he carried before.

"What is that pile?" asked Dr. Zhou.

"Just some reactive materials for testing. I keep them under high-temp silicone blankets just in case a fire broke out. I couldn't tell you how they would combine with heat. Just a precaution."

Dr. Zhou nodded slowly, shrugged and moved on. Alex led them away from the pile to a stack of dull grey, interlocking bricks that stood a little over a meter tall and two meters square. A solid, thick sheet of the same material covered the top of the assemblage. A large U-shape bar was raised within the middle of the plate. Attached to it was a large hook and chain connected to an overhead winch. Several wires and pipes entered the walls of brick through sealed orifices. Another stack of bricks were to the side, appearing to Josh as extras to change the configuration of the experimental unit.

Alex pointed to the square, "This is made of interlocking ingots of lead. There is also an impervious liner within. We inject sample environments, ah, air samples, from various reactors in order to identify and measure rogue particles. Every reactor produces some. But each has a unique signature. This way we can monitor the external environment of each reactor to see if there is any change going on internally. It's just another safety measure. If anything out-of-sync starts to occur, this may give us the critical extra time to assess and react. Any questions?"

As there were none, Dr. Zhou thanked Alex for his time and the group left the lab. They headed across the bustling transition mall towards a portal on the right side of the oval, beyond the elevator doors.

The door was a cross between a bank vault and a ship's hatch. It was round, over two meters thick and two-and-a half meters wide. It was half opened. Dr. Zhou explained it would normally be closed, but was open for their visit. The Chinese stepped over the quarter meter bottom transom and signaled for the others to follow. They entered a vestibule that ran straight and further than the ability to see. The corridor had a vaulted ceiling, twenty meters overhead, with a line of caged lights fastened to the top and spaced several meters apart. As the door closed behind, the Doctor pointed out that this side of the door, as well as the run of walls, ceiling and floor, were coated with a burnt-orange colored material. He explained it as a heat-resistant composite epoxy that could withstand temperatures over twenty-seven hundred degrees Celsius. It was technology developed by NASA for space craft heat shields.

Thirty meters ahead, on the left, was another vault door. Peering down the dimly lit corridor, Josh could make out one more door at the edge of his vision. He surmised there must be more doors equidistant the length of the passageway. Dr. Zhou and Samantha walked the textured surface to the closest door and repeated security procedures. It opened outward and against the hinged wall, revealing another thick door, with a large, clear portal centered within. Immediately, bluish light spilt out into the corridor. Heat radiated from the viewing portal material.

Governor Hughes remarked, "Feels like Vegas in August."

Dr. Zhou nodded, "It runs around thirty-eight, thirty-nine degrees C. Anyone working inside uses air-conditioned, closed-breathing suits that are shielded for radioactive contamination. We put this clear door in for visitor viewing. This is the only reactor to have it. All are monitoried through wireless sensors and wireless cameras. You can see the monitors on the wall to your right. We also have monitors mounted within the chamber for personnel viewing. "

The audience had a good view due to the size of the portal. The ceiling was vaulted as the corridor, but not as high. The walls were similarly orange-coated as the vestibule outside.

Governor Fodor spoke, "Okay, you've got me. What is it? A Fusion experiment?"

Dr. Zhou frowned, "We are not experimenting here, Governor. Everything you see is commercially viable and producing revenue."

"Didn't mean to offend, Doc. Then what is this commercially-viable, revenue-producer before us?"

"It is a PBR. A Pebble-Bed Reactor, a fission reactor."

"Whoa, FISSION! As in spent rods, contaminated water and nuclear waste dumping into the atmosphere?!"

"You have just described the potential problems of a conventional, water-cooled nuclear power plant. It is also the source of its high cost to build and maintain. The cooling system is of such complexity it requires extensive safety systems with several, redundant backups. When you look at a conventional nuclear station, the vast majority seen is actually the cooling system, not the reactor. Conventional systems also have a core that bombards the water with neutrons. This allows the water to become radioactive. Additionally, it causes the high pressure piping system to become brittle requiring constant inspection and periodic replacement.

As you can see by the smaller size and minimal amount of pipes, pebble bed reactors do not have these liabilities. The PBR is a VHTR, or very-high-temperature reactor. It is gas-cooled, not water cooled."

"Where are the rods?"

"It doesn't use rods. Instead it uses round fuel elements called "pebbles." They are fuel particles, or TRISO particles, consisting of U235 within pyrolytic graphite and coated with a ceramic layer of Silicone Carbonate. The pebbles are about the size of a tennis ball, and when they are stacked in certain geometric progression, become critical. There are over three-hundred and sixty-thousand of these balls within a reactor, producing an abundance of heat. In actuality, one reactor produces forty-percent more heat than a comparable water-cooled reactor. And, more heat translates to more power generation for less money."

"So what makes it any safer than water-cooled systems?"

"First is the lack of cooling pumps, water and redundant backup systems."

"That makes it safer? Sounds to me like an accident waiting to happen. Redundancy is safety, and you're telling us you don't have it."

"Redundancy means multiple back-ups: more pumps, more pipes, more valves. It means more complexity. And when there is an accident in one of those conventional plants, it all goes south in a cascading effect, with everyone running around trying to figure out from where the problem stems. By the time the initial problem is isolated, another pops up, and so on until you have a cascading catastrophe. Contaminated water becomes steam and has to be vented. The disappearing water has to be replenished before the rods are uncovered or you have meltdown."

"And you propose that cannot happen with this system? I don't want to be around here if you're wrong."

"As I said earlier, this reactor is air-cooled. Inert gas, we use helium, circulates around the stack of pebbles, carrying heat away. The lack of complexity lowers the chance of accidents to very low possibilities. We could use the heated helium directly to turn turbines. Helium doesn't easily absorb neutrons or dissolve contaminants. But as an even greater consideration to safety, we run it through heat diffusers converting water to steam to drive our turbines. We are studying the use of helium gas directly and will consider it as we gain experience and confidence in the future."

"So, there's absolutely nothing that can go wrong, is that what you're telling us?

"No, I am not. There is inherent risk with any technology. The key is to minimize the risk while achieving maximum reward for mankind. Airplanes are inherently dangerous, yet we have tried to minimize this risk."

"Yeah, but if an airplane goes down, it only takes the people on board with it."

"Really? Perhaps you'd like to address that point to those that did not survive Nine-Eleven."

All were silent for a moment.

"We have written off promising technologies because of isolated accidents. Yes, they may have been deadly and threatening to whole communities. But lessons learned should improve the technology, not shelve it, particularly in the area of energy production. Oil spills from off-shore drilling rigs shut down that supply of domestic petroleum. Three-Mile-Island's dispersal of radioactive steam into the atmosphere killed the growth of the nuclear industry. Both should have been studied with the intent of developing new methods, improvements in technologies and oversight. Instead, we run away from them in fear and kill the exact things that provide the best hope."

"To answer your concerns directly, Governor, if the reactor vessel is breached and oxygen introduced, the graphite can cause a fire, accompanied by dispersal of radioactivity. However, there are no pipes within the core. The helium naturally flows around the voids of the stacked pebbles. It is a low-pressure system that contains its own passive safety feature. The gas acts as the coolant: the more pumped in, the more heat carried away and the slower the reaction. There are no control rods required to constantly adjust the fission reaction. A PBR is much less complex and many times more self-regulating than conventional light-water reactors. Not to get too technical, but there is a phenomena known as Doppler Broadening. Essentially this occurs when nuclear fuel increases in temperature. There is rapid motion of the atoms. U238 is likely to absorb these fast neutrons at higher temperatures. Less neutrons available for fission means a lower reaction in the chamber. We call this a negative feedback. As temperature increases, power decreases."

"But it can burn up, right?"

"If oxygen is present, yes. However, the vessel containment is airtight. The only gas present is inert helium. Even the external environment of the chamber is helium. This area in which we are standing doubles as a pressurization chamber. If any personnel need enter the reactor area, they would first enter here, wearing a pressure suit, and close the door behind. This area would have the ambient air, which contains oxygen, removed. Then helium would replace the air before the person entered. This thick, clear portal in front of you does not exist in the other reactors. It is strictly for tours like this. And, as you may note, attached to it is a covering hatch that is now open. The other chambers have a solid metal door similar to the one behind you."

And because helium does not easily absorb neutrons or contaminants, this hazardous offal is not passed to outside pipes, which could cause embrittlement. A pebble-bed reactor can have all of its supporting machinery fail and the reactor will not crack, melt, explode or spew hazardous wastes. It simply goes up to a designed "idle" temperature, and stays there. In that state, the reactor vessel radiates heat, but the vessel and fuel spheres remain intact and undamaged. The machinery can be repaired or the fuel can be removed. These safety features were tested, and filmed, within a Chinese reactor. The coolant flow was halted. Afterward, the fuel balls were sampled and examined for damage and there was none.

I already discussed the fire resistance of the composite on the walls, floor and ceiling. But I did not tell you of the one-meter thick lining of lead beneath the concrete floor. Plus we are nearly a mile underneath the ground. All in all, we feel quite safe with our design. And each one of these reactors produces 120 megawatts of electricity every day."

"Each one? How many do you have?"

"If you walked down this corridor to the end, you would have covered nearly two miles and passed by fifty PBR's."

"FIFTY! Good God! What do the Feds have to say about that?"

"You cannot comment about that which you have no knowledge."

Governor Fodor appeared stunned. The Utah Governor spoke, "I have a question."

"Go ahead, Liz."

"What do you do with the waste? I mean, there is nuclear waste material from all of this, isn't there?"

"Yes, there is waste. But the graphite core and silicone carbonate surrounding is so tough, stable and resistant to fire, some propose it can be stored geologically without concern. However, for added safety, we enclose the spent balls within lead-lined concrete coffins stored in a nearby facility where we reprocess other nuclear waste. Some of the waste is used for the blanket of the **Wystar**. And due to the size difference between the balls and conventional rods, we have enough storage facilities already constructed to store two hundred years of waste from all of these reactors."

Governor Almondo was surprised no one had asked his question, "Why a fission reactor? I thought we were here to view a Fusion reactor."

"And you shall, shortly," answered Dr. Zhou. "The reason for these reactors is that we needed to begin producing a revenue-generating product: electricity. Fusion was not developed fully when we installed these reactors. These have been on-line for ten years; **WyStar**, our fusion reactor, only one."

The California Governor followed up, "So, now you can shut these down?"

Dr. Zhou looked confused, "Why would we do such a thing? We understand the process intimately. These reactors are productive. They are safe. We have an investment here, and there is at least twenty-five years' more life in these reactors."

"That may all be true, but wouldn't your people feel better if you shut these down?" asked Governor Almondo.

Samantha touched Zhou's shoulder, indicating she would handle the answer, "Mario, we are not a touchy-feely State. We do things because it makes sense, not to score political points. Our people are aware that these reactors exist. They understand the need, the benefit and the risk. We have told them all three in very truthful terms. If I proposed shutting these reactors down for the worries you have stated, I would be voted out of office tomorrow.

She continued, "And on that note, let's proceed to our crowning jewel."

# Chapter 4

## WyStar

Samantha and Dr. Zhou led the group from the fission vestibule out and across the transition mall to another large vault door on the opposing wall. They passed through the opened portal into another intermittently lit hall that extended beyond their vision. There was only one door along this travel.

Dr. Zhou addressed the group, "We currently have only one Fusion reactor on-line. However," he pointed down the lengthy cavern, "we have already excavated for future expansion. Through the door to our right is **WyStar**."

He walked through a door similar to the PBR entry, stepped over a metal threshold and signaled for the group to follow. Inside he and Sam scooped up a stack of booties, caps and jumpsuits made from a paper-like product. As he and Samantha passed out the clean-room attire, Zhou instructed everyone to watch as he donned the outer garb. Leg ends and sleeve ends were elastic, held snug to the body. Same was true for the cap applied over hair and booties over shoes. The group climbed a flight of stairs and entered through a clear door surrounded by a thick seal. When pulled open there was a noticeable whoosh, indicating greater air pressure on the other side. They were upon a metal catwalk raised three meters above the floor of the reactor room. Another thick window ran the length and ended at another clear door. On the other side were stairs leading downward to the floor. Josh felt a constant vibration in his head. It wasn't terribly irritating, just more like background static.

Zhou explained the need for their personal coverings, "This building houses the world's most powerful lasers. Lasers are beams of light and, therefore, very sensitive to any particulate contamination. This entire building is a M6.5, or Class 8 clean room, meaning there are only 0.5 particulates per three-thousand cubic meters of air. Behind this glass panel, one is able to view **WyStar** without a respirator. However, those within the chamber must wear such equipment."

Zhou gave a short wave to a man down on the main floor. He was dressed as they, with the added accessory of tight fitting gloves, respirator within a full face mask and a thin belt with small attachments. Acknowledging Zhou, he nodded and headed to in front of the window.. He pressed a button on the belt allowing his voice to come through speakers within the platform area.

*"Gut Morgan."* From his greeting and accent, Josh thought the man to be German. "I am Dr. Gleispach, Director of Operations for **WyStar**. I begin by saying zat I am Austrian, not German." He nodded his head quickly in punctuation to this seemingly important point. He turned and pointed to another, similarly clad floor person. "And that gentleman is Dr. Leo Viloshensky." The indicated man gave a short wave and proceeded with his work.

"Dr. Zhou, azzked I explain vat you zee. Zat pro-nounced hum pul-zing in your head iz coming from zese rows of laser amplifiers. Zere are vun-hundred und ninety-two channels zat take zee weak laser beam and increaze power many times over. Zee beam is shplit and pazzed tru glass slabs. Inzide slabs xenon lamp eggzite neodymium. Dis deposit energy into zee beam. Zee laser beam is sent tru zis proocess fifty-two times before iz directed to zee Fuzion chamber. Mit each slab, it iz amplified twenty-five per-zent over previous strength. Pleaze give me a moment vile I valk vere zee real action occurs."

"Sure sounds German to me," mumbled Josh. Elizabeth Brigham snickered into her hand.

Dr. Gleispach walked to a center aisle and turned right towards the front of the building. He passed along several extensive rows of one-meter high cabinets. Occasionally he would point to one of the boxes calling out a designation amplifier or preamplifier. The walk ended at a three-story tall, round chamber perched upon large metal legs. The chamber had several protrusions radiating outward, as well as cables, tubing and lrger pipes. To the right was a graphic, similar to the one in the presentation. It was a cut-out representation of the massive ball. There were depictions of the inner core lining, the electro-magnets surrounding the inner core lining, lasers penetrating the core, a charged-ion bombardment ring, the waste blanket within the outer core and a lead covering around the entire unit, nearly two meters thick. In the center of the chamber, beams of light were firing into a glowing, bright core labeled plasma.

Dr. Gleispach explained, "To create initial ignition, ve use the laser beam. The beamz are cone-verted from red vavelength to ultraviolet. When zey cone-verge on the target pellet, over vun-hundred tousand Kelvin is reached. Zis crushes zee pellet into a denzity vun-hundred timez zat of lead. Immediately upon ignition plasma is generated. At zis zame time a current is passed through zee plasma to zus-tain it. Zen ve inject more hydrogen isotope in zee form of deuterium into zee plasma. A fixed, magnetic field zus-pends the plasma. Zee secondary, ion belt zurrounds zee mag-field and, tru repulzion, aid in maintaining plasmatic core, Zis for over six minutes. Zis zecond, charged bombardment haz been zee key to zus-daining zee plasma state."

A row of buttons ran down the hand rail in front of the group. Dr. Zhou pressed the one in front, allowing him to be heard by the floor personnel, "And after the six minutes?"

"At five minutes, fifty-tree and two ten-zousandths of a zecond, anutter pellet iz fired into zee plasma. Laser ignition must reoccur becauze zee plasma core cools zlightly by zis time and needs a boost to reheat and re-prezzurize zee incoming pellet. In zis manner, the plasmatic core iz cone-tinuous and zo too zee heat generated." Dr. Gleispach pointed to a tube leading to another chamber, "Zat is transfer tube for fuel pellet. It iz cone-nected on zis end to plasma chamber, vere it iz fired into the plasma via a linear accelerator. At zee other end is rotational molding unit for pellet fabreecation."

"Zurrounding zee chamber iz a blanket of radioactive izotopes. As, I believe, your prior pre-zentation dis-cuzed, zeese are capturing zee extra neutrons egz-pelled during Hydrogen Fuzion. Zee heat from zee core, coom-bined with zee blanket, heat zee liquid in zose tubes. In turn, zee tubes run tru a heat egzhanger vere vater is turned to shteam and uzed to drive electrical tur-bines. Zee electrical generating units are directly behind zat vall."

Governor Fodor punched the button in front of him. "Your 'blanket' doesn't look much like a real blanket."

Dr. Gleispach nodded, "Ya, zee 'blanket' iz ach-chewally curved sheets of lead wrapped within a proprietary alloy of utter metals. On top of zat iz a specialty zeramic developed here in Wyoming."

*"And no doubt Jimmy Dillon had somethin' to do with the ceramic,"* mused Josh.

Gleispach continued, "Zee radioactive product derived from Fuzion processes elze-vere and here are embedded wit-in zee lead base, but not to a tickness zat inhibits zee rogue neutron from penetrating. Ve use zee term 'blanket' in zee sense of a covering, not regarding its coom-posite material."

"That's clear as mud," whispered Josh into Brigham's ear. She spit out a short laugh.

Sam looked in their direction, "You two can stay after class."

The Utah Governor elbowed Josh, "Nice job, cowboy. Now we've got detention."

Sam turned to the others within the small audience, "I think since Scott has started us off, this would be a good opportunity for other questions. Just press the button in front of you."

"Well, I have a question that's been nagging me for the last few hours." Governor Almondo was pressing his button. "If Fusion is so safe, then what caused the European version, the...ah...ITER, to blow up?"

Governor Fodor confirmed the question by nodding his head vigorously.

Gleispach looked to Sam. She was already reaching for her button. "I'll field this one, Doctor." Sam turned to Almondo. "Mario, the ITER was sabotaged. It was deliberately destroyed."

"WHAT?" It was Governor Fodor who was most shocked, "It was blown up on purpose? How do you know that? There was never any mention of it by the French or anyone else. They said a fault in the chamber during initial startup caused the accident."

"Yes they did, Scott. And as far as I know, they still believe it was an accident. However, we know otherwise. Many of the scientists here were working on ITER and are thought to have died in that explosion."

"This is crazy," whined Fodor. "You telling me these gentlemen here were at the ITER when it exploded. That story doesn't hold water, Sam. Sorry. The press said that all of the important scientists were killed."

"True, they did say that, Scott, because that's what we wanted them to believe" answered Sam calmly.

"You wanted….. I still don't get it Sam. Unless you, or some henchmen for, you actually blew up the damn thing. Were you getting rid of the competition?"

"HOW RUDE, SCOTT!" Elizabeth Brigham chimed in. "You know damn well Sam isn't capable of such a thing. My God, have a little class."

"I don't know what to think at this revelation," added Governor Hughes.

Sam's composure remained serene, "Scott, John...to enlighten you, the ITER *was* destroyed by a competitor. But not us. It was the Russians. They could see the end game: the end of fossil fuel demand for transportation and electrical generation. Their entire economic future is pinned on Europe's dependency upon their natural gas and oil. The eventual development of Fusion would bankrupt them.

The Mossad learned of the pending sabotage and informed us. Israel is banking a lot of money on our successful development of Fusion. However, the Israeli's saw the French security of ITER as poor, if non-existent. They knew if the Russians were thwarted this time, there would be other attempts. And sooner than later, one would be successful. So we developed a plan to extract the scientists just moments before the explosion and bring them here to aid in **WyStar**'s development. We were already three years into development and, technologically, beyond ITER. The scientists like Dr. Gleispach here, were excited to become part of our team."

"Wait a minute," Fodor maintained his skeptical look. "How did you know the precise moment to remove these guys….timing the explosion, extraction and all that stuff?"

"Because one of the scientists here set the charges. He knew the most vulnerable points on ITER and therefore where to exactly set the charges." Sam said this with almost nonchalance.

"ONE OF THESE GUYS BLEW UP THE ITER? WHICH BASTARD? HE SHOULD BE HANGED!" Scott Fodor's voice was so many octaves high it almost squeaked.

Dr. Leo Viloshensky appeared to monitor one of the laser units, but was listening to the conversation intently. At Fodor's outburst, he hung his head and shuffled towards the end of the room.

"Scott, I wouldn't begin to tell you who caused the explosion. The man involved was being blackmailed by the Russians. His family was under a death threat if he did not succeed. His first instinct was to refuse his orders. But the Mossad told him to proceed. They rewired the explosives so as to localize the damage and ensure no human lives were lost. In a very dangerous mission, the Mossad also extracted the man's family from Russia and brought them here. The man has dealt with enough fear and anguish over this, Scott. And no one here heaps the slightest blame upon him. Even if he had refused the Russians, the result would have been the death of himself and his family. Then the Russians would have revised their plan, been more determined and their inevitable success would have caused the deaths of hundreds. So consider these facts, Scott, before condemning the man. Fortunately, none of us has had to face such choices….yet."

"It all makes sense to me," said Governor Brigham supportively.

Scott Fodor mumbled a comeback that was unintelligible to the others.

Stillwater slowly moved his head to look in the direction of Leo and thought, *He has a Russian-sounding name to me. I'm not sure if he did the right thing, but he's probably been to hell and back over the decision.* Then another point came to mind.

"Sam, aren't you nervous they might try it here? I mean, the Russians trying to sabotage **Wystar**?"

Sam nodded, "Yes, they and our own Federal government. That is why we have implemented the security measures we all went through to get down here."

"Won't help if it's an inside job," offered Josh.

"That's true. However, we have thoroughly vetted all personnel. And access to this **WyStar** part of the facility is even more restricted."

Josh nodded his support to her answer but thought, *I sure hope so.*

Dr. Zhou used the lull in conversation for redirection, "With that issue out of the way, let's return to the details of **WyStar**. Let's focus on the economics of Fusion."

"Good idea, Doctor," assisted John Hughes. "I was thinking that very point as I noted all the energy poured into this process. Are you even close to breaking even? What do you get out of **WyStar**, other than dimming the lights in the nearest city?"

Liz Brigham chuckled, trying to lighten the mood.

Samantha appreciated her efforts, "That, Governor, is a perfectly succinct question. After all, it is the point of building all of this, spending all this money. This is not a research center to prove out theoretical propositions. It is an energy facility. To answer your question, seven-point-five percent, soon to be eight-point three percent."

"Excuse me, I don't understand?"

"What I was saying, a bit cryptically, is that we have currently generated a seven-point-five net return. And soon, it will be eight-point three percent."

"That's all? Seems like an enormous waste of resources. Why would you do all of this for a seven-point five percent return on investment."

Samantha looked at Hughes, "I think you are not clear, John. That means for every Kelvin or kilowatt of energy we put into this plant, we receive seven-point-five-percent more energy out of it? You know how perpetual motion machines were, at one time, the holy grail of machinery? Imagine if you had a perpetual motion machine that not only kept going forever, but produced seven-point-five percent more energy than went into it."

Governor Hughes appeared confused. Sam knew it was a difficult concept for people to grasp, at first. Zhou jumped in. "Let us make it more relative this way, Governor. If you were running an energy-producing, turbine-power plant, it would take one-hundred percent of the energy of the natural gas or synthetic gas to produce somewhere between forty to sixty percent of the energy received in the form of electricity. Does that make sense?"

Hughes pondered that a moment and slowly answered, "Okay, I'm with you so far. I understand that energy conversion, whether natural gas, coal or oil, loses energy during its conversion to electricity. In that way, it's a losing proposition. Is that what you mean?"

"Exactly, but in dollars it is the consumer who is losing. Power-generating utilities charge for the total cost of the energy required to create a kilowatt of electrical energy. Additionally, they add profit, overhead, maintenance and all other costs. So,..."

"Hold on!" The Governor's eyes were saucer-shaped. "You mean that every dollar spent on raw materials to drive this plant produces revenue of one-dollar, seven-and-a-half-cents?"

Zhou and Sam looked at each other. This wasn't the point. "No, but close." Sam was trying to aid the understanding. "Actually, the raw materials, the deuterium and trintium, are, more or less, free. The electrical cost to drive the lasers is a major portion of the total cost. And, no, we don't dim cities to accomplish it. Initially, we used power from the fission processes across the transit area.

What we are talking about is gross energy consumption versus net energy output, which can eventually be calculated as costs and revenues. See,

John, if you add up the kilowatts used to produce the lasers and the ionic and magnetic fields to create and maintain the plasmatic core, there is enough heat generated to create the steam that drives the turbine to produce seven-and-a-half percent more electricity than went into the creation of the plasma in the first place."

Governor Hughes' face screwed into contemplation as mental gears shifted into high. Then he got their point. He said with suspicion. "Wait a minute. That is *beyond* a perpetual machine. You're saying you get more energy out of this thing than is put into it."

"Welcome aboard, Governor. After all, that is the point of Fusion."

"OK, say I buy your premise, which I still find dubious, what about all the money you poured into this in the first place. You actually think you're going to make a profit on this someday?"

"A skeptical politician, the hope of the future." Sam smiled. "We have been conservative, Governor, and calculated a twenty-percent drop in reactor costs from this to the next reactor and subsequent ten percent drops for the next two facilities. Then it should be much smaller drops after this thirty-five percent. And remember, we are basing the starting cost on the physical facility. The initial research costs need not be included. Naturally, we will continue research on improvements and better methods, but it will never get close to the costs we incurred for this initial **WyStar**. As an example, we are already researching the elimination of radioactive waste as the absorbent for the rogue neutron. The point of everything here is to solve the near future and of driving turbines directly with the molten sodium. However, we are continuously looking to the future. We believe with money and emphasis, we can solve anything within fifty years. WyStar will provide its own money for its own improvements."

Governor Hughes interjected, "This is well and good, Samantha. But I am sure your estimates are based on returns compared against the outrageous prices now paid for imported oil. Once your production ramps up and hits the market, you know what the Middle East oil producers will do: drop their prices fifty percent just to drive you out of the market. What happens then to your projections?"

"They stay right on target."

"How can you say that?"

"Because, by our laws, and those of nine of our international partners, we maintain an all-electric requirement for powering transportation, manufacturing, all motors, commercial buildings, and home residences. We provide an exclusion to the transportation category for aviation fuel. Additionally, our laws require no air pollution from electrical generation. We believe many of the States, hopefully yours, will have the same requirements soon. The areas mandated represent eighty-five percent of oil's use within the United States. Two-thirds, sixty-six percent is for transportation alone. We have already developed within Wyoming enough oil production to cover the other fifteen percent, this mainly for polymers, lubricants, feed stocks, fertilizers and other miscellaneous uses."

"So you force a monopoly upon your people." Governor Fodor looked smugly around.

"Price levels are set by the State in the same manner Public Utilities were before the public was duped into deregulation." Sam paused a moment before continuing, "Let me ask you Scott, would your Citizens rather purchase their power from a State-regulated utility, or from an international oligarchy called OPEC? I think the fact that most members of OPEC use our money in attempts to destroy Western Civilization might be deterrent enough, don't you?

Governor Fodor grumbled.

Sam followed on, "If the Federal Government had developed a real energy policy after the Oil Shock of the late nineteen-seventies, the United States would not be in half the hole it currently is and would not require a military presence in that part of the world. What was needed then and now was an immediate, domestic production plan, a long-range production plan and a flooring price for imported oil. Any difference below the floor should have been used for domestic development only. That's what we originally did here."

"Wow! That must have made the public real happy! How did you pull that off?"

"We didn't 'pull-off' anything, Scott. We explained the plan to our Citizens. We had town hall debates. We made some compromises on timing of implementation and interim financial assistance. Then we voted. It passed by a sixty-seven percent majority."

"Why, in God's name, would any taxpayer ever agree to tax themselves? Our legislature uses every shenanigan in the book to increase taxes without a public vote because it would be defeated."

"And that's why your Citizens would never vote for a tax. First, they figure you've already taxed them without their permission. And this makes them mad. Voting NO is their only way to fight back. Second, there is a supreme arrogance of deciding what is best for people without asking them. You are treating them like children. And this makes them even madder. If you trust your Citizens, treat them like adults; inform them completely of what is involved in any proposal. You might be pleasantly surprised as to how they will step up to the plate and do the right thing. People will sacrifice their immediate needs for a brighter future. But they have to trust the sacrifice will be used wisely and honestly. Most State governments, and definitely the Federal government, have broken so many promises and consistently lied to their Citizens, that any potential trust has been destroyed. It is going to take a real commitment on the part of government to repair the breach. For some governments, it may take their elimination, replaced with a new beginning."

Governor Hughes was thoughtful, "What about the switch in transportation? How could all your Citizens afford to switch to electric? I mean you also have hydrogen fuel cell technology for cars, trucks, tractors. Wasn't it tough on farmers and business, let alone individuals?"

"First, we gave them ten years to replace their combustion vehicles. That's why we pumped oil from within our State and invested in oil sands in Canada and oil shale from Scott's State, Colorado. Then we provided everyone a low interest, long term loan to switch to electric. Actually, for farmers we increased their profits, dramatically, through the drop in oil prices for feed and fertilizers. And prices of our electricity are the lowest in the world. This is a boon to industry and individuals. For instance, a hydrogen-fuel cell vehicle costs forty percent less per mile to run than a gasoline-powered car in any of your States. Our farmers and ranchers' energy costs are only thirty-five percent of other States. With our ramped-up oil production, we actually have the beginning of a glut of oil's derivative products. Prices on fertilizers have fallen dramatically. Companies flock here for many reasons, but energy and low-cost plastics are near the top of the list. In fact, we just authorized the export of a certain percentage of these derivatives at handsome profits."

"I concede, you have a good thing going here. So what stops the rest of the world from copying you and taking away your competitive advantage?" asked Governor Brigham.

"Well, you have a lot of the world involved right here. And they will receive the benefits."

"You mean the technology."

"If they can afford it."

"You mean they can pay to develop this one, proto-type facility, but they can't afford to develop their own facilities?"

"Well. Your question is not entirely correct, Liz. Only four countries paid for these facilities: Wyoming, China, Japan and Israel. Each will partake in the direct fruits of this development. Each will have detailed knowledge of how to reproduce this facility."

"What about the other twelve countries represented."

"If their people can carry in their heads the knowledge to build this facility to their own countries, and if they have the money and the will of the people to build it, they can do so. However, what each has earned is a significant discount in the cost of energy derived from all of our energy production methods. For many of them, it makes far greater sense to buy our competitive energy to supplement their own, rather than duplicating our entire structure. Even with our primary partners we hope to be so price-competitive for delivered electricity, they will see the economics of keeping us as a supplier even after deciding to build a Fusion facility."

Governor Fodor scoffed, "Discounted energy? How are you going to sell them energy? Some of these countries are over twelve thousand miles away. You telling me you're going to ship energy that far? If so that's ridiculous. Did you find out Tesla's secret to send electricity through the earth?"

"Not ridiculous, Governor, sublime. And ask no more questions on that subject as you will receive no more answers."

"Yea, get the message Scott. They're not going to tell you how they ship their electricity all over the place," said Governor Hughes. Josh restrained a smirk, for he already had the answer. Hughes continued, "Here's another question. If this is your only fusion reactor, how is your electricity so bountiful and cheap now? Do those PBR's provide all the State's needs?"

Sam answered, "No, we have one-hundred and twenty-nine, natural gas powered turbines combined with HRSG or heat-recovery-steam-generators, seventy-eight of the turbines run on UCG,...."

Governor Fodor interrupted, "What is ...."

Governor Brigham interrupted him, "Lordie, Scott, let the lady finish her sentence."

He harrumphed and turned back to Sam, nodding for her to continue."

"Thank you, Liz. As I was saying, seventy-eight UCG/HRSG plants. To explain the acronym, Governor, it stands for 'Underground Coal Gasification.' I will explain it simply, as I am not an expert in the subject. It is essentially pumping oxidates into seams of underground coal. With ignition and pressurization, it produces synthetic gas. The gas is then used in turbines for electricity production, along with the heat recovered from the gas turbines to power steam turbines."

"You burn the coal underground?"

"Yes, but technically we are oxidizing the coal to produce gas. With advances we have developed, it is much more economical than mining bulk coal. It is easier and cheaper to transport the fuel. It is far less polluting than burning coal above ground. And it is more efficient than burning natural gas. In fact, we have either converted or shut down our twenty-three coal fired plants that were running at the beginning of this century. An additional bonus of UCG is one of its by-products, hydrogen. And we've already covered how we are putting this to use."

"To continue with our list, we have seventeen large-scale hydroelectric plants, seventy-two mini-hydroelectric units rivers, and over six hundred micro hydro-electric units along creeks and streams. Additionally we have over three thousand wind-powered units, three geothermal plants, eleven full-scale hydrogen plants, water based, not methane, over twelve-thousand micro hydrogen generators, nine-hundred and eleven mini hydrogen generators, fifty fission plants, and one Fusion plant."

"Jeesh! No wonder you have such an abundance of cheap energy. You must be producing ten percent of the entire nation's electricity."

Sam gave a self-satisfied chuckle, "Actually, we are closer to thirty-one percent."

Governor Fodor was dismissive, "I think we are doing a little over-estimation now. I know how pride can influence numbers."

"It's not pride, Scott, it's fact. You seem to have forgotten how much capacity has withered. By the beginning of the recession in 2008, electricity demand fell. There was actually a glut. By the time of the Greatest Depression, electricity consumption fell even further. Due to economics, new plants were put on hold. Old plants were closed. The environmentalist saw this as a perfect time to strike. Stringent pollution requirements forced moth-balling, rather than updating of marginal plants. Environmentalists then demanded laws specifying fixed percentages of energy to come from passive sources: wind, solar, geothermal, and tidal. This caused an even greater glut of conventional power generation, as another ten percent was carved from the conventional-powered plants' market. The environmentalists' next attack was nuclear. They had Federal courts rule that, with all the waste product sitting in vulnerable 'coffins,' the plants had to stop producing more radioactive waste. In other words, the plants were out of business in one stroke. The industry screamed at Congress to open Yucca Flats in order to safely store the waste. But the pleas fell on deaf ears. Bye-bye clean, low-cost, non-imported energy.

This pulled twenty percent of our electrical energy off the grid. It was just enough to stabilize the conventional power suppliers. However, they had scrapped all plans for any expansion and any new developments. With the Federal Department of Energy recently given re-regulation of all utilities, the plants make a small margin. But their energy and maintenance costs are so high, electricity prices have begun to skyrocket again. And any uptick in economic activity, along with increased oil demand sends electrical price soaring. Then the economic upturn sputters, falls, and we go right back into the dumpster."

"So how does Wyoming make money on electricity?"

"First, we consume a lot of it ourselves. But the great percentage is not for consumption, it's for production. We produce products we can sell to the world. This brings us revenue. Second, we export energy to markets that are doing well and need extra supplies."

"I still don't get how you deliver it. Aren't all the transmission lines under the control of DOE?"

"Yes, Governor. And as before, don't ask 'cause we won't tell."

Josh's thoughts harkened back to his conversation with Jimmy regarding Wyoming's growing network of high-speed trains, accompanied by the superconducting, electrical transmission lines buried between the rails. No wonder the State required ownership of right-of-ways within other States.

"Josh?"

Stillwater was jarred from his thought. He felt like a schoolboy caught daydreaming, "Huh?"

Sam said, "I was asking if anyone had any further questions before heading back."

"Nope."

# Chapter 5

## A Pleased President

## Oval Office, White House

President Rivera stood at a window within the Oval Office. He gazed upon the rose garden and sighed.

"Guess they're through blooming."

His Chief of Staff, William Dormier, was the only other person in the room.

"Sir?"

"The roses. I said they must be through blooming for the year."

The comment threw Dormier off kilter. George Rivera had never commented on the roses during his six years in office except to curse them for aggravating his allergies. Dormier was becoming increasingly concerned about the man. The President's mood swings and vitriolic outbursts were becoming more frequent. The ever-increasing power demanded by this President, and ceded by Congress and the Supreme Court, had fueled Rivera's megalomania and emboldened his moves towards an autocratic, if not despotic Executive.

The carnage the Federal government had subjected the dollar to allowed Rivera to declare the economy a national emergency. And emergencies always allowed Presidents to expand their powers with public acquiescence. Lincoln suspended *habeous corpus*. Adams and Wilson banned traitorous speech. Roosevelt instituted and banned gold ownership. Now, Rivera raised the Executive Order to an entirely new level, creating laws at whim. If Congress finally uttered a protest at his excesses, he merely bullied them into approving law that extended the power requested. Congress could claim they had exercised their Constitutional powers; had pruned back the Chief Executives overreach. And all were mollified.

But Rivera learned that with such extensive power came ever-increasing responsibility to show results. The majority of the time he reveled in being the single source of action. When he finally fixed all the problems of the nation through his sole leadership, all credit would be his. There would be no sharing, no compromising, no back slapping of Congress. He would claim it all as his victory. This would be his legacy.

However, the nation's problems were becoming more and more intractable. Unemployment was stuck at nearly fourteen percent. And this was the officially released number. He knew it was closer to twenty-two percent. But juggling of the numbers and constant changes to the formulae masked the real extent of the problem. Inflation was running at nearly forty percent a year. Foreign nations that the U.S. depended on for oil and natural gas imports no longer honored the Dollar as payment. Instead, they demanded gold. The GDP – Gross Domestic Product – of the nation was nearly thirty percent lower than the national debt. Any attempt to stimulate the economy through deficit spending or the Fed pumping in more money was ineffective. Rivera finally understood the economic rule that any increase in debt spending above the GDP equaled inflation.

Yet, in spite of these mountainous problems, the President still pulled the nation inexorably towards a socialist system. Taxes on the 'rich' were increased nearly every year to the current rate of ninety-five percent. Capital gains were at the same rate. Individual gold ownership was banned. Railroads, automobile manufacturers, defense contractors, newspapers, energy companies and many other industries had wailed for Federal bailouts and protectionism. Rivera had horse-collared Congress into granting these requests. But it came at a price for the capitalists; fifty-one percent Federal ownership of the companies.

Rivera had finally gained the 'organized' economy that he, and all of his liberal/socialist fellow travelers, had envisioned. But for reasons that always baffle socialists, the goose stopped laying golden eggs while demanding more and more grain; i.e. more bailouts. The economy sank and the national debt ballooned. The United States of America was broke. There was nothing more to tax and everything for the government to control, and feed. The economy was a mess. The whole purpose of socialism was to 'organize' it; tidy things up. It was perplexing to the Chief Executive. And sometimes it made him tired, like now.

Dormier looked anxious, "Mr. President, are you feeling all right?"

The words broke off Rivera's gaze of the outside. He turned and barked at his Aide, "I'm fine, Bill! Jeeze, I take five minutes to literally smell the roses and you're sizing me up for a straightjacket. Well, I don't like it. So knock it off!"

Dormier was actually relieved at the rebuff. Rivera was back to his old self. There was business to attend, the country's business.

"Yes sir. Which do you wish to talk about first?"

Rivera thought a moment, "Tell me, how is the money exchange going?" The President was referring to what had become known as the 'Big Swap,' or, as it was jokingly referred to by the citizenry: BS.

In order to combat inflation, Rivera had concocted a plan whereby ten 'Old' U.S. Dollars were to be exchanged for one 'New" U.S. Dollar, commonly stated as NUS. The President, without input of his Treasury Secretary, had surmised that reducing the amount of available script in circulation by ten times would reduce inflation by the same amount. It had possibilities of success, if Federal spending had been cut by ten times. But this was never to happen. Instead, inflation picked up because of the 'Swap' stripping away the last vestige of confidence residing in the currency.

"It's going well, sir. In fact Treasury Secretary Halston calculates that nearly seventy-five percent of the 'Old' bills have been exchanged. It would appear we are ahead of schedule." Of course Halston had never done any calculation of the sort. The percent number quoted was decided upon by Dormier and the Secretary during a midnight call.

"Seventy-five percent, imagine that. Tell Halston 'good job,' Bill." The President was pleased. And he had not been pleased over many things lately.

"Will do, sir. Next subject?"

"Wyoming, definitely Wyoming. Where's Declamore at on moving his toy soldiers around his game board?"

Never having served within the armed forces, Rivera nursed a loathing of all things military. He attributed it to his liberal bent that the military wanted, even sought out, unnecessary wars, thereby upsetting other countries and creating bad juju for the U.S. He never once considered who had ordered the troops to far-off lands to die in those unnecessary wars.

In truth, Rivera's anathema for all things military derived from lack of service. Many other politicians proudly hailed their call to duty. This handicap to his career irked him. Many politicians that had not served officially honored the troops and the officers that led them. Rivera decried this as phony patriotism and mere pandering for votes. Deep down he felt inferior to those that had put their lives on the line for the nation. This inadequacy led to a political career of denigrating the military. This made him feel superior and accredited him an ideological star of the Left.

"The seventy-five thousand troops just south of Wyoming's border, Mr. President. They are awaiting supplies and then your orders."

"About time," Rivera was pacing. "I'm going to give that State two weeks to capitulate to my demands or I'm giving Declamore the go ahead."

"Invasion, sir?" This entire approach made Dormier nervous. He didn't like to think of the potential fallout from the other States if the Federal government, using U.S. Army troops, invaded one of their brethren.

"You damn right, Bill. Invasion." Rivera punched a fist into the other open hand. "I'll show that Nevin Stiles he doesn't talk to the President of the United States the way he did."

Nevin Stiles was a Wyoming tycoon as well as one of their Senators. He had known George Rivera from the days of Senator Rivera. The two had been friends until, shortly after Rivera's inauguration, Stiles fiscally conservative advice to the new President was completely spurned for Rivera's hard turn to socialism. The last time the two had met was in the Oval Office and Stiles had reiterated his formula for Rivera to 'right' the nation's economic ship. Rivera felt the advice was draconian and Stiles to be a broken record on the subject. The original subject of the meeting had been the President's demand that Wyoming stop ignoring Federal laws, restart payments of Federal taxes, the overall capitulation of Wyoming and the return of the State to the Federal fold.

The meeting ended badly.

"That might not be the correct motivation to invade a State, sir."

"Lincoln did it and got away with it, Bill"

"The situation was substantially different. It was multiple States he invaded. He had the military support of numerous other States. And the invaded States had unconstitutionally seceded. Additionally, Lincoln had the impetus of the immorality of slavery. I think it's difficult to compare the Civil War to this situation with Wyoming."

"Who's side are you on, Dormier? This State has basically seceded and I have the power, and the *moral imperative* to bring them back in line."

"I have always been on your side. I am on your side now. That's why I am trying to help you avoid a misstep that could be potentially damaging. Wyoming has not seceded. They are ignoring Federal law. The first you handle with U.S. troops. The second you handle in U.S. Federal courts. If they ignore the Supreme Court, you send in U.S. Marshalls, the FBI, even the DDD. That keeps us legal and with the moral upper hand."

"Dishwater, that's all you offer, tepid, used dishwater, Dormier. Remember Teddy Roosevelt: 'Talk softly and carry a big stick.' Well I'm going to spank that State royally with a big stick, the United States Army."

Dormier wished to remind the President that Roosevelt had said the phrase regarding other countries, not his own citizenry. But Dormier thought better of this. *If Rivera is off on this bent, so be it. Let him clean up his own mess, for once. There won't be anyone to blame but himself.*

"What's the name of that General in charge out there, Declamore's chum from the Academy?" asked Rivera.

"Maxwell, Mr. President. General Vernon Maxwell."

"Well I certainly hope the all-mighty Chairman of the Joint-Chiefs-of-Staff, General Horace Declamore doesn't 'screw-the-pooch' on this one." Rivera didn't really look worried.

But Dormier was as he thought, *God let's hope not. If Wyoming ties or wins this match, we're the pooch that'll get screwed."*

# Chapter 6

## Checking Trains

### Fort Hood, Texas

The gasoline-powered sedan sailed up I35 from Austin and looped west on I190 until the driver saw the south entrance of Fort Hood. He pulled off the interstate and worked his way through waiting cars up to one of the guard gates. An Army MP emerged from the guard house, raised and dropped his gloved hand indicating to the driver to lower his window.

"ID, Sir," requested the guard. A leather holder was flipped open displaying the Army identification of Major James Wilkerson, Command Coordination. The MP didn't know the Major, but he was fully aware of Command Coordination status. The officer before him certainly worked out of the Pentagon and was attached to Army Intelligence. The young guard snapped a salute and indicated the car to continue. The Driver casually returned the salute and drove past.

Ben Warner wore a hint of smile. The forged ID worked perfectly. He really had no prior apprehension. He knew the designation of Command Coordination was the ultimate hall-pass onto any Army military base in the world. He knew it because he had once worked for the unit. The guard knew the name on the ID was false. For all within the CC used aliases. So there would be no calls to the base commander for authorization as all guards were prior notified that announcing the arrival of CC personnel was *verboten*. The official mission of the CC was to perform snap inspections of bases, looking for actual or potential breeches of security. How a terrorist could infiltrate a camp or a civilian contractor could smuggle out pictures or data were just a few of the CC officer's objectives. And a CC ID gave the person holding it carte blanche to roam a base. Warner shook his head at the irony. The perfect cover for a potential terrorist was to enter under the guise of hunting terrorists.

He followed the four-lane road to the first turn-off, Railhead Drive and proceeded west until he found, first, the deployment area and then the railhead. The installation boasted the Army's largest and most technology sophisticated railhead with twelve spurs and nine sorting tracks. The facilities were impressive.

Ben entered a second secured area and flashed his ID to another set of guards. One MP read the wallet carefully and, while handing it back to

Ben, said in a deep Texas drawl, "The General ain't gonna be pleased to see ya'll. Not at this time."

Ben responded seriously, "General Brock's concerns are not mine, Sergeant. Not unless he has something to be concerned about. Either way, it's none of your business, now is it Sergeant." The noncom snapped to attention. "Sir, no Sir!"

"Good," replied Ben. "And make sure you keep this between us. You know the rules, Sergeant."

The guard gave a curt nod and waived his hand for Ben to pass. Ben drove on, found Visitor parking and pulled in. He grabbed his valise, for a valise always made an officer look more officious, and bounded up a set of concrete steps. At the top of the stairs he stopped and surveyed a frenetic activity. The metal roof covering over the raised concrete pad was enormous. On the opposing side sat a train exceeding fifty cars in length. The loading pad was level with the flatbed railcars and the open doors of the box cars. Tow motors and overhead cranes were loading flatbeds with the Army's latest heavy and light armor, with self-propelled equipment driven on. Even a few Cheyenne and Apache helicopters were being secured to the rolling stock, overhead blades lined up forward and aft. They drooped at both ends, giving a tired look to the crafts. Ben knew this changed quickly when they began rotation, as the air foil design lifted them onto a flat plane perpendicular to the craft. Ben was awed. It had been a plan on paper up to this point. And all the posturing of his State had been mostly bluff. But with what was before him now, nobody would think it a bluff anymore.

Filling his lungs with air and resolve, Ben quick-stepped to a clump of Brass huddled fifty yards away. He could make out two generals, a colonel, three majors and five captains. As he approached, his posture stiffened. He stopped outside of the conference circle and waited to be acknowledged. A General with his back to Ben spoke while writing on a clipboard. "What is it Major. We're busy."

Ben was impressed that his rank had been noted even though the officer had not turned round.

"In case you're wondering, I saw you at the top of the stairs. Now get on with it."

Ben snapped a regulation salute, "Sir, Major James Wilkerson, Command Coordination."

Now the general turned and faced Ben. "CC, huh. One of Ballard's boys. Picked a helluva day for a snap inspection. As you can see, we have a train to load."

"And you are, Sir?" Ben asked.

"Major General Alvin Palmer, TRANSCOM."

"Sir, General Ballard picked today precisely because of this train. Can you explain the purpose of all this materiel, where it is going and why?"

The other General spoke hesitantly, "Yes, and why only a minimum guard. Hell, this train has half of our armor and artillery on board."

General Palmer frowned. He was not used to being questioned. He ignored the other general, "It's destined for Ft. Collins, Colorado, to the request of USNORTHCOM, Commanding General Vernon Maxwell. As to its use, you'd have to ask him. Call him if you wish."

"Well, sir, we received a copy of the manifest. What has General Ballard most concerned is the transfer of four DARTS units. What could the General possibly do with these in Ft. Collins?"

'DARTS' was the designation of the latest U.S. SAM – Surface to Air Missile. It was an outgrowth of the PATRIOT system with much greater velocity, tracking and maneuvering capabilities.

The General standing to the right of Palmer nodded his head up and down. It was General Brock. Ben recognized him from Intel photos. Brock spoke up, "I told you this didn't smell kosher, Al. Jeese, you sure of this? Now you've got CC down on our necks."

General Palmer sighed, "Gentlemen, first of all, this is a 'follow-on' requisition from different origin. You're off the hook, Brock."

Ben gave the General a puzzled look. He wasn't acting as he had no idea what this meant.

"What this means, Major, are that those DARTS launchers and missiles are coming up from Fort Bliss. That is where the PATRIOTS units are posted. Those two cars will meet up with this train just below Albuquerque. Hood supplies the light and heavy armor and artillery. Everything else, including personnel, left yesterday via trucks."

Brock thought it a little strange that Palmer was sharing these details with a lowly Major.

Palmer continued, "There are seventy-five thousand troops standing on the Colorado – Wyoming border, waiting to carry out Presidential orders. All they are waiting for is this shipment. I have a manifest with General Declamore's personal signature. I also have verbal orders from him to get this train on the way. It's the damn reason I flew out here. If any of you have any doubts, give him a call, although he's probably at home by now. Or you can call General Maxwell. In either case, I have my orders, you have yours and this train better be loaded within the hour or your asses are grass and I'm the lawn mower. Am I clear?"

All officers expect Brock and Ben snapped at attention and the Colonel, Majors and Captains responded in unison, "Crystal, Sir!"

General Palmer nodded his head sharply. "Now, let's get this train loaded, gentlemen."

Hands flew to caps and pulled salutes. All officers but Brock and Ben spun on heels and marched off. General Palmer turned back to Ben. The General's face screwed into a look of annoyance. Ben was on his cell phone.

"Who you talking to, Major?"

Ben put his hand over the mouthpiece and said, "My Commanding Officer, Sir, General Ballard." Palmer ripped the phone from his hand and put it to his ear.

"Stinky? Al. I don't mind you sending this prick Major to do your snooping, just keep him out of my way while my men do their jobs." He was listening to a response, "I don't know and I don't give a shit. Get Dec or Norm on the phone and ask them. You know that none of this is by my request. Yes, I mean it. I'll hang on." Now it was General Palmer's turn to cover the mouthpiece. He glared at Ben, "Major, you and your people are a pain in the ass." Ben just stared. General Palmer shot a glance to General Brock who rolled his eyes.

After several minutes of silence, General Palmer spoke into the phone, "Well, I'm glad everything's hunky dory on your end. Because I now have less than fifty-five minutes to get this train rolling." He sounded exasperated. But at the end he paused and softened his voice, "And Stinky, tell Carol Hello." He flipped the phone closed and tossed it back to Ben.

General Palmer turned round, "Brock, you got this under control? This train has to get out of here on time."

Brock raised his hand lazily in acquiescence. "Sure, General. I was just a little concerned, you know, the minimum detail and all." He shrugged, "But, what the hell, if CC is OK with it, who am I to question?" He looked at Ben who gave a curt nod.

Palmer said, "The Major and I are going to have a small conversation about a big subject."

Brock again waived him away, turned and started walking toward one of his Majors that was berating one of his Captains. Over his shoulder he shouted, "Have a nice interview, Major." It was in a sarcastic tone.

General Palmer grabbed Ben by the arm and gruffly marched him back towards the stairs. In a low voice he said, "Perfect timing, Warner. Brock was starting to ask too many questions. I don't blame him. And I sure as hell wouldn't want to be in his shoes when this all goes down."

Ben nodded, holding his face in a grimace as if Palmer were dressing him down. He said softly, "How many is a minimum detail?"

Palmer answered off handedly, "Twenty-six."

"Twenty-six!" responded Ben, "When you said minimal support personnel, I thought we were talking about four or five. But twenty-six, hell, that's a platoon. Why didn't you just arm it with a company?"

Palmer's features stiffened. His jaw clinched, "Listen, son, this whole plan was of your design. You saw how suspicious Brock was. Imagine if I put a smaller number on board. He would definitely have been on the phone to somebody, and somebody way up the food chain and I'd be on the menu. Besides, only two are in the cab and the rest are in the troop transport hooked to the end. Just proceed with the plan and the odds will be fine. But don't underestimate those two up front. They can kill without hesitation."

Ben stared a long distance off, trying to run different scenarios through his mind. "It will be dark in seventy minutes. Think you can stall this from leaving till then? It would certainly increase my odds of getting aboard unnoticed."

"I think that can be arranged. They're behind schedule anyway. A move like this usually takes two weeks to organize. And these poor bastards were notified forty-eight hours ago. In fact, I don't see it rolling for another two hours. Should be nice and dark by then. That work for you?

Ben nodded. "That works. You've done your job, General. And your State is proud of you. The curtain is down on Act I. Now I have to get dressed for Act II."

Palmer looked at him with concern, "Be safe, son." He looked hard into Ben's eyes, "And try not to kill anyone, please. You know from your time in the Army, GI's don't sit still for their buddies being killed." His face softened, "See you at home." It came out more as a question than a statement.

Ben smiled, "See you at home, General." Then he turned deadly serious, stiffened to attention, saluted crisply and said in a loud voice for all to hear, "Sir, Yes Sir! I will notify General Ballard of your opinions." He spun on one heal, stepped onto the metal platform and descended the stairs.

Brock, hearing and watching the scene thought, *Well, at least Al put that punk in his place.* Not to be outdone by Palmer, he turned back to a Major and commenced his own tongue lashing.

# Chapter 7

## Local News

### Cheyenne, Wyoming

After the motor coach returned to Cheyenne, Josh had given up on trying to get Sam alone. All of the Governors agreed they wished to return to their hotel and could fend for themselves that evening. Sam acquiesced, but reminded them of their tight schedule the next day. She asked them if they still all had their hotel business cards and they nodded. Josh didn't understand the question. Sam said it would be clear in a moment. The Governors said their good-evenings to Sam and Josh and walked over to CityCars waiting passengers. They split into pairs with one of each group holding a business card to the screen of their respective CityCar. The entered and the Cars sped away.

Sam waved until they were out of sight and then turned to Josh.

"Here's the card I mentioned." It was a Westin Hotel card. "Most businesses here print company cards with a barcode on back. The CityCar system recognizes the business location so the address doesn't have to be manually entered. Also, nearly all our handheld devices can read the card and bring up the location in most navigation applications."

"Neat," replied Josh as he accepted the card from Sam.

She continued, "I reserved a room there for you. It's all prepaid. We're departing from here at nine-thirty tomorrow, so please be on time." She looked at Josh. For the first time there was emotion in her eyes. "I am so glad you are here. You've been missed."

Josh looked at her as if a puppy expecting a pat, "By you?"

She slapped him on the side of his arm, like a kid, "Of course, by me, silly. But a whole lot of people have missed you. I hope you've got that feeling the last few days."

Josh nodded, "But you missing me means the most."

She smiled, then dropped her eyes, "Josh, we can't,.......emmm, it's difficult to discuss the past with so much....."

Josh held up his index finger and pressed it to her lips, "Shhhhh...I understand. It's been fifteen years and I just come waltzing back in here.

You made a new life, an impressive life, without me. All I'm going to say on the subject, Sam.....and I swear I will never mention it again, but I love you. I've always loved you. And I'll be there for you in any way I can, friend or whatever...."

He looked at her but received no response. He gave a slight sigh, "So I guess it's friend"

She said, "I think of you more like a brother," and held his eyes with hers.

"God, I hate that phrase. Makes me sound harmless. And you know I'm not harmless, girl." He smiled.

She nodded. Her eyes were glistening with moisture. Josh started to get choked up himself. "Give me that card. I need a big drink, a big meal and a good night's sleep, in that order."

It was Sam's turn to smile while she handed him the card. He turned and walked directly to the remaining CityCar. He never looked back at her as he sped away.


***


The Westin Cheyenne was a remarkable hotel. His room had a hundred-and-eighty degree view of the lit-up city. He plopped his large frame onto the even-larger bed. The pillow-topped mattress was like lying on a bed of down, yet firmly supporting. There was an abundance of pillows stacked against the headboard, many with different firmness or softness, foam or down. After a restless fifteen minutes, Stillwater rose, showered and dressed. He then headed down to the restaurant.

He was enjoying his second incredible steak of the trip and savoring every mouthful when the chair across his table pulled out. A skinny but tall man sat down. He was wearing a Western Shirt, Wrangler jeans and alligator cowboy boots. His hair was greasy and combed straight back, long over the ears and well past his shirt collar.

"You must be on a different expense per diem than me, being able to stay and eat at this place." His grin was actually a sneer.

"ID'ing your voice, I'd say you were *Canary*, or can we skip the birdcalls and I'll just call you Tex." Josh sliced off another piece of beef and stuck it into his mouth. He was pissed this guy was here. He didn't want to be seen in public with another agent, particularly this guy. Yet he wouldn't give a hint Tex was ruining his evening.

"Yeah, I'm Canary, Tex, whatever you want to call me. And your boss wants to know why the hell you don't call him and tell him what's going on."

"Keep your voice down, asshole. Didn't they teach you not to draw attention to yourself in public. Seems you've got a training gap."

"Don't get cute with me, Stillwater."

Josh cut him off, "And that's another thing. How come you know my name and I don't know yours? What the hell is your name?"

"They trust me and they don't trust you. Tex work's just fine. Stay with it."

Josh nodded nonchanlantly. "Obviously you haven't talked to Maxton since after ten today, 'cause I already called him. He was pretty pleased with what I told him. I think you're the one that needs to update his resume."

Tex fumed. Josh could tell he had gotten his goat. Tex's call to Maxton, if it occurred, must have been before Josh's.

"So what did you find out that got you back in good graces?"

Josh knew he held all the Aces on this hand. He shook his head while cutting off another piece of steak, "You first."

"Okay, I'll play your game. I switched targets when you went on your little huntin' excursion. You can stop looking over your shoulder. I'm on Benjamin Warner now, the Lt. Governor of this damn State."

Josh had to give up a few of his Aces, "Warner? Huntin'? What the hell you following us for? Was that you that shot him?"

"Naw, wished it was." Tex took out a huge knife and started cleaning underneath a finger nail with it. "Baby and I like our wet work up close and personal." Tex was stroking the blade lovingly.

Josh had known guys like this from his Army days. Some had pet names for their rifle, sidearm, knife or some other ordnance. *This guy has a screw loose. I wonder if that knife talks to him,* he thought.

Tex remained fixated on 'Baby' as he continued, "Saw your target wriggling away. You almost had him. Too bad you spent your lucky shot on the buck."

Josh was getting pissed, "Who the hell you think you are, Jim Bowie? Put that damn knife away or I'll shove it up your ass." He was curious though, "Could you ID the guy?"

Tex frowned as he replaced "Baby" and gave the boot's upper a pat. Stillwater just dropped his head in disgust.

"Naw," responded Tex. "Couldn't even tell if he was Chinc, Wap, or Wasp. I was farther away than you. And the guy had his face covered with grease. Now your turn. What'd you tell Maxton."

"Ask him yourself." Josh raised his hand to get the waitress' attention. He wanted dessert, if for no other reason than to piss off Tex.

The lanky Texan burned. He knew he had been stiffed. He changed horses.

"So what was that bus ride about, today? Tried to follow but got stopped by a roadblock."

Josh wanted to smile. *Seems Sam wasn't bluffing about security measures.* "I'll call my boss tonight and let him know." The waitress arrived and he requested a dessert menu. She pulled one out of her apron, handed it to Josh and left.

Tex slammed his fist down on the table, rattling silverware. He hissed, "You'll tell me now or you might never report again."

"You might not want to make a scene in public, honey." Josh surveyed the other eyes upon them from within the room. He thought of an idea that might be fun, at least from his perspective. He straightened up, wiped his face with his napkin and said, "OK, I'll tell you. We went to a nuclear facility. They have it."

"They have what? Don't be coy, Stretch."

Josh acted exasperated, "Come on, Tex. They're producing plutonium. What do you think they're using that for? Haven't you heard the news? This State's on the brink of war with the Federal government. Use your brain, man."

Tex thought for a second and his eyes widened, "A bomb? They're making a nuclear weapon?"

Josh raised his eyebrows in the *Now you've got it* sense. Tex exhaled a small whistle and said, "Jesus be with us now. God Almighty, you know what this could mean?"

Josh shrugged, returning his eyes to the menu. He asked, "Why're you here if you're supposed to be on Warner."

"Don't worry your pretty lil' head over him. I've got him covered by a partner in Texas. That's where he's headed. Saw him get on the plane myself. I'm heading there right now. Maxton has a private jet standing by for me. But with what you just said, think I'll make a short call first. Maxton always favors the first one to report in. I'll be sure to tell him you're enjoying a fine meal before you get around to him."

Tex stood up quickly, his Tony Lama heels clicking upon the ceramic tile as he quick-stepped from the dining area.

Josh sat back and smiled. He signaled the waiter over, "Another glass of this great red wine, ma'am. Oh, and no dessert." He thought about Tex following Ben. Was Warner in danger from this screwball? He grew concerned, but knew of no way to contact Ben without blowing his own cover.

***

Returning to his room, Josh pulled off his boots and flopped his long body back onto the bed in one jump. He picked up his cell phone and checked the phone log. Maxton had called him once when he was underground at the Energy Facility. But then there were another eleven calls from his boss in the thirty minutes. He smiled, knowing Tex had planted a mighty big burr under Maxton's saddle. Josh checked his watch. *Just seven-thirty here. Makes it nine-thirty for him. Nope, not late enough.* He grabbed the remote and clicked on the TV.

The difference from national news to local was marked. National was reporting a flurry of numbers showing up-tic's to the economy and down-tic's to the unemployment figures. He knew it was all BS. Josh had devised a little system long ago that served him well. Whatever figures the Federal government pumped out, he just reversed them. Whatever statements the White House issued, he assumed the opposite. The method worked, so far.

He changed the channel to local news and caught film highlights of a high school football game. Competitive team sports had long disappeared throughout most of the nation. The schools were so strapped for money that all after-school activities nearly ceased. PC - Politically Correct – parents had convinced school boards that competition destroyed a child's self-esteem, but not in Wyoming. Football was big here and a major high school rivalry would draw crowds in excess of ten to fifteen thousand people. It would have been more, but the stadiums weren't big enough.

Josh wondered about one of the games. It was between *Seimens Tech* and *Cheyenne North*. He had never heard of *Seimens High* or *Tech* before. The news then switched to weather. He found it interesting that, after covering the State region-by-region, the newscaster expanded to international weather, focusing on Asia and Europe. Josh had seen firsthand how interdependent this State was on those regions. So it shouldn't really be a surprise that they kept their Citizens and international visitors up on travel weather.

After the weather came financial news. The numbers were not dramatic. All Wyoming indices were up, but by small tics. A year-long time graph showed a slow, stable growth. The only strong rises were within export prices. Lamb, beef, coal and electricity showed major gains on the futures markets. The announcer said that the gain was attributable to continued-falling production within the rest of the nation and further strengthening of the WC against the NUS.

The price of gold per-ounce against the WC traded within a narrow range. This was true of gold against a few other international currencies: Yuan, Yen, Australian Dollar, Swiss Franc and even the Deutschmark. The last one still confounded Josh. The Euro still existed, yet the Germans used the Deutschmark outside of their continent. *Weren't the Germans the movers behind the Euro in the first place?* Josh puzzled. He knew Europe's EMU – Economic and Monetary Union had fallen apart. Individual countries had reinstated tariffs and quotas. A strike by French farmers that had effectively shut down their country resulted in reinstatement of trade barriers removed nearly twenty-five years earlier. France was making noise about abandoning the *Euro* and returning to the *Franc*. Germany was effectively gutting the *Euro* by paying for energy imports with *Deutschmarks*.

The financial news switched to interest rates and something called *leverage*. Mentally searching his long-dormant college education, Josh remembered accounting terms: negative and positive financial leverage; negative and positive operating leverage. Appling the terms to banks was a fuzzier subject. He remembered something about a minimum ratio of Tier 1 capital to total average adjusted assets. But he also remembered his senior econ professor, Dr. Milton Bern's derision of the formula:

*A financial formula that allows financial institutions to select which items are considered liabilities, which are assets, which of these assets are considered the standard of 'risk', and then to park, off-balance-sheet, any items not within the norm, is no standard at all. It is obfuscation in order to hide risk and potential danger. The only formula that should be considered is whereby all assets are valued at a percentage of their risk-value, as determined by a truly independent, if not government, agency. And assets should value first position derivatives at market-to-market pricing by a central clearing house, and ban derivatives of derivatives. Then liabilities, including intra-bank loans, should be divided by the asset number. It becomes a simple formula, one that we can all understand and compare. That is why financial institutions will never agree to this; for the resulting numbers would be so poor as to disqualify the institution from playing the high-yield game, known by the rest of us as high-risk.*

Reflecting on this memory, Josh recalled an article he had read about some international bank agreement, *Basel II*, that allowed the banks to choose those assets that were deemed 'most risky' to represent off-sheet assets: assets not reported on the balance sheet. *What a bunch of hooey that was*, he thought. Naturally, the banks and other financial institutions didn't pick the riskiest assets for their evaluations. This would have raised their leverage ratio too high and reduced the amount of money they could gamble.

Initially, however, he didn't correlate the importance of the individual bank leverage numbers being reported. The announcer had introduced this segment with a simple explanation of leverage. In Wyoming they defined it as the ratio between bank assets and reserves minus liabilities. They had their own twist and footnotes. No off-balance-sheet items allowed. No loans to other banks were considered an asset, but were considered a liability. *Now that's a real twist*, he thought. And all derivatives were valued at market-to-market rates, with a State agency acting as the clearing house, publishing 'Bid' and 'Asked' and providing bond ratings.

Josh smiled. It was Dr. Bern's formula. *I guess someone's listening to the man.*

Through the numerous banking crises of the last many years, financial institutions were always on the verge of collapsing because their leverage numbers were too high. The institutions had borrowed billions, often from each other, and used the funds to acquire assets providing the highest yields. These assets also provided the highest risks. But it wasn't the banks' money, individual traders surmised. So, they rolled the dice; all-in. When they 'made the point' they were rich. When it came up 'snake-eyes,' they shrugged and waited for the game to restart.

During these financial downturns, banks stopped loaning to each other. The financial institutions with cash still on hand knew their compatriots were a bad credit risk. Self-preservation became the mantra. They wanted to protect the only viable asset in their inventory: cash. The institutions that were without a seat when the music stopped, begged the Federal government for loans. If an institution was 'too big to fail,' meaning it had borrowed and gambled in such extraordinary amounts that its failure could wipe out a large swath of lenders, Federal money was forth-coming. If the numbers were less spectacular, the institution was allowed to fail. Incompetence and fraud trumped. This meant giving financial institutions staggering sums in order to pay each other off. The Federal government rationalized these moves by saying that trillions of dollars had evaporated. And they, through the Federal Reserve, were just *re-monetizing* the system. Later it was called *Quantitative Easing*. There was no need for the taxpayer to worry because the money was just replacing that which had been lost.

*Bullshit*, thought Josh. *That money was, and is, still out there. It never evaporated. Where do they think all the inflation came from?*

The leverage numbers the announcer displayed on-screen were surprising to Josh. Bank's leverage numbers ran from three to twelve. The bank names were grouped by Retail, Commercial, Investment, and Speculative. The leverage number increased from the first to the last group, with each grouping's range within one and several decimal places either added to the one or below it. And logically, to Josh, the interest rates, both savings and credit, mirrored the leverage number. If the leverage number was higher, the savings rate was higher because depositors were gambling with a higher-leveraged bank. Concurrently the credit rate was higher because the bank was paying a higher savings rate.

The surprise for Josh was how low the leverage numbers were. When the national financial collapse occurred, these numbers ranged from thirty-two to sixty-four. For the highest number, that meant the bank had borrowed sixty-four dollars for every one dollar it had in capital assets. *With a leverage range of three to six*, Josh thought, *these Wyoming banks are incredibly strong.*

The next news item was a recap of current interest rates. In Wyoming, savings and credit rates reported by individual institutions averaged two percent for savings and four percent for credit. A five-year chart showed no more than quarter-point changes for the entire period. *Now that's stability*, Josh thought.

When the financial news segment ended, Josh found it interesting the lengthy amount of broadcast time focused on money. If broadcast time equaled interest, Wyomingans must be paying attention. In the rest of the nation, the show would have already lost its audience.

It was nearing twenty-hundred hours and the announcer was recapping the day's top story:

"And to wrap up the evening's news, it is reported that Federal Troops are being assembled between Fort Collins and the Wyoming border. There is no firm number of troops reported. But informed sources estimate the number to be in excess of seventy-five thousand. Plan 1 is now in effect: All Wyoming Citizens and Residents should have reported to their Wyoming Army unit. If you have not already done so, we remind you that delay is unacceptable. Children requiring shelter and attendance should be dropped off at their schools. You will be notified if your child is moved to a safer facility as per Plan Nine. We will continue to provide updates as events unfold."

Josh had lain prostrate upon the bed, but now propped up his head upon hand and bent elbow. *Sure confirms why Wyoming's mobilizing. Everyone in this State is getting ready for something big to happen,* he thought.

*Even me.*

He reached for his cell phone to dial Maxton. It was late enough.

# Chapter 8

## Trust

### Cheyenne, Wyoming

The four Governors met Josh in the hotel lobby the next morning. Scott Fodor was in an agitated mood. Governors Almondo and Hughes were deep in thought. Only Governor Brigham seemed her normal self, pleasant and affable. She was first to acknowledge Josh.

"Good morning!"

Josh mustered an appropriate response.

Governor Fodor nervously blurted, "See the TV last night? We're going to be in a war zone, pretty damn soon. The morning news said the road is blocked by the military between here and Denver. And the airport is closed to domestic flights. How the hell am I supposed to get home?"

Governor Brigham's response was upbeat, "Relax, Scott. I'm sure Sam is on top of it. Let's ask her what we should do when we see her this morning. By the way, we have thirty minutes to be at the mansion."

*This lady has a lot of cool*, thought Josh. *Fodor looks like he's gonna wet his pants.*

"Well, I'm going to rent a car and drive south. There's no way the Army's going to mess with the Governor of a State!" Fodor said this with more bravado than confidence.

"I wouldn't count on that, Scott." Governor Hughes spoke up. "They seem to be messing with this State's Governor. And to prove that we Governors are not so lofty, I ask you one thing. Did Washington notify you they were putting seventy-five thousand Federal troops on your inviolate State's soil?"

Scott Fodor hadn't even considered the point until this moment.

"Yeah! What the hell are they doing in Colorado! I never even got a call from the President."

Elizabeth Brigham laughed, "Haven't you learned by now, Scott. We're just puppets of the President. The man can do whatever he wants, including peeing all over the Constitution. Now, relax. Let's hop in one of these CityCars and go see Sam. I'm anxious to hear her take on things."

The male Governors mulled this over for a moment. Governor Almondo and Hughes looked at each other. Both gave a crisp nod and followed Brigham and Josh outside. Fodor begrudgingly followed.

\*\*\*

Sam was standing outside, at the top of the Mansion drive. She waved as the Cars approached.

"She doesn't look too concerned," said Governor Brigham to Josh. "She's either got nerves of steel or massive confidence."

Josh replied, "Both. Known her for most of her life. She's always been,...ah...unflappable."

"Good word," agreed Brigham. She looked at Josh sympathetically, "You're in love with her, Joshua Stillwater."

Josh didn't know if it was a statement or a question. He turned his head and looked out the window.

Brigham sighed and said softly, "Unrequited love, the stuff of broken hearts and endless novels."

The CityCar had come to a stop and Josh jumped out as soon as the doors opened. Samantha greeted him, Brigham and the male Governors exiting from the second car. Her demeanor was airy.

"Good morning, one and all. You're on time and we're all set to go. Today, we shall see some amazing ways that we have solved….."

"Hold on," said Governor Fodor. "Let's talk about this invasion thing, shall we? I mean, you don't look too worried, but the rest of us are very concerned."

"Speak for yourself, Scott." It was Elizabeth Brigham.

"Yeah!" confirmed Governor John Hughes. Mario Almondo was silent.

Sam looked at Josh. He just shrugged. She smiled and looked at Governor Fodor, "Scott, there is no invasion."

"Yet," he grumbled.

"No, not today and not tomorrow. We have an Ace in the hole. They will not invade. This is all bluster and bravado on part of Rivera. It will become a stalemate. I can assure you of this."

Again, Fodor was grumbling, "Yeah, and on my State's soil."

Sam nodded enthusiastically, "Exactly! And what have you done about it?"

Fodor raised his hands to shoulder level, "What the hell am I supposed to do about it? It's not like I have an army that can take his on."

Sam nodded, "That's your first mistake, but one easily rectified after the main event is over." Fodor looked at her like she had lost her mind. Sam continued, "Now, here is what you do. You march right into my office, sit down, and, calmly, get Rivera on the phone. Then chew him a new one. You tell him he's got twenty-four hours to get those troops off your soil. You threaten to mobilize your National Guard and have them confront his troops. Then you call your Attorney General and get a warrant for the arrest of the General in-charge and the President. Any Judge stays your action, you get it immediately heard by your State Supreme Court. Do not take it to any Federal court, because you already know the outcome. Then you send out State law enforcement to arrest the General, and to Washington D.C. to arrest the President. This is all for show, so make sure you have a huge press entourage for each event. Then the ball's in Rivera's court. It's all simple."

Fodor's jaw dropped. He couldn't say a word.

Sam looked at him, annoyed, "Come on Scott. Chop, Chop. We have a full schedule ahead of us." She looked at her watch, "And we're already late."

Joshua struggled not to smile. He thought about Sam's instructions to Fodor, *Somewhere there's a brass monkey missing a pair of balls.*

All Scott Fodor could muster was, "I'll think about it." He turned and, defeated, headed to a CityCar with the door held open by Paul, the security man.

Governor Brigham slowly shook her head, "Poor Scott, he's just now coming to terms with the fact Rivera owns him and his State."

Governor Hughes asked Sam, "Anybody shoot holes in that Ace you're holding, Samantha?"

"Not yet, John. Not yet."

The guard had three CityCars waiting. He said, "Ms. Governor," while gesturing to the second. Sam entered and signaled to Joshua to join her. Then the guard entered instructions into the Car's outside screen, escorted the four governors to the third and fourth and entered similar instructions into the screens. With doors closed, both cars headed down the drive. The guard stood in the front car facing forward, scanning for possible threats.

Sam sat across from Josh. Both were in silent contemplation. Josh was mentally replaying last night's conversation with Maxton.

***

Maxton had been in his standard surly mood, "I just talked to *Canary*. Why didn't you call me the minute you found out what those people are up to? How big does it have to be to call in on time?" Maxton's voice was terse but low. Josh knew a major eruption was just ahead.

"Gosh, I guess I didn't know nuclear power would be the end all for you. I'm letting you know now. That's how their generating so much electrical power. I'm glad you feel it's that important."

"Nuclear power! What the hell are you talking about? If this is one of your little jokes, I'll have your head for this." Maxton sounded more panicky than angry.

"Whadaya jumpin' all over me for? You asked and I'm telling you. These people have nuclear power and it's way down deep underground. I don't have any idea where it's at because basically we were blindfolded for the trip there. I'll try and find out, but that's all I can do, try."

"I'm not talking about nuclear power, you idiot. I'm talking about a nuclear bomb. That's what *Canary* told me. They have a nuclear bomb. Is this right or not?!!"

"Jeese, I never said nothing to Tex about a nuclear bomb. He must have misunderstood. You know, he did kinda run away from our meeting real quick. Said he had to call you, but I told him I was gonna report in. Guess he jumped the gun a bit." Josh enjoyed the game so far.

"Ya think! Hell, I've already told my brother-in-law, ah, I mean, my boss. And I'm sure he's already told the President. Good God, what am I going to say? Alder Manning is going to have my head for this. He may even throw me out of the family!"

Josh found the scenario terribly entertaining. Maxton's voice was the whiney equivalent of hand wringing.

"I'm going to kill that damn Texan over this!" There was a long pause. Josh just let Maxton slowly twist in the wind.

"Wait a minute, wait a minute, I've got it!" Maxton sounded almost relieved.

Josh broke in, "You're gonna lay it all off on Tex, aren't you. Because you sure aren't going to put that horse in my corral."

"Shut up, you shit kicker." Maxton's words never failed to sting Stillwater. "No, I'm not laying it off on either of you. Rivera wouldn't stop with you piss ants. He'd make sure Manning chopped my head off too. If not Manning, then Dormier would definitely step in and do the honors. No, my plan......and you listen to me close, Stillwater. My plan is to say *nothing*. Let them think Wyoming has nuclear weapons. What difference does it make?"

"But..." Josh tried to interrupt. The game was turning dangerous.

"Shaddup! That's the plan. Rivera has his smoking gun and can tell the world. Then he can use his big stick with full impunity. It's perfect. And if you breathe one word of this to anyone, then your carcass is fried. I wouldn't be surprised if the President sanctioned your ass. So keep your mouth shut."

"But it's going to come out at some point." Josh was floundering to throw up some sort of roadblock to Maxton's plan.

"Who gives a shit. It's over by that point, *fait accompli*. Just like Iraq with Bush and the WMD's. So what if they didn't exist? Bush got his invasion and sat in the hot seat for a while afterwards. It all blew over."

Josh felt bile rising in his throat. He knew he had handed the keys to Wyoming's destruction over to Maxton. It had all been a childish game to get Tex in hot water. Now that water was at a full boil. What was he going to do? He had to tell Sam. She was calculating moves based on bad Intel. The players had moved on the board and she had no idea. It was all Josh's fault. As his mind returned to the present, and to Sam, he didn't know how to begin.

***

"Ah, Sam?"

She turned her face and thoughts to Joshua. "Sorry, just running some problems through my head."

*I'm sure you are*, he thought. "Sam, ah, well,…let me start this way…How big is that Ace in the hole?"

Sam stared intently into his eyes. She was deciding something and Josh didn't move or say a word. He knew it was important. She was deciding whether to trust him, or not.

"Josh, my ace-in-the-hole is known by only those I trust the most. Can I trust you Josh? It's been fifteen years, and you do work for the Federal Government. Would you put my future and the future of everyone in this State in jeopardy? Can I really trust you?"

Here was the crux. He knew this moment was coming and he dreaded it. There was no way to sidestep it, to placate both sides, to run a scam on his boss or on the woman he loved. It had been a game up to this point. But now it was over. He had to decide. What did he want, accolades from Washington? A way back into the military? Or did he want his life back, his life in Wyoming before Charlie Warner knocked it out from under him? It all came down to this choice. Sam would believe him whichever way he answered. Could he betray that trust? Even if she didn't love him,…what did Liz say….unrequited…even if his love were unrequited, could he betray Sam? Whether she loved him or not, she was at least honest, the most honest person he ever knew. It was a large part of his love for her.

He decided, "No. You can't trust me, Sam. Not right now anyway, until I figure some things out."

She reached over and grasped both his hands, "That is the most honest answer anyone has ever given me, Josh. It must have been difficult. Glad to have all of you back."

His head hung down. He couldn't look at her. He just slowly nodded, still grasping her hands, still hanging on to the only truth he had ever known.

# Chapter 9

## Ramping Pressure

### Oval Office, The White House

President Rivera grasped his hands together in delight and looked at Dormier. "Do we really have them, Bill? I mean, won't I be applauded for invading a State that threatened the rest of the nation with a nuclear weapon?

Dormier checked his finger nails. It was an interesting prospect, but something about the whole thing didn't seem on-the-square. "Well, yes it would, sir. But we have to examine this from all angles."

"Always angles with you," mumbled the President.

Director of National Intelligence, Blaine Fisk interjected, "Here's the problem in my mind. First of all, what kind of bomb is it: air-burst or just a dirty bomb? Second, how do they plan to deliver it? Do they plan to drop it by plane or missile? Or have they already planted it somewhere for maximum effect?"

Rivera followed up, "Like in New York, Times Square? That sort of thing? If so, it might not be bad to wipe out a few thousand Americans. It would really make the rest mad as a hornet towards Wyoming."

This President never failed to take Fisk's breath away. "Or it might be in this building, perhaps right underneath us, in the Sit room. You're not a favorite of the military, sir."

Rivera would have jingled change in his pocket to relieve nervousness, but he never carried money since becoming President. "You mean those bastards might try to blow me up?"

Fisk shrugged, "Who knows? Hitler's Generals tired."

Rivera glared at his intelligence advisor, "You comparing me to Hitler?"

Fisk hurriedly explained, "No sir. It was only by way of historical context, the military killing a leader. There's still those who think the Military was involved in Kennedy's assassination."

"Great, just great. Now I have to watch my ass with the Military. I get it. So Wyoming has a bomb. We don't know the size or composition. And we don't know how, when or where it will be delivered. And you want me to just wait. Act like I don't know what they're up to."

"For the moment, sir. I believe you still continue to arm General Maxwell's forces and get them in position to push forward. When Wyoming sees these troops directly on their border, armed to the teeth, I think they'll get a message to us. It would be suicidal for them just to explode one nuclear device. They would lose their one bargaining chip. And what would be their justification to the world? The Nation would be on our side and we would have a free hand to respond anyway we choose. The Federal press would make sure of this."

"How do you know they only have one device, Blaine?" It was Dormier's question.

"Well, not only from Manning's Intel, but also facts. It took Iran thirty years to put in place enough centrifuges to make multiple bombs. I don't think they've had the time, money or expertise."

"They could have bought them on the black market," offered Rivera.

"True enough, but again it requires a lot of money. But more than that, we've had them embargoed for two years, checking every shipment in and out. Part of that has been radioactive scans and they've shown nothing. How could they have even got them in?"

"Anything's possible. But let's get back to the one device. Here's a question: what if they drop it right on our troops at the border?" Rivera was proud of his proposal.

"I think the reaction would be the same by the nation. Perhaps the outcry would be even louder against the deaths of our young men and women in uniform."

Rivera thought about Fisk's response, "Hmmm, yes. I can see that." Rivera stood up, "Good advice, Blaine." He shook the man's hand. "We keep pressing them on their border and see what pops."

Fisk looked at Dormier who slightly smiled. The Chief-of-Staff was infamous on his ability to steer the President towards a predetermined outcome. He and Fisk had worked out the tactics before the meeting.

# Chapter 10

## Wellness

## Cheyenne, Wyoming

The CityCars entered an elevated expressway running down the middle of Interstate Twenty-Five. As overpasses were encountered, the expressway did not duck underneath or rise above. It was level with it and the Cars ran at cross direction to stopped traffic on the overpass. Joshua didn't know if the cross-traffic was stopped because the expressway had precedence or the Governor did. He found it to be the later when the car exited the elevated and proceeded through city streets unabated, while others were slowed and moved to the side. Joshua knew the computerized system had given their cars priority. It wasn't just a status thing, it was for security reasons. It's pretty tough to chase a car on foot. He wondered about a stationary shooter taking a shot at the passing Governor. There was a lot of glass to take a clean shot through. Then he noticed the seat upholstery. He had missed it when they had first entered the car. It was in the furry cowhide, just like the couch in the mansion.

Trying to recover from their emotional moment, he asked "This a special car?"

She nodded. "Bullet proof glass. Special Kevlar armored sides, top and floor. No luggage area on top, just more head room for us. A nice work table. That's about it. We keep the outside looking as a regular CityCar so that an attacker would think it had the same lack of protection and, hopefully, underestimate."

Joshua understood. To appear vulnerable sometimes dissuaded a terrorist from using his strongest munitions or explosive. Those precious resources could be used later for a more hardened target. "You have any of the local nut-jobs try taking you out?" He was surprised to find himself talking in law-enforcement jargon to her. He had left her as a young girl. But now she seemed, what was the word he searched for, *capable*, that was it, very capable.

She shook her head determinedly, "We don't worry about any Wyomingans. It's those from outside that pose the threat. That's one reason for our visa system. We have a chance to perform background checks on new entrants. Of course this system still has its porosity."

*Outside*, thought Josh. *Outside where? This town, the State, the Nation?* He would bide his time on this subject as the car was now slowing.

They stopped before a large glass building that had a concrete edifice built into its center. At the top it announced, "Cheyenne Memorial Hospital" in relief lettering. Sam grabbed him by the arm and said, "This way. I want to take you in via the Emergency Room."

*A hospital?*, he thought. *Are we visiting a sick person or taking a tour of the medical facility? She's probably started some program to take care of the indigent and wants to show it off.* He braced himself for crying kids, gurneys blocking halls, moaning patients, people shouting in foreign tongues and crushing crowds trying to get to the receptionist.

National Health Care may have given everyone medical coverage, but the quality of care, in Josh's mind, had fallen to an abysmal state. An exodus of skilled doctors from the U.S. had left corps of newbies or incompetents behind. This left nurses to pick up the slack. But even they had become disgusted with the hours, the pay and the stress of making medical decisions way above their pay grade. This caused nursing ranks to thin. Hospitals had become overwhelmed with patients. With no co-pay, patients invaded waiting rooms for the smallest of reasons. And the inclusion of illegal immigrants within the system added to crammed emergency rooms, many seeking care for a child with a cold. Serious surgeries, such as bypasses, required months of waiting for a specialist. In a strange turn of events, Americans with financial means were flocking to Canada for medical care. An underground of Canadian doctors willing to handle U.S. patients, for cash, had developed in America's neighbor to the north.

U.S. Hospitals were nightmares, and Stillwater wished Sam had picked someplace a little more cheery for their first stop.

Around the side of the building, they followed signs pointing towards EMERGENCY that ended at steps leading up to the loading dock. One ambulance was parked against the dock, while another, with back-up bells dinging, eased into another slot. Sam and Josh entered two glass doors and proceeded into a waiting area that, oddly, had no one waiting. A lone receptionist jumped to her feet and spoke, "Ms. Governor, we were informed of your visit. We thought you would be entering through the front. Can I be of assistance?"

"No thank you, eh," Sam looked at her name plate pinned to her blouse, "Jenny. I know my way around. If you would just buzz us in, please."

"Yes Ma'am." The big door beyond the desk buzzed and Sam pushed it open, leading the way for Josh and the Governors. Inside the corridor they saw to their right the ambulance that had been backing in. Two EMT's rolled out a gurney containing an elderly woman with an oxygen mask over nose and mouth. A nurse was walking alongside the rolling bed holding a small hand-held electronic pad. She tapped the screen a few times and then, gently removed the patient's hand from underneath a blanket. The nurse pressed the patient's thumb against the screen, asked the patient to verbally say her name into the electronic device and told the EMT's, "Room Nine." They nodded and rolled the gurney down the hall before Josh and Sam.

Sam said, "Well, what did you think of that?" She pointed at the disappearing gurney.

Josh had no idea what he was supposed to say. The Governors were quizzical as well. It was a hospital. Sick people come into a hospital and were taken into rooms to be looked at by a doctor. What were they supposed to see that was so marvelous? All Josh could do was shrug. Sam appeared a little exasperated.

"First of all, how many people did you see in the waiting room?" she asked.

Governor Brigham answered, "Well, ah, none, but I thought they had cleared it out for your visit. You know, the Governor VIP treatment, shine the shoes, hide the dirty laundry."

Sam shook her head strongly. "No way. They knew I was coming, yes, but not when, and they expected us at the front. There are no police out there blocking patients from getting in here. Not even the Governor could stop a mom from bringing her kid to the emergency room. And what about that elderly woman arriving on the ambulance?"

"What about her?" Scott Fodor's mind was still on an invasion. He wasn't focused on the tour.

"Did you see her delayed outside? Did you see a nurse asking twenty questions while the poor woman struggled to sign ten admission forms or locate her insurance cards? Did you see her gurney get abandoned in the hall until a room was ready? You didn't see any of that, did you?

"No." Elizabeth Brigham responded brightly. She was catching up to Samantha's point.

"That is right," said Sam. "Now let's go upstairs and I'll show you how this miracle, you just unknowingly witnessed, works.

***

They stood in a large, open room with individual, two-person tables organized into 'U's. Posters covered most of the open wall space. Several were warnings as to the dangers of obesity. Some showed before-and-after pictures of young and old people: the first obese and sad, the second smiling and thin. There was a large chart of the food group, a little different than Josh had known as a child. Delicious smells wafted from a room beyond. Obviously someone was cooking a meal.

Children and adults were sitting before desktop computers that had, what looked to Josh, medical instruments attached. The instruments went to a white box that was about nine centimeters long and five centimeters wide. In turn, the box was connected to the back of the computer. Young men and women were showing the sitting persons how to use the instruments as well as the computer.

Sam swept her arm and hand across the scene. "What you see here is a big part of our health care secret: home diagnosis. The persons in white coats are volunteers, high-schoolers, college students and insurance recipients unable to pay the entire or portions of their fees.

This State has achieved quality health insurance for all its citizens. Not that garbage the Fed's pass-off as National Health Care. I wouldn't take my dog to any U.S. hospital outside of Wyoming."

Josh felt a little out of his element. The group nodded. They agreed that NHC was a complete failure. The entire system was bankrupt and it showed in old equipment, run-down facilities and lack of proper medical supplies. It was a system teetering on the verge of complete collapse, just as Social Security had collapsed.

As with the city transportation system, Josh felt another lesson coming as to how this State had outdone the rest of the country in health care. It was probably something spectacular, so he tried to pay attention. Obviously Sam had a major role in this and he wanted her to know he was interested.

"It's a government program in that we demand one hundred percent of our residents be enrolled. But it is all done through private insurance companies. The government is involved also in that every three years a government commission acts as an arbitrator between hospital accountants and the insurance companies. Doctors and nurses are represented as well as a patients' advocacy group. A fee for every possible procedure is agreed upon and then adopted for the intermittent three years. We have one standard insurance rate for every person, regardless of age or pre-existing condition. Naturally fees are higher for a family. But overall rates are lower, in Old US dollars, then before the turn of the millennium.

"How do you accomplish that?" Governor Hugh's interest grew.

"John, it took six big steps to get started," Said Sam. "First we had to get every Citizen on board. That was no small task. There were so many concerns about choosing one's own doctor, prescription costs, mandatory insurance fees, on and on. After addressing all these, we had a strong consensus."

"Second was to abandon Medicare. We convinced seniors that they were at a disadvantage being on Medicare. Doctors treated them differently because Medicare set treatment and payment edicts in Washington. There was little regard for the patient, just the bottom line. And more and more doctors were refusing Medicare patients because they did not get paid a fair fee and, worse, never got paid in a timely manner. Many doctors had to hire extra personnel just to handle the paperwork and keep on the government to get paid. So we opted out of the program."

"Opted out?" Governor Almondo asked. "What does that mean?"

"We told the Fed's we were not subsidizing Medicare or Medicaid anymore and they did not have to reimburse doctors. That's opting out.'"

"What did the Fed's say?"

Sam smiled, thinly, "They said 'No.' But we just ignored them, and stopped any participation."

"And they did what?"

"They sued us, naturally. Took it all the way to the U.S. Supreme Court, and won. And we have ignored that as well," said Sam, calmly.

"How can you ignore the Federal Government or the Supreme Court?" asked Governor Almondo. "If we did that, it would be the last we saw of FUSS payments to our State. We would completely collapse."

Samantha slowly nodded her head, "Yes, Mario, you probably would. And your State should never have allowed itself to be in that position. You will have to strengthen your economy first. Then remove yourself from the Federal dole, no matter how painful. As long as you are suckling the teat, they own you. It's going to be a long, hard trail back, but you owe it to your Citizens

"We haven't taken a dime of their worthless money!" said Governor Brigham, pridefully.

"Yes," nodded Sam, "And you are much stronger for it today. Your State has earned its independence, Liz. Now, let's move on.

Third, we had to make sure our insurance rates stayed low. In fact, we have actually driven down rates through our Wellness Program. You are looking at a big part of it in front of you. I will explain it all in detail in a few minutes."

"Fourth, we had to gain levels of efficiency that individual hospitals could not do alone. Here, our State government acts as an agent on behalf of the patient and the medical community. We centralized all patient records. This was a massive undertaking, but with volunteers we accomplished it in two years. No longer are their individual records at every doctor's office. Every visit, every procedure, every prescription is entered into our central data base. The efficiency of this has been amazing, not only in cost reductions but in faster and better care for the patient. Doctors don't have to keep all their office files. All they need is a wireless hand-held. Whether the patient goes to a doctor's office or a hospital, their records are immediately available for recall. Even appointments are done by computer through our system. You want to see Dr. 'X', you pull him up and check his calendar. Then you make your own appointment. "

Josh spotted something wrong with this centralization, "But what about a patient's right of privacy? Now the state has all of the individual's health history. What stops that info from being disseminated to, let's say, insurance companies that deny coverage based on it?"

"Good point," replied Sam. "But remember, no one can be denied health coverage for any reason and everyone pays the same rate. So what if an insurance company gets ahold of records? We have already given them a statistical breakdown of the pool from which they will be assigned clients. Age, weights, dependents, non-dependents, pre-existing conditions: all the info is provided to them prior to the bidding process, but it is devoid of names, patient numbers or any identifiers. All companies receive nearly the same percentage from each category. The only choice they have is the number of pools they want to insure, and we have a minimum on that. So what is their incentive to find out individual names?"

Josh thought for a second. There was still a snag and it came to him, "Here's two other areas that I wouldn't like for my medical records to be disclosed: a life insurer and a potential employer. How are you protected in those areas?"

"Again, excellent questions. I am so glad you are paying attention. First, life insurance; as part of our medical coverage, we include a ten-thousand Credits life insurance policy. It may not sound like a large amount. But remember, we are talking Wyoming Credits here, not the NUS.

But to expand on this and answer your question about a potential employer seeing your records, I have to tell you about our security. Our centralized computer has never been hacked. We have probably the world's best team on encryption and security right here, working in our State. When you get a chance, look into a company call **CrypSurity**. They have an incredible staff and incredible track record. In fact, they are working on a large project for our State right now. So the only way we can see the records becoming public is through an employee or doctor letting them out. As part of our law creating the health insurance plan, the State has assumed the same patient-doctor confidentiality. All records are encrypted and can only be accessed by a key that is sent out daily. Doctors, health care workers and State employees working in the health care office have their individual password. When a record is accessed, a central log is updated and the patient receives an email. Any individual releasing confidential records faces immediate dismissal and banning of future employment with the State or within the health care field, five years in prison and a one-thousand Credits fine, for each incident. You may not trust your national government, Josh. But Wyomingans trust their State because we have not given them reason to doubt.

"But the biggest gain has been in billing. Because ours is a comprehensive insurance plan, we add a standard five credit co-pay. It's really designed to make sure visits aren't just frivolous for lonely Aunt Martha to have someone listen to her for an hour. The doctor keeps the co-pay. After the visit, the doctor enters his diagnosis and the bill is electronically sent to the State payment center. The computer checks for anything unusual or possible fraud, and is compared to a statistical algorithm. With everything approved, the State pays the doctor within twenty four hours. At the same time the State is reimbursed from an account each insurance company maintains up-front. It's part of our agreement with any insurance company that they have to maintain this account at a pre-set level.   Otherwise, they lose their license to operate here.   With our centralized purchasing power, these companies comply rather willingly. They've seen our fraud detection software and our enforcement policies, so the majority of insurers process their payments to us without even going through the hassle of checking each bill.   They use their own statistical analysis of the bills to see if they are falling into their anticipated payments.   Insurance companies are not allowed to refuse payment.   If they have a dispute, they take it up with a joint- arbitration board we assembled.   A hearing and decision must take place within ten days of the insurance company's filing.   There is a single appeal process as well. Actually, the insurers have found our system provides major cost savings for them.   Many are listed on the WSE – Wyoming Stock Exchange – and are a favorite investment of State pension funds.   They pay excellent dividends.

We also created quite a savings in the prescription drug arena.   The State negotiates directly with pharmaceutical companies for the top generic drugs.   We make these purchases available at no profit to pharmacies throughout the state, with a proviso.   They must sell them at our designated fixed price, which is low.   Also, we make them directly available to physicians who provide them free-of-charge to patients without means to pay.   For all non-generic drugs, we encourage our patients to shop prices."

She looked at Joshua to see if he was still with her, "Want me to go on?"

The Governors nodded.   Josh was neutral.   He wasn't too interested in medical payments.

Sam pressed on, "The Fifth area was liability.   It was a huge hurdle.   We had lawyers from all over the country popping up here to fight us.   Most we never let through immigration.   In order to succeed, our program had to control liability costs in two areas, law suits and mal-practice insurance. The State proposed to assume all liability for our doctors.   This removed the burden of doctors from paying mal-practice fees.   These fees had been jumping thirty percent a year, every year, and forcing doctors to abandon individual practices.   It also was a discouraging factor for increasing our corps of new doctors.   But remember, when you gain something you have to give up something.   We put doctors on an annual review.   Our medical review board contains not only doctors, but lawyers and representatives of patient advocacy groups.   Every doctor's record is reviewed throughout the year.   If he is found derelict, he is subject to a hearing.   A simple majority against him can strip him of his license.   He is immune from civil suit, but not criminal.   And doctors are not immune to monthly wellness tests. These are mandatory, at random appointments and must be done in person. It's sad to find how many good doctors become addicts through their own self-prescription. And we are not easy on them when it comes to weight, alcohol or tobacco use, either. Part of being a doctor in this State is to set a good example for the patient."

Patients have to give up something too: the right to sue. We have established a table of conceivable injuries and assigned each a reasonable maximum amount payable to the patient. The same panel that reviews doctors also hears these mal-practice cases. There are no punitive damages allowed. Pain and suffering are already calculated into the table of reimbursements. If mal-practice is found, the patient is paid by the State. Handling this one issue, we dropped over-head costs to the doctors by nearly sixty percent. That meant we could lower our payments for procedures. And the real boon is that our door is being knocked down by doctors wanting to practice here. We have a two-year waiting list for the review committee."

Scott Fodor had put away his invasion fears and was listening intently. He wanted to bring up another point, "It sounds like you covered most bases. But what do you do when an insurance company decides it's been a bad year for healthcare, so they pull out, leaving you high and dry. Who takes care of their clients?"

Sam responded, "Remember, the insurance companies have fronted monies into an account on behalf of the State. It amounts to twenty-five percent of the coming year's anticipated payments. And they cannot dip into it until the last quarter of the year. They can invest it and reap the gains under two conditions, the State has the right to spend the principal reserve amount to pay any claims that the insurer has defaulted on, and two, it's invested in low risk items. A lot of times they choose our own State bonds because of safety. We have a State commission that approves every investment. If an insurance company decides to leave, naturally we have no way to stop them. Within six months of close of the State fiscal year and payment of all claims, they are returned any left-over funds, plus interest. And if they owe us money, they will never get back into our State unless they make good on the funding." She chuckled, "But we certainly don't have that problem. We have insurance companies from all over the world trying set up shop here. With our Wellness programs, we have one of the healthiest populations in the world."

"You've mentioned this Wellness program a couple of times," Josh said. "Tell me what it includes."

"Better yet, I am going to show you," answered Sam. "But first, let me cover the last point. It's the stickiest."

Josh nodded.

"The sixth was a major challenge, Illegal immigration. The first thing we had to do was develop an effective illegal immigration control system."

Josh's interest perked up. After the discussion with the Dillons, he wanted Sam's take on this policy. Certainly she couldn't feel the system was fair. Wyoming had strict laws against illegals along with strict immigration procedures.

Sam explained, "Any businessman hiring, or landlord renting to, an illegal faces two years in jail for each offence and a five thousand WC fine. With a tight immigration system, every visitor is provided an ALIEN identity card containing picture and biometrics: voice, fingerprint and retinal scan. CITIZENS and RESIDENTS had their own status and their own cards. A businessman or landlord is required by law to scan the card through a reader and receive an on-line verification of the person's immigration status. The card is next to impossible to duplicate. Additionally, law requires any captured illegals to spend six months in a camp that provides extensive, ah... exercise and restricted, bland food. It is not a pleasant experience, but one that is not physically threatening. It is the State's opinion that six months in one of its camps is a lifetime deterrent to repeat offenders. It is also hoped that the State has developed a callous reputation to dissuade other interlopers.

Governor Almondo spoke, "We were briefed on your immigration policy. A little severe, don't you think?"

Sam shook her head, "No I don't." Josh's thoughts of Sam's leniency were dashed. "Mario, I do not wish to be harsh, but your State, California, is a disaster. If you wish to be concerned about an invasion, please do not worry about Wyoming. It is California that has, and is, being invaded. Nearly forty percent of your Southern California residents are illegal. These people are not usually at the top of the socio-economic scale, so they become the State's largest burden when it comes to social services. And they are the group least likely to pay for it through taxes. If you do not establish an effective immigration program, and protect your borders, then California is finished."

"But how can we? President Rivera has given the vote to these people. There is no way we can propose changes that would win at the ballot box. Even you, Sam, have preached about having the support of the people."

Sam again shook her head, "I never said that, Mario. I said to gain the support of your *Citizens*. If you consider anyone walking across California's border to be a Citizen, then all hope is lost. My advice, disregard Rivera. He has no Constitutional right to give the vote to anyone. And stop saying 'we.' You are the Governor, Mario. Sign an executive order. Disenfranchise these non-citizens before it's too late. The ones that earned, or their great-grandparents earned, Citizenship will thank you and support you."

"God Almighty! We, ah, I would have riots in the street if I did that."

Sam nodded, "Probably. That's what your National Guard is for. Call them out. Quell the riots. Induct legal Citizens if you require the manpower. But you better do something soon, if it's not already too late."

"You're talking war, Sam." Almondo sounded as if he were pleading with her.

"Mario, you are already at war. You just refuse to recognize it. And you are losing through inaction."

Governor Almondo dropped his head in acquiescence. She was right. He knew it and so did the other Governors consoling their brethren.

Sam continued in a lighter voice, "But let's table this debate for now. I want to explain our Wellness program. Most of it is represented right here," again she pointed towards the room they stood before.

Sam said, "It starts with weight. When we initially looked at wellness, we tracked almost fifty percent of preventable health costs to obesity, improper diet and lack of exercise. Heart disease, strokes, diabetes, even depression caused by the social stigma of being obese. We believe that many cancers are directly related to excessive consumption of animal fats and proteins. Obesity was our first target to conquer. And I think we have made a good dent," she chuckled at her own pun. "How many obese people have you seen since you've been in our State?"

Josh ran street scenes through his mind. He couldn't really say he saw anyone who would be considered fat. 'No big percentage, I guess. What, do you throw them in camps as well?'

103

The Governors chuckled at this rebuke.

Sam shot back, "We have less than three percent of Wyomingans in the obese category. We have biomass tables, created by health studies, as to what acceptable weights are for people of certain heights and ages. It's pretty reasonable. We don't want a state full of bulemics or anorexics."

Josh laughed, "And you tax them by the pound, right?"

Sam remained serious, "In a way. But taxes are punitive. We always try to work from incentive. If you are within your weight category, you get a discount on your monthly insurance premium."

Josh said, "I thought you said everyone pays the same. Now you're making amendments?"

"No," replied Sam, "I stand by that statement. We have one standard fee for health care. But there is a discount available if you take care of yourself. It's an incentive."

"Sounds pretty punitive to me, for the fatties I mean," Governor Fodor groused.

Sam responded, "Why? Insurance companies have done it for years with Life Insurance. If you're overweight, you pay more. Who is responsible for your health, you or society? It's definitely you and you need to have control over it. And we teach people how to accomplish it."

Josh said, being serious this time, "Maybe you do need to throw some of them into exercise camps. I saw firsthand how boot camp cleaned up a lot of fatties. Always thought everyone should go through bootcamp."

Sam replied, "Please, Josh. Let's refrain from the word fatties."

He nodded.

"However, to your point, if we took that path, we would lose all support for our program, not to mention ending up with a forty percent heart attack rate of those Citizens. No, our solution is not that drastic. We identify who has problems and then we help them solve their weight issues. They are encouraged to take our free cooking and nutrition classes. That's what you smell coming from the back room. They can also receive psychiatric help, to find out if there is an underlying emotional issue. They are given physicals to see if the problem is glandular or a disease precursor. They are enrolled with other over-weight people in exercise classes, not camps. They are encouraged to attend health classes. We even allow them to witness an open heart surgery."

Josh questioned, "And this works? People voluntarily subject themselves to this?"

Sam answered, "We use a lot of societal pressure as well. We constantly run ads in the local media. We recognize, in the media, winners that have lost substantial weight. We send out volunteers that have successfully completed our programs to meet obese persons. But the real way many see the light is through kids.

In school, we reinstituted mandatory physical education. Each child is tested, just like old times. But more, we make health class mandatory through grammar and middle schools. It's not the mamby-pamby health class taught by the gym coach. We put a nutritionist and nurse in charge. We show them the insides of healthy bodies and diseased ones. They are taught a real food triangle that puts eighty percent fruits and vegetables at the top, then fish and chicken, then red meat and dairy at the bottom." Sam laughed, "The ranchers and dairymen sure didn't like that, especially my father."

"And in our school cafeterias, we do not serve the slop that you and I grew up with. Fresh vegetables, good carbs and small portions of lean protein are for lunch. Cereal, oatmeal, whole grain bread, fruit and non-fat milk or juice for breakfast. And we don't count catsup as a vegetable.

We have the kids keep a journal as to what they eat outside of school. Of course this reflects what Mom or Dad is serving at home for dinner. When we show what alternatives should be served, or how the food could be prepared more healthy, then the child becomes an effective messenger back to the parents. It caused some consternation at first. But we stuck with it and have seen good results. Societal change is always more successful through positive peer pressure than government bullying."

"Sounds a little like Big Brother to me," scoffed Fodor.

"How is it any different than anti-littering campaigns in the nineteen-fifties, or seatbelt ads in the nineteen-sixties, or anti-drug lectures in the nineteen-seventies?

Further, we instituted mandatory Home-Ec for both boys and girls. For two semesters in middle school, all children have to learn to prepare home menus and cook healthy foods. And I mean all children: boys, girls, jocks, computer nerds. They have an incentive in that the entire school eats what they cook. Trust me, you don't want kids on your back for serving them slop. Part of these two classes is on basic economics, balancing a check book, living within a household budget, the evils of credit, the rewards of saving and basic, sound investing. We open a savings account for every child and let them voluntarily deposit even the smallest fractional Credits each week. But I do not wish to stray too far from our Wellness program.

So with proper diet and exercise, we have removed a huge burden from our health care system."

She searched each for questions. Finding none, she continued, "Now to an explanation of the people at the computers. After months of laying out the parameters of our Wellness program, getting it to the floor of our State Congress, having it pass, and then receiving a priority from the Technology Committee, we were on our way. In short, what we accomplished was an at-home-diagnosis system. Let's say you wake up and feel like you're coming down with a cold. You know enough to stay in bed, because of our educational programs. You take aspirin and eat chicken soup. But now you have a raging fever and lumps rising in your neck. What to do? Go to the doctor, right? But if it's two AM, maybe you're rushed to the hospital emergency room. With our program, you go to a computer that is provided by the State for every household. We needed to provide this for our educational programs anyway.

You click on the Wellness icon. It asks MONTHLY CHECKUP, or ILLNESS. For this example, you would select Illness and prepare the attachments. That is what the young lady over to the right is showing that elderly gentleman. She is teaching him how to use the thermometer to take his temperature, the blood pressure cuff, the tongue depressor and throat swab, an ear and throat probe, this one gets a little trickey as you have to look at the monitor at the time you are manipulating the instrument, then the weigh scale, a blood test that involves a similar instrument as a diabetes test. It is a quick pin-prick and a squeeze onto the diagnostic pad. And finally a closeup camera-shot of the lumps. As you focus and zoom the camera, the image the doctor will see is on the screen, so you can make adjustments. Then the patient pops the throat and blood swabs into their separate readers. They fill out a questionnaire as to possible symptoms. Every instrument is attached to the computer through that white box. The doctor has most of the information required to make a diagnosis. If it's something puzzling or serious, you are notified to go to the emergency room at the nearest hospital. The computer asks if you need emergency services to come to you. If you say no, you punch in an estimated ETA and the computer schedules your visit with the emergency room. The computerized file is waiting for the on-call doctor. There is no need to fill out any paperwork or insurance. That is all on file in the computer. Even your copay is automatically charged to your WC account on file. You go straight into care with just a thumb print and verbal confirmation of your name, if you are conscious. If the doctor requires X-rays, additional blood tests, or different scans, this is scheduled beforehand and is handled by technicians even before you are seen by the doctor. Emergency services, in contact with a doctor, also perform many of these tests on-board during transit and send the info to a waiting physician. Or they can schedule tests electronically before arrival. This is why the elderly lady at the beginning of our tour was wheeled right to the required care area. The doctor can also tie a genealogy to a patient for comparison with other family members.

But, we're still back at the home. You click SUBMIT and go back to bed. Within no more than an hour, a PA – Physician's Assistant - is on-line, dinging you from your sleep. You get up and go to the computer. The PA has run a computerized diagnosis of your symptoms and vitals and forwarded it to a doctor for his review. It had listed earlier all possibilities of what you could have. The doctor eliminates most. Because you entered that you haven't traveled outside the State for six months, he can eliminate things like African sleeping-sickness. So the PA tells you what you already know. You have the flu, including ear and throat infection. She, or he, sends you the serial number of the prescription that she has already sent to your requested pharmacy; provides dosage information and schedules a follow-up with the doctor within forty-eight hours. The message covers any prescription or other questions and then signs off. Voila! No emergency room visit. The majority of our pharmacies now offer home delivery within four hours at no additional cost. We didn't mandate this. They do it as a competitive offering. And, as an added incentive, we charge no co-pay if you use the at-home system and skip the emergency room.

As part of the educational system, we give students at every grade level training on the instruments and the computer. We've had six year olds do exams for their eighty-year-old grandmothers. Children are capable of a lot more than we give them credit for. They just have to be instructed properly.

Our doctors and PA's are the most efficient in the world, seeing over seventy patients within a ten hour shift. And our emergency rooms have the lowest case load in the world. It has already saved Wyomingans millions of Credits. Our Citizen's prefer it. It is silly that when you are sick, you have to wait until morning to call a doctor. Then get an appointment time that might not even be the same day. Then have someone stay home from work to drive you to the appointment. Then wait in a room with other sick, and well, people, some coughing and hacking while others breathe it in. Then wait in an exam room for a busy doctor to tell you that you have the flu. Then get your prescription and take it to a pharmacy that makes you wait while you infect another twenty people."

Josh broke in, "You said something earlier about using the same computer and instruments for a monthly thing? What's that about?"

Sam answered, "I'm glad you remembered. Shows me you were listening instead of thinking I was just droning on about my pet project. It's what we call Monthly Wellness Checkup. A lot of things, if caught early, are more successfully attacked during treatment. And that treatment can be a lot cheaper than if the disease becomes full-blown.

The program is simple. You examine yourself monthly with all the instruments and then fill out a lengthy questionnaire. You can also input any aches, pains or conditions you have been experiencing. The computer scans for any abnormalities against thousands of possible diseases or conditions. Then it forwards any suspicious files to the PA who reviews the file with a doctor. If further tests are required, the patient is notified by computer. Different than other health systems, the computer keeps the patient, or the responsible party, in the loop with all computer file updates. You can't expect people to be responsible individuals when you treat them like children.

I think our system is not only incredibly efficient, but better at taking care of the individual: good investment all the way around."

Governor Hughes said, "Sounds good. Have to try it before I comment, though."

Governor Fodor said, with some sarcasm, "Glad to see you have escaped the evil government intrusion into your daily lives that everyone here talks about, you know, pioneer freedom. And kids keeping parents in line, a bit fascist isn't it?"

Sam didn't react to the baiting, and instead answered calmly, "Scott, there are things we can accomplish as individuals. There are things we must band together to accomplish. People do not hate government. They hate a government that doesn't ask their permission. They hate a government that wastes their money. They hate a government that takes away from them that which they have worked hard for, yet returns nothing. They hate a government that lies to them or manipulates them for some hidden agenda. They hate a government that promises something but never tells them what it will cost, either financially or in personal liberty. They hate a government that doesn't protect them from harm. They hate a government that tries to destroy their culture, their history. They hate a government that is too big and too far away to hear them.

We don't mandate anything without a vote. Most of our programs are voluntary. Sure we use social pressure to achieve a good for not only society, but the individual as well. The greatest blessing of our democracy is freedom. But in the last analysis, our only freedom is the freedom to discipline ourselves. That government is best which governs the least, because its people discipline themselves. Thomas Jefferson said, A successful society needs disciplined individuals practicing self-control. I don't care if it's personal health, dealing with personal finances or obeying laws when no one's looking. The people of this State decided, through a democratic vote with an overwhelming majority, that they wanted health insurance for all. They were told upfront what was needed to make it happen, and they chose that path. I hardly call that facist. As to intrusive, anytime you want to receive something you have to give up something. Yes, our system may appear intrusive, to a degree. But our Citizens knew what they were signing up for. It wasn't some self-serving, patchwork legislation coming from on high down to the masses from elitists; with no way to pay for it except a massive new tax or burgeoning deficits. We leave that style to D.C. It took a lot of town meetings and a lot of compromise. In the end, they, we, all said yes.

It has been successful. As I said, our State is one of the healthiest in the world. And I give a lot of the credit to the Wellness program. It has dropped our emergency room costs nearly fifty percent."

She looked at the group for further comments. Meeting silence, she said, "Okay, I think that's about all on health care for today. Let's head out to see another area that we tackled, education."

She quick-stepped towards the door and signaled the others to follow. Governor Brigham hesitated a moment. Something in that back room kitchen sure smelled good.

# Chapter 11

## In the Dark

### Outside Fort Hood, Texas

This day had been strange, very strange. Tex had no idea as to what this Ben Warner was up to. He initially wasn't sure if his decision to break away from Stillwater was smart. But Maxton saw the possibilities in changing quarries. A quick background search of Warner by Maxton had piqued the DDD Director's interest. Warner was the Lieutenant Governor of the troublesome State. But he had a background of a more clandestine nature: a U.S. Army Intelligence officer, involvement with classified, dark op's; a hero of the Iran affair, yet an informal reprimand in his file regarding leaks of information to the Mossad. Yes, Tex thought, this guy is definitely a more interesting target. And now he's dressed up as an Army Major and entering a U.S. military base. This just gets better. After review of the information, Maxton had authorized a sanction on Warner. This was right up Tex's skill set. He was through with being just a spy. Wet-work was his specialty. He smiled and thought of the custom Bowie knife in his boot. It was his killing instrument of choice. *Baby, you and I finally get to have some fun.*

Tex had met up with his former partner, Osmond. The other man had been watching Warner since he landed in Texas.

"Where we at?" asked Tex.

Osmond was sitting in a car below an overpass in front of the Fort Hood base. He was eating an egg and bacon sandwich. The hood was up on the car, giving him cover of a break-down while waiting. "Went in there about thirty minutes ago and hasn't come out. There are other exits. But I figured he'd come out the same way he entered. Couldn't follow him inside unless I pulled out my DDD badge. Didn't think that would be too smart. He's driving a Ford-Nissan blue sedan with black-walls and no wheel covers."

Tex nodded, "OK. I got it from here. Take my car and I'll wait in yours. You go around to one of the other exits just in case. I'll give you a call in about thirty minutes."

Osmond mumbled something while chewing a bite from his sandwich. He grabbed his coffee cup and exited the vehicle, "Keys are in it."

Tex handed his keys over and Osmond left in the rental car. Tex left up the hood of Osmond's car, continuing the ruse. It didn't make sense that he had car trouble yet the engine was running, so he turned it off and began to bake in the penetrating Texas sun. Even though the afternoon was slipping towards evening, it was still thirty-seven C outside. The only blessing for Tex was that this was West Texas. Humidity was a little less than if he were in Houston, his home town. The base sat just outside Killeen, not far from Austin. This part of the State was considered downright dry by those living near the Gulf.

He was dripping sweat as he sat inside the car, windows down. His long sleeve shirt may have appeared hot, but it kept his bent arm from being burnt on the metal door frame. He kept his eye upon the rear view mirror, looking for Warner's sedan. This caused him to miss the State Trooper coming the other way. The State vehicle spun a 'U' behind Tex's car. Now he filled the rear view.

"Afternoon, officer," Tex drawled deep and friendly as the Trooper approached. "Just having some car problems. Think it's the thermostat. Either that, or the water pump is out."

"I'll take a look for you," offered the officer.

"Naw," replied Tex casually. "I already called Triple A. They're sending a tow truck."

"That's all right," said the officer. "I don't mind. Be good if we can get it running to have a little air conditioning. You're gonna melt in this heat."

Tex got out of the car and followed the Trooper up to the engine. The officer said, "You know, those thermostat trouble indicators go bad all the time on this manufacturer's cars. It's probably a faulty light. Why don't you start it up and I'll see if she gets hot."

Tex sighed. He reached in his back pocket and pulled out his DDD identification. He tapped the Trooper on the shoulder and stuck it in front of his face, "Ok, you got me, officer. I'm on a stake-out. There's a guy that just went onto the base and we have cause to think he's a terrorist."

The State Trooper frowned at the ID. He looked up at Tex, his face hardened, "We really don't like your kind down here. Why don't you stay in the North where they all quake in their boots when you flip that out."

Tex didn't like this guy's tone. "Don't get tough with me, cop. I can have your badge in twenty-four hours for obstructing justice."

The officer looked down at his name tag pinned to his shirt. "Hoffsteader, Alec J., Sergeant. Make sure you get it wrote down correctly, slime ball. By our laws, any Fed policing agent must report to the county sherrif and present a warrant, unless you plan to arrest someone on a Federal military base. But I don't think the Army would take kindly to your sort. You're in Texas, boy. I know we don't take kindly to Yankees coming down here and messing in our State."

Tex's face had reddened, more anger than the relentless heat, "You dimwitted redneck, I was born and raised in Houston. And we'll mess around anywhere we want."

"Well, that makes you worse than a Yankee, mister. A Texan working for that outfit is just a damn traitor." The cop folded his arms on his substantial chest. "And what the hell is the DDD doing in the terrorist business? That's FBI territory. You're probably lying like all you bastards do. I'd say you're probably trying to bust some poor schmuck that called your President a bad name. And you'll give him twenty years for it, too. So why not just get out of my State, and pronto."

At this very moment, Ben's sedan rolled by. He was oblivious to the row taking place on the roadside. Tex caught sight of the car, pocketed his ID and slammed the hood shut. He trotted back to the door, jerked it open, jumped in and fired up the engine. As he spun rubber pulling away, he stuck his hand out the open window, flipped a bird and yelled, "Screw you, Officer Asshole!"

The State Trooper shook his head. He was contemplating putting out a BOLO - Be-On-Lookout - for the guy just to bust his chops. He could say the Fed assaulted him. He thought about it for a moment and then decided it was just too much paperwork.


Ben drove east, back towards Killeen. He turned into the Dove & Quail motel, pulling into a parking space that fronted outward-facing room doors. He grabbed his valise from the passenger seat and a rucksack from the trunk. He then unlocked and entered room number fifteen. Tex swung his rental into a Whataburger parking lot across the street to wait and watch. Being hungry and not knowing how long until his quarry reappeared, he swung into the drive-thru lane and ordered a Double

Whooper with double cheese, no veggies, extra mayo. Tex then parked, facing the motel, and tore into the burger. Chewing joyfully he thought, *"God, I've missed Whataburger!"* The fast-food chain was headquartered in Corpus Christi with locations predominantly the South.

Thirty minutes later, Warner reappeared. He was dressed in black with the rucksack slung over one shoulder. He jumped into his car and headed back east. It was just starting to get dark. *Is he headed back to Fort Hood?* Tex pondered, starting his car to follow. With the waning light, Tex followed at a safe distance, trying to decide if he should turn on his headlamps. The sudden appearance of lights could catch Warner's eye. On the other hand, if the Wyomingan saw the silhouette of a car with no lights, tailing him, this would certainly arouse suspicions. Besides, there were still plenty of other cars on the road. He turned the knob and the lights popped on.

Warner zipped past the Fort Hood turnoff and continued west. Several miles later he pulled into the right lane and slowed. Tex didn't think he had been spotted. Warner appeared as if he were looking for a road sign. But there weren't any paved roads let alone road signs. They had passed Fort Hood's fence line about a kilometer back.

Warner made an abrupt turn onto a dirt road and stopped. Tex kept his head forward as he cruised past, never chancing a look. He looked in the rearview mirror to watch Warner's next move. Tex kept his sedan traveling away at a constant speed, thinking, *Warner's probably checking to see if he has a tail. This could play out one of three ways. Either he turns around and goes back from the direction we just came, he continues on the dirt road, or he pulls back onto the main road and continues in my direction.* If it were the latter, Tex would see some lights soon. This didn't happen. He pulled his car off onto the side of the road, leaving the engine running, headlamps on and even turned on the interior light. With flat fields extending for miles from both sides of the road, there was nowhere to hide a car. His only option was to pull out a road map and act as if lost.

# Chapter 12

## An Education

### Cheyenne, Wyoming

Sam and Josh were rolling down another city street, Paul still in the first car keeping vigilance. They had been silent since leaving the hospital and Josh felt a need to restart the conversation.

"You said you provide each family with a computer for schooling?

Sam nodded, "It's a tablet, actually."

Josh asked, "Must have been expensive. Where did the money come from?"

Sam, "Well , first of all, we are a rich State. But we are not extravagant. We purchased the tablets from a Chinese company that decided to set up shop here in Wyoming. The tablets aren't what you think of in the conventional sense of the word. Our term is 'scrolls.' They actually roll up and are very durable. When unrolled they are stiff and can be expanded left and right to create a twenty-five by fifteen centimeter tablet. They can display video, play audio, be written upon with a special pen and can even be typed upon."

Josh remembered seeing the same technology used by a waitress at the 'Gold is King' steakhouse and bar in Casper. It was quite unique in that, after placing his order on the pad, she had rolled it up and put it into her pocket.

Sam continued, "It was a win-win for the Chinese and us. We licensed them the technology of the scroll, as it was developed at our University and patented here in Wyoming. We provided the Chinese company an exclusive sales agreement within China while we share in the profits. Additionally, they are the exclusive manufacturer for Wyoming State government and schools. Our initial order was for three hundred thousand units: a nice incentive for them to set up shop here and meet our terms. After they saw all the advantages to our State: no corporate, personal, property, or inventory taxes; an educated, disciplined work force; a company union modeled upon the Japanese method; it was a win-win for all. And the fact that the State invested, and owns, ten percent of the company via preferred stock, we are first in line for some hefty dividends. We do that with a lot of companies. It gives them Credits to get started and we get a continued return. "

115

The CityCars rolled to a stop in front of an elementary school. Paul stood guard as Sam exited the Car and led the group through the front doors. She was explaining the scroll technology to the Governors as she walked, "So we provide a scroll to each child. But here is the caveat. The entire family must come to the school for a weekend education seminar on the technology's basics. One Saturday and Sunday out of your life is pretty cheap for free, advanced electronics. And we have continuing classes if they wish to continue learning."

Inside the school hallway, an older lady met them and shook Sam's hand. She was introduced by Sam to the group as Ms. Helspar, the principal. After introductions, they were ushered by the woman into a third grade classroom. The principal nodded to the teacher who nodded back. The teacher brought her hands up in a sweeping motion and all the children rose to their feet. They said in unison, "Good morning, Ms. Governor Warner and guests."

Sam smiled and bowed slightly. "And good morning to all of you, as well," she said. "Please, take your seats so we can begin."

Sam looked at the Principal who began to describe events within. Sam and her entourage followed as her explanation took them to different areas of the classroom.

"Every student has a scroll open on their desk. They are connected, via WiFi, to the school's central server along with the teacher's console. If you notice, on her desk is a very large monitor, I believe one-hundred and twenty centimeters?" she moved her eyes to the teacher, questioning. The teacher nodded again.

"This allows the teacher to have a split screen with a space for every student's response. As she writes a question on her pad, it transfers to the students' scroll. When it's a question, the students respond by writing the answer onto their scroll. The teacher can quickly see who has the correct or incorrect answer. This way there is no need to embarrass a student or force a shyer child to shout out answers. If there is a small core of children not understanding properly, then the others can view a learning video of new, upcoming material. This is done silently as each student has wireless, stereo earpieces. You can barely see them protruding from their ears. They have them in their ears during classroom time as this is how the teacher communicates with them. This way she can isolate one child for a detailed explanation or speak to the entire class. It has been a boon to teaching while reducing boredom and misbehavior."

"Each child having a scroll has been a large boost to our homework programs. Homework is given out starting in the first grade. But it is provided and completed on the scroll, with parents notified of the assignment. Any required writing is accomplished via typing or writing directly upon the scroll, same as they have here. After school, at a time predetermined by parents, children are expected to log-in to their scrolls. Anyone not logged-in is beeped. If still no response, the parents are contacted. If still no response, then we have PTA volunteers start calling until either the child or a responsible adult is located. So back to the homework.

The child is expected to begin the lesson. It is usually divided into small sections which, after completion, is checked by our central computer for accuracy and even penmanship. We are fortunate to have a very advanced voice and hand-writing recognition program developed right here in Wyoming. This way, teachers are spared the drudgery of correcting homework the majority of assignments. Naturally, if the homework is of essay form, the teacher has a corrected copy sent to her for review of content, syntax and writing style.

If there are incorrect answers, the child is shown a short video by a very personable teacher explaining the problem and how to solve it. Then the child is given another question of the same nature first missed. If he or she fails to answer this category of question three times, the lesson moves on. But a note is recorded for the teacher to focus on this child and this part of the lesson. It achieves wondrous results.

The great thing is we can get around the snow days as well, using the scrolls. Winter snow can disrupt several days of school."

Josh groaned, "Oh God, don't tell me you make the kids go online even when it snows. That's downright vicious. I used to pray for snow days, especially if we had a test scheduled." The kids laughed. This earned them a stern look from Ms. Helspar, which slowly turned upon Josh. He looked down and coughed. Sam raised a hand to hide her smile.

The principal continued, "Yes, just as with the post office: rain or shine, snow or sleet, etc. Our computers are interactive. As in the classroom, the teacher is seen by all the children when he or she is talking. In turn, the teacher has a split screen, with all the children's faces on her monitor. She can see who is and who isn't paying attention. She can even talk to them individually to correct them without all the other children hearing. It's a real plus for discipline. And, if she calls on a child, she can direct the child to be seen by all the other students while replying. We can make it interactive for just one child also.  Say your child has something contagious but might feel well enough to continue learning.  We encourage parents to contact the teacher, by computer, and have little Jack or Jill stay home, but tune in on the computer.  Absenteeism is cut to a minimum.  Using the computer in the educational arena has been a boon to large reductions in absenteeism and has boosted test scores"

Additionally, the scrolls double as portable e-readers.  Many of our children read on the bus during transit time, which has decreased discipline problems in that arena.  And for beginning readers, we created reading groups whereby students, after school, read aloud through their scrolls to other students.  Our first graders are reading three grade levels higher than the nation's average."

"This whole 'free scroll' program must be expensive," interjected Governor Brigham.

Sam answered, "Not really, Liz.  One of the beauties of the scroll is its simple design and simple manufacturing steps.  Although it's a new technology, we purchase them at about the price of an old technology: smart phones.  Another cost benefit is books.  Think of all the funding you waste on text books.  They get damaged, wear out, are lost; require transport and storage and have to be tossed when information is updated.  Add to the textbook cost the required supplies of paper, pencils and workbooks.  For us, it is far cheaper to provide each child a scroll than the old technology of printed materials.  The cost of all the scrolls we have provided equals one year of text books and supplies.  Yet the child has the scroll for their entire education.  It is actually a huge savings."

Ms. Helspar nodded agreement.

This raised a question with Governor Hughes, "What about internet costs.  Now you've made the parents responsible to buy internet service and a wireless system for their homes.  Your State may be rich, Sam, but ours still has some pretty poor people that can't afford such luxuries."

"Good point, John," responded Sam.  "That is why our entire State provides wireless free."

"God, talk about expensive!"  It was Scott Fodor responding.

"It could have been, but save one technology, Scott.  We looked at cabling the entire State.  It was too cost prohibitive.  But an independent R&D company that the State aided during startup, developed a new, cost-effective way in splitting transceiver bands. I am no techie. So my explanation may be a bit simplistic.

The favored phone transmission is GSM. It has a broad reach. WiFi is designed for shorter reach, yet can process larger amounts of data via the internet. The women, yes it was two women that developed this, found a way to route transmission packets from GSM to WiFi automatically. This was a boon to cellphone operators in that their GSM towers were not only becoming overloaded with voice traffic, but also the ever-increasing demand of data processing. The new technology recognizes data from voice thereby routing data through the internet. The two ladies dubbed their invention G-WiF. We put together a contract that allowed the cellular companies discounted prices on the small, add-on equipment required, in turn for free wireless throughout the State. However, we didn't wish to step on the toes of internet providers, so the scrolls are designated to receive and send over a band reserved exclusively for their use. Additionally, the cellular companies agreed to erect towers where, previously, reception was spotty or non-existent. We were up and rolling in eighteen months as most of the equipment required was retro-fitted to existing. Naturally, our companies can make this technology available to your States…at an excellent price."

"Naturally," muttered Mario Almondo to Sam's smile.

"Okay, you have complete wireless coverage. Your kids can be on-line if they're sick or it's a snow day," Governor Fodor recapped. "So why not go total interactive. Eliminate schools."

The principal flinched and Sam intervened, "Actually, we thought about it. But the advantage of motivation, social competiveness and social interaction is too beneficial. Sports, arts, drama, music: all are important afterschool disciplines. But they are the wallpaper of life, not the wall. More important is for little Jack or Jill to develop competiveness within the group through the power of accolades and peer recognition; yet learning cooperation, politeness, manners and team work. Additionally, he or she needs to learn how to handle tedium, boredom and frustration. It's called discipline. All are essential to successfully compete in this world."

Governor Almondo broke in, "Competiveness is a bad word to the PC – Politically Correct - crowd."

Sam smiled, "Maybe that's why your State is uncompetitive, Mario."

119

"Ouch," the Governor replied.

Sam softened her tone, "I don't mean to be insulting, Mario. But people have taken PC to extremes. What does it accomplish to keep a child locked in a protective bubble? At some point he or she is going to come face-to-face with a competitive environment; if not in our nation than within the world. Political Correctness acts just like drugs on a child, it merely delay's child development and causes a greater pain in the future. It's not just competiveness, either. Every child here and every child in our educational system participates in martial arts training every day. Bullies are out there and have to be dealt with. And we use the opportunity to not only allow our children to defend themselves from schoolyard bullies, but the real bullies that surround our State. These children are tomorrow's defenders of Wyoming. And they will be prepared."

She gave a hard look to Josh and continued. He remained expressionless.

"Racial slurs, religious exclusion, sexual-orientation persecution, gender harassment: yes we consider these unacceptable and teach our children so. But we don't kick a nine-year-old boy out of school because he inappropriately touched a girl. Under our liability laws, any suit brought against the child, his family or the school system would never be heard. The boy gets a stern lecture with both parents present. Then he has to attend two Saturday classes on appropriate versus non-appropriate behavior. Stealing a kid's Saturday is pretty stiff punishment. This is usually sufficient to correct future misbehavior.

We praise achievement at all levels, but only if the individual gave one-hundred and ten percent. It's important to engender competitiveness within children, especially competitiveness with themselves. This is how humans maximize their potentials."

"I understand," acquiesced the Governor. "And I agree. But the PC people are organized, pervasive and persuasive."

"I am sure if you properly explained the situation to all of your Citizens, the fanatics would be berated, if not shouted down. As a politician, Mario, you think that answering or catering to the extremists on one or both sides of the spectrum is required. I tell you it is not. Instead, talk *with*, not *to*, the center. These are the vast majority and they are waiting for someone that cares about their views, their lives. They revile extremists and are tired of being pulled in opposite directions."

Governor Almondo snorted, waving his hand around the classroom, "And you don't call this extreme."

Sam shook her head, "We call it common sense, Mario. And that is the domain of the center. It is also the domain of Statesmen. Become a Statesman, Mario, not a politician."

The Governor didn't know if he were just insulted or exalted to new heights. He remained silent and thoughtful.

"The real benefit to educating kids together, in a classroom is building pride, an *esprit de corps* as you would say. It's pride in our State; all we have accomplished and all we will accomplish. We need defenders of our values and we are building them every day in our schools. It's tough to do that for a kid sitting at home, working on a computer."

She turned towards the children and half-shouted, "What State is this kids!"

They all shouted loudly, "This State of Mine!"

Sam nodded while laughing and clapping. It made Josh a little mad. Aside, he said to Sam, "How about making them proud of their nation, as well as their State."

Sam hesitated for a moment, considering her answer. "Maybe, Josh, our State serves as our nation in our minds. What could we possibly point to for our children to be proud of in this country, outside of Wyoming?"

*Again, the State versus the nation,* Josh thought. *These people are living in a fairy tale if they think they can take a path separate from their country. The Feds are too powerful and are going to squash them like a bug if they don't get back in line.*

Elizabeth Brigham directed her question to the Principal, "How long does it take to get your children back up to speed after the summer break?"

Ms. Helspar shook her head, "We do not have a summer break. At least not the three-month lay-off to which I believe you refer. All schools in Wyoming are year-around."

Josh groaned.

"I know, Mr. Stillwater, a year-around school sounds evil to someone brought up on the lazy, whimsical days of summer."

"It's downright cruel," replied Josh. The other adults chuckled.

"With the old system, it would take us three months of review just to get children back to where they ended their education the prior year. The brain is a muscle. Three-months of inactivity makes it flabby and soft. Our children need to be educated on a world-class basis, as they must compete within that world. The United States is the only industrialized country in the world that still adheres to a three-month summer vacation. But don't despair, Mr. Stillwater. Children in our system still have plenty of free time. We have a two-week summer break, two-weeks in the fall, winter and spring as well. This is plenty of time to frolic. This is the equivalent of two-months off, but is provided in breaks that the child looks forward to, yet is still capable of picking up where he or she left off. Any child in our system is three grades of material ahead of any other child within the national, public-school system."

It still left a sour taste to Josh. They were probably right, but summer being lost to school time sounded wrong. He shrugged.

Ms. Helspar asked for questions. As there were none, she thanked the group for coming. The teacher raised her hand, affecting the children to rise from their seats and, in a chorus, say, "Thank you for coming, Ms. Governor."

Sam smiled, shook the hand of the Principal and Teacher, complimented them on their presentation, and waved to the kids as she shouted out a 'Good-by'.

As they returned to the Cars, Governor Brigham said, "Nice educational system. All this pioneering and debugging is going to be a boon to our States."

She smiled, "Thank you, Liz. Remember, we offer scrolls and GWiF technology in bulk discounts. Additionally we provide education-redesign consultation and development services; at a fee, naturally."

Elizabeth Brigham laughed, "Mario's right. You are the consummate salesperson."

Sam smiled, "Only because I believe in the product. You have not seen it all, yet. We have one more stop."

## Chapter 13

## The Wrong One

## Wyoming

Dr. Leo Viloshensky's plea was passionate and heavily laden with his Russian accent, "Pleazzze helps me.  You are dee only one I  trust."

"And why is that, Leo?" asked the other man.

"Because you my best fwend here in Amareka."

He nodded, "I'm flattered at your trust.  But what're you asking of me?

"Take my Sasha for time till Ben Warner finds this man and den my Sasha, she is safe again."

He pondered the point for a moment and asked, "Why not send her back to your Mother's in Jackson."

Leo shook his head, "No good.  Dey know I am here in Wyomink, den dey know Sasha's babushka here too.  No good.  Must be someone dey know not so much about.  Someone dey not know am my good trust friend.  Dis way I tink of you."

***

Leo Viloshinsky had been Russia's gift to the European ITER program located near Cadarache, France.  It was the stunning apex of his career; selection by his country to participate in the development of ITER.  At least he thought it was until that fateful night when an agent of the FSB, modern Russia's spawn of the defunct Soviet Union's KGB, burst into his apartment.

The agent, Zhukov, was a hulk of a man, nearly seven feet tall.  His face and neck displayed a jagged, red scar: a souvenir from three Bosnian attackers that he had dispatched from their earthly bonds with his bare hands.

Zhukov informed the good doctor that his mission to the ITER had another component:  he was to destroy the hope for Fusion.  Zhukov thrust the explosive device into Viloshensky's hands with the demand that the ITER be destroyed upon his call to the physics doctor.  And to ensure Leo's cooperation, his daughter Sasha would stay behind in Russia as the FSB's hostage.  Any deviation by Leo of his instructions would result in his daughter's, his mother's and his own death. Viloshensky was devastated by his proposed role in the sabotage. He saw no way out. That is until a Mossad agent in Moscow made contact. Israel was aware of the plot and informed Leo to call them for help after Zhukov made contact with Leo in France.

The fateful day arrived. After the call from Zhukov, Leo agonized over his limited options. Should he set the explosive device and destroy the ITER? Failure to follow Moscow's instructions meant the death of his most precious item: his daughter Sasha. Resolving his quandary, he made the difficult decision to contact the Mossad, knowing even the call could result in Sasha's death. He prayed the call was not monitored or traced.

His satellite call to a man known to Leo only as 'Eagle' resulted in even greater consternation. First, Eagle had a very pronounced English accent. Secondly, the voice instructed Leo to proceed with ITER's destruction. The second point caused the Russian near apoplexy. He couldn't believe it. He demanded reasons. And the Brit supplied them.

Eagle told Leo that the Russians were determined to destroy ITER. The state of French security at the facility had more holes than a sieve. The Russians would be successful, either now or in the future. Russian motivation was driven by that nation's future ability to survive. The entire Russian economy was propped up by energy exports. Oil and natural gas shipments to neighboring countries ensured its financial future. Nothing could threaten that future. And unlimited, cheap energy provided by ITER's potential success was a threat. In Russian leaders eyes there was no question that ITER had to be destroyed.

And Leo was the instrument of that destruction, whether he was willing or coerced.

Dr. Leo Viloshensky understood the Brit's reasoning, and it made a convoluted sense. *Only in Russia does destruction make sense*, thought Leo.

The Mossad plan called for Leo to make contact with a dependable ally of Israel, a man identified only as Eagle. He had a striking resemblance to Benjamin Warner. Wyoming and Israel were natural allies; both were small states facing much larger foes. They both inhabited a dangerous sphere within the world. Additionally, Israel was a major partner in Wyoming's Fusion development. The Jewish State would soon possess a **WyStar** cloned Fusion plant of its own.

Eagle, aka Ben Warner, was successful in extracting not only Leo, but the leading Fusion scientists working at ITER. Their escape was in the darkness of night, aboard another miracle of *Dillon and Dillon*, an LTA – Lighter Than Air- craft. It was the Jules Verne update of the dirigible; hydrogen-fueled, superconducting turbine engines combined with a chameleon outer skin that mimicked its surroundings. The craft was nearly invisible, to the human eye and to radar. It was this craft that whisked the ITER brain trust and plans to Wyoming. **Wystar** was already a year under construction, but now its development would dramatically accelerate. And the world believed all of these top scientists had been vaporized in the massive explosion of the ITER.

During the exodus, Israel had been true to its word for Leo. Mossad agents produced another trademark operation; this one in Moscow right under FSB noses. Leo's daughter and mother were snatched from the jaws of potential death and reunited with the doctor in their new, adopted homeland: Wyoming.

All had been good in this new land for the Russian immigrants until a chance sighting of Zhukov within Casper's airport reignited Leo's fear for his family's safety. It was within this anxiety that he had turned to an old friend to hide Sasha until Ben Warner could find and eliminate Zhukov. Leo's friend acted honored that Leo would entrust his daughter's safety with him.

***

"Again, thanks Leo." He dipped his head and rubbed his chin for a few minutes, minutes excruciating to Leo. Then he raised his eyes, smiled and said, "Sure Leo, no problem. I will hide Sasha until Warner returns. I'll put her on an old friend's farm. Nice people. Practically raised me. That way, if my name enters the fray and they come to my place, it won't do them any good."

"Dis good idee,. Who iz dis people?"

"You really want me to give you their names? What if the big Russian scar-face you're so terrified of tries to get it out of you? I mean, I'll tell you if you really want to know. You're decision." He shrugged.

Now it was Leo's turn to think. Finally he shook his head firmly, "Nyet. You be only one who knows. Iz best way. I agrees."

The other man nodded, "She can go with me after the Governor's dinner. That sound okay?"

Leo's response was to hug the man and kiss both his cheeks.

After the two went their separate ways, Leo's friend retrieved a cellphone from his back pocket and dialed a number.

To the other person on the line, he spoke Russian for several minutes.

# Chapter 14

## From the Floor Up

### Cheyenne, Wyoming

The three CityCars were traveling outside the downtown of Cheyenne. Josh had endured the tour not so much to be educated as to Wyoming's success, rather to be near Sam. Originally, it had been his hope that some spark of their prior relationship would reemerge. But he knew this was not in the cards. He would have to be content with only her friendship and trust. And from this accomplished, strong lady, he was beginning to treasure both.

"So where we headed now, a high school or what?" asked Josh sounding bored.

Sam looked at him askance, "I thought you were enjoying this outing. I can drop you off and you can grab a returning Car if you prefer."

Josh tried to perk up, "No! It's been great. I'm very impressed with what you, I mean, the State has accomplished."

Sam said, "Well the answer to your question is Yes and Yes. We are going to a high school, in a way, so that would include the 'what' of your comment."

Both Cars pulled to the entrance of a large commercial building on the city outskirts. The sign on top of the building read *Siemens Electronics & Technical School*. Josh, confused, looked through the open doors and asked, "This a school?"

Sam rose and stepped out of the car, "Yes," was her sole response. "You coming?"

Joshua stood and followed.

He fell to the back of the group as they walked the lengthy side walk. She began the explanation, "Let me tell you one fact that is true from any perspective. We have the lowest dropout rate through high school than any other State. We graduate ninety-eight percent of our students, a rate comparable to Japan, Switzerland or Germany. In fact we rely upon the German model for some interesting differences to your States' educational programs.

127

We found out early on that students failing to graduate were lost to the system before they even entered high school. At about fourteen, children, especially boys, can just tune-out school. They don't see relevance between school and life and are just plain bored. Their boredom leads to bad grades, bad friends, distance from family members, getting girls pregnant, and, God save us, drugs. So, at the age of fourteen, we review their school progress, speak with their teachers, have a counselor speak with the student and give him or her an aptitude test. There is no pass or fail. It's just to decide which path will be best for the child. Those testing higher and having the motivation and past grades to go on to regular high school and, eventually, college take the traditional high school route. Those interviewed with low testing, lower motivation and poor grades go to our tech schools.

Governor Fodor was a little surprised, "Oh great, you pigeon-hole a kid at fourteen, blue collar vs. white collar, low pay vs. high pay. This is pretty elitist, even for you Sam."

Sam was annoyed by the supposition, "That's the same response we received from a majority of our parents when we presented the program. So, we began a pilot program with only volunteers. Not to be sexist, but we started with boys. Most would be considered low-performers, troubled or at-risk children. We explained what we had in mind. A few of them were quite excited after seeing the opportunities at the company we are now entering. After they enthusiastically spoke of it with other boys, the others wanted the same opportunity. We sat down with the won-over boys and their parents. We explained the goals and that there was no stigma attached. Eighty percent allowed their children to follow this path. It was our first class along the tech route and one-hundred percent of the first twenty-six boys graduated. You will meet a few of the students now participating in the program. I hope you don't insult them with your ignorance. They might knock your block off."

Fodor sniffed at the thought of a fourteen-year-old taking a swing at him. He'd take the kid and hang him in the nearest closet. He had liked Sam's fire, but wasn't sure if he enjoyed her superiority.

They entered the company and were met by a gentleman in a white lab coat. His badge ID had the name 'Muller, Hans S.' under his picture with the number '4'. He greeted Sam with a dip of his head. Josh expected him to complete the picture by clicking his heels. "Ms. Governor Varner. How pleased ve are to have you and your friends wisit our facilities," the man said. Josh noticed the same 'V' and 'W' switching as Dr. Gleispach at the Energy Facility. Other than the two-letter reversal, his accent was not near Gleispach's.

Sam shook his hand and turned towards her group, "I wish to introduce Dr. H…"

Josh interrupted, "Don't tell me, Hans, right? Hans Muller." He grabbed the man's hand and shook it mightily. The man was puzzled at Josh knowing his name.

Josh pointed at his badge, "The ID,….kinda gave you away."

Sam was not amused. The Seimens director merely turned towards the to the inner building and grumbled something in German.

"Nice going, Josh. I think you just set back German-Wyoming relations by a decade," scorned Sam.

Josh raised his hands in defense, his face wide-eyed with innocence and looked around the pool of Governors, "What did I do. How'd I know the man lacked a funnybone. Jeeeseh."

Sam slugged him in the arm and Josh feigned pain. At least, he thought, I got her to be playful and touch me.

She said to the others, "Please excuse him. He was kicked in the head by a mule at a young age."

All but Josh chuckled.

As they marched down corridors and out onto the factory floor, Muller began his dissertation. He seemed as if he had done this sort of tour before as he began attacking preconceived notions.

"First of all, there is no stigma in not attending college. Our youth find great careers without a sheepskin. They are happy and complete. Every parent vants their child to go to college. I understand that. It is the same in Germany. But not every child wants to go. What to do?

"And vat does it accomplish most time? More lawyers taking our money and more frivolous law suits? More history majors selling shoes at mall outlets? Another MBA to figure out how to get us to buy more cheesey biscuits? Our tech school graduates often earn more than college graduates fresh from academia. Vyoming is being very vize, rebuilding its industrial base, just like Germany after second big war. It needs fresh minds with the working, not theoretical, knowledge to accomplish this."

Sam entered the discussion at this point, "Granted, we always need more math, engineering and science majors. We encourage any child with an inkling of interest in these fields to go on to college and advanced degrees. In fact the State pays for it. So now, Hans will show you how it works."

Fodor displayed his, now, typical skepticism. "I don't think I'm going to enjoy this." The others ignored him.

Hans took over the discussion again, "When a child heads along the tech path, they actually get hands-on education. Many are taught right here, the production floor of our factories. When they are not learning how a piece of equipment or an instrument works, they are sitting in chairs listening to a school master at a white board. Here, we can see instruction in progress. Mr. Heinz is explaining the theory behind the reality they have just touched with their hands. The teacher is explaining the math and the science needed for the machine works."

The seven stopped outside a rectangle painted upon the glistening factory floor. Twelve young men and four young women were seated in schoolroom chairs, writing upon scrolls with rapt attention the subject being covered upon an enormous flat, digital screen. The instructor stood to the side, watching the same presentation. The students excited to listen and learn. All were wearing headsets with built-in microphones. Josh knew it was so they could hear over the hum of the factory's machinery. Although the visitors could not hear the presentation, the visually detailed CGI of an electronics chip rotated as an moving arrow pointed out different components of the chip. When the arrow would stop, the presentation panned into the inner workings, moving down to the level of electron flow. The word RESISTANCE appeared to the side, and a hand-written formula began scrolling underneath.

Josh started to see Sam's view point. Anything that kept a kid learning couldn't be that bad.

Sam took up the lead, "For the first time in a long time, or even the first time, they are motivated. They begin to absorb geometry, algebra, trig, even calculus and physics at rates higher than average high schoolers. We have many instances where test scores from these students surpass equivalent high school requirements. That is why, each year, we retest these students. If their scores are up to par with the high school level, they can jump right back into that level. Oddly enough, when this happens a majority choose to stay on the tech path.    Even when they graduate with a high school tech degree, they can still apply to colleges by taking an SAT test.    Our colleges encourage them to do so because they have found these students to be more motivated and more disciplined than many of their standard high school counterparts.    In fact, students that have gone from the tech route to college have a ninety-nine percent graduation rate from college."

Hans jumped in, "And for those that don't get a satisfactory SAT number, they can still apply to the community college in preparation to move to higher college level.    We are helping to graduate a waluable item, youth vith a skill."

It was Sam's turn, "The rest of the nation sits at an overall forty-five percent high school graduation rate.    And most companies think those degrees aren't worth the paper they are written on.    They complain that kids come to them for interviews unable to read or write or do the simplest math.    Now, that's disgraceful.    And, if you want to really pigeon-hole a young adult, have him hit the bricks as a drop out.

We have the highest educated workforce in the nation and one of the highest in the world.    We have to in order to maintain this vibrant economy you see all around you.    Remember, we only have a population of just over seven-hundred-and-fifty thousand for the entire state.    We cannot afford to lose one child."

Hans' turn, "The companies vere these youth get their tech training, companies like Seimens, try to keep them with the company.    In fact, we have to compete with wages, offering more than other companies to keep the graduates.    Many of them become managers and are sent to night business school, paid for by our company."

Sam's turn, "Our unemployment rate is at two percent, two percent! Most any economist would tell you that two percent can well be accounted for by people transiting from one job to another, people going back to school to re-tool their education or receive a higher degree, women taking time off to have a child or to raise that child, and the just-plain-hardcore unemployed, those that don't want to work no matter what you do for them.    I'm pretty satisfied with that number.    I see it as full employment.    What's the national average right now, thirty percent unemployed?"

Fodor was pleased to correct her, "According to last night's news, it's at twenty-five percent and falling."

Governor Hughes could not let this pass, "Oh, come on, Scott. They changed the formula again. Heck, it might be forty percent. You can't tell with those liars in Washington."

Fodor grumbled.

Hans followed up, "Please vait a moment. Gunter." He spoke into his microphone.

A tall, youthful man came round the chalkboard after exiting the production area, "Ya vol, Heir Muller?"

Hans said, "Gunter, I want you to meet some people." The man came forward and instantly recognized the Governor.

"Ms. Governor, we meet again."

Sam shook his hand and smiled. She said to the group, "Gunter was in our first graduation class. He has performed remarkably here at Seimens and is attending night college. I use him as our poster boy for these tours. However, there are many other success stories working here."

Hans put a hand on the young man's shoulder. The youth was at least a foot taller than his director. "This young man came to us at fourteen. He is now nineteen. We convinced him to stay on with us and now he attends night engineering school, at company expense. He is an electronic vizard. He is a major contributor to our new products development team. And he has become quite fluent in German. All students in the technical school programs are encouraged to learn the native language of the company: German, Japanese, Chinese, Korean and so on."

Sam interjected, "And last year Gunter was quarterback of the Siemen Tech Wizards. He led his team to their first State championship in football."

Josh thought of the local news from the night before and now understood the sports reference to Siemen Tech.

Gunter hung his head. Hans continued, "False modesty, Gunter." Turning towards the group, Hans said, "Someday I plan for him to take my position, he is that good. He has already given us several ideas for large cost savings. We are quite proud of Gunter." Hans finished his last sentence with a hardy slap to Gunter's back. The young man just nodded.

Fodor looked at Sam and raised his eyebrows, "Okay, I'm impressed."

Hans spun on his heels and took off, instructing, "Come, I vill show you more students in class and on production floor."

When Hans was out of hearing distance, Gunter approached and said, "My name's actually Gunther. Because of my State Army service, all my friends call me 'Gunny.' But round here you go with the flow. Know what I mean."

They all laughed and Josh responded, "Sure do, Gunny. I know it more than you think." Then he looked at Sam who was a little exasperated. He said, again acting innocent, "What?"

Josh thought of something, "Hey, Gunny, why haven't you reported for duty. I heard about the emergency call-up on the news last night."

Gunny nodded, "We are finishing up some electronics for the Military right now. They gave us what I guess you'd call, a special dispensation until we are done. Then I'll be right up there on the front lines." He was smiling. Josh gave him a salute and Gunny returned it, crisply.

This brought back Governor Fodor's invasion fears with a rush. He moaned, "Oh, God." Governor Brigham patted his back gently.

# Chapter 15

## A Feast Full Of Ideas

### Governor's Mansion, Cheyenne

When the group returned to the Governor's mansion, Josh lagged behind and watched the entourage of Governors animated in conversation with Sam. He appraised her. She had led this State out of the wilderness into the light of prosperity and personal enrichment of its Citizenry.

And he was there to help tear it all down.

Words from a former life flooded his mind. Before each Army mission, Sergeant Jackson would recite Robert Oppenheimer's quote from the Hindu scripture, the Bhagavad-Gita, 'Now I am become Death, the Destroyer of Worlds.'

Then, they were words of inspiration to kill the enemy. Now, they were words to kill a dream.

As Sam answered one question after another, she noticed the absence of Josh, turned and found him some distance back. She raised her hand to hail him, but he shook his head. She finished some comments with the group, asked them to proceed to the Mansion and waited for Josh. He strolled up, smiling.

"You really are a wonder, Ms. Governor. All of those other governors hang on your every word."

Sam pishawed, "Don't be ridiculous." They are just trying to pick my brains so they can return to their States and claim to have all the answers. So why the drop back? You want to talk to me?"

Josh said, "Yeah. I just wanted to tell you I had a great time. It was wonderful to see you again. I don't want to cut into your life any more. I need to get back to my life. It was a mistake for me to come here, I mean Wyoming. I see that now. You people have sacrificed so much and worked so hard, I, well….ah, I'm just an interloper. I'm gonna head on out and wanted to say good-bye."

Sam locked her arm within his, "Don't be ridiculous. We're having a big bash here tonight. Cocktail hour is just starting and I need you by my side."

Her touch melted Joshua. Even after all these years, she owned his soul. "Sam, I'm,…I don't want to see you hurt. All of this," he waved his hand in a small circle, "everything you and this State have accomplished is in jeopardy. I put it there. You're better off with me gone."

His words provoked no surprise on her part, just determination. "Whatever has been done, can be undone, Josh."

He shook his head without breaking eye contact, "You are too trusting, Sam."

"This State was built on trust, Joshua Stillwater. We are not naïve. We need you, at this time of our greatest peril. Any personal success God has granted me has come from the ability to read people, to know what is in their hearts. And I know you have a good heart, Josh. You just have to listen to it."

Josh dropped his head and eyes. She released his arm, put her hand below his chin and lifted his head gently. "Don't give me that hang-dog look. One thing about us Wyomingans, and, yes, you are a Wyomingan whether you carry a card or not, we deal with reality and make the best of it. Fate has decided you and I will never be together in the way you want, Josh. But it didn't decide we can't be together, period. I need you, Josh. Wyoming needs you. And if you haven't figured it out yet, you need Wyoming. You have never fought for a worthy cause your entire life. This isn't any fault of yours, it's the fault of those that commanded your loyalty and abused it. Is it a cause worth fighting for when you are forced to kill a twelve-year old boy?"

Her words stung Josh hard. He didn't know whether to be angry or ashamed. He clinched his jaw tight, not knowing what words would emerge if he opened his mouth.

"We, this State, Josh, are that worthy cause and we are worthy of your loyalty. You may wonder from where I gain my confidence and determination. I'll tell you. From all these magnificent people that make up this State. We are loyal to each other. We would die for each other. And we are waiting to embrace you. All you have to do is open the door and let us in. This is your life. You're home, Josh and your family is waiting for you inside."

She paused. Josh's eyes began to moisten. The word 'family' hit him like a sledgehammer. He understood at that moment that it was family he had been searching for his entire life. His father had deserted him. His

136

mother died when he was young. The man Josh had adopted as a father figure, Charlie Warner, always kept him at arms' length and finally punched him in the face. So the Army had become his home, only to betray him.

He considered turning and running to the CityCar. He couldn't. Instead he looked at her. No, there would be no more running. After a long moment, they broke eye contact. Sam cleared her throat and said, "Now walk me in, tall dark and naughty. And don't you dare disappear again, Joshua Stillwater."

Joshua looked into her eyes, smiled and nodded his head, rasping out, "OK, you got me. I'll stick around."

She turned, tugged on his arm and they headed up the concrete path.

***

As Josh and Sam entered the foyer, a young man in a red waistcoat greeted them, "Ms. Governor, nearly everyone has arrived. Shall I take your coats?" Both offered up their coats, hats and gloves and then were shown in to the great room. "I have already taken drink orders from the other guests. May I get something for you and the gentleman?"

Sam replied, "That will be fine, George. I'll have my usual. Josh, what are you drinking these days?"

"Bourbon and branch water," he replied. The Jack Daniels had been a concession to Jeff's taste, and Jake's Johnny Walker scotch was a little sharp for his taste. Charlie had taught him to like bourbon and branch water and the taste stuck, even though it carried the memory of someone best forgotten.

George nodded at Josh and turned to Sam, "That will be fine, madam." Josh found it interesting how Sam handled her station with such poise. He always saw her as charming. But in their youth, she was a rough and tumble cowgirl who could out-rope, out-ride, out-shoot and out-wrestle both her younger brother and Josh. To see her in this setting seemed a bit strange. But in another way it reflected her style and grace that Josh had seen developing within her before he left. She felt a princess to him then, and even more now.

Inside the great-room were close to thirty people standing in smaller groups, all deep in conversation. To Josh it appeared more as an after-convention cocktail hour of professionals talking over the day's presentations. A few looked up and acknowledged the entrance of Sam and she lightly waved. She took her arm from within Josh's and now placed her hand on his elbow. She steered him towards the temporary bar that had been set up and to where George was collecting drinks upon a tray.

"I thought we could reduce your load a bit, George. We'll take them from here," she said. George handed a cosmopolitan to Sam and the bourbon neat to Josh. He then picked up a double shot glass filled with branch water. "Would you like it all, Sir, or just a splash?" Josh actually wanted it straight, and then a refill after he swilled it. But he thought better of getting soused in front of present company.

"Pour it all in, George"

Crowds of strangers made him self-conscious. Since the military, he was a loner, the kind that has only one friend at a time, if that. Small talk wasn't his forte and usually led to awkward silences and nervousness. But he was determined to just sip the drink. Sam, with drink in one hand and Josh's elbow in the other, moved along to the first set of guests. They stopped their conversation as the two approached. Josh suspected that it was in deference to them, for their conversation volume kept reducing as Josh and Sam drew near. They obviously didn't want to continue the subject in front of a stranger.

Sam spoke, "Gentlemen, enjoying the State's alcohol, I see." They looked at their drinks and smiled. Sam continued, "I wish you to meet a dear friend from my past and fellow Wyomingan, Joshua Stillwater. Josh, this gentleman is Dr. Milton Bern, our State's Treasurer." A short man with disheveled salt and pepper hair shook his hand. Josh remembered him from his days at the University.

"Professor Bern, right?" The man was pleased to be identified more as an educator than a government employee.

"Yes, that's right. And I remember you in a class of mine."

Josh smiled, "Well, that's a compliment, seeing as you had so many students pass through over the years."

"Being of diminutive stature, one tends to remember people of physical prominence. Nearly two meters is it?" said Bern, measuring Joshua with his eyes.

"Close, six-foot four," replied Josh, taking another sip of his drink.

"You and Ben Warner went into the military together, if I remember. How was that experience? Still in?" asked the Professor.

Josh's face darkened. He didn't like anyone bringing up his past, or his present for that matter, "No. But I found it interesting." The Professor nodded. Sam then moved her attention to the other gentleman.

"Josh, this is our own U.S. Senator, Russell Colter. Senator Colter, Joshua Stillwater."

The Senator was just shy of six feet, with wisps of grey hair slapped down sideways across a shiny, bare head, a bad comb-over. He grasped Joshua's hand with a strong shake and said, "Any friend of Samantha's is a friend of mine." He looked at Sam, "But I don't like them so young, tall, or handsome. It's just more competition to elbow me to the back of the line for your affections, Ms. Governor."

Sam responded with a short giggle, "Senator, you flatter me. But you know you've always been at the front of my line."

The Senator waved his hand strongly to Sam and said, "I like to hear a good line of BS as much as the next guy. But I think, in this case, you should leave it up to a professional, like a U.S. Senator."

Sam openly laughed. "You make a good case, Russell. So it shall be in the future. Now if you gentlemen will excuse us, I have some others I wish Joshua to meet."

Sam directed him to a pod of seven men and one young lady standing in a circle. One was looking upwards, his lips moving as if he were working out a problem. Another was leading a group discussion by drawing imaginary figures in the air while another objected and pantomimed an erasure of the drawing. They both acted as if an actual chalk board were in front of them. Five were dressed casual with pressed slacks, dress shirts open at the top, and a variety of sport coats. One was well beyond casual, somewhere between disheveled and homeless. His shirt was half-tucked, buttons were unbuttoned, stains spotted his clothing, his pants were wrinkled and his shoes......Joshua almost laughed. They were a pair of slippers, with no socks. The young lady stood close to this vagabond, her hand clasped within his. She looked about sixteen to Josh. She had black hair swirled into a bun and wore a simple, white dress with black pumps, half heels. Her features were not striking, not beautiful. But they were strong, giving her an air of confidence and sophistication. *Slavick* thought Josh, *Just like the guy she's holding onto.*

The circle was comprised of the scientists from the Energy Facility they had visited yesterday.

The first to notice Josh and Sam's approach was the only American, Alec Sidney. He was dressed Western, as he was at the Facility. But it was a notch up, Saturday Best. He wore shined snake skin boots, denim jeans with an ironed-in, razor crease, a wide leather belt with a large silver belt buckle and a crisply ironed Western shirt. Josh casually looked at the buckle. He could make out most of the words bannered across. It was a prize buckle for bull riding from some high school rodeo with a district number embossed. Josh had won a few of these for not only bull riding, but roping. The only part of the man's apparel out of place was the hat. It was the same straw that had, at one time, been white but now was swirls of different beige hues caused by grime. The brim edges were frayed and the tight weave was unraveling. The only thing remotely formal about it was a new, red silk band.

He held up a beer bottle in greeting, "Evenin', Ms Governor."

"Hello Alex," returned Sam.

The others turned round to see who had broken their spell. The homeless looking one was Leo Viloshensky, shorter than the rest, with a large belly splashing over the rolled waistband of his pants. He immediately broke into exhuberance. "Miss Samanta, Dee luff of my life." His accent was heavy to the point of being barely understandable.

The man nearly stepped out of his house slippers trying to grab Sam's hand within his pudgy fingers. He excitedly kissed her hand while she applied full force to extricate it.

The young lady at Leo's side spoke up, "Daddy, stop pawing the Governor. You are going to chap her hand."

Leo let go, his face still bubbling with smile.

Sam nudged Josh forward. The circle had widened to include them. Leo was to Josh's right, looking down at his slippers and pouting.

Sam said, "Gentlemen, you might remember this man. He visited the Energy Facility yesterday. He is Joshua Stillwater. And Josh, you are in the presence of the brightest group of physicists ever assembled since the 'Manhattan Project."

Josh mentally confirmed that **Wystar** was definitely their 'Manhattan Project. And these geniuses were the underpinning of the entire development. He hoped the term was only a reference to the peaceful generation of energy and not a bomb. *Wait a minute*, he thought, *Maybe that's the meaning of Sam's reference to an Ace-in-the-hole. Maybe my game with Tex wasn't so far from the mark.*

Alex turned to Sam, "Lady, just to put you on notice, you have more brain power assembled here than all the two hundred physicists at Los Alamos combined. Oppie was mediocre at best. Now if Ferme had left Chicago and joined them, then that would have made it a horse race." Alex raised the beer bottle to his lips and took a chug.

Sam said, "Point well taken, Alex. So Josh, next to you is Dr. Leo Viloshensky, you saw him on the reactor floor with Dr. Gleispach yesterday."

Josh nodded.

"Next to Leo is his daughter, Sasha." Sasha leaned in front of her father, smiled and gave a short wave. "Next to him Dr. Franz Gleispach, whom you've met. And, as I am often reminded, I am duty bound to inform you that he is not German but rather Austrian." Gleispach gave a short nod. "Next is Dr. Zhou Li, who you have already met. Then Alex. He's our local boy, born and raised in Laramie. Then Dr. Daruka Bharat from New Delhi, Dr. Kenji Yazaki from Osaka, and Dr. Hadar Weinberger of Israel."

"I am very impressed with your Energy Facility," offered Josh. "I think you have created something for the benefit of the entire world."

Alex spoke, "If they're willing to pay for it. Right, Sam?"

She smiled, "TANSTAAFL, Alex, TANSTAAFL."

Josh searched his memory for the acronym and admitted defeat with a questioning brow.

"'There Ain't No Such Thing As A Free Lunch.' Robert Heinlein, Moon Is A Harsh Mistress." said Sam.

Josh nodded.

Sam bid their adieu, "Gentlemen, thank you for the interruption. And a special thanks to all of you for your efforts, not only on the behalf of Wyoming but of the entire world."

The physicists beamed. Sasha appeared bored. Sam grabbed Josh's elbow and turned him to walk away.

"So, Sam, why the dirty straw on Alex? Nobody ever told him it was black for night and white for day? Besides, that straw's more beat up than my old work hat." said Josh.

"He wears that straw because it's his lucky hat. He was wearing it during a high school rodeo, where he won the belt buckle. He successfully went the eight seconds, but when he dismounted, his boot snagged on the belly strap and he got wrapped up with the bucking bull. Apparently, he got the snot kicked out of him and almost died in the hospital. The weird thing is that his hat never fell off the entire time, or so he says. So he chalks it up to some sort of lucky charm. You're welcome to ask him about it. He's not shy about re-telling it."

"Naw, it's probably bullpucky anyway. He's probably going bald and doesn't want anyone to notice the shiny hole in back. This way he has an excuse to keep his hat on indoors."

Sam chuckled, "Now Josh, when did any of you cowboys ever need an excuse to keep a hat on indoors?"

Josh smiled, "Yeah, guess you're right about that. And thanks for still thinking of me as a cowboy. Kinda missed that designation over the years."

Sam stopped their walking and looked seriously into his eyes, "Josh, none of us care what you were, or are, out there. You're home now. And here, you're a cowboy." She walked him towards another introduction.

The next group included two men Joshua knew from childhood. They were big scale ranchers like Charlie and were both dressed in Cowboy finest: Western cut suits, white Western shirts with pearl snaps for buttons, bolo ties, black felt hats and animal skin boots. The first was Harley Stevens whose spread was northeast of Casper and shared part of the fence line with Warner's. The other was Denny Watson, whom Jake had spoken of his son, Blake, dying from drugs. He had the largest ranch in the Cheyenne area, and second in the State only to Warner's *Five Fingers*. Josh never thought these men interested in politics, so it was somewhat unusual for them to be invited this evening.

Sam introduced Joshua, "Harley, Denny, you might member this gentleman, Joshua Stillwater." Watson looked askance at Josh for a moment. "You worked for Charlie, didn't you?"

Sam interjected, "He was born and raised on our ranch. I grew up with Josh. He was like a brother to me."

Josh cringed slightly.

Harley now had the connection, "You were Shirley's pup, weren't you?"

Denny Watson asked, "Who?"

"Shirley," said Harley, "Worked for Charlie. Lived in the bunkhouse. Cooked and washed for the men."

Josh felt his face flush, "We didn't *live* in the bunkhouse. Had a house connected to it so my Mom could go back and forth out of the snow."

Harley only said, "Ah." Both he and Watson took a tug on their drinks while looking at each other. The embarrassment was palpable, so Sam said, "Well, nice of you gentlemen to come. We have other people for Josh to meet." She turned Josh's arm and started to escort him away when Denny Watson spoke up.

"So, Sam, where's Charlie. He's coming isn't he?"

Sam was walking away and said over her shoulder, "No. He was unable to make it this evening. Maybe next time."

Something about Watson's attitude and the timing of the question pissed Josh, he shot back, "Sorry to hear about Blake." He noticed Watson's shoulders sag and Harley Stevens scowl.

Sam tugged harder at Josh's arm, "That was not necessary."

Josh shrugged innocently, "Just giving my condolences, that's all."

Sam's eyes narrowed.

Josh knew it best to change the subject, "Charlie was invited?"

Sam shook her head and said, "No, Josh. I wouldn't do that to you." She then smiled, "What am I saying? I wouldn't do that to me!" Both chuckled as they moved towards another group.

# Chapter 16

## Train Racing

## Fort Hood, Texas

Ben Warner slapped his neck as silently as possible. He missed the mosquito that, a split second before, was drilling into his neck. He pulled a large backpack from his shoulders, reached inside and removed a power bar and a jug of water. *God*, he thought, *the heat! And humidity*! Texas during October was still hot. In Wyoming he'd be wearing his Gortex underskins by now. Instead, he was wearing a thick balaclava over his head. At least the sun had gone down. He looked at his watch. It was nineteen-thirty hours. General Palmer had successfully held off the train till darkness.

His legs were starting to feel the burn from squatting for over an hour in the small draw. He stood up and stretched against one of the scrub oaks that dotted the wash. Although he was far enough down the rail line to avoid the flood lights of the army base he wasn't immune to discovery from guards that manned the gate which served as egress for trains. He perched himself far enough away to avoid detection yet close enough that the exiting train would not have significant momentum before he chose his time to board. This compromise had landed him in this mini canyon containing ankle-depth, stagnant water. It was just enough to breed a mass of mosquitoes. The attacks of the swarm were maddening. As if the multiple penetrations of his skin were not enough, the ones that flew into his ears and up his nose would have sent most sane men running in a screaming flail. These mosquitoes lived up to their nickname, the State Bird of Texas.

Over the years he had overcome things much worse than mosquitoes. The annoying buzzing took him to another place and time.

**\*\*\***

It was during the Iran war. He had been night-dropped well outside of Esfahan. Before the bombings it was the third largest city in Iran. South of Teheran, it sat in the center of the country's crossroads and had once been capital of ancient Persia. Having landed in the Zayaden River north of the city, he swam, with over thirty kilos of gear on his back. Reaching the river's side, he burrowed a hole into the muddy bank large enough for his pack and covered it with river reeds.

Like tonight, it was October, but in Iran the nights were close to zero C. His clothes being wet began to freeze and stiffen. His only relief was to pack river mud over him during the night. The bank allowed him a good vantage to report troop movements and, more important, mobile SAM units. On one occasion, a patrol happened nearby and was running a routine check of the bank where he lay. Using his KA-bar knife, he cut a reed and lay on his back in three feet of muddy water. His lips twitched for days after from holding the natural breathing tube between them. Soldiers walked in the muck where the water lapped while an officer rode above in an enclosed vehicle. At the critical moment that the troops slogged past his position, something in the water wiggled into Ben's pants leg. Normally he tucked his pants into his boot. But after three days both pants legs had pulled out and he saw no urgency in re-tucking them. Lesson learned. The unknown intruder was making its way to his crotch just as troops passed. It took all his mental discipline not to move, not to cause any suspicious ripple. He clamped his jaws so tight that later he found he had fractured one molar and cracked a crown completely in half. Yet he never moved a fraction of a millimeter. And his adversaries passed by unsuspecting. Finally convinced he was undetected and the enemy soldiers long gone, he jumped from the water, reached into his pants and retrieved the eel from his boxers. *From now on, only briefs!* he thought, as he sliced off the eels head and ate the bloody meat.

***

The rumble at the end of the draw brought his mind back to present. The headlight from the train's lead locomotive reflected upon the rails thirty meters before it. Ben knew the train was over fifty cars in length so the column hadn't had time to build up any great momentum. He ran, crouched over, to the lip of the draw nearest the tracks. He had to time it right, but which car? There were some boxcars interspersed. But most were flatbeds loaded with war materiel. He had a moment's hesitation until the train was close enough for details. The box cars had no grips or ledges on their sides. And their doors were all padlocked. The flatbeds further down the line would be his best bet. He reached in his rucksack and pulled out a light-weight grappling hook attached to a knotted nylon line. The ends of the hooks were rubber coated so as to be nearly noiseless when hitting metal.

While bent forward, waiting for his opportunity to spring forth, it went unnoticed to Ben that another traveler was also hidden. He was twenty meters further down the tracks, lying in the tallest grass he could find. The interloper hoped he wasn't too exposed. He kept moving his attention from Ben to the train, back to Ben. When he saw Ben holding what looked as if a grappling hook, he groaned.

*That crazy bastard is going to board this train with a grappling hook. How the hell do I follow that act?* thought Tex.

Earlier, when Ben hadn't pulled back onto the main highway, Tex had U-turned and found the dirt road. He proceeded as cautiously as he could, until spying Ben's car. He pulled out his night vision monocular and scanned the vehicle. The engine still reflected heat, but it appeared unmanned. He went on the assumption that Ben was afoot. He pulled up next to the other car and parked, threw his hat on the passenger seat and got out. He locked the door by key as he didn't want an alarm chirping, or headlamps flashing. He noticed his car charger attached to the cellphone sitting in the ashtray. Did he need it? He dismissed it for time sake and the fact he had lost reception after pulling off the main highway. His quarry was on the move. Besides, he'd have to light up the phone face to locate the vibrate command. He also dismissed needing his forty-five in the trunk. The darkness of night and 'Baby,' the bowie knife in his boot, would suffice. He took off, tracking Ben's path through crushed weeds and boot prints. He scanned through the monocular into the distance and saw a man's heat signature disappear down into a small draw. When Tex stumbled across the rails, he looked at them and pondered. Then he looked at the military gate. *What's this guy up to? Is he going to sneak onto the base through the rail route? Is he gonna meet someone out here? Is he gonna blow up the train?* He ran bent over into the tallest grass he could find, laid down and hoped the darkness was cover enough. Whatever Warner was up to, he would catch him at it from this vantage.

Now it dawned on Tex that Warner was attempting to board the train. He rued his choice of footwear, coveting Warner's advantage of flexible hiking boots. Tex was facing a sprint wearing stiff, slick-soled, cowboy boots.

After the locomotives and several cars passed his position, Ben judged the distance his best chance to board undiscovered: midpoint between the engines and the rear troop-transport. He sprang from the draw readied himself near the gravel rail bed edge. He watched as boxcar after boxcar passed, waiting for the moment a flatbed would appear. He looked down the convoy and finally saw one emerge in the base flood lights. When it was within two car lengths of his position, Ben took off sprinting parallel to a box car. The train was picking up momentum and Ben was hard pressed to keep up. He pumped his legs while swinging overhead as if a lasso, the rope tied to the grappling. From his peripheral vision, he saw the beginning of the flatbed come into view. He redoubled his efforts to increase speed while he turned his head to catch a glimpse of what rode upon the car deck. Still pumping, he swung the grappling high into the air, over the top of whatever was tarpaulin'd down, and onto its other side. He pulled on the rope and felt it go taut. He was now running fastener than he thought possible, reeling in the rope, like a fish pulling itself to shore. When he thought he had removed the slack, he jumped forward, hanging from the rope, his feet and legs extended before him. His rear was barely ten centimeters from the gravel bed that raced underneath. He pulled himself up the rope. Reaching the flatbed's side, he released one hand and quickly grabbed above where the rope was angled and rubbing against the metal edge. This action spun him so that his outstretched legs rotated underneath the car. He sure hoped his hands didn't slip. He was in prime position to fall under the wheels. His boot hit some metal bracket under the car. He shoved against it and spun his body back from where it started. Once his feet had cleared the side, he jerked his boots straight up until they were above the floor of the flatbed. Then he slammed them down on the floor. Securing this position, he pulled up his torso and rolled onto the deck. He was breathing hard, so he lay there for a moment. His pulse and breathing returning near normal, he stood up on the car deck and slapped a curling run of loose rope, freeing the grappling from the other side. Then he slowly reeled it in and put it back into the rucksack. He caught a lung full of air and began tugging at a heavy plastic covering of whatever had been chained down. The tarpaulin had a thick bungee cord woven taught through eyelets at its base. He pulled mightily until there was a space between the plastic and the deck that allowed him and rucksack to slither under. Now he was completely enclosed in darkness. He rubbed his sore arms and hoped that his attempt to ride the rails had gone unnoticed by the engineer and the base guards.

Watching Warner's escapade, Tex was doubtful of his own odds in boarding successfully. He had none of Warner's equipment, especially boots for running. He had a decision to make quickly. Run back to the car for the phone and get instructions from Maxton or run for the train.

He had a pretty good idea as to Maxton's probable response. Why hadn't he, Tex, jumped on the train and continued following his orders to tail Warner?

*Asshole*, thought Tex about Maxton. Tex sprang from the weeds and began to mimic Ben's initial move, running parallel to a car. He was at a large disadvantage, though. Cowboy boots are designed for stirrups; not for running. The high heels and pointed toes dug into the gravel while the slick soles offered little traction. He leaned forward, bit his lip and ran with maximum effort. He was surprised by the height of a flatbed from the slanted roadbed. During a stride, he sprung upward and grabbed a handful of chain links. He furiously pumped his legs to keep upright. It was in vain as he stumbled. He maintained his grip but this resulted in being dragged along and savaged by the gravel. With his feet and legs bumping along, he managed to raise his free hand and grab part of the chain below the death grip of the first. With maximum effort, he pulled his body upward of the flatbed. He was doing a sideways pull-up with his body torqued downward at a forty-five degree angle. Slowly he gained centimeters until one of his was boots was ripped off by the gravel. He flopped his upper torso onto the platform. Although his lower half still dangled over the edge, he laid there for a moment, trying to recover from effort manifesting in terror. He felt for the knife in his remaining boot. When his hand slid round the handle he let out an utterance of relief saying "Baby." His heart rate beginning to lower, Tex pressed down on the flooring and slithered forward until completely aboard. Mimicking Warner, he squeezed underneath a tarpaulin, there to nurse his wounded body and wonder what this crazy stunt was about. He wanted desperately to call Maxton to hear some credit about putting his life on the line for this worthless assignment. But he had no phone. His only excuse was that no one could have fathomed Warner was going to hop on a train bound for God-knows-where.

This salved his self-esteem not one bit.

*** 

As if part of a planned routine, a third body popped from the grass following Tex's pitiful performance. This human form exuded agility, speed and coordination. Even though the train's pace had quickened, the form smoothly matched tempo. It ran aside a box car, waiting for the end of the car to come abreast. Then it sprang high for a ladder welded to the backside. This was a more dangerous maneuver as the leap was made between two cars. A misstep and the silhouette would have been mangled underneath passing cars. The form gracefully pulled hand-over-hand up the rungs until it gained footing on the bottom rung. Then it flipped itself around, holding the ladder to its back and sprang, chest out and arms back, toward a flatbed coupled behind. Hitting the floor, it rolled directly towards and under a strapped-down tarpaulin.

# Chapter 17

## Bank On It

### Governor's Mansion, Cheyenne

Sam stopped before two men deep in conversation. One listened while the other punctuated his verbal points with a sloshing glass.

Sam stepped forward, "Gentlemen, if I may be so rude as to interrupt, I wish to introduce someone." She presented Josh. Then she introduced the 'slosher' as Howard Finkel and the 'listener' as Frank Dunleavy. Sam informed Josh that Mr. Dunleavy was a family friend and, ten years past, had relocated from New York City to Cheyenne. He was head of the Wyoming investment house *Dunleavy and Greenberg.*

Dunleavy's name was not unfamiliar to Josh. It had been associated with Wall Street and power for nearly three decades. But Josh had thought the man retired. There had been some article in the news about him stepping down as CEO of the largest investment house a few years back. Josh wondered how this man was now found to be in Wyoming. *It's eighteen hundred miles from New York City to Wyoming*, thought Josh, *but light years in culture.*

Dunleavy stood around six-foot, trim and well-tailored. His suit was definitely not off-the-rack, nor his shoes. The grey pin-striped suit framed a dark blue tie against a white background of crisp shirt. His wavy salt-and-peppered hair was neatly coifed. He appeared to be about fifty years old, younger than Josh would have expected for a man that had been at the top of the financial world for several decades. Josh surmised the man's fame had come a young age. Dunleavy put forth his hand to shake Josh's.

"Nice to meet you, Josh." His voice was low but confident, his demeanor affable. "And this is Mr. Howard Finkel, CEO of *Silverman & Boxe.* It's an investment house on Wall Street."

Josh almost smiled. It was like someone saying, 'This is Julius Caeser. He's from a little place called Rome. Perhaps you've heard of it?'

Josh shook Finkel's hand. Howard Finkel was taller than Dunleavy, but shorter than Josh. He had a few excess pounds packed around his midsection, stretching the buttoned coat to the max. Although obviously younger than Dunleavy, deep lines in his face and small red veins running

151

at the surface of his nose said his miles had been harder. He looked to Josh as to be a drinker.

Sam politely excused herself, saying she had to check on other guests. Sam's eyes settled upon Dunleavy's for a beat. He nodded and she smiled as she turned and walked away.

With disinterest, Finkel mumbled "Hi" to Josh while turning his attention back to Dunleavy.

"When are we going to talk business, Frank? I have to get back tomorrow."

Dunleavy answered, "I thought right now would be a good time."

"Here?" Finkel looked at Josh and then back to Dunleavy. Obviously he did not wish to talk business in front of a stranger, or at a cocktail party.

"You can speak freely in front of Mr. Stillwater. He's nothing to do with the world of finance. In fact, he is with the Department of Homeland Security. Am I right, Mr. Stillwater?" He looked causally at Josh for confirmation.

Josh was miffed. *How does this guy know who I work for? Sam said nothing in introductions.* She obviously had filled Dunleavy in earlier, so that meant Sam wanted him to be here and to listen to these guys. *Has she always been this manipulating?* he wondered."

"Yeah, that's right. Homeland."

Finkel seemed to perk up, "Fed, good. Ah, I mean I can talk in front of you. Who's your boss, Alder Manning?"

"No," answered Josh. "Higher than my pay grade. He's my boss's boss."

"Oh," Finkel seemed pensive, a little confused why someone so far down the ladder would be at this dinner. Josh had an instant dislike for this guy.

Noting Josh's discomfort at Finkel's slight, Frank Dunleavy picked up the conversation.

"So, Josh, to bring you up to date on our conversation, Howie here was telling me all the reasons why other financial institutions from New York would like to open offices here in Wyoming. And I was just about to explain that I do not think it would be a profitable move."

Dunleavy turned to Finkel, "I don't think you're going to like it here, Howie. Wyoming is quite risk averse."

Finkel laughed, "Yeah, right, and so that's why they tell D.C. where to stick it. Come on, Frank, these are our kind of people."

Dunleavy shook his head, "You don't get it, Howie. These people are building something here; have built something. And it is rock solid. They are very conservative when it comes to their hard-earned capital."

"Well, that's because they haven't seen what *Wall Street* can do for *Main Street*. This may be a shit-kicking backwater, but they're awash in money and we're going to show them how to get a proper return."

"You've already made your first mistake, Howie, calling this place a backwater. But I will give you *shit-kicking* because they are going to kick the shit out of you and your brand of hustlers. They've already seen how The Street gets a proper return. We both know that's just a catch phrase for unconscionable risk; buyer beware and let the public face the music when it all collapses."

"So everyone in this State is happy with their little-piddling five percent returns and wouldn't even look at someone who could make them twenty-to-forty percent?"

"Well, actually they are in the two-to-four percent return area. And, yes, they are happy with that. And, no, they won't listen to your schemes. The main reason is that your schemes were a major player in bankrupting the country. That combined with D.C.'s drunken spending, massive deficits and socialist destruction of the real market place: goods and services. They don't need to earn forty percent here because they don't have the forty percent inflation of the dollar."

"Even better! It's the reason the rest of Wall Street wants a presence here. It's why the Big Five Houses sent me. The dollar is shit and we can't keep the returns up high enough to counter the depreciation caused by inflation. The entire Street is thinking of adopting the Wyoming Credits as our trading currency. This solid currency mated to our innovative financial instruments is a win-win all the way around."

It was Dunleavy's turn to laugh, "And you think they'll buy that; give you boys a chance to destroy their capital all the while skimming off the cream. I don't think so. They know all about The Street's so-called *innovation* and, here, it's a dirty word when applied to financial instruments.

Their laws are set up to make sure your style of innovation never sees the light of day."

"Oh, Frank, don't be so dramatic. You know laws can be circumvented."

"Not these," Dunleavy sipped his drink.

"How can you be so certain?" Finkel was smiling.

"Because I helped write them. It's always smart to consult an accomplished thief to find flaws in your security system."

Finkel's smile faded, "Come on, Frank. They just need a little education. We talk to the big dogs in the government, throw money around for reelection campaigns, or fill up some numbered accounts in Geneva and they're throwing the golden gates open for us. Don't try to tell me that money doesn't buy power here. Hell, we've had four of the last six Treasury Secretaries come right from The Street, including the current one. Plus we own the Chair of the House Banking Committee along with Senate Finance. Why else do you think there has never been any real reform after each crisis. We made it through 1984, '87, '90, '94, '97, '08 through '011 and even '018 without any real reform. Hell, they even got rid of the last vestiges of Glass-Steagall so Citigroup could go full-service. We keep coming back. The players may change seats, Banking houses may merge, new ones emerge, but we just keep coming back. Whichever instruments played out badly and caused a downturn, we make revisions and restart the game. No big deal. Right Josh? You're a government guy. You know how it works."

Josh sipped his drink non-committedly. He didn't understand five percent of what these guys were jabbering about. But he knew one thing. *This Howie guy's crooked as a hound dog's back leg.* Josh had an immediate dislike for him, finally responding with the Wyoming shrug.

Frank Dunleavy's face turned taciturn. "I think I'd lower my voice if I were you, Howie. You are an invited guest of these people, so I wouldn't be insulting them so easily. And you just violated one of their laws by even discussing a bribe of an elected official. Their elections campaigns allow no placards, no advertising and no money, even personal money. Anyone seeking office has one year to collect signatures from a specified percentage of qualified voters. That accomplished, candidates are included in publically aired town-meetings once a week for twelve months. And no corporation can contribute to, or endorse, any candidate. There is no corporate income tax, so a corporation fails the

Supreme Court test of having rights of *personhood*. Laws protecting their elections have stiff penalties, and jail time. Continue such rude comments and you may find yourself escorted to the border tonight. Or you could end up looking outward from the inside of a jail."

"Don't try and scare me, Frank." He looked from Dunleavy to Josh and noted the seriousness, "Really?"

Josh nodded his head and looked very somber. *This is starting to get fun*, he thought.

Dunleavy's glower caused Finkel to fidget. It made him nervous that Frank was so serious. This wasn't the cocky *wunderkind* that created blockbuster trades in the last decade. Frank had changed. The brashness was gone. *Maybe the guy's lost his edge*, thought Howie. Frank seemed intimidated by this State. *No, that isn't the word*, Finkel thought as he searched for the appropriate term. He had it: *respect. Frank actually has respect for this place and the people in it.* Howie was confused. That was a near impossibility. No one on The Street had respect for anything except how much they pocketed from their own trades. Clients, stockholders, friends, mentors, bosses, subordinates, competitors, government regulators, politicians, even laws: they were all something to be manipulated or circumvented, not respected. It was dog-eat-dog, buyer beware, survival of the fittest. It was one day up, the other down. Traders had a lot of acquaintances, but no friends. Friendship made it harder if, someday, the friend had to be screwed.

Frank had been one of The Street's kings of aggressiveness and arrogance. He had developed the no-respect attitude to an art form. He was famous for it. When Frank Dunleavy had resigned as CEO from *Merrick-Wolf* and Greenberg, CEO from the same company which Finkel was now CEO, *Silverman & Boxe*, the Street was stunned. A year later, when the two reemerged in Wyoming as partners of the investment house *Dunleavy & Greenberg*, speculation soared as to what the two legends were up to. It was the reason Finkel was here: find out how Dunleavy and his partner Greenberg were fleecing this golden flock. On Wall Street, if anyone made substantial profits on a new idea, a new financial instrument or a new market, the rest of The Street wanted in on the winning formula. Howie wanted to know Frank's game so that his and other institutions could play. The biggest players on The Street had sent Finkel as their emissary to Wyoming. It was like the old days when Moss Greenberg represented Wall Street to a Maoist China.

But not seeing Frank for over five years, Finkel saw something different in the man. Finkel thought maybe it was an act. Maybe Frank was trying to scare him and the rest of The Street's players from horning in on Dunleavy's new gig. *Well,* Howie thought, *he's not going to get away with it.* Finkel discovered, while researching Wyoming's money - the WC - that there was plenty to go around. And Frank Dunleavy, along with Moss Greenberg, weren't going to be allowed to pluck all the low hanging fruit. Finkel reapplied his aura of self-confidence.

"So, Frank, this little act of you and Moss supposedly *going native*, you really think it's going to work on Howie Finkel?"

"If by *going native* you mean I believe in these people and what they've built; and Moss and I want to be part of it, to build not bilk, if that's your definition, then yes, definitely. Moss Greenberg and Frank Dunleavy have gone native in Wyoming."

Finkel just smirked. He would let Dunleavy keep up the act. He was probably doing so for the sake of the tall government guy listening. Besides, he was there to find out what type of products Frank was trading. This, after all, was what his compatriots from the Street really wanted to know.

"Okay, Frank, whatever you say. Let's talk business, not philosophies. What are you trading these days, CMO's? CMO's squared?"

"You can leave your alphabet soup at the door, Howie. Those don't exist here."

"So you've got different names. Just what are you securitizing, collateralizing?"

"Straight loans, one at a time, that's it"

"Huh? What are you talking? Me, I'm talking about trading. You do remember trading, don't you?"

"Yes, we trade: bonds, commodities, equities."

"Okay!" Finkel brightened up, "Tell me about the bonds."

"Well, unlike instruments you're used to, these are fairly straight forward: State bonds, muni's and commercial paper are about it."

"Come on, Frank. Stop gaming me. You know I mean derivatives. How are you spinning out the mortgage paper? You keeping the strips for yourself? Looks like a lot of building going on. Bought a mortgage broker yet?"

Josh was wondering if this was a good time to start wandering off. He had promised Sam he would wait here for her, but he had no idea what these guys were saying. It was like they were speaking Swahili. Frank Dunleavy noted Josh's disinterest and felt it only polite to include Samantha's guest in the discussion.

"I apologize to you, Mr. Stillwater, for the arcane discussion."

"Please call me Josh."

"Josh it is. And I am Frank. Mr. Finkel here, as well as myself, come from the so-called "investment" side of the banking business."

"You sell people bonds," ventured Josh, trying to show he wasn't completely ignorant.

"Well, that is one aspect. We do not really sell the individual, unless he or she is very wealthy and has the money to buy large blocks of stocks or bonds. We also are an underwriter for bonds."

"I've always wondered what that term meant," queried Josh. "You mean you insure the bond to the buyer or the seller?"

"Well, in a way, for the issuer, ah, the seller. Underwriting means we create a market for the bond. The insurance you speak of is that we commit to buy a large block of the bonds, thus ensuring their sale. For this, we get a discount from the bond price. See, an underwriter, with agreement from the issuer, prices the bond offering, sets the interest rate and sells it to clients."

"The discount is how you make your money?

"Yes, and associated fees as well."

Finkel interjected, "Yeah, and tell him how lousy the spread is on the whole thing, particularly if you don't sell the entire lot at first offer."

"It's a matter of perspective, Howie. Underwriting, IPO's, equities trading, bond trading and client advisory fees were how investment houses made their living for generations."

157

"Yeah, and it sucked. Margins were so thin and competition so fierce, you had to be a surgeon to slice the pie."

Dunleavy looked at a confused Josh, "Don't be concerned, Josh. I don't understand that simile myself. Of course, our industry tends to make things up as we go."

Josh chuckled while Finkel glared.

Josh said, "So what changed so much from then to now? I guess these derivatives are the reason? I've heard about the term before, but really don't understand it. All I know is a lot of people have lost their shirts on them, right?

Dunleavy nodded, "And a lot of those people have been financial institutions. They are the people that create most of them."

"So, they are a bond, right?"

"Well, some are. Let me explain. A derivative is exactly what it's named. It *derives* its value from something else; hence it is a derivative of something else. For example, if you buy an equity, a stock, let's say Sumitomo Motors, you actually own the stock and, hence, part of Sumitomo Motors. You with me so far?"

Josh nodded.

"Now, let's say I think Sumitomo's stock is going to rise in the future. But either I'm not sure enough to buy it now and wait, or my cash is tied up till sometime in the future."

Finkel interrupted, "Or you don't want to tie up your money in a dog stock, but still want to make a little gain."

"Sumitomo is not a dog stock, Howie. They are one of my best clients."

"All stocks are dogs, Frank. It's why we don't screw around with them anymore, unless you got someone on the inside."

Even Josh knew the inference was shorthand for insider trading. *What a sleazebag*, he thought.

"And it's also why your economy is in the toilet and will remain so," retorted Dunleavy.

"MY Economy! Yours' too, Frank."

Dunleavy looked coolly at Finkel, "Not anymore, Howie."

It appeared to Josh that Dunleavy's explanations were more than just for Josh's ears. He was stating an argument to Finkel, all the while forcing him to endure the rudimentary as explained to Josh. *Maybe the man needs some re-education*, thought Josh as Dunleavy returned to him.

"Where was I? Oh, yes. So I want to be able to buy a stock in the future but not pay the full purchase price. What to do? Simple, I buy a stock option. This financial instrument is exactly what it is named. It is an option to purchase a stock in the future at some given price. The reverse side of this transaction is the person selling the option that you chose to buy."

"So the person selling the option owns the stock," Josh asked, thinking he was coming up to speed.

"Maybe, maybe not," answered Dunleavy.

"Why own the damn stock to sell an option?" Finkel sounded disgusted. "You're just tying up capital you could invest somewhere else."

Josh returned to being confused, "How can you sell something you don't own?"

Finkel's chuckle was abbreviated by Dunleavy's eyes shooting darts at him.

Frank answered, "It's done all the time Josh, and in many different ways. That's why Wall Street focuses on *controlling* assets more than *owning* assets. You can *control* assets worth several multiples more than what is required to *own* them. This way you can buy many more assets with limited money and reap profits from asset sales many times greater than if you had to own them. Options are this way. You can control assets worth ten times more than the price of the option."

Finkel busted in, "And that's the only way to be involved with equities, unless you want to own them long, and that's just stupid."

Dunleavy controlled his anger, "It's not stupid, Howie. It's how it is done here. We invest in corporations for the long haul, five to fifteen years. The capital appreciation has been exceptional and the dividend yields keep ramping up each year, based on your original purchase price. And capital gains laws here encourage the *long* view."

"Capital gains?? You said there were no corporate taxes and no personal taxes, Frank." Finkel was definitely put off.

"Income taxes, Howie, income taxes. There are no personal or corporate income taxes. However, there *are* capital gains taxes." Dunleavy turned to Josh, "Capital assets are things like land, buildings, machinery, a patent and stocks and bonds. When a government taxes the gain, or profit, a person or company makes upon the sale of these assets, it's referred to as a capital gains tax."

"What's the rate," demanded Finkel.

"Fifty percent the first year, forty the next, thirty, twenty, ten the fifth year, then zero after that."

"THAT'S INSANE!" Finkel was nearly shouting, and attracting attention.

Dunleavy looked around at the crowd and smiled, "Keep it down, Howie"

"How can you make any money trading if you have to give all the gains to the government? These people are nothing but socialists!"

"You don't give the government a dime, Howie, if you hold an investment for at least five years. But you are correct that it has a dramatic impact on short-range trades. That's exactly how they designed it."

"But why?" Finkel's voice was plaintiff. Josh was curious for an answer as well.

"Howie, it's simple. They don't like *Casino* Capitalists. They want *Creation* Capitalists investing here."

"*Casino? Creation?* This some New Age religion?" Finkel was confused.

Dunleavy smiled, "In a way, I guess. They *are* religious about their economy and their money. They want everything on an even keel at all times. They don't like big run-ups of markets because they know it results in big down-turns. Creation Capitalism is a term they coined meaning to create new business and new jobs. This kind of investing they want, they encourage. Casino Capitalists describes quick money made from other people's money. It describes the Street. It describes you, Howie. And it describes what I used to be, but am no more.

160

Dunleavy focused on Josh, "Casino Capitalists bet on the short term. They thrive on volatility, the rapid ups and downs of markets. If they can anticipate these turns, they can make a lot of money. Every day when the market bell rings, traders start shouting their buy and sell orders. Volatility is based on time. And a trade made a minute too late can wipe out millions, or even billions in profit. The din of noise on the trading floor always reminds me of a crowd shouting for a hot craps thrower trying to make point.

Wyoming, Howie, doesn't like that image. They want cool, calm, well-researched, deliberated decisions on where capital is to be invested. They want sustainable, long-term returns from profitable companies selling real goods and services, not short-term pieces of paper dubbed so-called *assets*. They want their CEO's and corporate presidents rising from bed each morning thinking about improvements to their products or services; how to lower their unit costs; what M&A's – Mergers and Acquisitions – would lead to long-range growth of the company. They don't want these officers wasting time thinking of ways to manipulate their stock so that they can bail out with their golden parachutes."

Howie shook his head slowly, "Jeese, Frank, I think you've been drinking the Kool-Aid here too long."

Dunleavy openly laughed, "I hope so, Howie, because it's damn good Kool-Aid."

Josh, who was initially bored, now gained some enthusiasm for the conversation. He was beginning to see how the nation's economy was manipulated by these capital overlords. He particularly enjoyed Dunleavy's term of Casino Capitalists. He asked of Frank, "Tell me more about the derivatives. I know they caused a lot of problems going all the way back to 2007."

"First of all, let me say that not all derivatives are a bad thing. Some derivatives have been around for ages and actually 'smooth-out' market swings. Some provide great service to business and even to governments. Take for example Forward Fx – foreign exchange – contracts. If a business sells internationally and receives foreign currency from its sale of products or services, it might wish to escape the potential swings of currency valuations in order to present a stable price to its international customer. So it purchases a Forward Fx contract. This means it buys the rights to another currency for future delivery, hence the Forward, based on a discount from the spot market, or today's price. The company can now set its price level, in the currency of its customer for whatever number of months in the future, or Forward.

An Fx contract is a derivative in that it derives its value from an underlying asset, in this case the actual currency to be delivered, or made available in the future. Fx contracts are important to Wyoming due to its business with so many international customers, suppliers and partners. Although the WC is very stable against gold, moving up or down about one percent during a twelve-month period, some of its trading partners' currencies fluctuate to a greater degree. Buying Forward Fx contracts provides price and profit stability longer range. And if this State is about anything, stability and profit are its catch words.

Another example of a derivative is a Commodity Future. This is very similar to a Forward Fx contract except the underlying asset is a commodity instead of a currency. Commodities can be oil, coal, precious metals, orange juice, pork bellies, and, most important to Wyoming's ranchers: beef and lamb. A rancher smoothes out swings in his annual profit by offering some or all of his animals for sale in the future at a fixed price today. Additionally, many of these ranchers purchase feed the same way. Farmers use the same financial instrument for the sale of their crops and anticipated purchases of fertilizers.

These financial instruments represent real assets and assist in the production of future goods. Although they carry the stigma of being derivatives, they are vital to an economy's long range stability."

Josh nodded, "I never knew they were considered derivatives, but I know their value. By the way, you know a kid named Bernie Dillon?"

Frank Dunleavy laughed, "Oh, yes…but I think you mean *Bernard* Dillon. We wouldn't want to be corrected by William Dillon." He shook his head slowly, "That kid is a walking, steel-trapped brain. He's made his Grandpa Jake a lot of money on lamb futures."

Josh also laughed, "I'm sure he has. I heard him work out this coming spring sales with Jake. I think it took him all of ten minutes. The kid's probably got the combined IQ of both his fathers, William *and* Jimmie. It's got to be off the charts."

"No doubt," replied Dunleavy. "Anyway, do you want me to keep going on about derivatives?"

"Sure," said Josh. "I think I'm mentally getting in the swing of it. You getting close to the bad derivatives."

Dunleavy nodded, "Right now. It isn't that their bad, Josh. It's that they have potential for misuse. 'Bad' derivatives have one thing in common: they are derivatives of derivatives, another step away from the asset they represent; another layer of potential confusion, obfuscation and even corruption; another layer of credit inflation that can burst. They are potentially harmful to an economy, and they've proved this."

Finkel's face was contorted, "Name them, Frank, cause I'm not following. And I'm considered an expert."

"Howie, you may be an expert in trading these animals, but no one is an expert in what's in them or their provenance," answered Frank. "But I'll list them: CDS –Collateralized Debt Swap - or Swaps, CMO – Collateralized Mortgage Obligations, SMBS - Stripped Mortgage-Backed Securities, CDO – Collateralized Debt Obligations, even stock options."

"Whoa, wait a minute. These aren't derivatives-of-derivatives. These are only one step away from the assets that back them, especially options. I think you've goofed-up your definition on this one, big man of finance." Finkel seemed please to trim Dunleavy's sails.

"I do not agree, Howie. A stock option is derived from a stock certificate."

Finkel fired back, "Yeah, and a stock certificate *is* the underlying asset,"

"Not really, Howie. Maybe through accounting methods a stock is considered an asset. But the real asset it represents is the potential profits and worth of a company. It represents the goods and services produced by the people of that company. In itself, it is a piece of paper. It isn't even a claim upon the company's assets as a secured note is."

"That's baloney, Frank. It is ownership in the company. How much closer to the assets can you get?"

Dunleavy coolly responded, "Unless you have a seat on the board, Howie, you have absolutely no control over those assets. And those on the outside-looking-in would be 99.99% of people trading stocks. Just go to a bankruptcy auction of a corporation and see what your stock ownership gets you. You'll be at the end of a long line: preferred stockholders, banks with secured loans, other secured creditors, accounts receivable holders, underfunded pension retirees, unsecured creditors, and, unless I left out anyone else, you with your piece of paper."

Finkel rubbed his chin, deep in thought. Then he lit up, "Wait a minute. You've still got a problem with your definition. Okay, commodity futures I'll give you as being backed up by real assets that you have claim to. But what about a Futures Fx? What is currency except a representation of the productivity of a nation's people?"

"Close, Howie, but no cigar. There is one major difference between a stock certificate and a currency. Currency, or money, is universal. I can trade my currency for a car or a loaf of bread. Try and do that with a stock certificate. Currency is far beyond the *representation* of an asset. It is the transportable store of value of the assets of a nation. This makes it an asset unto itself."

Howie searched for a comeback as Josh jumped into the conversation.

"Hey guys, you're gettin' a little esoteric for me. Let's get back on point here. You can duke this out later behind the corrals... Okay, let's say I agree that all of these derivatives are actually a derivative of a derivative. What makes them so bad?"

"Different things for different derivatives. For example, Swaps really aren't bad as they allow exchanges of varying interest rate structures or credit commitments. This can be useful for corporations or wealthy individuals that know how these instruments work and their potential hazards. The problem is they can morph, such as CDOs squared. I will not get into its details, but it is a further step away from the real asset."

"CMO's, a specialized type of CDO, spawned the mortgage collapse beginning in 2006. And they also spawned the Mortgage-backed Strips, a very risky instrument that wasn't understood fully by anyone I knew."

"Beyond not knowing what was within a lot of these instruments and what their worth was, here are the two biggest problems with such *innovative* instruments: they expand credit bubbles and they are a lousy use of capital for a society."

Finkel grunted, "Lousy use of capital? You know better than anyone, Frank, the returns available on derivatives. Why do you think they were gobbled up?"

"Again, lack of listening skills, Howie. I said 'lousy use of capital *for a society.*' Granted, most people try to maximize their gains. And derivatives provided maximum gains for some people....for a while. But the capital did nothing for society. They are elitist financial instruments in that there is no long-range gain for society."

"Are you trying to say that CMOs didn't cause the biggest housing boom since just after World War II? Come on, Frank."

"No, I don't deny that. It also caused the largest drop in housing starts in our nation's history and the collapse of the residential construction industry. For all those that lost their homes to foreclosure or lost their good-paying job, CMO's were a pretty bad creation."

Dunleavy focused on Stillwater, "You see, Josh, the reason these instruments come into existence is to sop up excess cash. When a nation exercises poor fiscal and monetary policy, money becomes too abundant. Valuations of real assets become unrealistic and cannot absorb the excess funds. Fiscally, the U.S. has continually increased deficit spending until its national debt exceeded its GDP. Combined with poor money policy pumping unlimited funds into the financial system, the U.S. economy fell off a cliff into an inflation-driven depression.

Prior to this collapse, the excess money had to go somewhere. Competition for financial institutions to profit from this money whirling through ledgers became fierce. New instruments were created to win an edge in the game to attract these funds. Naturally these instruments had to return dazzling rates in order for a gain to exceed rampant inflation numbers.

The real problem is that the excess money stayed in the stratosphere, circulating internationally within so-called assets that are not really assets. The financial instruments most used for this were, and are, derivatives.

Derivatives allow money to be made from money while creating no real assets. That is why the Great Recession beginning in 2007 was bereft of jobs. Of the billions of dollars pumped into the system via 'stimulus' or 'quantitative easing' or deficit spending in general, very little found its way into new technologies, new products, new industries, new commercial research, new IPOs or new small-business loans. It just circled in the stratosphere fueling the up-and-down roller-coaster ride of stock markets and commodity prices. And this stratosphere is the realm of the Casino Capitalists. Whereas the rest of society craves stability, these adrenaline junkies...and I was one of them... love volatility. When their bets pay off, individuals reap huge rewards, but the general economy does not. When their bets go bust, their clients lose money and the damage to an economy moves from struggling to crippling."

"Got it," said Josh. "These financial instruments are high-risk bets in a game for the rich with a nation's economy used as the stake. But, long range, the nation only shares in the losses, not the winnings."

"Exactly." Dunleavy raised his glass in salute to Josh.

"But what about that credit bubble thing. Is that the cause of busts?"

Dunleavy nodded, "Every single time, Josh. When you have too much money chasing too few assets, the financial world thinks they solve the problem by creating so-called new *assets* out of thin air. These are the *innovative* financial instruments. These are the derivatives. There aren't enough assets of worth to absorb the extra money, so they create another layer of so-called assets. But here is the real crux; you can buy these instruments on *credit*. Although credit is a direct response to money supply levels, credit *expands* money supply much faster than a government pumping money into the system. And the worst part, it's *exponential*.

"Really?" It surprised Josh that privately extended credit was more impactive to an economy than governmental actions. "How is it exponential?"

Dunleavy nodded, "Think of it this way. If something costs $100 and you only have $100, then you can only buy one, right?"

Josh knew it was a rhetorical question and did not respond.

"But if the seller only required twenty percent down..."

Josh brightened, "I get it. You could actually buy five on credit."

"Exactly," replied Dunleavy. "And this is true for original assets as well as stocks representing that asset and derivatives of the stock. Let me explain. Let's say someone buys five assets at twenty percent down each. He leveraged his money five to one. In other words, every dollar he used bought him five-dollars of assets. Now, someone buys the stock of the company that leveraged its assets in this manner. But the stock buyer also is extended credit at twenty percent down. So he is leveraging the original company's asset another five times, or twenty-five to one. Now the stock owner sells an option on his stock and the option buyer is extended credit by a brokerage firm of twenty percent down. That's another five times, or one-hundred-and-twenty-five-to-one leverage..."

"Wow!" exclaimed Josh, "No wonder..."

Dunleavy held up a hand to stop Josh, "I'm not finished. Let's say the option buyer was an ETF fund that leveraged itself five-to-one to buy, not only this option, but thousands of others. Then it creates an option market for its ETF fund, and buyers purchase the options on credit...."

"Options squared," mumbled Finkel.

Josh did the math, "If that's another five-to-one leverage, then we're up to six-hundred-and-twenty-five-to-one. Amazing!" He thought of last night's TV financial news. *No wonder this State watches leverage so closely. These bankers could gamble the store away, and with other people's money.*

"Not amazing, scary," frowned Dunleavy. "If the economy slows and the original company can't meet its credit obligation and goes bust, and everyone in the pipeline of instrument ownership - instruments based on the original assets - cannot cover the eighty percent call – the money owed on credit – then the house of cards collapses. And with it goes the economy, leveraged into a hole so deep that it cannot climb out for a long time.

Now you know why this State does not like derivatives that are not tied directly - meaning one-step - from an actual asset. They have seen the devastation caused by Casino Capitalists on Credit."

"God, Frank, you make it sound like we're all strung out on drugs." Finkel was disgusted.

"You are, Howie. It's a designer drug containing the ingredients maximum-risk and maximum-credit. You even gave the drug a street name: max leverage.

Finkel looked at Josh, "If you watch your markets carefully, you aren't left without a chair when the music stops. You unwind your deals beforehand. That is unless one of your traders goes 'rogue' on you."

Dunleavy gave a dark chuckle. "How come when a trader loses billions, he's gone *rogue*. But if those same trades go the other way, he is revered, exalted and promoted?

Have you learned nothing Howie? When you are the CEO it's all your responsibility. You can't lay it off on one person. You are the ultimate responsible party. You set the culture, the risk threshold. I know it is the way of our industry to take your attitude. But enough is enough. Take responsibility. For me, I approved every penny of capital of our shareholder's and client's money we poured into risky instruments. I also approved the risk models we incorporated into our computer system. It was just plain stupidity on my part. The difference is, Howie, I learned from it and the rest of you haven't."

"Yeah, Frank, I see how you learned. You ran away to cow country and, supposedly, scrape by on the old-institution model. You know it's dead. So what are you doing, Frank, penance?"

Josh's face was screwed up in confusion and Dunleavy noticed.

"What Howie's saying is that Moss and I now run our business the way banks ran after the Glass-Steagall Act, until the late nineteen-seventies. We provide advice to our clients, trade stocks and bonds, underwrite new bonds and IPO's - initial public offerings of new companies."

Josh was impressed with a man that admitted his failings and changed his ways. In the military, you either did that or soldiers died, "What happened afterwards? I mean from the seventies on up to today? What changed?"

"Our souls, Josh. We became gamblers, not investors. Suddenly it was not enough to make money the old-fashioned way. The new model was *proprietary*. What it means is to have a product that is proprietary to your house. That way you can set the price and reap all the rewards. And you are responsible for the maximum risk."

"How does an investment house get a proprietary product?" asked Josh.

Finkel puffed himself up to answer, "You invent it, son."

"Huh?"

Dunleavy put his hand on Josh's shoulder, "He means high-yield instruments that are also high-risk. He's talking about derivatives. You see, Josh, Howie has a short memory. All traders do. Otherwise they couldn't live with themselves."

"I'm damn good at trading, Frank, and my memory's not that short." Finkel looked indignant.

"Really, Howie? I imagine you would rather forget 2006." Dunleavy looked at Josh to explain, "In 2006, when everything collapsed, starting with the housing market, there existed over ten-trillion dollars of CMOs - Collateralized Mortgage Obligations. And nobody even knew what they were worth. A large portion was still in the inventory of the investment houses. They had violated the number one rule: never eat your own rat poison, even if it's wrapped in candy."

Josh chimed in, "So why didn't these banking houses just hold on to them until the market turned?"

Finkel gave a low, short laugh, "Two big reasons. The houses had borrowed the money to buy them in the first place. We were leveraged thirty-to-one, meaning we had borrowed thirty dollars for every one dollar of our own money. And we weren't the most leveraged on The Street.

The second reason was that nobody knew what was in the bond. The CDOs could contain a thousand auto and credit-card loans. The CMOs had morphed into PACs, TACs an VADMs, all with their own *tranches* – bonds sliced into different risk instruments. With so many foreclosures and consumer loan defaults, no one knew which bonds contained how many bad loans. They were all essentially worthless. We've still got inventory from back then."

"Is that what they call toxic assets?" asked Josh.

Dunleavy nodded, "And thank God the Fed and other nations allowed the industry to price them anyway we wanted. Otherwise half of the financial institutions in the world would have been declared insolvent."

Josh was surprised by this comment, "You mean financial institutions could say they were worth whatever they wanted? Aren't there standard accounting rules or some agency that says what they're worth?"

Dunleavy appeared saddened, "Not really. There was no clearing house, no government oversight of these instruments. Moody's and S&P had given them all triple-A ratings. Why not? They were backed by mortgages and high-interest consumer loans. They were collateralized. When the market collapsed, no one really knew how to price the bonds.

You see, Josh, these instruments were traded directly from seller to buyer. There was no intermediary, no clearing house as exists for stocks and bonds. Therefore all controls were circumvented. There were no real standards of compliance in place. For balance sheets, they could be valued at Market-to-Model. This means, whatever a company's computer model said it was worth, then that's what the company priced it at. And of course these models never said it was worth less than what the company paid for it. If the Market-to-Market price was applied, meaning the price the market would currently pay for the asset, the game was up. Everyone, including nations, would be bankrupt. When the collapse occurred, the markets froze. Nobody was buying. Nobody was lending. There was no way to tell what was toxic and what had value. So, essentially it was all toxic. When you encounter a sign that reads MINEFIELD AHEAD, you tend to avoid it rather than try and pick your way through it."

Josh shook his head, "I always thought you guys knew what you were doing, knew more than the rest of us. Hell, you were just a bunch of shysters playing craps with our money. And it sounds like nobody ever thought it could come up snake eyes. Even a dumb Army grunt has learned that lesson."

Dunleavy looked at his shoes, "I think your analogy is very succinct. The problem is that the grunt is only using *his* money and he wins or loses on every throw of the dice. We, however, were paid handsomely when we won. The only thing we lost when things went the other way was our commissions; and, for some of us, our self-respect."

Josh was becoming incensed with this enlightenment.

Finkel smiled, "At the peak of things, I made twenty-two million. Say what you want, Frank. That buys a lot of self-respect." He cast his eyes to Stillwater. "Think of me whatever you want, Josh. But I'll match bank accounts with you any day."

Josh's dislike for this guy increased every time he opened his mouth, "Yeah, and I will match cocks with you any day. You need to grow up. I don't think bragging about how much you make when every five or ten years you ruin millions of lives by losing so much of other people's money is very smart."

It was Dunleavy's turn to smile, "I think he has a point Howie. Josh, that's the number one reason I came here, to get away from a world that thinks like Finkel here."

"Oh, bullshit Frank." Finkel was annoyed, "Don't tell me that you aren't trading the same stuff we do on The Street. Hell, you've probably invented some new twist on mortgage bonds. I see all the building going on here."

Dunleavy shook his head. "No, Howie. Couldn't do it if I wanted to. Wyoming law prohibits bundling of financial insturments."

"What are you talking about, Frank? No bundling! Where's the cash coming from?"

"A lot of it comes from the buyer. The rest is financed initially by the State."

"No way! I didn't think these people were a bunch of socialists. Doesn't the State sell the loans off? They couldn't have enough money to finance all this."

"Well, yes, they sell off the loans. But you're wrong about not having the money, Howie. The State government here is beyond solvent. It has reserves that can carry it through five years of the worst downturn.

They handle their loan re-sells unlike Freddie There is no bundling. Each loan has to stand on its own merit at auction. The loan doc's and credit history of the borrower are available to the bidding parties sixty days before the auction. And here's your twist: these loans are not backed by the government. And no loan exceeds fifteen years."

"Okay, so the State's in the loop, big deal. You just buy up a bunch, bundle them and issue bonds. *Voila,* you're in the CMO biz."

"No-can-do, Howie. It's illegal to bundle mortgage loans here. The only way you can sell groupings of assets is in a mutual fund. Even there, you have to list each asset and its rating. And the mutual fund itself has a rating by an approved agency. Every investment available in this State includes not only a rating, but a leverage ratio of what is backing it. Whether an individual for a mortgage, or a business for corporate bonds, all have a leverage ratios.

Additionally, every sale of financial instruments in this State has to go through a government-approved clearing house and have a rating from one of the four government-approved ratings firms. It is very difficult to start a rating company or a clearing house. Government accountants and advisors sit on their boards and keep a close eye on every transaction. They have the right to delay any clearing or assessment until the government is satisfied with the efficacy of the product. It may slow some trades down, but that is a price these people are willing to pay for economic stability. The rules are never changed and there is no political access to change them for some short term political gain.

The rating also determines what tier of financial institution can buy, sell or hold the bonds. They do not use letters here; rather it is risk percentage. There are five percentage rankingss: 5, 10, 15, 20, 25. Dunleavy & Greene is an investment house. So we can participate in upto15% risk instruments. Only speculative banks can go higher, up to 25%. This works with our loan patterns as well. We can only make loans with a 15% risk factor. And this is not an average of all our loans. This is the max of any single loan or asset purchase. On top of this, we have to maintain an overall rating below that for our total banking business. It keeps us pretty conservative and very stable."

"Still sounds like socialism, the government having that much power over capital. It's anti-American," grumbled Finkel

"Wrong, Howie. It's pro Citizen. Don't talk to me about 'drinking the Kool-Aid' if you buy that freedom-of-the-market crap the Street has propagandized for years."

Dunleavy turned to Stillwater, "You see, Josh, the Street always tries to rig the laws and the economy to its benefit. They don't care whose money is at stake or how many people have jobs. They just want freedom to gamble other people's money. Wyoming calls it Casino Capitalism. When regulation is put upon them, the Street wails against loss of freedom; government socialism destroying markets. But when they crap out of the game, when the markets collapse, they are the first to scream for government intervention: re-capitalize the banks, re-inflate the economy. They threaten the nation with 'too big to fail.' So the great invisible hand Adam Smith wrote of does not ever get to wipe the slate clean; isn't allowed to punish those that gambled all and lost."

He turned back to Finkel, "It's not capitalism you're protecting, Howie. Otherwise you'd be forced to learn from your errors and your arrogance. If you really knew there was no backstop and that no one was 'too big to fail' then maybe you'd think twice about where you put other people's money.

This State has designed an economic system that keeps the hands of Casino Capitalists out of the State's economic cookie jar. Its legacy is throughout the system."

"God, I hate to ask, what else do they have their fingers into?"

"Not just their fingers, their entire fist, Howie."

Josh was enjoying the anguish on Finkel's face. It was as if a kid had his candy bar stolen. It was refreshing to hear that Wyoming had stopped the barbarians at the gate. This was definitely something the rest of the country could learn.

Dunlavey began, "First of all, just as in the rest of the country, the State collects payroll taxes through businesses. But there is no matching, no increased amounts, no social cost for business. Unemployment, health care, savings and pensions are all deducted from wages and each is deposited into the State Bank under the name of the individual. The State cannot touch it for expenses. They can lend it to financial institutions at a fixed rate and with very tight reins on its investment."

"There's a State Bank?"

"Yes, it controls all the gold and the computerized currency it backs: Wyoming Credits."

"And they have all the pension and health care funds?"

"Yes. And it can only be spent on the Citizen and his or her dependents that are named on the individual account."

"Good God, and what measly interest do they lend it out for?"

"Banks that desire State funds issue notes to the State at two percent interest. The caveat is that the money can only be loaned for housing loans and only at a four percent interest rate. Additionally, no single loan can be for more than fifteen percent above the average amount of all loans issued by the bank over the last twenty-four months. This way no individual customer or bank director can get a million Credit loan of the people's money to blow on a mansion. Such money would have to come from either an investment or speculative bank as these institutions cannot borrow public money for home construction."

"So the State borrows money from individual deposits of payroll, health and pension withholdings and does with it what it wants.?"

"You weren't listening, Howie," Dunleavy shook his head. "This isn't the shell the game the Federal government used for Social Security; stealing the money for inflated social programs and putting an IOU in the so-called *lockbox*. Here, the individual holders of the State accounts actually own fractional shares of State bonds issued at two percent when the money is loaned to the banks. The notes are five year notes. They can be renewed, but the interest has to be paid at each maturity. This way, the State is guaranteeing to the individual the resulting bank loan. The investment is secure and will be there when needed by the individual. They can even ask for their pension pay-out in gold, if desired."

"Gold," snorted Finkel. "Just try to get gold out of any person, let alone a State."

"It's easy here," Dunleavy looked at his hands with nonchalance. "You can request your pension before any Friday and receive your gold no later than the following Thursday."

Finkel looked as a small child, "Really?"

"Truly, Howie. When these people say 'Gold-Backed', they mean it. You can also redeem Wyoming Credits at any bank following the same rules."

Finkel searched for something to criticize, "Well, two percent return is kind of a lousy rate, Frank."

"Not here, where inflation is nearly zero. Remember, the two percent return is compounded. These people will end up with over a million Credits if they make the minimum contributions for the forty-five years of their working lives. And a million Credits here far exceed the comforts and joy of a life lived to one-hundred years old. Most will have a lot of money to leave their children."

"So, getting back to mortgages, Frank, what are these 'stringent' requirements you said there were for a loan?"

"Thirty percent down, fifteen years pay-off, a nearly spotless credit record and a maximum amount loaned that, amortized monthly, is no more than two weeks of your monthly salary averaged over the last five years."

"That's inhumane. Who could afford a home?" demanded Finkel.

"A lot of people, Howie. You already said how much construction you saw. A home is the goal for these people. Most scrimp and save, avoiding the lure of expensive cars, electronic toys, lavish vacations and all the other garbage that the rest of the country used to go into debt for. These people are savers, along the model of the Asians. The savings rate here is over twenty-five percent.

With thirty percent down and only four percent interest over fifteen years, and property taxes capped for life of ownership at the first year property assessment, the monthly payments are very affordable. Citizens here don't go overboard on homes. Most of the homes you saw are below six-hundred square meters. And a lot of the construction you saw is land development; no houses, just lots, roads and utilities. Inflation for desirable land, meaning near or in a CityCar district, is higher than building costs. So many younger Citizens buy their plot of land first. Most developers provide five-year land loans at cheaper rates than banks offer. When the land is paid off, they get another loan for building the actual house. A person in their early twenties who buys his or her land is usually ready to build their house in their early thirties."

"And they have to cough up thirty percent of the total cost?"

"No. Paid-off, developed land is usually sufficient to cover the thirty percent down. If not, there is usually less than five percent additional down required."

"And banks only charge four percent. But what if, after scrimping to save, interest rates jump up? The schmuck is screwed."

Dunleavy's eyes flared, "Watch your mouth, Howie. There are no schmucks here. To answer your question, the four percent rate is frozen in their Constitution. It would take a two-thirds vote to change it."

"So the Bank is paying two percent to the State for money. And the State pays two percent to the individual pension-account holders. How does the State make any money on the deal?"

"Why should the State make money, Howie? Government is not a for-profit entity. The State is the people, it doesn't need to profit from them. The State has many other avenues of revenue: two percent sales tax on all finished goods and royalties on energy resources consumed or exported, dividends from corporations that the State holds shares of. This State is a partner with its Citizens and its businesses. Although laws encourage investment, and the State knows business lays the golden eggs, business is considered as serving the overall welfare of the Citizens, not the other way around."

The conversation had not changed Finkel's perspective, "Still seems silly to miss out on potential mortgage bonds. The State could pick up easy cash with a small income tax. Big returns equal big cash flow."

Dunleavy sighed, "You just can't let it go, Frank. There is no income tax and they don't want mortgages to be a cash cow for anyone. They want stability. That is their mantra, stability, along with slow, steady growth.

Because of the housing down-payment requirement, there is no explosion in home building and no bubble of an inflationary spiral. If you think you saw a lot of homes being built, it would be ten times that if they applied the old down payment and qualifying models that caused the 2006 bubble.

Housing price inflation is less than one percent per year, with developed land averaging about a percent-and-a-half, even in this hot market. There is no new-home construction inventory, because a new home is not built until there is a buyer. No bank here would loan to a developer that did it any other way. On used homes, inventory turn is between six and twelve months. There is no rush in buying a home here. And that keeps prices down. Now, what's more inhumane; people waiting and saving for a house they can afford, or issuing loans at inflated interest rates, a loan they are not qualified for, and then watching as they fall and take the entire economy with them?"

Josh broke in, "I got a question." Dunleavy nodded.

"Well, with this payroll deduction thing, it sounds like what you're talkin' bout is a pay-as-you-go system instead of a younger generation payin' for the older, right."

Again Dunleavy nodded and Josh continued, "What about those that can't pay? What about the ones that don't have forty working years left when this whole thing here got started? Are they just out in the cold?"

"No. The State, meaning all of us, picks up the tab for unemployment and health care benefits for those retired, retiring soon, or are completely, and I mean certifiably, unable to work. Those that are age-eligible receive a livable pension. You're right about the pay-as-you-go, but to get it started this working generation has to shoulder those of their parents' generation that have no money. And they have to pay for themselves at the same time. It is quite a burden, but is being shouldered willingly.

Times are good and they are making the most of it. Social Security in inflated New, Old whatever dollars, wouldn't have solved their problems anyway. The lockbox was broken into decades ago and the money stolen by the general fund. That's why the age limit has been raised to eighty-five. The Federal government does not want its Citizens to live long enough to collect Social Security because the money isn't there.

Do you know why Franklin Roosevelt set the original retirement age at sixty-five when he created Social Security?"

Josh pondered for a moment, but had no response.

"Because it was the average life-expectancy at that time. He knew the government couldn't afford a majority of old-persons living long enough to collect a pension.

The younger, working generation in this State was prepared for this initial, one-time burden. They overwhelmingly voted for it because they knew it would benefit their parents. After this generation, each subsequent generation will be paying only for themselves. This current generation may be sacrificing short-term pleasures. But they will be heralded as heroes by future generations. There is no deficit, no unpaid bills for the following generations. And if one generation explodes like the baby boomers, there's no problem because each person is paying their way. So far, we've been lucky. The economy here is strong, creating enough earnings to manage this one-time tax burden. In actuality, the sales tax burden has been temporarily reduced because the State has been running such large surpluses. When was the last time you heard of a State running surpluses, and then reducing taxes instead of finding ridiculous things to spend the surplus on?"

Josh interjected, "OK, impressive. So the State is haulin' in enough money to cover the shortages and the working stiffs are kicking in extra. But how much can this generation afford without corporations kicking in matching amounts. Isn't business getting a free ride?"

Dunleavy shook his head, "No, and let me tell you why. These people have created one of the best educated and highly motivated people I've seen in a long time. Yes, corporations pay no matching on payroll deductions. But they also are aware there is a limited resource here called people. And they have to compete for these people. Salaries have increased nearly forty percent in the last ten years. But so has productivity. These people put out for what they get paid. And the increased wages and subsequent increase in withholdings more than make up for any corporate matching.

Finkel rubbed his chin in thought, "Hit me on the income tax thing. It didn't soak in the first time."

"Unconstitutional, for individuals and business."

"Really! Well, there's a positive. So if there's no corporate tax and no payroll taxes and no health care or pension costs, then corporations should be rolling in dough. What do they invest in? Is that your secret treasure mine? Are you rolling them into high-yields?"

"No, not the ones you're thinking about. Most of them reinvest in their own business. Corporations also buy significant chunks of IPO's, hedging that a new company might have a promising technology. Also, they pay large dividends. That is how a stock is really judged here, by how much cash it generates and then distributes to its shareholders. If you are a public corporation and your dividends are less than a ten-to-twenty percent yield, your shares are not looked upon with great favor."

"Ten-to-twenty percent yield! Why would they distribute it to shareholders?"

"This is going to be difficult for you to understand, Howie. But there is a complete different corporate culture here. Although employees are paid exceptionally well because there is a limited pool of them, shareholders are the first in line for distribution of profits. Corporate executives don't run public corporations as their private fiefdoms and personal source of boundless wealth. Officers of companies are responsible to boards. Board members are, by law, major shareholders, with the proviso that at least two seats are for shareholders of less than one-tenth of a percent of the outstanding shares and can serve only one year. Board members cannot be employees of the company. One cannot be an officer and a board member. And board members receive no compensation except for direct expenses. Trust me, there are no golden parachutes….. or private jets, or corporate retreats or penthouse suites or parties in the Bahamas. Public corporations exist to make money for shareholders, period. The number of top executives is held to a minimum. And bonuses can only be paid in a percentage of the bottom line *cash* generated. Not profit, Cash. Executives are well compensated. But it is more along the Japanese model, not the prima donna model that the U.S. allows."

"This includes you, Frank? Doesn't sound like your style."

"It is now, Howie. But these rules don't legally apply to Dunleavy and Greenberg. We are not a public corporation. We are privately held. But Moss and I answer to six shareholders other than ourselves. And they all have strong opinions as to how their money is spent and even stronger inclination to risk-avoidance."

"And you say this State believes in capitalism? I still say its socialism."

Dunleavy responded, "I told you they do not believe in *your* kind of capitalism: Casino Capitalism. They believe that capital is precious and is the source of a society's potential wealth and success. That's why they have such tight rules and reins upon it. Investment persons like myself know we don't own all the capital we make decisions for. Nor do we personally reap the majority rewards. That *is* socialism. We believe capital should not be squandered on schemes to make money from money. It's pure gambling.

What *is* respected, Howie, is Creation Capitalism. It has nothing to do with God. It means capitalism that creates wealth, not just money. And wealth means new technologies, new products, new factories and new, high-paying jobs. What every Citizen in Wyoming deeply believes in, Howie, is free enterprise."

Finkel snorted his disdain, "It's all sentimental gobbledygook in my book."

"Then your book needs editing. Casino Capitalism does not produce goods and services. Yes, free enterprise requires capital to run on. It is the fuel. That is why they respect Creation Capitalism. Gambling all the money produced by hard-working individuals and dedicated entrepreneurs on higher-yield, obscure and obfuscated trading instruments is reckless. When capital is solely earned by an individual, he or she can do whatever they choose. They can gamble it away. They can burn it if it gives them pleasure. Although with the WC, lighting a cigar with plastic is difficult, and stinky."

Josh chuckled.

"But, as in our industry, when it is the capital of our clients or the capital we borrow from other banks, or capital we borrow from government, then we have an obligation of careful investment. We are entrusted with a precious commodity, a people's wealth. And we have the duty to be trusted with its use. Our industry has violated that trust on many occasions. This State wants business to survive and thrive. It is what employs their people and it is their future. This they are certain of. And what else they are certain of is that people like you and me aren't going to get our hands on the earnings, the future of their people, and go hit the casino with it. They have structured their entire financial system to make sure this doesn't happen."

"Tell me they didn't resurrect Glass-Steagall, Frank."

"Well beyond that, Howie. By your thinking, they have created the Frankenstein of Glass-Steagall."

"You mean banks can't sell derivatives?

"*Way* beyond that, Howie. There are four levels of private banks here: retail, commercial, investment and speculative."

Josh's ears perked up as this was something he hadn't understood completely during the TV news broadcast.

"As we already discussed, the State bank controls all pensions, mortgages and tier-one savings, three areas that are key to the average Citizen's future."

"Wait. What do you mean by tier-one savings?"

"It is the individual's savings account that must be maxed out before money can be put into higher tiers within the banking system."

"Christ, how much is that?"

"One-thousand WC, about sixty-thousand of your dollars."

Finkel shook his head, "This on top of their State pension fund?

"Yes"

"OK, they hit tier-one, that's a retail bank, right?"

"Yes. When they hit the minimum savings level, they can go up to tier-two: commercial, then tier-three: investor and finally, for millionaires: speculative. Corporations, naturally, can start at tier two. But they have to maintain one million WC at this level to go to tier three. And that's if they are a private company. Public companies cannot have money in speculative banks."

"What the hell is a speculative bank. What are they into?"

Essentially, they are a combination of a Wall-Street investment bank, hedge fund and arbitrage. But they have limits too. They can only be funded by wealthy individuals, privately-held corporations or loans from other speculative banks as no bank below their level can lend to them. Also, banks can only sell loans or assets to another bank at their level, for example commercial to commercial, retail to retail. And no loans or obligations can be bundled into any financial instrument. They have to be bought and sold as individual instruments."

"So there are no derivatives?"

"Only futures and fx contracts. But those are even limited because they cannot be sold on margin. Every transaction has to have complete visibility. And there are many other regulations that are too numerous for evening talk. Reserves are higher. No off-books or off-shore transacting allowed. All the things we thought of to get around control. And if you think of anything new, it is illegal to sell or trade it until it has been submitted to the Wyoming SEC for evaluation. The minimum evaluation period is three years, with a mandatory, four-public-hearings and a vote in the legislature and signature of the Governor."

"Jeesh, Frank, no margins? You're kidding."

Dunleavy shook his head, "I am not. The State can control money supply, but we all know that credit is the real beast. They are tired of Casino Capitalists end-running monetary policies and creating enormous credit bubbles that eventually implode and destroy economies. The majority of economic and business laws passed are aimed at thwarting people like you, Howie. Public credit is controlled tightly and is not adjusted through interest rates. What rates we banks charge, except for housing loans, are our business. But the environment is very competitive to keep them low. They don't want us to be selling assets on margin because it inflates the credit market and allows room for all the tricks you call innovation. Consumer credit is capped by a required ratio of the individual's monthly *cash-flow* to debt, not assets to debt. And an individual's home can never be considered an asset for loan consideration unless it is for direct improvement of the home or property.

This State has done well at avoiding what we called the business cycle; what the public refers to as boom and bust. We all know that credit bubbles are at the core of these cycles. But this State doesn't play the constant money supply game. It has fixed interest rates, both paid and charged with funds controlled by the State Bank."

"How do they control the money supply if not through constant interest rate adjustments?" Finkel was baffled and Josh saw this as humerous.

"Gold. They are on the gold standard, Howie. They have a fixed price that they endeavor to keep the WC valued against gold. As the State becomes wealthier and gold drops in value against the WC, it issues more WC against its surpluses. When gold starts to rise, it takes the surplus and buys more gold with the funds."

"This *is* a Frankenstein," Finkel mumbled. "If there are not constantly fluctuating interest rates, how do you speculate? How can you make any money without volatility? How can you make a killing without insider info on when the Fed is going to raise or lower interest rates?"

"'Killings' here, Howie, are left for hunting season." Dunleavy answered. "Capital growth, rising dividend yields, expanding job base and stability are prized terms within this State."

Finkel shook his head sadly, "You've been nutted, Frank. I feel sorry for you."

"Don't Howie. These people have given me the greatest gift of my life, a second chance. And I'm using that chance to become what I always wanted to be…..a banker. Not a Casino gambler losing other people's stakes, but a *real* banker. So go back to The Street and tell them how Frank Dunleavy and Moss Greenberg went native. How this State can smell their kind a mile away and how it won't tolerate their ways. Tell them to stay back east, toast their martinis to the glorious tales of how they screwed this competitor, and how they ripped off that client and how they bribed a government to deceive its own people. There's nothing here for them, Howie. And there's certainly nothing here for you."

Josh raised the bourbon glass to lips, trying to hide his grin. Dunleavy and Finkel glared at one another.

With perfect timing, Sam appeared at Josh's side and wrapped her arms around his, "Having a lively discussion, gentlemen? So, Mr. Finkel, I hope Mr. Dunleavy here has been a most capable diplomat on behalf of our State. We are certainly fortunate to have a man of his character participate in our State's renaissance. His judgment is completely trusted as to who is allowed to participate in our little financial miracle. I will be interested to receive his thinking on the institutions you represent. His opinion is so valued, that Mr. Dunleavy is retiring from his investment house at the end of the year to become Chairman of our Wyoming Securities and Exchange Commission. We could not be more pleased." Sam smiled while Finkel choked on his drink.

"SEC, *you* Frank?"

Dunleavy's smile was larger than Sam's, "Yes, and I am deeply honored. Not only will I make sure existing law is enforced, with vigor, Howie, but our discussion tonight has given me ideas of some new regulations I think should be proposed."

Finkel was ashen. Josh chuckled as Sam squeezed his arm slightly, "So, please excuse me as I am going to steal Josh for a while. There are some others I wish him to meet."

She spun away from the two men, leading Josh as she spoke, "I hope that wasn't too dry or taxing for you?"

"You knew they were going to have that conversation." It was a statement, not a question.

"I knew why Mr. Finkel was here. He originally requested talks with me regarding participation in our financial system by the largest houses on Wall Street. I thought it more prudent to have the new, incoming Chairman of the SEC explain our rules. Franklin Roosevelt thought it smart to put a former fox in charge of the hen house when he named Joseph Kennedy as Chairman of the Federal SEC. I understand the President's thinking. Sinful men can be deceitful to everyone but a reformed sinner. Don't you think?" Sam laughed heartily as she led Josh through the crowd.

Josh looked down his shoulder towards her glowing face. She was simply amazing.

# Chapter 18

## A Lot of Brass

## Governor's Mansion, Cheyenne

Sam looked across the crowd, smiled and waved at someone, while pulling Josh along, "Here's some gentlemen that speak your language."

Stillwater asked. "And what language is that?"

"Military, silly. Generals!" Four men in full dress uniforms turned in Sam's direction. Two Air Force uniforms each bore two stars, indicating the rank of general. The other two were Army three-stars. One wore a Wyoming Army insignia. Their greeting was in unison ,"Ma'am."

"Gentlemen, I want to thank you for coming. I have a new guest to introduce. Actually, he is an old guest in that we grew up together. He is also former military. This is Joshua Stillwater. Joshua, General William Toomey, Commander of Minot Air Force Base. General Thomas Grant, Commander of Warren Air Force Base. Army General Alvin Palmer, Deputy Commander of Transcom. And Wyoming Army Commander, General Douglas Roughton. So Doug, how did things go today?"

"A-One, Ms. Governor, everyone is where they should be."

"Excellent, General. And you Al?"

"Smooth as silk, Ms. Samantha. Everyone is, what's the expression, on board."

Sam chuckled as the assembled brass smiled. Josh felt he was missing an inside joke. He felt just like a former Captain should before this group; small.

She spoke, "That is good news, Al. Are you settling in ok? Anything I can do to help?"

General Palmer shook his head, "Nope, just glad to be on the other side of the bridge, finally."

*Wonder what that means?* Josh thought.

"Well, we could not be more pleased to have you. And Bill, everything to your satisfaction?"

"Tell you tomorrow, Ms. Governor. Haven't really been all that briefed yet. But from what Ben told me, it should be an interesting command."

*Ben?* thought Josh. *Why would a State's Lieutenant Governor be briefing an Air Force General on anything? And what's so damn important for him to miss this party?*

"We can definitely make that promise, General. Well, if you gentlemen would talk to Joshua for a bit, I have some other Governors that I must check on."

The Generals nodded. After Sam walked away, all three Generals sipped on their drinks, silently. They were appraising Joshua before speaking. Stillwater mirrored their actions. He felt as though Sam's chit-chat with the four was a lot more than casual. He wished that everyone would stop talking in code so he would have some idea as to what was going on.

General Palmer broke the silence, "So, Captain, enjoying our State?"

"What I've seen of it. But that's Captain, retired," stumbled Josh.

"Not in my book, Captain. I knew Colonel Denning. Damn shame he resigned. Heard it was over you."

Josh tried to maintain a poker face. He hadn't followed anything in the military after his dismissal. He didn't know Denning had resigned, let alone over him. It appeared that these men were clued in on his past by Sam. *God,* he thought, *Is there anybody in this room that doesn't know the story of my life?* He felt a small shiver down his spine. *Maybe they also know what part of DHS I work for and why I'm here.*

"Don't know. Didn't keep in touch. We weren't buddies, him being a Colonel and me being a Captain."

Palmer's gaze softened, "Read your file, impressive, your field service, right up till you got shafted by politicians. Never personally experienced that shit so far down into the ranks before. Of course the four of us dealt with it on a daily basis. I'd apologize to you, but really wouldn't be worth much."

Josh just shrugged. No one had ever acknowledged his shafting before, and certainly not someone of these men's ranks. Josh stood a little taller and a little straighter, regaining some military bearing against the sulking stoop he had adopted over his past years of personal disgrace.

"You involved with Ben in Iran?"

"Iran? Ben?" was all he could respond.

Palmer nodded, knowing he had caught Stillwater off guard.

Josh tried to cover his surprise. *Ben had been in Iran? When, where?* Josh had always thought of him as a deskman in Intelligence, not a field Op. His mind flipped back to the KA-bar knife and the manner in which Ben had sloughed off the assassination attempt. Maybe there was more to Ben then he first thought. Maybe a whole lot more.

"I thought we sat that one out," was all Josh could muster.

Palmer nodded, "Officially, but Ben was in the thick of it."

Josh struggled to hide his shock. His best chance was to change the subject, "So what are your gentlemen's postings? I know General Roughton is Wyoming National Guard."

"Wyoming State Army," he corrected.

Josh nodded, not knowing what to say.

Palmer said, "I'm retired."

Josh wasn't going to let it drop there, "And before?"

"TRANSCOM. Supply"

Josh nodded. He knew what TRANSCOM was. He looked at Toomey for a response.

"Just took over Minot."

*Now this is interesting*, thought Josh, "Minot, huh. That's Minutemen III silos, isn't it?"

Toomey offered a brief nod, "Part of it. We have other Wings there too."

"Kind of a powerful command, holding so many nukes in your hand." commented Josh casually.

"Actually they are in the President's hand, along with Command Central. We really don't control anything from here unless they say push a button.

Even then, I don't know what would really happen. Our real job is to make sure they're ready to go and nobody gets to them before they fly."

Josh didn't take the comment as a rebuff. He knew it was how military men spoke.

"And you, General Grant. Warren's Minuteman also, isn't it?"

Grant shrugged, "Just like Minot, part of it."

Another round of silence fell before General Palmer spoke up, "What was your MOS – Military Occupational Specialty -?"

It gave him pride to say, "Special Forces, A-Team Leader."

Palmer raised his eyebrows in respect. Palmer spoke next, "See any action beyond Georgia?"

Josh sipped his drink and answered casually, "Nine major, and a baker's dozen of side jobs. All classified." He was telling them that if they didn't want to talk expansively, either would he.

Roughton followed up, "You went DHS?" His face appeared to sour at the speaking of the acronym.

Suddenly Josh felt ashamed. He again gave the all-purpose shrug, "Had to eat."

"What about contract work? Hear that pays real well," asked Roughton.

"I don't kill for money, General; bad Karma."

"And working for DHS is good Karma?" It was one of the Air Force Generals. Josh tried to recall his name; Toomey, that was it.

"General, Sir, I was, shall we say, *requested* to join DHS. I had the option of that or a six-by-eight in Leavenworth. They told me they didn't want my skill set to go to waste. Looking at the situation, I saw it the best option, at the time."

"And now?" The General wasn't fazed by his response.

Josh responded with a stony glare. Enough was enough. He wasn't in the military anymore and didn't have to endure a grilling. Besides, he was here as a guest, or so he had thought. He felt it was their turn to answer some questions. He turned to Palmer.

"General, what did you mean earlier that you were glad to be on this side of the bridge?"

"Well Captain, it means after serving the Federal Government honorably for thirty-two years, I am glad to be home."

Josh thought his use of the Federal Government strange. Any military man would have said my *Country* or our *Nation*.

"You originally from Wyoming?"

Palmer nodded, "All of us. Sam had to bestow Honorary Citizenship on Toomey, though. Poor bastard has to serve his time in South Dakota."

The four military leaders laughed. Josh didn't join in. *There it is, again. This Citizen bullshit*, he thought.

"Aren't all four of you Citizens of the United States of America? And don't you, General Toomey, General Grant, still work for the President of same country?"

Four pairs of eyes looked at each other conspiratorially.

"I currently serve at the President's pleasure."

"Currently?" asked Josh.

Again Toomey looked at the other Air Force officer. "I might be resigning soon."

"Resigning or retiring?" pressed Josh.

"Same difference," shrugged Toomey.

"Not when it comes to pensions." Josh gave no quarter.

The General stiffened and bore his eyes upon Josh, "Captain, I find your comments bordering on impudent. However, I will tell you there are ideals worth fighting for far more important than a pension." He turned to his cohorts, "Generals, excuse me for a moment. My drink needs freshening." Grant followed.

Roughton gave Stillwater a tight look and then turned, "Hold up, I'll join you."

Palmer stayed in place, appraising Josh while sipping his drink.

"Didn't mean to knock anybody on their brass," Josh's tone was affable.

"Yes you did." Palmer smiled. "I remember when I was a Captain, Josh. I didn't much care for the brass either. Can't imagine how you feel after being shafted by them."

"No you couldn't, General. But that's neither here or there. I want to know why you four consider being a Citizen of Wyoming a higher station than a Citizen of our Nation?"

"You can be pretty direct for a Wyoming boy, Josh."

"I passed *boy* a long time ago, just about the time I left this State."

"Ran away, don't you mean?"

Josh's face burned. He knew the General was baiting him, but he didn't know why. He wasn't about to turn from this confrontation. He wanted some answers.

"You going to answer the question, or just try to get me riled."

Palmer gave him a half smile, "That 'bridge' I spoke of crossing with Governor Warner, it was over my personal Rubicon. If you want a direct answer, Josh, I do not consider my Citizenship within the United States my first loyalty. The State of Wyoming comes first in that department. That direct enough for you?"

Josh wasn't backing down, "And the other three?"

"They will have to decide, on their own, if they are crossing that same bridge, and soon."

"Why soon?"

"Because the timing of events dictates so."

"What events?" Josh felt as though he were chasing this elusive rabbit down the hole.

"My God, Stillwater. Don't you watch the news? There's seventy-five thousand Federal troops less than fifty miles from this city."

"And how does that play with your former position in the U.S. Army?

"When it comes to my State or the Federal Army, I am on the righteous side of my State. As for the others, you would have to ask them. Now, if you excuse Captain, I'm going to reload." He smiled, lifted his empty glass, jingled the ice cubes and walked away.

## Chapter 19

## Riding the Rails

Ben knew it was going to be a rough ride, but he had no idea how rough. Army boxcars and flatbeds weren't spec'd with the cushioned ride of passenger trains. And nearly thirty hours later, his body had been shaken and pounded to the degree that he didn't know if his outsides or insides hurt worst. He had laid out his foam sleeping pad when he first set up bivouc under the tarpaulin. Yet now it felt as thin as paper between his bruised rear and the steel deck below. It had been his first priority to cut a slit in the covering so he could peer out and keep track of the trip. But sitting up undera low-belly mobile cannon had put the punishment squarely on his posterior. So he reverted to spending hours laying on his back, side or belly, spreading the jarring load over a greater surface area. He checked his watch often, calculating the train's speed and estimating the distance covered. Outside the dark silhouettes of the countryside appeared the same, mile after mile. Seeing out did not have the same urgency as in the beginning. Now he just lay on his back,

Again, he scanned his luminescent wristwatch and mentally clicked off the hours before he would go into action.

He played the small beam of his flashlight along the underside of the heavy armament hovering above. He had read a thousand times the words NOT FOR FIELD SERVICE stenciled upon an access plate. By now he had memorized every tread and torsion bar of the MGV, or Manned Ground Vehicle. It was a self-propelled artillery piece, this one specific to the NLOS - Non Line Of Sight-, one-hundred and fifty-five millimeter cannon. The advantages of this powerful weapon excited Ben. It was light-weight and maneuverable, weighing less than twenty-five tons, cannon mounted. It was rapid fire, laying a barrage down with only nine seconds between shell explosions. It handled a variety of shells that could be interspersed during action: air burst, impact, illumination, even tactical nuclear. And it could do it all from ten kilometers away without visual contact of the enemy, hence the NLOS designation. Firing solutions were plotted via GPS and networking systems. A real advantage to Wyoming was the weapon only required a two-man crew. Ben knew there were four of these mobile cannons aboard the train. This combination could break the back of a tank assault, annihilate armored convoys, pound dug-in or hardened enemy positions. But Ben had a different use in mind.

Even if this crazy plan worked, Ben wondered if all this materiel would actually make a difference. It was in the field that he was most sanguine about the odds of their plans' success. Although the armaments aboard this train were enough to equip his State's warriors, it was only a fraction of what the combined U.S. military forces could bring to bear against their small revolt. At home, he always felt buoyed by the 'can do' spirit of his Wyoming brethren. But out here among their adversary it seemed as if they were playing at toy soldiers. Still, he would not fail to do his part. If it didn't work out, he was probably going to be one the first in line for the firing squad. But, he knew, he would be within the finest company. He actually loved his role. He had been trained for it and his exploits during his tenure in Military Intelligence showed he was good at it. He just wished he had someone else he could rely on. Someone that had survived situations as desperate as those demanding his best talents. He thought, *Josh Stillwell can fill the bill, if Sam works her magic.*

When it came to the Wyoming cause, no one was more persuasive than his sister. And Ben knew Josh was vulnerable to more than Sam's logic. He was in love with her. Ben thought that if his father had not been so stiff-minded and arrogant, Josh might be sitting next to him right now. Under the best circumstances, it was a tall order to convince a dedicated and hardened soldier to switch sides. Josh's sense of duty, honor and loyalty, blended with his personal antipathy of Charlie Warner, would be a tough nut to crack. Yet Sam seemed so positive that Josh would come around. Ben had no idea from where her confidence sprang. But he knew Sam's indomitable spirit had brought the miracle of Wyoming into being. A rose in the desert, she had called the transformation of their State into a social and economic success. And that's how most viewed his sister, a rose in the desert. Maybe she could bring Josh around. Ben had grown up with Josh and would have trusted him with his life. *But does the returning man still have the same heart as the boy who left? Probably not,* Ben thought as he crawled from underneath the artillery piece and peered once more through the knife slit into the darkening night.

## Chapter 20

## Lightoiler

### Governor's Mansion, Cheyenne

Cocktails greased the gears of conversation that wound upward in volume. The next two greetings were more relaxed for Josh. The first was Jake Dillon and the second was a round-faced man with a full beard. He was of medium height, thin and dressed rather nondescript. But Joshua was struck by his face. Something about this man was definitely familiar to Josh. He felt he knew him, but from where? Maybe he was the father of one of his school mates. The thought wouldn't come and he just waited for an introduction.

"The first one will be easy," Sam said to Josh. "Hello, Jake. How is Louise? She busy for tonight's dinner?"

Jake had already stuck his hand out and was shaking Josh's, "Naw, she didn't want to come. It's her bridge night. You'd think it was a high stakes poker game with the importance she puts on it. Besides, I didn't invite her. Told her it was stag. But I got tripped up when I said it was at the Governor's. She said last time she checked, you were no man. I told her she should stop checking things like that. They have laws against it, don't they Guv?"

The four had a good laugh and then Sam introduced the other man. "Joshua Stillwater, Charles Lightoiler. Charles, Joshua." The man shook Josh's hand. Josh did not let go for a few seconds. He stared deep into the man's eyes and said, "Have we met before? You look awfully familiar."

Lightoiler thought for a moment and shook his head, "No, I can't say I recognize you, or the name. I think I'd remember a big guy like you."

Joshua was irritated at himself. In his line of work facial recognition was a necessary skill. Even posture and gait could give a disguised perp – perpetrator - away. But Charles didn't seem like a guy that had committed some crime. He was relaxed, even casual and looked Josh directly in the eyes, unblinking.

"Your name sounds familiar, too."

Charles chuckled. "I get that a lot. Same name as the second officer on the Titanic. Enforced the Women-and-children-only rule up to the last lifeboat. He was washed overboard as the ship sank and was the last survivor picked up by the *Carpathia*, perhaps a metaphor for the nation and Wyoming."

Joshua didn't know this guy's role in the State, but a metaphor could provide his thinking, "How so?"

"Easy. Wyoming tossed me a lifeline while I thrashed about in tumultuous seas, brought on by the sinking of the nation."

*Another deserter*, thought Josh. "So, what do you do here?"

Lightoiler thought a moment before answering, "I'm a type of….painter: one of landscapes. I am painting landscapes of Wyoming for the rest of the nation to see what I see. It is such a magnificent State. Don't you agree?"

Josh shrugged, "Parts, I guess." *There's more to this guy than this BS*, he thought.

Lightoiler tacked away from himself, "Stillwater, huh. I fancy myself an amateur genealogist; trace back names to countries and such. Your name English?"

Josh didn't release his stare, "No."

Sam entered the conversation, "Josh is half Indian, or Native American if you choose. Stillwater was his father's tribal name. Shoshoni, wasn't it Josh?"

Josh felt the weight of the large chip on his shoulder. *Why say* half *Indian? Sam knows I'm sensitive to that. It's like saying* half-breed. She had never goaded him before. Maybe the comment was innocent. He tried to hide his annoyance when he answered, "Yeah, Shoshoni."

Lightoiler nodded as if this had some significance, "Should have guessed. Your darker complexion and that massive head of dark hair. Gives new meaning to the 'jet' in 'jet black'."

*What the hell does that mean*, Joshua thought? He started to get irritated and didn't know what to say. He just shrugged. Jake noticed him becoming uncomfortable and intervened, "Josh, Jeff is here. He's standing over there with Jimmy. Why don't you go regulate his alcohol consumption? He gets all sad-sack when he drinks too much."

***

Jeff and Jimmy Dillon were brothers, yet the two were different in so many ways. Physically, they were both tall, six-feet-two. But where Jeff was stout, even developing a 'spare tire' around the middle, Jimmy was trim and athletic. Jeff was the successful director of the family company, *Dillon Enterprises* which focused on markets that his father had exploited for a lifetime: beef, lamb, coal, uranium and real estate. He was affable, out-going and wore emotions upon his sleeve. This last characteristic became more pronounced with the addition of large quantities of alcohol. His drinking was prodigious, if not legendary. In college, Josh had suffered this same reputation. But the military's discipline put his self-destruction behind.

Excepting their mutual heights, Jimmy could not be more different from his brother. He was lanky, sporting a runner or swimmer's body. He was friendly to those he trusted and guarded to all others; over the years it was his shield for secreting his sexual preference. Jimmy was gay.

Next to Jimmy was his life-partner William. For twelve years they had been married; a marriage recognized under a Wyoming constitutional law had been debated, voted upon and approved by a two-thirds majority. At five foot eight, bearing small features, William could be considered petite. His wavy hair, bronzed skin and nearly-feminine features produced a scaled Adonis.

William and Jimmy's union had produced a child via surrogacy. With Jimmy's and William's sister's contribution, the couple had created their son, Bernard. Both Jimmy and William were graduated PHD's from MIT; specializing in electro, chemical and nano-engineering. Their union had birthed not only Bernard, but an increasingly successful company: *Dillon & Dillon, Inc.* Harnessing their stratospheric IQ's to their educational foci, the male pair developed a profusion of futuristic products: quick-charging battery skins; superconducting, mag-lev, high-speed trains; superconducting, underground electrical transmission lines; and the *360i* : a round wheel/tire assembly able to rotate upon any three-hundred-and-sixty degree plane. It had become a mainstay of Wyoming's advanced automobile industry.

And, suspected by Josh, the wheel had transformed from civilian use to a military weapon.

During his visit to *Dillon & Dillon,* Josh had ignored Jimmy's instructions to avoid a specific, restricted manufacturing area. Seeking information for the DDD, Josh surreptitiously gained discovery of the *360i* being mated to weaponry. His brief glance of the assembly had produced a sea of questions and, to date, no answers for Josh. His information gathering had been truncated by a weapon-toting, serious-looking Wyoming Army squad. Since this moment, Jimmy had become wary of Josh's intentions.

*And with good reason*, thought Josh trying to wash the guilt from his mind.

***

Sam had also picked up on Josh's discomfort at the Indian comments. She said, "Yes, Josh. Why don't you do that? I certainly don't have to introduce you. I'll go check on the other guests. No telling what wild stories are circulating within this bunch. Alright with you?" She was gently rubbing his arm while she spoke.

Josh nodded and took one more look at Lightoiler. He knew this guy, somehow, and was sure he didn't like him. Lightoiler said, casually, "Nice to meet you, Josh. I'm sure we'll talk more this evening."

Josh turned back his head as Sam led him away, "Count on it."

# Chapter 21

## Wait And Watch

## On Board

The darkened mood with which Ben pondered the future seemed almost cheery compared to another car down the line. Tex had gone from fear at nearly killing himself during boarding to anger over his lost Tony Lamas boot, to self-pity over the continuous pounding of his all-ready bruised body; to, finally, a permanent brooding fueled by lack of food and water. How the hell was he expected to know this fanatic's plan was to jump a freight train and take a ride across the country? Sure, Warner knew where *he* was going, so he was prepared with *his* precious backpack, probably loaded with food and water. Tex had not one opportunity to track his location.

In the early hours of the next morning, the train had stopped and backed onto a spur. The resulting jolt led Tex to think they were coupling or uncoupling cars. He took the opportunity to read station signs on the track switches. They all began with the same stenciled letters, Albuq. It wasn't difficult to deduce they were in Albuquerque, New Mexico. *But why?* He had no idea. He furiously calculated if it would be a good opportunity to jump off, find a phone and call Maxton. But odds were that Warner would see him either disembark or re-board. Maybe he could abandon the mission, saying Warner had jumped and then Tex lost him during pursuit. Maxton would be furious and berate the agent. Then Tex's effort and suffering to this moment were for naught. And if the train departed without him, Maxton would chew him out for not sticking with the target. There really wasn't an upside, so he stayed put.

After the train pulled out from Albuquerque and gained speed northward Tex continued to mentally chide himself for leaving his cellphone behind. He had no idea where the assemblage of train, military hardware, Ben Warner and he were headed. With a phone he could have called in reinforcements or had supplies waiting up the line; or had gotten info on his location and possible destination. He tried to lick his cracked and wind-burnt lips, but had no moisture left upon his tongue.

While Warner could sit around and wait or even sleep, Tex had to maintain a constant vigil. He had no idea how or when Ben would make his next move. So Tex sat upright under the tarp, peering through a slice in a tarpaulin similar to Ben's. Instead of looking at the countryside, Tex had knifed his slot towards the front. This way he could, hopefully, keep an eye on his target. The problem with this strategy was that the wind blew directly into his eyes. He had no way to protect them except to continually turn away and blink back some moisture. His eyes were red, itchy and blurry. The monocular had fallen from his pants pocket during the tumultuous boarding. He couldn't use it during daylight hours. But it would have been a lot easier at night.

Enduring another day under cover, Tex noted the train's reduced speed as it struggled up an increasing grade. They were definitely climbing. The ascent took most of the daylight hours. He surmised they were ascending the plateau that was eastern Colorado. At the top it would be flat until, to the West, it met the Rocky Mountains. The encroaching darkness of another nightfall brought relief from the stifling heat under the tarpaulin. But one extreme led to another as the elevation cooled off the air beyond Tex's comfort. It was downright cold. Tex shivered in his lightweight clothing.

Rubbing his eyes once more, Tex peered through his slit and tensed when he thought he saw movement. Four flatbeds up, a dark figure crawled from underneath a tarp. Tex watched it stand, pull on a pair of goggles and look in his direction. Tex jerked his head away from the slit and sat back. *It has to be Warner*, he thought. *Which way is he heading?* He watched the figure as best he could in the rushing wind. It seemed to have something strapped to its waist. Tex was pretty sure it was a side arm. He thought, *Guess I brought a knife to a gun fight. But if* Baby *and me get the drop on him, he won't stand a chance.* He patted the knife stuck in his lone boot and sneered.

***

Four cars north of Tex, Ben shook away any doubts and rechecked his watch. It was action time. In Albuquerque, the train had joined up with the DARTS launchers. At present, they were just clearing Denver and the engulfing darkness meant 'show time!' He ate an MRE and chugged the last of his water. He felt rejuvenated as he was an action junkie, relishing the adrenaline rush that now pulsed within. He grabbed the rucksack with one hand and slithered out from underneath the tarpaulin.

His mission was to keep the train rolling north, without the scheduled stop at Ft. Collins. Free from the stale odors underneath the heavy plastic, he sucked in fifty-mile-per-hour air rushing at him. It was a relief to be out of the heat and humidity of the South. Now up on the Colorado plains, the cool night air was as dry as in Wyoming. He pulled down night vision goggles over his eyes and surveyed the train following behind. There were nine flatbeds before he hit a boxcar. This would speed things up for he only had to jump between these before having to scale boxcars. He reached in the backpack and pulled out a holster with a gun strapped inside. It was an unusual looking weapon with a long narrow barrel and a plastic grip. The holster had no waist belt, but clipped onto his belt, with the bottom toe attaching itself to Velcro sewn onto his pants. On the side of the holster was a strip containing five cartridges. The unusual bullets had red plastic end caps where normally would be the primer pin. Next, he retrieved a stick of black camo grease, raised his NVA's to the top of his night cap, and then used the stick to draw irregular streaks of black across his face and neck.

Retrieving the rucksack, Ben dropped the grease stick within, removed a bundle of black sticks and dropped the bag to the steel deck. He tugged the sticks outward, pulling at the elastic cord that connected them. To the unknowing it looked similar to flexible camping tent struts that, decades past, had replaced wooden poles. He spun the system of struts around so that one end, perpendicular to the frame, was at top. He bent over and rummaged through the rucksack until he found a pair of large rubber blocks. These he snapped onto the top protruding struts. Each rubber foot was formed with large saw-like teeth. He looked appraisingly at the assembled ladder and nodded. He muttered, "That William is pretty damn creative."

He picked up the knapsack, unfurled the straps, feed his arms through and hefted the bag high up his shoulders. He grabbed the ultra-light ladder, and slid his hand along the strut until it reached the balance point. He pulled down the goggles, let his eyes orient to the greenish glow and calculated his distance. Then he took off in a run towards the rear of the train. He cleared the first void easily, jumping from his flatbed to the next, aided by the wind at his back. He kept running and repeated the maneuver again and again.

***

Ben unknowingly ran past Tex who was taking in the scene from his slit in the tarp. Tex straightened as the moonlit outline ran past him towards the end of the flatbed. The figure leaped, cleared the gap between cars, and landed while maintaining a sprint.

Tex hesitated to attack Warner as he passed. There were still too many questions as to the purpose of this train ride. He had to scope things out until he had more answers.

*What in the hell is he up to?* Tex quizzed. *Thought for sure he'd be going forward toward the engines. Where the hell did he get a ladder?* Tex thought about following, but had no idea how he could do it and still keep out of sight. *Has to come back this way*, he tried to convince himself. His options were limited    so    he    thought    it    best    to    wait    and    see.

# Chapter 22

## Gold

### Governor's Mansion, Cheyenne

Before Josh had made his way to Jeff, a word spoken from his right caught his attention. It was *gold* and appeared to be central to a roundhouse conversation with a group containing the four visiting Governors plus Senator Russell Colter, Dr. Milton Bern, and a new face Josh had not seen prior. As he sauntered towards the group, he grabbed hors d'oeuvres from a platter circulated by a member of the staff. Looking towards the group, he asked to the waiter aside, "Who is that man over there with the Governors, the one in the gray suit?"

She looked over her shoulder, spotted the reference and said, "Him? That's Nevin Stiles, one of the richest men in this room, advisor to four Presidents, including President Rivera. But he walked away from that gig. Apparently the President didn't like what Mr. Stiles had to tell him."

Josh looked at the server with some surprise on his face. He wasn't expecting such an in-depth bio from one of the staff. He was even more surprised to recognize Sam's EA wearing a waiter's waist coat. She noted his look and smiled, "Remember me? His eyes surveyed the tall woman. He had not paid sufficient attention to her physical details when they first met. His thoughts had been completely upon Sam. But now he noted her remarkable beauty. She was young, under thirty, svelte with an athletic shape. Her hair was bobbed shoulder-length, not quite as blonde as Sam's, but more brunette with interwoven golden strands. Her face was flawless, sporting minimal makeup. Her smile was large, exposing perfectly white teeth.

Josh stumbled in response to his new found assessment of this beauty, "Ah, jeese…ah, I'm sorry, Caroline. I didn't recognize you before…I, ah mean, I didn't recognize you tonight."

She chuckled, "It's alright. I understand completely, particularly being dressed in this outfit. One of the staff had to go home early, family emergency. So I offered to pick up the slack. Must pitch in where needed, right?"

Josh nodded and smiled, "Thank you, Caroline, and please call me Josh."

"No problem, Josh. You need the 411 on anybody else, just come find me. I'm here till the last dog is hung." She and the platter moved on to another group.

Josh laughed to himself. He hadn't heard the *dog hung* phrase since he left Wyoming. He watched her walk with a flowing grace. The view from behind was as stimulating as the front. He shook his head, trying to remember what caught his attention before Caroline. In a moment, he grabbed the thread, *Gold.*

He tore his eyes away from Caroline's departure, turned and walked over to the group and sidled up behind the current speaker, Governor John Hughes of Nevada.

"I've seen the New York Reserve's pile of gold. Can you match theirs?"

"Seen it recently?" asked Professor Bern, casually.

"No, it was about ten years ago, actually."

Bern nodded, a thin smile pressed on his lips, "The State's reserves are impressive. And we guard them zealously. It represents over fifteen years effort of a people dedicated to a cause: the financial stability of the Wyoming Credits along with the stability of their futures."

Governor Hughes followed up. "So what gives your currency stability? The NUS is pegged to gold, although they constantly adjust the rate. Why isn't it stable?"

Stiles responded, "That's a joke. The Federal Government can adjust all they want. They are trying to sell a fraud to the international gold markets. No industrialized country on earth will accept the NUS as payment. They want gold. So the Federal Government attempts to fight off the inflationary wolves by artificially pegging gold to an arbitrary, and may I say, unrealistically low amount of NUS. But their trading partners aren't buying it. As I said, the markets set the rate. So the Feds are forced to constantly raise the amount of NUS against an ounce of gold.

The Federal government has tried to mask bad fiscal policy through monetary policy. It doesn't work. Constant deficit spending combined with massive pumping of the money supply has produced one notable record for this government. At sixty trillion dollars, the U.S. national debt is nearly forty percent greater than the GDP – Gross Domestic Product – of the country. When debt exceeds GDP, every single dollar spent is pure inflation. And we can certainly see the results of this."

Governor Fodor of Colorado spoke up, "Rivera says we can grow the economy past the debt and then begin to pay it off with cheaper dollars."

Bern chuckled, "Well, he has one part right: cheaper dollars." He turned serious, "As to 'outgrowing' the debt, let me provide a salient point. *If* U.S. economic growth were at zero today, it would take twenty years of ten percent growth for GDP to surpass the debt. But the economy is not even at zero. It is currently running at a negative three to five percent each year. This translates to a requirement of thirteen to fifteen percent growth annually just to overcome the debt level. When was the last time you heard of any industrialized economy growing at that rate? Maybe some third world nation that ultimately collapses in a monetary heap.

And adding fuel to the inflationary flame, Rivera and Congress continue to increase deficits to make up for a failing economy. This adds to inflation, increases the debt and increases the interest on the debt. In order to finance this debt, interest rates continue to spiral to astronomical levels, sopping up desperately needed capital for business. And the economy staggers further into negative territory."

Governor Almondo asked, "So attaching the dollar to a gold standard would solve the U.S's economic woes?"

Bern shook his head, "Absolutely not. In the first place, a gold standard is nothing more than an unbiased assessor of fiscal and monetary policy. If there is no discipline, the dollar will still be ravaged by rising gold prices. Nothing has been accomplished."

"So what's the point of gold?" sniffed Governor Fodor. "Why put your economy under the thumb of a metal ore? Sure, it's shiny, but what's the big deal? We've been off the gold standard for over a half century. Most of that time, our economy was in pretty good shape. Isn't everything based upon faith and credit, either an individual or a nation?"

Bern smiled, "Politicians wish it were so. In reality, the world has always been on the gold standard, Governor. After the Second Great War, we were on it. This ended in the seventies and our world economic dominance allowed us to roll along, printing more specie each year, far beyond our economic growth. The world was always measuring us through gold. It measured as gold was at one-hundred-and forty-Old-US-per-ounce of gold when President Nixon abandoned the *Bretton Woods Agreement*. It measured as gold soared to eight-hundred Old US in the nineteen-eighties. It measured as gold began its real climb in the beginning of this new millinnium so that it is over six-thousand New US per ounce, and rising. You see, Governor, the world has always been measuring us. And gold has always been the yardstick. What changed is that, in the distant past, our credit was worthy enough that other countries accepted our payment of trade deficits in dollars, based on what gold said it was worth. When we abandoned any sense of fiscal discipline in 2009 and beyond, the world said our credit was no longer good. Payment would only be accepted in gold."

"Okay, but why gold? Why not coal, or diamonds?" pestered Fodor.

"Gold has history. It has always been recognized as *the* royal metal, going back to such disparate civilizations as Egyptian Pharos and Incan Indians. It's value as a medium of exchange is that it cannot be artificially manufactured; it is a scarce ore; it is immune to physical degradation; it is easily recognizable in purest form; it has a low melting point for smelting and, due to its malleability, can be stamped into coins. Because of its intrinsic value, gold gained an acquired value by all nations on earth; this translates to universal acceptance, a world standard. All nations and all people agree that gold is *the* universal medium of exchange. This was decided millenniums ago. All of these factors led gold to become the medium of value. True, there have been wild swings in the gold's value against one currency or another. But that is reflective of the oscillations of the currency, not of gold. Generally, these swings are in direct correlation to the money policies of the society issuing the currency."

Governor Hughes interjected, "Okay, here's a criticism of gold I've heard from economists: due to its scarcity, gold supply cannot expand at the same rate as a growing economy."

The comment caused Bern to scrunch his nose as if he had smelled something bad, "This is absurd drivel. A nation has the ability to grow their currency at any rate it chooses. What so-called economists are really demeaning is the ability of a universally accepted measurement of the value of their currency. If you had one bar of gold and only one printed note, or specie, the note would be valued at a one-to-one ratio with the value of the gold bar. Add another specie and the value of each is one-half the value of the gold bar. This is not good or bad. It is simply a valuation that is non-arguable in a foreign currency exchange market. What allows specie to grow in volume without appreciably dropping its valuation against the gold bar is what the society does with the specie. If it is used to create goods and services valued by the rest of the world, and those goods and services are exported, then the value of the specie vis-à-vis gold is relatively stable, the reason being that new wealth has been acquired by the society. That wealth generally takes form of receiving other currencies, if they are deemed credit worthy in relation to gold. These currencies can be used to produce more wealth or to buy more gold."

"But isn't investing in your people and your society a form of wealth generation? Isn't an educated man, a healthy society, or a new highway as much an investment as a new factory? You seem to put a high degree of importance on it here in Wyoming, social programs I mean." Governor Almondo was pleased with his observation.

Nevin Stiles touched Bern's leg, "Let me field this one, Milton. Bern nodded and Stiles began, "Well, yes and no. We care about our Citizens. We want them educated. We want them healthy. We want them to enjoy the world around them. But, this is not wealth generation in and of itself. Actually it is the opposite. An educated man who spends his day contemplating the number of angels on a pin head, or a well society that goes off hiking all day, every day, or a society spending its transportation budget on building roads only to resorts, all have one thing in common. Nothing is produced yet it all must be maintained. These are *expenses* to society, not wealth producers. An investment in education should result in new industries, more efficient manufacturing processes or new and innovative goods and services. A well society should have people in a better condition to do their daily tasks and to miss less sick days from that task. A new road should carry more goods, faster and cheaper to new markets. If this is accomplished, then all the above *is* an investment. Otherwise it is just a drag upon the economic wheel of a society. It becomes an expense."

"I apologize for jumping from one point to the next, but could you explain something? How did you get the Wyoming Credit started? I mean, how did you acquire the gold to support it? What did you buy the gold with? Utah used to accept gold and silver as legal tender but now are stuck with the dollar." queried Governor Elizabeth Brigham.

Bern resumed answering, "Asset pledging. Many of the people in this room pledged their life's work, their net worth to get us started. These men received large, fixed loans in dollars by pledging their lands, their buildings, their businesses, and their savings. They negotiated a moratorium of one year on payments. They gave our Central Bank the dollars and the Bank issued them interest-bearing bonds in WC. The State then issued as many bonds, in Old US, as the bond markets could swallow. Then we did a little foreign currency speculation, primarily shorting the dollar, and used our proceeds to purchase gold. We started paying our own Citizenry in Wyoming Credits and made all payments to the State mandatory in WC's.  Once other States and other nations knew our Credits were not only backed by gold, but convertible to the precious metal, the WC became much more valuable than the ever-falling dollar.  This accomplished, we started paying off the bonds the State had issued in an even cheaper currency, the NUS.  Rivera could not have done us a bigger favor than devaluing the dollar by replacing it with New U.S.  Destabilizing any remaining faith in U.S. currency increased inflation of the specie against gold even more dramatically.  As gold gained nearly six-thousand percent against the NUS, the President had successfully cut our State's debt, and that of our benefactors, by six-thousand percent.  Our timing, or actually Rivera's timing, could not have been better, for us.  So in a major way, we have the Federal Government to thank for our success.  Their irresponsible fiscal policies actually bankrolled our WC.

Governor Fodor asked, "So what is the value of a WC against gold.  What have you pegged it at?"

"We don't".

"I don't understand," queried the Governor.  "Doesn't any government on the gold standard specify what the convertible rate of their currency is against gold?"

"Yes, most do.  But this is a bit fraudulent.  If I tell you what the value of my currency is, you have two choices.  Accept it or not.  I am still free to pursue any monetary policy I wish, because I am only going to pay so much gold no matter how much specie I print.  Currency markets will play this game only so long.  The valuation of one currency against the other is not controlled by any government.  It is controlled by markets.  In the past, currencies were pegged against gold at fixed prices mainly for stability between governments as regards currency exchanges.  It worked as long as governments within the agreement maintained some semblance of a sound fiscal and monetary policy.  By the 1970's, this had pretty well ended and Nixon stopped the charade by removing the U.S. from a fixed gold standard.  Within five years, gold rose over fifty percent as valued against the Old US dollar.

So, no, we skipped that game.  We have nothing like the Federal Reserve.  We have no economists consulting magic eight-balls to decide our monetary and fiscal policies.  The WC floats on the open gold market and every day we issue, publicly, the size of our gold reserves.  We have set a fixed-range within which we must keep the WC.  It is 34 to 35 WC per ounce of gold.  This amounts to a three percent fluctuation.  And this rate is cast in stone within our constitution.  We adjust our money supply to maintain this range. We do not adjust the rate to accommodate an arbitrary money supply. We have an algorithm that was developed by leading mathematicians and statisticians over a ten year period. This is also now incorporated into our constitution and cannot be changed without great effort. The value of the WC against gold is on automatic pilot. Our economy has grown at enviable rates as compared to the nation. But the WC stays at the same rate. The world values this stability. Therefore it values Wyoming Credits."

This spiked a thought from Fodor, "What about world fluctuations? I mean, every time there is some crisis in some part of the world, everyone races into gold. Doesn't that create wild swings in the WC?"

Bern nodded, "Yes it can. However, a growing situation we've found is that these same persons, multi-national corporations and nations flock not only to gold but to our WC as well. Much as the Swiss Franc, the WC has become an international 'haven' currency. There are two solutions to this. The first is to do nothing. What I mean is that as there is a 'run' or panic buying of gold, many also buy the WC, as it is convertible to gold." The older man chuckled, "They consider it 'diversifying.' Yet, in actuality, they are buying gold in both instances.

What occurs is that the WC and gold track nearly at the same ratio. It is against other currencies that the WC rate substantially changes, not against gold. But I do not deny there are times of substantial flux. Due to this, we only make adjustments via our currency issuance or buying every six months and we use a running prior-six-month valuation of gold. This substantially smoothes the curve and allows fluctuations to have less impact."

Most of the group nodded understanding while Governor Fodor pressed on, "What is your economy's rate of growth?"

"Four percent. It was lower in the beginning as we scrimped to build our gold reserves. But now it remains stable at four percent."

"Four percent? That's certainly not great. The Chinese beat that number." Fodor's response was acerbic.

"True. They also have a billion people to feed on limited resources. And they constantly have to be vigilant of inflation creeping into the Yuan. Their economy has performed remarkably while the West has been in economic decline. But with such population pressure, China has to grow their economy faster or face civil unrest. It is a balancing game for them, one I do not envy.

On the other hand, our economy grows at a very stable rate. We control our population numbers by tightly controlling immigration. We want to take care of *our* Citizens, not those of the world. A four percent growth rate keeps our Citizens near full employment, our factories running near full capacity, and our inflation rate nearly zero. Our Citizens value stability over inflationary booms and deflationary busts that could wipe out their previous efforts."

"Beings you brought up the word 'deflation,'" interjected Governor Almondo, "What about the deflationary aspects of a gold standard. Isn't that what happened in the last depression, the one of the nineteen-thirties. The dollar became worth more and there were less dollars."

Bern replied, "Yes, there was deflation. However, there was not less dollars, in the sense that they had disappeared. What really happened was a loss of credit. The credit bubble burst. In this instance it was credit of margin on stock purchases. And after the bust, those holding dollars did not have faith enough to reinvest in economy. Roosevelt lashed out at those holding their money tightly as *hoarders*. He tried to paint the monied as unpatriotic. Yet, at the same time he was proposing a slurry of programs considered socialistic, raising income taxes, passing detrimental economic laws and began deficit spending in earnest. I would have thought twice about investing my money as well. That is a real problem with socialist Presidents, be they Roosevelt or Rivera and all shades of pink in between. They think that a President actually controls an economy and can dictate how individuals should respond. Of course they are constantly thwarted. This leads to their frustration and increasing tendency to autocracy.

What these President's seem to miss, term after term, is that constant meddling within an economy, constant money supply swings, deficit spending, new economic and regulatory laws, increased social programs…all of this leads to volatility. And only Casino Capitalists gain from volatility, not the economy. It is the function of government to provide a solid fiscal system, unburden free enterprise from social costs and minimize government intrusion into the market place. This provides stability. And stability is the environment in which Creation Capitalists and entrepreneurs thrive. Stability is the fertile soil of real investment; investment that leads to an expanding economy, new industries and quality jobs. Money does not require faith if it is backed by gold. But an economy grows on faith that one's investment will not be confiscated and shall be returned, with a gain. This is pure logic, not rocket science. If you explain it to your Citizens properly, they will never buy the socialist promises of blue skies, a life of leisure and free desserts.

As to deflation, yes it occurred in the nineteen-thirties. However, it was not caused by a gold standard. In reality, a fixed-range gold standard would have prevented the economic collapse of the thirties. If such a standard existed, the Federal Reserve would have increased the money supply by nearly thirty-three percent. The reason: in 1933 the Fed had an increase in their gold supply exceeding thirty-three percent. The increase was due to a sharp rise in American exports and the subsequent receipt of international gold payments. But the Fed took the opposite step. Instead of increasing the money supply, the Fed raised interest rates in response to the credit bubble of 1928, even though it had burst in 1929. That is exactly why we do not rely upon human intervention for calculating when and not when to buy gold."

"So who is to say that you actually have the gold in reserve that you say you do?" Governor Almondo asked skeptically.

Stiles answered, "We have an international commission. Members from India, China, Japan, Switzerland and Germany evaluate and publish our gold reserves. They weigh it, randomly assay it, count it and publish a value that has always matched what we publish. In the beginning, they came once a month. Now it is twice a year and they have requested to change it to an annual audit. We are so inclined if it is acceptable to our major trading partners."

"So do you have more gold than Fort Knox?" asked Governor Brigham. Josh was definitely interested in this answer.

Nevin Stiles harrumphed, "Fort Knox has been empty for years. Our President used it as a last ditch effort to support the dollar. He went on the open market and bought as many dollars as he could, using the gold in Fort Knox and the New York Reserve. And, if you're not aware, most of the gold in N.Y. Reserve actually belongs to other countries. It was an honor system that Rivera dishonored. No one should be surprised that the world insists on gold as payment versus the NUS. When countries like China found out, it almost caused a war. Rivera issued them variable-interest I.O.U.'s in the form of thirty-year T-Bills. But he could have issued them toilet paper for any faith they put in those instruments. It was all a waste of motion on the President's part anyway. His gold stealing had no impact on the NUS as the same amount of currency that he retired had been printed and spent before the dollar purchasing even concluded."

Governor Fodor wasn't buying this story, "Very few persons are allowed into the New York Reserve or Fort Knox. You know this for sure?"

"Yes. First, because China is one of our largest trading partners and their President, Win-Shi, told us of Rivera's shenanigans. And second, we bought the U.S. insignia gold bars from the foreign treasuries that sold the dollars. " Stiles face hinted at sadness.

Utah Governor Brigham stated almost innocently, "I don't think the American people would be too happy if they found out all their gold was gone."

Bern sadly shook his head, "I think they are beyond caring. Their currency has already fallen six thousand percent against gold prices. Should that not have been enough of a clarion call? The public cannot claim ignorance when the facts are readily available."

Governor Hughes emphasized her first statement, "Still, I think some heads will roll if they find out."

Stiles interceded, "*When* they find out, you mean. And yes, heads will roll. That is the mentality of the mob, or as the rest of the country refers to them, the electorate. They vote someone into office that promises to fix all their problems without ever saying how he or she will do it. A people deserve the government they receive. They don't want to hear the truth because the truth might involve discipline, sacrifice and pain. They would rather take the slow downward spiral of a worse tomorrow than face their problems today."

"So where do you keep all this gold?" Governor Fodor asked.

Stiles answered, "There are only eleven people in our government who know that answer, and I am not one of them. Nor do I wish to be. I, like the people of the commission, have seen it. But it was only after a lengthy bus ride. It was in the same motor coach with blacked-out windows in which you traveled to our energy facility. It would be too tempting for the Feds to steal our reserves if they knew where they were. For the length of drive we all took, it could be in another State or even Canada."

Josh floated a trial balloon, "Well, if it were me, I would keep it in the middle of a military base, just like Fort Knox." He looked at Bern and Stiles, but received no reaction.

Governor Hughes asked, "Getting back to the gold standard, one of the criticisms I've heard is that it restricts the money supply from growing fast enough to sustain economic growth?"

"Again, a worn out axiom. There are two pricks to that balloon. First, if you are producing and securing wealth through exports, then you can purchase more gold with the foreign currency received. Then you issue more WC's in order to keep the money within a fixed range. But the other fallacy is that there has to be more currency for economic growth. Let's take a loaf of bread, and say that today it takes one credit to buy it. Then let's say that, through added wealth and, hence, greater value to the currency, now it cost only point five for the loaf of bread. Has not the currency been expanded in that only half is needed to buy bread, as well as other goods?"

"You just described deflation," Fodor pronounced *deflation* as if he had sucked a lemon.

"You are correct. Deflation has gained bitter enemies within economists and most politicians because of falling asset values during the Great Depression. However, that was *sustained* deflation. It persisted over a long time due to the complete loss of faith in the economy. The WC has periods of deflation as it gains value and inflation when it loses value. But these swings are small and are of short duration as our algorithm adjusts the currency through the buying or selling of gold. The deflation and inflation cancel each other, providing major stability of the currency and the economy. If, as most economists pitch, some inflation is natural and even encouraged, then why should not some deflation be natural? The only reason moderate inflation is touted as an economic positive is to, supposedly, allow politicians to pay off national debt increases with cheaper dollars. As Andrew Jackson in 1835 was the only President to pay off the national debt, this *cheaper dollar* payoff of the debt is a complete ruse. What they really mean is that the *interest* on the debt can be paid in cheaper dollars. This theory is absurd. Iincreasing debt derives from either fiscal or monetary policies. Either way inflation is increased and natural laws of economics counter inflation through increased interest rates. So I guess I require a primer on how cheaper dollars are such a good thing."

"You said earlier that a destabilizing item is laws interfering with economics. Can you give me an example as I don't see the difference between this and economic policies?" asked Almondo.

"Sure. Economic laws are part of policy. One glaring example is Roosevelt's outlawing of gold ownership."

Governor Brigham corrected Bern, "I think you meant to say 'Rivera,' not Roosevelt."

"No, I meant Roosevelt. Where do you think Rivera got the idea from?"

Brigham was surprised, "I knew President Rivera had outlawed individual ownership of gold. It killed our system of accepting gold and silver as legal tender. I never figured out what his motivation was."

Bern reached into his front pocket and retrieved a small scrap of paper, folded in half. It was dog-eared and appeared yellow. He unfolded the piece and waved it as if it were a trophy for all to see. "I have had this for years. It is a good reminder that absolute power corrupts absolutely...and that bad laws are often ignored." He installed a pair of reading glasses perched near the end of his nose and read from the paper. "I will read you just a portion, as it is a very lengthy law:"

*All persons are hereby required to deliver on or before May 1, to a Federal Reserve Bank or a branch or agency thereof or to any member bank of the Federal Reserve System all gold coin, gold bullion and gold certificates now owned by them or coming into their ownership on or before April 28....*

Brigham followed up her surprise, "That sounds like part of Rivera's law. But you said you've had the paper for many years."

"Yes I have. And yes, it should sound like Rivera's law, because word-for-word it is. You see, when it comes to pure politics, I have never accused the President of being stupid. In fact, he uses rat-like cunning to ram his ideas through the political labyrinth. This is actually the wording of Roosevelt's law from nineteen-thirty-three. Rivera used it without change as he knew there could be no challenge to a law previously upheld."

"But I ask again. Why institute such a law? What does it accomplish?"

Bern was subdued, "Because it removes a competitor from the Federal Government. You see, nations may abuse their citizenry by practicing bad economic policy. But when it comes to nation-versus-nation, 'the jig is up,' as they say. Countries trying to survive an international, economic collapse have no confidence in each other's currency. They demand gold as payment, especially from a debtor nation. If the American people are so lacking in confidence of their own government, and begin dumping dollars for gold, the price of gold increases precipitously against the dollar. This makes it even more difficult for the Feds to ante up gold for balance-of-payments to other countries. This is exemplified by Middle Eastern countries not accepting NUS for oil payments. Gold, Yuan and the Swiss Franc are the only acceptable mediums of payment. And with the Federal government having no gold reserves, it has to enter the spot market to meet these needs. It certainly doesn't want to compete against its own citizenry bidding up the price of gold."

"Has it done any good, I mean the gold law?" asked Fodor.

"No, and it never will just as in Roosevelt's day. All such laws do is to destroy any remaining confidence in the currency, the economy, and the government. Persons owning large quantities of gold merely transfer them to safer locations, such as Switzerland or Australia. This occurred in Roosevelt's time and now. Wyoming has been a large recipient of much of this gold. The owners were well satisfied to convert their holdings to WC's.

But, Rivera has a much bigger sieve to plug than gold in the possession of the nation's Citizens."

"And what's that hole?" asked Elizabeth Brigham.

"Illegal aliens. There are over fifty-five million illegals here now. And they have even less confidence in the NUS than the rest of the country. Remember, these people come from countries that, generally, have destroyed their own currency value. Therefore, they know bad value when they see it. Instead of saddling their relatives back home, where most of their money goes, with paper script that continues to lose value during transit, they wire money back in gold denominations. Those paycheck-cashing kiosks you see all over major cities, do not only cash checks. They convert the NUS at a large discount, sometimes fifty-to-sixty percent from illegals, into gold vouchers. These are wired to their offices or affiliates within other countries and redeemed in gold; gold that was purchased with NUS currency. This further exacerbates the rising world's valuation of gold against the NUS. It is a huge inflationary drain upon the U.S. economy."

"I never even thought of that one. Is Rivera aware?" asked Governor Almondo.

"Oh, he's aware. But he can do nothing without upsetting Mexico. And we all know his feelings towards that country."

All four Governors nodded.

Governor Almondo asked, "I have another question regarding a gold standard. What about business cycles? Without manipulation of the money supply, how can we mitigate downturns?"

Bern chuckled, "A classic argument. Yes, there are business cycles and yes, there are downturns. But every time a government...what was your term? Oh, yes, *mitigates* it, there is only postponement. And the delayed response is worse than the initial downturn. What you are really saying when you say *mitigate* is to *deficit spend* or pump up the money supply.

Yes, downturns result in less revenue received by the government to pay for education, healthcare, public services and safety. That is why you plan for it. You design your budgets to produce a surplus that is accumulated over good economic times. Then, when downturns occur, government has a reserve to call upon in order to maintain basic services without raising taxes, waiting for the upturn that will produce future surpluses. We all remember the slogan of *saving for a rainy day*. It is not a trite saying, just as most time-tested axioms contain truth.

If you deficit spend; if you increase the money supply drastically to counter a downturn, all you have done is to exacerbate the problem. Increased money creates increased credit bubbles. And all bubbles burst, eventually. If you delay the bursting by increasing money and credit at an even greater pace, the bubble will be back. And each time it bursts, it is even larger and more difficult to recover from. If you continuously deficit-spend to forestall downturns, the world will stop accepting your debt. And that is all deficit spending is, credit markets absorbing your debt. This is what finally occurred in 2018 and why the rest of the country is now in the deepest, the greatest of depressions."

Almondo followed on, "So you adhere to a fixed number of WC to gold. And when these bubbles burst, you just tell everyone to ride it out, every man and woman for themselves."

"No, as I said, if you put money away during good times, you have it to spend on social nets during downturns. We do not abandon our Citizenry. Nor do we allow any free rides. If a person is out of work, they can go back to school to re-tool their skills for a different position. Or they can go on interviews with leads we provide. Or they can assist in a social program or government position until they find an opening in the private sector. What they cannot do is sit at home, watch soaps and hope a job will find them. The State provides assistance, not charity."

Bern continued, "But your statement speaks to bubbles and downturns. To date, we have not experienced any such drastic condition. We've had growth slow to one percent or even zero on two occasions. But the economy picked up within twelve months. We actually call these 'rests.' They are natural to even the most stable economic system. Business takes breathers. These are times to access costs, expenditures and markets. There are times that no new technologies are ready for market in any industry. When these things occur across market segments, you have a 'rest.' It is natural and is short-lived as there is no major credit bubble bursting. We actually have the opposite situation. Due to high savings and investment levels within the State, banks are competing with one another to loan during these rests. This shortens the down cycle even more.

"I don't see any big difference between your algorithm and the Fed controlling interest rates."

"Actually, there is one large difference. The Fed adjusts money supply for a desired fiscal affect. It fidgets and tinkers with interest rates, fingers crossed that they will get this or that economic reaction. It is never sure if they left rates too low for too long or too high because the results are not seen for nearly a year to eighteen months.

We adjust our money supply to our wealth, as measured by international markets for gold. The economy is left free to adjust to the available money supply. We control no interest rates except for issuance of our State bonds, and they represent a small percentage of the money supply. There is no requirement for bank reserves to be in State bonds as the Fed requires of U.S. banks. Bank reserves in Wyoming are either in currency or gold. We live in the reality that we must adjust to the world's valuation of our wealth. The Federal government operates within some fantasy that it can dictate to the world what the American economy is worth. And we can see the negative effects of this self-delusion."

"So gold gets all the credit for your economic miracle," stated Scott Fodor.

Bern shook his head, "Not really. Gold is strictly a discipline, a yardstick. I give the credit to the foresight of the people of this State to put sacrifice, hard work and personal discipline before their wants and desires. They have paid the price and they are now reaping the benefits. When I was teaching, I began each new freshman class with the following quote; *A peoples' money is their reflection. If it is strong and respected, so too are they. If it be weak and debased, so too are the makers.*

The soft tinkling of a crystal bell caught their attention. George was announcing the commencement of dinner.

As the assemblage rose and began moving towards the dining tables, Governor Hughes sidled next to Milton Bern and asked "Who's quote is that, Adam Smith?"

Bern smiled, "No…it's mine."

# Chapter 23

## Tex's Edge

## On Board

Ben had cleared nine flatbeds and was at his first boxcar. While he paused for a moment to catch his breath, another set of eyes were upon him from between the chained crates directly behind. If Ben had been aware of two people watching him, he would have been chagrined at his *secret* mission being not so secret.

Warner studied the boxcar end up to the roof where he pondered the implications of a six inch overhang. He noted the thick framed metal ladder welded to the back. It went partially upward the ten foot car's end about four feet and stopped. On modern boxcars, the brake wheel had been brought down from the roof and now stuck out from the back. Apparently the ladder was only needed for access to the brake wheel and, therefore, did not proceed to the roof. The boxcar end was of corrugated construction with each rib sticking out about ten centimeters. It would have been exhausting and time consuming to scale, hence the ladder. He raised it straight up and slammed it down upon the car roof. Then he pulled backwards on the frame's side rails. The gripping blocks on the ladder top gave only slightly and then moved not an inch.

Tex was three cars away and felt secure enough to lift up the back of the tarp to view Ben's progress. He now understood the purpose of the ladder. Having no ladder affirmed his decision to stay put unless Ben left his ladder in place. Then he would follow.

Climbing the ladder to atop the boxcar, Ben steadied his wobbly stance. He pulled the night vision goggles up on his forehead allowing his eyes to adjust to the darkness. NVGs were OK to see what was in front of you, but they distorted depth of field. Ben needed this sense to make his way along the roof. Up here there was nothing to break the wind that preceding cars provided when he was on the flatbeds. He stowed the NVG's into his rucksack and retrieved a pair of clear goggles.

He surveyed the roof top and was glad to see they still had the walking-boards. On older trains they were wooden and ran along the center of the boxcar roof. This allowed a brakeman to walk along the roof tops, providing access to the brake wheels. On newer cars, like this one, the board was actually formed from the same steel as the roof.

Ben reached around and pulled up the ladder. He walked to the other end and mentally measured the distance to the next boxcar roof. It was the same as the flatbed distance, but he had to hit the narrow 'boards' upon landing as the roof slanted away from the ridge. He bucked himself up by muttering, "No big deal," retraced his steps halfway back, turned, hitched the rucksack high on his back and began running. He cleared the distance by nearly three feet, but stumbled slightly on the landing. The ladder he carried in his left hand banged sideways onto the roof, stopping his near tumble. He would need some adjustment to the equipment as he had four more boxcars to clear. He adjusted the rucksack lower on his back. It was too high for the first jump. As he landed and bent over, the pack's inertia almost pulled him over. He started his run again. This landing was spot on, and his center of balance was so perfect that he just kept running until he cleared the next two cars in a row. Then he used the ladder to lower himself back to a series of flatcars. The process continued: jumping between flatcars, climbing up boxcars, jumping between boxcars, climbing down boxcars and back onto flatcars again. He was growing tired of the pace when his destination finally appeared. It was the end of the train.

Lying prone upon a boxcar roof, he regained the NVG's and peered over the edge. The last car attached to the end of the train was a troop transport. The door facing front opened to nothing as there was no platform on the coupling end. There was probably one on the back, he thought. It was fortunate for Ben, as this way no Army personnel would have to be taken out first. General Palmer's words harkened, "Try not to kill anyone." He could only hope no one would catch a glimpse of him through the door's window. The chances were fifty-fifty.

He removed the NVG's, stuffed them into his rucksack and replaced them with the clear goggles. He swung the ladder downward between the two cars. He pushed on the blocks to make sure they were secure and spun his body around. He inched his way backwards, feet first, until his waist was at the roof edge. He bent the lower half of his body downward, allowing his boots to find purchase on the rungs. He climbed down to the last step. The next maneuver was to be the most difficult, and the most dangerous.

Ben grasped the rungs tightly, lifted his feet and slid them through until the creases at the back of his knees were positioned on the bottom rung. He was now thankful for the six inch roof overhang as it gave him a space for his legs between the boxcar end wall and the ladder. Then he skid his hands down the side frames until his upper torso was even with his thighs. He reached into one of his cargo pants outside pockets, retrieving an LED penlight that he held between his teeth. He then released his grip and flipped over and downward, dangling from legs and ladder-locked boots. He was now facing the troop car, upside down, and could hear laughing, sex stories and rough language. He hung there for a few moments, listening to any change in conversation that might indicate he was seen. Nothing; the conversations went on as before. He bent his head backwards in order to see downward, turning on the light that now faced the complex coupling. All that was between his acrobatic position and roadbed whizzing by was the coupling. It all made him nauseous. He swallowed bile and urged himself on.

He examined the coupling, moving the light by moving his head. He mentally compared it to the spec sheet he had studied two days prior. Finding what he was looking for, he manually closed the angle cock. Then he grabbed the cut-lever and tugged. It didn't move. He knew his time was limited as the blood was rushing to his head and his bent legs were growing numb. At this moment he noticed a diminishing of the light from the door's window of the troop car. He rolled his eyes upward as far as possible and found himself staring, upside down, at a soldier looking through the glass. The GI's face was a mixture of shock and confusion.

Ben said loud enough to hear over the rushing wind and wheels, "Shit!" The penlight fell from his dental grasp, bouncing off the coupling and disappearing onto the roadbed now far behind. Time remaining was counted in seconds before the soldier gathered his wits and reacted. Ben redoubled his efforts with great urgency. He pressed his boots against the boxcar end, grabbed the cut-lever with both hands and grunted as he exerted a force that lifted the coupler's lock to allow release of the car's mechanical couplers. Just then the soldier opened the door and, grabbing the threshold with both hands, hung out the door. He leaned down to get as close to Ben as possible and shouted, "What the hell are you doing, mister?"

It was at this instant that the air hose glad-hands automatically released upon the car-to-car separation. This caused the remaining air pressure still in the brake pipe line to escape. Apparently, Ben had not closed the valve far enough. The hoses and glad-hands nearly missed Ben's head, then whipped backwards and cracked the soldier on the head. He fell forward, unconscious. Ben quickly reached out and grabbed him, stopping his fall beneath the car. He tried to shimmy the limp body backwards into the car, but the trains were now separating quickly. Upside down, Ben pushed on the young man's shoulders. The now uncoupled troop transport car fell back from the train faster as the normally-closed brakes began applying pressure automatically to the wheels. Ben, holding onto the soldier's uniform, was pulled away from the boxcar, the ladder angling outward with him. He had to make a quick decision and reluctantly let go. The ladder and his body swung back to the boxcar and both banged into the steel wall. His head hit first, causing him to see stars. But he was still conscious. He looked back at the troop transport and was relieved to see the soldier still attached to it, laying half way out and down the back. Two of his buddies were tugging on his legs, reeling the body back in. One of the soldiers stepped over the unconscious man and leaned out the open door. He shouted to the upside down silhouette on the distancing boxcar, "HALT! Or I'll shoot! Jefferson, go get me my piece!"

Ben had recovered from the thumping against the boxcar, but was quickly becoming light-headed quickly. He swung his body back and forth trying to get a pendulum action started. On the third return he strained every abdominal muscle to the max and gave out a loud grunt until his hands found the frame side. He pulled himself up and grasped an upper rung. Then he pulled his body upward, releasing his legs and allowing his boots to slam down onto the bottom rung. While hanging from his knees, the rung had cut off the blood flow to his legs. His legs tingled as they came back to life, slowly. They were still rubbery underneath him as he spasmodically ascended the ladder. Behind, he heard a distant yell, "I told you to HALT!"

Ben kept climbing without looking back. He willed his legs up the ladder. Reaching the top, he flopped over. He heard the sound of the shot just as the bullet whizzed by. He didn't know if it was a warning shot or if the soldier was a lousy marksman. He hoped the later. He snaked his way along the roof, trying to get small as fast as possible. There were three more shots, but none found their mark. The angle of shooting from the troop transport's door upwards to a boxcar roof that was quickly disappearing into the darkness of night was nearly impossible. Or so Ben hoped.

When the receding car became a small speck, Ben felt it safe to rise and begin to retrieve his ladder. When his legs felt normal, he began retracing his recent trek, bounding the distance between boxcars and flatcars until reaching the run of flatbeds he recognized as containing his. Kneeling on the last boxcar roof, he spun his ladder round, secured it and climbed down. He jumped to the flatbed, retrieved the ladder and began his dash along the metal deck. He leaped from this first flatbed to the next and resumed his sprint until he jumped to the third. As he passed a tarp'd and chained self-propelled mortar, a hand reached out and grabbed his foot. Ben was caught completely off-guard. He stumbled and fell forward.

The ladder skidded half way down the car deck as he went head first into a metal tie-down. Holding the chain from the deck to the gun was a welded, metal ring. This is where Ben's forehead collided. His body flipped to the side and his head was concussed again when the back of his skull hit the metal deck. Somehow he maintained consciousness. But his vision blurred and the night's stars above rippled in waves. He felt a surge of nausea and feared he would vomit while on his back. Blood from the cut on his forehead leaked down, pooled in his eyebrows and ran down the bridge of his nose. He tried to turn over on his side. But there was now a pressure on his chest and he could make out a large shiny object waving before his face.

Tex was sitting on Ben's chest moving the large knife inches from the bloodied face. Lying in wait, luck had been with him that Ben would be coming back. When his target ran by, Tex had reached out from underneath the tarp and grabbed his ankle. Watching Ben sprawl onto the deck, Tex moved quickly to take the advantage. He pulled the big Bowie knife from his remaining boot, rolled from under the tarp and jumped to his feet. He covered the distance to Ben in two steps and sat on the wounded man's chest.

"Hello, Warner," shouted the lanky Texan over the train noise with a sneer on his lips. "So, I suspect you're pretty tore up with that gash in your forehead and all." Tex brought the huge knife right up to Ben's eyes. "But me and Baby here," he twisted the knife back and forth, "we're gonna make you look a helluva lot worse. I'm gonna kill ya, but how I do it is up to you. It can be fast like your airport buddy in the hanger, or slow. You're gonna tell me why you're on this train, what you were doing at the back of the train, and where all this military stuff is headed. Then I can let you go to your Maker peaceably. If you don't answer me, I can show you Hell on earth before you go. I'll start by sticking this pointy end in your eyeballs and popping them out of their sockets one-by-one. Then I'm gonna start some serious carving on you. Your choice."

Ben was near passing out and his vision still blurry. But the ringing in his ears subsided. He heard the man's threats just fine. His mind frantically searched. *Who is this guy? Who's he saying he already killed? Someone at the airport?* Then he saw movement behind Tex. There was someone else that Ben had no idea as to identity. Ben tried to lift his head to get a better look at this second player, but this just put his eye even closer to the knife point. Tex noted Ben's line of sight. The Texan spun round, saw the shadowy figure and jumped to his feet. He held the knife out in attack mode. He shouted over the rush of wind and train noise, "Who the hell are you?"

Although Ben's vision was starting to clear, his head throbbed when he tried lifting it. He wanted to see this new guy and was able to get a glimpse before he dropped back onto the deck. The man was in his twenties, about six feet, thin and wiry. And he was Asian.

Tex demanded his identity again, but the Asian said nothing. He looked at the knife Tex menacingly waved, then at Ben on the steel deck and back to the knife. He calmly told Tex, "Put that knife down or you will have regrets." He had a slight Japanese accent. Tex laughed. "Unless you brought a gun to this knife fight, son, I think I have the advantage. Not you."

The younger man took two steps towards Tex. He then stopped abruptly, turned his body sideways, bent his knees, brought one arm down slowly until it pointed directly at Tex. Then he circled the other backwards as if he were cocking a weapon. The elbow of this arm was bent upwards to shoulder height. His thumbs and fingers were tight together and slightly bent at the ends. His face was expressionless. "Last chance, cowboy. Drop your knife."

Tex wasn't amused anymore. He jabbed the knife outward and bent his knees slightly. He then started swaying a little right and left. "Come on, Chinc, I'm gonna make noodles out of you."

"I am Japanese, not Chinese, you ignorant bastard."

"Whatever, slant eye. I think I'll make a little sushi out of you." Tex lunged and slashed. The Asian pivoted on his front leg while lowering his body nearly to the ground. His back leg swung and cracked into Tex's shin bones. His forward motion kept Tex stumbling backwards. The Taekwondo master completed his spin while rising up. Now he fairly pirouetted on his left foot as his right stiffened and crashed into Tex's side. The Japanese knew that he had cracked at least two of Tex's ribs. But Tex wasn't out of the fight yet. He winced at the injury and let the pain morph into rage. He straightened himself at the price of searing pain. Then he moved towards the Asian, slashing the knife back and forth. The Japanese gave ground and looked as if he had staggered, but it was only a feint. Tex saw the opportunity and thrust the knife straight towards his victim's torso. It was the move the Japanese was expecting. He turned his body sideways as the knife tore through his shirt. He brought his right hand up underneath Tex's arm and his left hand came full circle, down upon Tex's wrist. It was like a hammer hitting the anvil with Tex's wrist in between. A loud snap was heard and Tex yelled. But he didn't drop the knife. He retrieved it out of his right hand with his left and tried to jab at the Asian. The man of martial arts turned to face Tex. He stopped the thrust with his two hands out in front of him, both seizing Tex's knife arm in a vice grip. He pushed Tex's arm straight up and bent his wrist back so that the knife was now pointing at its owner's chest. The Japanese gave a high pitched yell and pushed full force. The Jim Bowie went through Tex's shirt. But only a small portion of the tip penetrated as the Japanese hesitated to kill him. Instead, he knocked the knife to the deck and sunk his knee into Tex's groin. Tex's cheeks bulged as the air rushed from his lungs. He doubled over in immense pain, covering his crotch with his remaining good hand. The Asian grabbed him by both shoulders, straightening him up. Then he brought back his hand, palm out, fingers up, and jabbed quickly at his nose. Cartilage snapped and blood shot out of the broken nose. Tex staggered backwards, howling in pain. His foot felt the flatbed edge and he flailed one arm for balance. The Japanese walked up to him, put out one finger and pushed him over the edge. Tex screamed as he fell from the moving train. When he hit the roadbed, his body bounced, then cart-wheeled and did another series of high and low bounces into the weeds, arms and legs flipping about like a ragdoll. The Asian leaned over the edge and witnessed Tex's acrobatics with no emotion. He said to the howling wind, "Who's sushi now, cowboy."

# Chapter 24

## A Friend in Need

## On Board

The Japanese was bending over Ben. He had removed a handkerchief from his back pocket and was trying to mop blood from Ben's forehead, nose and eyes. "How do you feel, Ben Warner?"

Ben's voice was gaining some strength. "Help me sit up and we'll both find out."

Ben's rescuer obliged. He grabbed Ben's right arm with both hands and pulled him up to a seated position. Ben took a few deep breaths and then focused his returning vision upon the Asian. Ben felt a rush to his head. It throbbed with an intensity that made him want to lie back down. After a moment it began to diminish. He tried to muster a smile for the concerned face in front of him. The blood began trickling down his face again.

The Japanese handed Ben his handkerchief and asked, "Who was that cowboy with the knife?"

Ben wound up the handkerchief and tied it tightly around his head, covering and compressing the forehead gash, "Beats me. I seem to be the only one around here that everyone knows. So, Hiroto, why are you here? I'm not complaining, mind you. That asshole would have cut my liver out and used it for pate. I thought you went back to Japan after delivering the recording."

Hiroto Ishikawa was an agent of Japan's intelligence service known as the *Jouhou Honbu*. Japan was an ally to Wyoming, a partner in **WyStar** and current recipient of electricity generated within the State. Ben and his State's welfare were paramount to the Asian island nation. Japan knew of Wyoming's many enemies, including the U.S. Federal government. This was why the head of the intelligence service, Daiichi Nagakawa, known within the intelligence community as 'The Elder', had assigned his top agent, Hiro, to remain in Wyoming after completing a courier mission. The initial mission was to deliver a recording to Ben in which Russian agents disclosed plans to eliminate Wyoming's Lt. Governor. The second part of Hiro's mission was to remain in the U.S. to discretely aid in Ben Warner's continued life expectancy. It was obvious to both men on the flatbed, it had been a wise decision.

"The Elder said I should keep an eye on you. He seems to think you have more enemies than you can handle."

Ben wanted to laugh, "Appears that Nagakawa has more insight of my life than I do."

"He is wise like an owl."

"Well, I'm sure glad for his foresight. But how did you know I was on this train?"

"I was following the cowboy because he was following you. It is true in reverse."

"What is?" asked Ben.

"The enemy of my friend is my enemy." Hiroto smiled and Ben tried to chuckle but it started his head pounding. "I thought you might need some help after I saw you were shot when out hunting with the other tall one."

Ben nodded, "Stillwater, Joshua Stillwater, old friend. Did you see who shot me? Was it that asshole you just threw off the train?"

Hiroto replied, "No, he was watching as was I. It was another wearing a sniper suit. He was as distant to me as he was to you. I did see him depart on a vehicle built for no road."

"A quad, a four-wheeler, all-terrain-vehicle, ATV," added Ben.

"I was pleased to see you rise from your shooting. Before, I thought you were with the ancients. How did you accomplish this? No bullet-proof vest we have would stop a sniper bullet."

"A new design we came up with," answered Ben. "I'll get you one, a little prize for saving me tonight."

Hiroto slightly bowed, "We would be grateful." Then he turned serious, "Twice fate has been kind to you. Once before, I saw the man with the knife. He should have thrown the knife and not try to kill me closely. That would have been more difficult to evade. He is quite skilled at this throwing."

Ben asked, "What're ya talkin' 'bout, Hiro?"

The Japanese man shook his head, "Not important. Perhaps a story for another time." He returned to the moment, "So, Ben Warner, I think you are on this train for a purpose. May I assist you?"

Ben smiled, "Be a darned fool to say 'No'. In fact, if you now help me stand, we need to get back on schedule. What time is it?"

Hiroto looked at his watch, "oh-three-oh-eight."

Ben shook his head, "Damn, I've got to get going or I'm gonna disappoint a lot of people, especially my sister. She doesn't accept failure very well."

"A very capable person. I agree. And most beautiful, too." added Hiroto.

Ben looked at him a little suspiciously. "You've met my sister?"

"Yes. However, I am known to her as Hiroaki Tanaka, a small subterfuge insisted upon by Nagakawa-san."

Both men were silent for a moment. Ben was rolling around in his mind the implications of the *Jouhou Honbu* nosing into Wyoming affairs. He shouldn't really be surprised. There was a lot riding on whether David could subdue Goliath. And he shouldn't be surprised at Japan's interest in the outcome. For the first time in a long time, he didn't feel quite so alone. There were probably other countries keeping their finger in Wyoming's pie. If so, he hoped they were as helpful as his Japanese partners.

Ben asked Hiroto, "Can you help me to my feet? We've got a schedule to keep."

Hiroto nodded, extended an arm and received Ben's Roman grasp. He leaned back and pulled him to his feet.

Hiroto then bent over and picked-up the large Jim Bowie knife. Examining it closely, he asked, "Ben-san, would you mind if I keep this unusual knife?"

Ben rummaged through his rucksack and found the clear goggles that he offered Hiroto, "Nope, and I don't think the owner cares much, now."

Hiroto smiled. He slid the knife between belt and pants while accepting the goggles with a dip of his head. Ben put on his NVG's, retrieved the ladder and led Hiroto flat car jumping and box car climbing for nearly thirty cars.   At the end of the final boxcar was the first of three engines. They were all facing the same direction and the last one had a large built-up steel box at the end of the cab.   Ben waited behind this box while Hiroto scrambled down the ladder.   Once together, Ben peered up the handrailed gangway running along each engine.   It was a long way to the first engine, but, from his vantage, didn't seem too difficult to traverse. He grabbed the rail and leaned into the rushing wind.

They worked their way to the back of the lead engine and peered down the last gangway.   It ran about twenty meters down the engine's side and then climbed a set of metal stairs up to the cab door directly behind the engineer.   He could make out a shadow of a back leaning against the door's window.   This was probably one of the two soldiers that Palmer had warned him were in the cab.   With the cab illuminated, the NVG's were useless.  Ben tore them off and stuffed them into the rucksack.

There didn't appear to be any rearview mirrors to betray their approach so they set out upon the last leg of the assault.   Pushing again against the wind, they made their way towards the stairs.   Ben un-holstered the air pistol and slammed the cartridge containing the five darts into the bottom opening within the handle.   Then he pulled up the velcro'd strap of a pants pocket and fished out a small metal container of compressed $CO_2$. This he quarter-turned into the end of the gun, in line with the barrel. When they made the stairs they slowly climbed, lowering their bodies with each step.   At the top platform they crawled on hands and knees to the door.   Staying low, they avoided the chance of being seen through the window.   Ben turned to Hiroto and held up two fingers.   Hiroto understood, there were two opponents on the other side of the door they must subdue. He pulled the knife from his belt and brandished it. Ben shook his head and raised his air pistol.   He looked from the pistol to Hiroto.   The Japanese got the point of using non-lethal means, nodded and returned the knife to the belt.   Ben gave a thumbs-up and Hiroto returned it.   He reached up and grabbed the handle, slowly pulling it downward, checking to see if it was unlocked.   He was prepared to blow a locked door with the small charge and fuse in his backpack.   He was glad this was unnecessary as they would have had to retreat down the stairs for the explosion and then charge back up.   He thought over his options of how to enter.   A 'flash bang' and smoke grenade were his two non-lethal choices.   But he really didn't think the two soldiers would be a problem, especially if the one against the door fell backwards and out of the cab. Besides, there was no need to blow anybody's ear drums out or blind them.  He needed the engineer in good shape to keep the train rolling. Ben pointed to the Army uniform in the window and pantomimed to

Hiroto how he would open the door, the soldier would fall backwards and then Hiroto would subdue him. Hiroto nodded.

He lifted off his knees and got into a crouch. He duck-walked backwards until he was tight against the cab's side. He told himself "On three" and then said aloud "Three!" He stood straight up and yanked the door open. The soldier staggered backwards out of the door. His face had a quizzical look as Hiroto grabbed his shirt and pulled him backwards even faster. When the soldier's boots hit the stairs, he couldn't keep up. Now he fell completely into Hiroto's arms. The Japanese reached up to the soldier's neck and pressed a pressure point that induced unconsciousness. He then jerked the limp body down the rest of the stairs and laid him out on the cat walk and rushed back up the stairs to aid Ben.

Ben had waited for the soldier to stumble backwards past him. He then ran into the cab, air pistol pointed skyward. He ignored the engineer who had turned around at the sound of the door opening. Instead, Ben scanned the cab for the other soldier. He found him leaning against the far back corner. The Soldier retrieved his rifle from behind and was leveling it at Ben. He made a critical mistake by taking the second required to put the piece to his shoulder when he should have hip-fired. Ben used this time to quickly kneel, aim his pistol and shoot the soldier in the abdomen. The GI dropped his weapon and grabbed at the dart in panic, but it was too late. His eyes rolled back into his head as he slumped back into the corner.

Ben pointed the hand gun at the engineer and told him to be a good boy and nobody would get hurt. At the same moment, he saw movement to his left. Someone had been standing in the open doorway that led to the huge diesel engines and their mating electrical generators. Ben swung the gun, but the person was gone. *Shit*, he thought. Now he had to keep an eye on the engineer while tracking down his cohort. It wasn't possible. While his attention was diverted, he heard the engineer shout, "CENTRAL, CENTRAL! This is northbound 708. ANSWER ME!" Ben spun the pistol round back to the engineer and jammed it into his neck.

"This isn't a toy, mister. If I fire this, you will be out for two hours and then wake up with one hell of headache. In the meantime, I will be forced to drive your precious train. And I don't know much about trains. Your choice."

Hiroto now came charging through the door. He quickly scanned the cab and concluded Ben had things under control.

The radio crackled, "This is Central. Stevens, that you? There a problem?"

Hiroto looked at Ben, who said, "Mister Engineer here got all heroic. But he's gonna fix it right now." Ben pushed the barrel into the engineer's neck even further. The engineer nodded, and then depressed the button on the microphone.

"No. No problem. Just thought I saw something on the tracks. Everything's OK, I guess."

The radio answered, "Well don't tie up the airwaves unless it's important. You know that."

He answered back, "Yeah, yeah."

The radio shot back, "You on time for Ft. Collins? I don't want any Army guys on my tail. They can ruin your whole day."

"Yeah, on schedule. Should be there in seventeen minutes."

"Good. Give me a shout after you're off-loaded. Central out."

Ben grabbed the mic out of his hand and stretched the coiled cord straight until it unplugged from the console. Then he threw it on the floor. "Good decision," he said.

Ben couldn't relax until he subdued whoever was back in the engine compartment. He was starting to hand his gun to Hiroto to keep the engineer guarded when he heard a voice call out from the doorway, "Mister, I don't who you are and I really don't care. But I have a Remington sawed-off and if you hurt a hair on Frank's head, I will kill you. Now why don't you just get out of here and off this train, PRONTO!"

Ben looked at the engineer, who had turned in his chair, and then at Hiroto who raised his eyebrows and forehead in a questioning manner.

The engineer had a small smile on his face. He nodded towards the open door and said In a Midwest accent, "That's Charlie. He's my fireman. And, yes, he does keep a shotgun back there. I'm Frank. And I suggest you do what the man says."

Hiroto didn't wait for instructions. He flattened himself against the cab bulkhead and worked his way slowly over to the opening. When he saw a gun barrel begin to peak out from the threshold, he grabbed the barrel and jerked it forward. Ben dove for the metal deck, air pistol out in front. A person connected to the stock of the gun stumbled out from back room. Ben fired a dart into his leg. But before the sedative worked, he tried to pull his gun backwards. This put pressure on his trigger finger and the gun roared.

Charlie, the fireman, dropped to the floor like a sack of potatoes. And the gun followed his descent. Ben looked over at Hiroto to see if he had been hit. Hiroto had let go of the barrel the moment it fired. He was checking his hand for burn marks. Other than that he appeared OK. Ben got to his feet and turned to speak to the engineer. But Frank wouldn't be talking to anyone for a while. He was slumped over his console and there were numerous small holes in his shirt.

"Oh crap!" moaned Ben. Hiroto looked from his hand to the engineer and understood the problem. When the shotgun went off, it was accidentally aimed at Frank.

Hiroto and Ben pulled the engineer from his command chair and laid him upon the deck. Ben removed his rucksack and put it under the engineer's head. Hiroto had already opened the shirt and was inspecting Frank's side.

"It is strange. The pellets are not so deep. I can pick them out with my fingers. And they do not look to be made of metal," said the Japanese.

Ben looked at a pellet Hiroto held between two fingers. "Rock salt," said Ben. Hiroto looked confused.

Ben elaborated, "Frank here is a lucky man. First of all, the sawed off barrel saved him. To shorten a shotgun barrel is to widen the shot pattern. The wider the pattern the less you're hit with and the less force it has. And using rock salt is a way to put someone down without necessarily killing them. But you still feel as if you've been kicked by a mule."

Hiroto nodded his understanding. Ben continued, "I'll look around for a first aid kit. They're bound to have one in the cab. You keep picking salt out of ol' Frank here."

Ben found the first aid kit under the fireman's console. He opened it up and took out some ointment, adhesive strips and an ammonia stick. He handed the assortment to Hiroto, "After you get the rock salt out, smear some of that ointment on the wounds and put adhesive strips over them.

Once you've got him patched up, crush the ammonia stick and wake him up. He'll be alright and we need him to drive this train. I'm going outside to retrieve the Army boy you put to sleep. Be right back." Hiroto nodded and handed Ben the clear goggles.

Ben found the soldier still passed out. He tugged him up far enough to get underneath and lay him over a shoulder. He then pushed forward against the pressing wind until both were through the door.

Once inside, he laid the soldier on the deck near his partner. He retrieved his rucksack from under Frank's head and pulled out twelve, plastic cinch ties. He looped one through its cinch and fed the second through the first. This formed a pair of handcuffs, with which he cuffed the two soldiers and the fireman, one to the other. After securing their wrists, he did the same to their ankles. Now he didn't have to worry about shooting anyone who woke up too early. By the time Ben was done, Hiroto had a moaning Frank awake and on his feet. He assisted the man over to his command chair and helped him sit down.

"How we doing Frank?" asked Ben in a light tone.

"How the hell you think I'm doing. I've been shot," growled Frank.

"Correction, Frank. You got rock-salted. It could have been a lot worse. You'll live."

"No thanks to you guys. What the hell you doing on my train anyway? It's kinda nuts to hijack a train. It's not like you can make me drive it to Cuba. They know where it is and can easily track us just by looking at a GPS map. Besides, I've got a stop coming up in exactly...," he looked at the digital clock in front of him, "four minutes. And there's a whole lot of mean soldiers that are gonna be pissed at you guys for shooting two of their buddies."

"We don't plan on making that stop, Frank," said Ben.

"What? You guys are nuts. You think they're gonna let you just roll on through and disappear with all their equipment?"

"That's exactly what they're gonna do, Frank. So keep this train rolling straight ahead," ordered Ben.

Frank shook his head vigorously, "No can do, Mr. Smart Guy. They've got us going off a siding for unloading. If I hit it at this speed, we will have one helluva derailment and we'll probably all be dead, not to mention all the troops connected to the back of this train."

Ben sighed, "Frank, Frank, Frank, this just isn't yours or the Army's day. You see I uncoupled that troop transport about a hundred miles back. They're wandering around Colorado in the dark trying to figure out which way is Denver."

Frank looked in disbelief. Ben continued, "Secondly, we aren't going off on any siding, least ways not yet. We are green lighted all the way to Wyoming."

"Wyoming? Why Wyoming? And what makes you think we're green-lighted all the way?"

"Well, I happen to like Wyoming. It's pretty this time of year. And we're green-lighted because I have a little birdie that left some poop in your switching programs. They couldn't reverse it if they had a week, which they don't. So you just keep the pedal to the metal, Frank, and all will be OK."

Frank turned round to face his chair forward. He just shook his head in disbelief         at         what         was         happening.

# Chapter 25

## Missed Schedule

## Ft. Collins, Colorado

General Vernon Maxwell peered down the tracks for the fifth time in as many minutes. He pulled up the sleeve of his uniform and checked the now luminescent dial.

"Where the hell is it? They're over eleven minutes late."

His aide-de-camp shared his concern. "Sir, yes sir. They were cleared as 'expedited' all the way from Texas. No excuse, no excuse. Got to expect it with civilians, sir."

"Go get that station master. He said he could radio the engineer. Tell him to get the guy on the horn now."

The captain snapped to attention and saluted, "Yes sir." He spun on one heal and the other toe and trotted off to the stairs that led upwards towards the master switching control. At just this moment a dim light appeared, steady in its course across the Colorado plains.

"Captain, belay that order. I see something coming." But the captain had not heard the repeal and continued into the upper offices.

The light became brighter along with a low rumble vibrating through the tracks before the General. A line of soldiers pressed shoulders to get a view of the oncoming train. A clear sky and full moon reflected off the rails as they stretched south from Ft. Collins. The General straightened himself and barked orders. "Colonel, get your men organized. As soon as that train is on the siding and off the main track, I want it off-loaded in record time. I want to be in position before the first rays of sun up, understand!" The colonel shot a salute and began issuing orders as men scurried in all directions.

The steadily increasing light grew in intensity until the large black void of an engine was distinct. A moment prior the train appeared to be slowing, as it should. But instead its whistle blew and the rumble of the roadbed indicated it was resuming prior speed. In front of Maxwell, the gravel began vibrating between the cross-ties. There seemed no attempt at slowing. Within the last four hundred meters of the station the train was at full throttle, giving no sign of the anticipated stop. The General looked around furiously, spinning his head left and right as if someone were supposed to step forward with an explanation. The dozen uniformed officers near him were as perplexed as their leader.

Now the lead engine's headlight raked all on the platform in stark whiteness. The concrete raised area vibrated from the surging wheels as they bore down upon the steel rails. The train roared past them in a cacophony of raging diesel, pounding steel, screaming whistle and a tornado of wind that sucked the General's cap from his head and thrashed it backwards underneath car after car. All he could do was to watch the load of his materiel speed north. The stunned General slowly regained his wits. "What in Sam Hell is going on? Where is that captain?" He turned and marched towards the metal stairs.

Entering the station master's door, he saw his subordinate throwing his arms about in frustration as he yelled at a man in fifties. The older man was short, with a large belly straining the buttons of a white dress shirt. A thin, black tie distinguished him as being in charge of the other four men and one woman. The men were focused on the verbal melee between boss and army. The woman furiously banged away on her computer key boards. The captain demanded an explanation. But the one provided by the station manager did not satisfy.

"What do you mean you can't stop it? Why isn't that train sitting on a siding right now?"

General Maxwell was now standing a few paces behind his captain. Unnoticed by the two verbal combatants, he actually felt the captain was voicing his shock and frustration as well as he could. He remained silent for the moment.

The station manager began frantically beating the keys in front of him. He turned his head to the officer in front of him. "Captain, we don't have any control over it!" He was bent over, peering at a small monitor. In surprise, he jerked straight up and yelled to anyone listening "Look at that!" All five of his subordinates followed his pointed finger to the large overhead digital board. Across it were lines indicating all main rails and side rails within a twenty-five mile radius of feeding through this epicenter. There were combinations of red and green lights where one track met another. A flashing light, a large asterisk was inching along a line that ran straight through the screen from bottom to top. All lights along its path were green.

"Someone's green-lighted that train all the way north." said the station manager in a disbelieving voice.

General Maxwell Vernon now stepped in. "Stop that train, mister. And I mean now."

The station master looked at the General incredulously. He stood straight up and put his hands on substantial hips. "And how do you propose I do that?" The station manager turned round and looked sternly at the five faces at their desks behind.

"I swear, if one of you guys is screwing around, you're in deep shit."

Maxwell turned to the captain, untethered the holster on his subordinate's hip and removed the side arm. He pulled back the top slide on the forty-five caliber automatic, loading a shell into the chamber. He turned and pointed the business end in the general direction of the five workers. "Gentlemen, and lady, the man is right. Someone is messing with my train. Whoever it is, I will ferret out later. The rest of you better get busy right now and figure out how to stop that train. This is a U.S. Army train and I am putting all of you under military arrest if this doesn't stop now. Press a button, make a phone call, I don't care. Just stop that train."

The four men immediately began to perspire, frozen to inaction. The woman just shrugged and bent over her console and began banging keys. The asterisk kept advancing north.

Maxwell turned back to the station manager. "Where do those tracks lead?"

"Next town, across the border. Cheyenne."

Defeated, Maxwell dropped the gun by his side and mumbled an expletive. "Captain, get through to the Pentagon and find me General Declamore. The officer snapped a salute and headed towards the door. He was nearly at a run."

Unnoticed by the others in the room, their female co-worker stopped banging on her keyboard and slowly retreated to a rear exit. She quickly descended a set of back stairs, briskly walked to her car and drove off east. In less than a mile she made a right turn onto a two-lane road heading north. A road sign read CHEYENNE 46 MILES.

## Chapter 26

## Full Steam Ahead

## On Board

Ben stood behind the engineer and peered into the night as far as the headlight carried. He was bone tired and his head hurt. He had found some aspirin in the first aid kit. But there were only two foil packets of two each. Their effect didn't last long. He was pretty sure he might have a concussion.

The run past Ft. Collins actually had an element of humor for him as he watched the shocked faces of soldiers, particularly the top brass. They were all waving their arms as if that could stop a train. But now it was going to get real serious. Frank was right about one thing. The Army was not going to take kindly to stealing this much of their materiel.

It didn't take long for the calls to start coming in. Ben had Frank ignore them. The calls continued and became more insistent. Ben was resolved not to answer. But after six more calls went unanswered from their side, Frank tried a different tack. Turning to Ben, he said, "You know, mister, if you don't answer they're going to get desperate, think we're a runaway."

"And then what?" replied Ben.

"Then they will probably try to derail us. They just throw a switch from their little computer and, BLAM, we're scooting along the dirt on our side, with thousands of tons from behind being shoved up our ass. Not a good way to go."

Ben just nodded and smiled, "You're right, Frank. But you keep forgetting something. Your people are not in control of the switches. Remember, Frank, green-light."

Frank was still worried. The maniac with the dart gun had never allowed him to reduce speed since the train was hijacked. He knew there hadn't been any improvements to the railroads since the government had nationalized them. The ties were rotting, the beds needed new gravel and even the rails were showing rust holes. "You just can't have a train barreling down this track. It's not safe. Heck, you've got me running at nearly sixty miles per hour on rails only rated for forty. They might not need to derail us if we do it for ourselves." Ben just shrugged. He was too tired for conversation. He looked over at Hiroto who was leaning against the bulk head, staring straight ahead. Ever since he and Ben had met on the flatbed, Hiroto had never asked what Ben's master plan was or why they were stealing this train. Maybe it was self-evident. But Ben thought it was more an incredible self-control on Hiroto's part. He was under orders to protect Ben. So wherever Ben went, Hiroto was along for the ride. Why they took the train or where they were going mattered not to Hiroto. *The guy has some 'cool'*, thought Ben.

# Chapter 27

## Smell of War

### Governor's Mansion, Cheyenne

In front of Josh was a formal setting: a delicately-thin dinner plate fired with a royal blue ceramic finish, trimmed in gold scroll repeating the words State of Wyoming separated by the WC symbol. This was placed within pewter chargers bearing the cast of the State seal. Leaded crystal glasses, a gift from the Chinese government, Sam noted, was part of each place setting, along with gold plated silverware and monogrammed napkins. The table was a cornucopia from the food-basket of Wyoming: beef, lamb, brook trout, antelope, venison, pheasant, dove, quail, sweet potatoes, russet potatoes, corn, beets, string beans, cabbage: all prepared four or five different ways with an accompanying assortment of breads. Sam had made sure that the entire fare was produced within Wyoming. With nearly ten-thousand farms and ranches covering over thirty million acres, the State was capable of feeding itself with plenty left over for export. Josh was amused that the male Governors seemed unfamiliar with nearly every dish, causing them to smell first and then experiment by tasting small samples. Only the female Governor, Elizabeth Brigham of Utah, dove in with enthusiasm. She relished each mouthful and nodded approvingly to Sam between bites.

The conversation at dinner was lively. Politics was the main discussion and references to the Federal government or President Rivera were pointed barbs. Sam sat at the table head with the Governors sitting at her left and right. Josh was at a table that was part of one leg of the 'U' layout. He was a few chairs down from Sam, close enough to hear her conversation. Sam participated in light banter, avoiding any remarks about the failings of the Feds. To Stillwater's left was Nevin Stiles and Milton Bern. The most animated in his talk was Lightoiler. He was one seat down and across the table from Josh. To his left was Frank Dunleavy. Across from these two, and to Josh's right were General Douglas Roughton, Wyoming State Army, and Howard Finkel.

*Charles Lightoiler is definitely a spokesman*, thought Josh. When involved he would set up his inquisitor with questions designed to lead a person to his conclusion. He was the type that knew the issues, knew his mind and didn't broach much disagreement. Those at the table were in general agreement, so debate aimed in his direction was small. Josh watched Lightoiler closely as he spoke. The familiarity of his face was only exceeded by his voice. Stillwater knew this guy from somewhere and it bugged him to no end not being able to remember.

When Joshua was asked his opinion on a politically charged point, he deferred by just shrugging and saying, "Never been political." He listened to the charges, counter-charges and finally spoke up.

"I have a question," he said.

The others quieted and Lightoiler nodded to Josh.

"I grant you, this place is humming along. You're successful, here. But why couldn't this same success be applied to the nation as a whole. I mean, why can't the Federal Government copy what you're doing?"

Lightoiler immediately filled the void, "If I may, I wish to field this one," he said looking at Bern and Niles. The dais was his.

"Joshua, the reason this cannot happen at the Federal level is for two reasons: lack of desire and distance. Let me explain. On the first point, lack of desire, the Federal government does not think our way. They have gone beyond full-blown Socialism to Autocracy. Communism's states that capitalism will be destroyed from within, not without. And this has happened. It started with populism, then progressivism, then liberalism, then creeping socialism, then, openly, socialism, and finally autocracy. It took their crowd over one-hundred years. But they were patient and they won. The nation stood by and allowed it. Hell, they even applauded. I remember a turning-point election where the candidate's, soon-to-be-President, rallying cry was *Change*. The masses cheered. They wanted change, alright, but never asked *what* change the candidate really had in mind. They soon found out. His first proposals were pure socialism.

So, if you worked one hundred years for an outcome, why would you be receptive to a complete U-turn, even if your way caused dire results? These people, the so-called leaders, are ideologues. They are completely devoted to an ideology that hails the destruction of free-enterprise and personal freedom. Both are anathema to them. They really don't care about the people. They care about the idea. And they believe they are the chosen ones to implement the idea. Therefore, they must retain the power or the idea dies."

Josh was conflicted, "But can't they see it's destroying our country?"

Lightoiler's face saddened, "Yes. It is the outcome for which they strived all those years. In their thinking, they had to destroy capitalism in order

242

to save the country. They aren't misguided. They are evil. They believe that democracy, free-enterprise, personal liberties, national patriotism, a strong military are the things *wrong* with this country, not what's *right*. And, naturally, they believe they know what is best for all of us. All we have to do is submit to their wisdom. Those of us that resist are not just misguided, we are dangerous. We have to be extinguished for the greater good. This has been the way with Autocrats for time immemorial."

"What about your second point, distance." Josh thought, *Lightoiler is a Svengali with words. There's something so damn familiar about this guy*, he thought. *It isn't just the face, it's the voice and words.* It nagged him. Intrinsically, Joshua disliked this guy. But he didn't know why. Everything the guy said was making sense.

Lightoiler picked up the thread, "Distance, yes. Essentially this means not only physical distance but lofty distance of the leaders from those governed. When one enters Washington, D.C., he, or she, enters a separate world. It is as if Roman Senators have arrived from their country villas mounting the steps of the Forum. The elite consort, confound and conspire. And they can only do this at a distance from those that elected them. It is a curtain they hide behind so that they can put into action their real plan. Few are there for the people's business. They are there for implementation of an ideology. They lied as to their true motivation, and distance gives them a shroud in which to hide their lies. They don't address what the people need, just what the people desire. It is as if shutting up a baby each time it cried by giving it sugar water. We all desire things, but that doesn't mean they don't have to be earned. Yet these ideologues care not a whit for the basics of a sound economy, a sound society. It is the implementation of their plan. The ones that occupy the seat of power require distance to provide the obscurity of their actual agenda: the destruction of our nation's economy and our culture. Distance allows this.

The further away a government is from those it is designed to serve, the more those with power can abuse it. The majority that shares the same view have successfully annulled the opposition through intimidation, parliamentary procedures and, now, threat from the 'Sedition Act.' There is no more oversight. The Fourth Estate, the Press, is their public relations arm, not an overseer. And distance has allowed this to occur. The people may be ill informed, but that does not mean they cannot see the end results: their money is worthless, their jobs are gone, their country is defenseless, their liberties are curtailed. But they don't know who to blame. The rulers all point to outside agitators and those few remaining inside who disagree. If only we could end these people's resistance, then we could solve these problems. That is what they tell the people. And the statement is true. Except that the problems are not the peoples. The people are confused. They do not know the truth. They have been so confounded; it takes time for them to recognize truth. All of this is accomplished with distance, physical and ethereal."

Josh interjected, "Why don't the people throw the bastards out at election time?"

Lightoiler nodded, "A good point. And, again the answer is distance. The elected official is one person in Washington D.C. and morphs into another before his electorate. He deflects all blame. He reminds all of the goodies he has delivered. He warns them that, in these difficult times, a district or State that sends opposition to Congress shall suffer the loss of Washington's largess. It is better to suffer the fool one knows than elect a new fool that might damage their allotment of the dole. But as the dole shrinks, meaning inflation reduces buying power, the natives are becoming restless. And this makes the Federal government even more autocratic and virulent against opposition. When Rivera's volume rises, it is because his efforts falter."

"So the people are basically stupid," Josh offered.

Lightoiler pondered his next statement, "Not stupid, but deluded by Washington and self-deluded because the alternative is too painful. We have been treated so long as naïve children that many act that way. They want quick fixes to problems that have built up over decades. They want no reduction in their entitlements, even though they wish to work less and pay less in taxes. Even the word entitlement was designed for the evil-doers' goals. If you create government programs that current recipients have not paid for, and you convince the public that they deserve the benefit, that they are *entitled*, then you have successfully put the country on the path to socialism. Man or woman is entitled to nothing except personal liberty and the fruit of their labors. Everything else is charity. These conspirators ended the use of the word charity, and replaced it with entitled. The reason? Charity is at the discretion of the givers and can be reduced or ended at their will.

But here is the real key to distance: it allows anonymity. It is conspirators stealing in the night. It's *sub rosa*. With the people so distant, the conspirators feel free to follow personal, and often, ideological agendas contrary to those they represent. And they get away with it."

"So what's the alternative?" Joshua's attention was rapt. This guy was outlining exactly what he had seen in the Nation's Capital, what he had been part of in the DDD, why he felt so sleazy working for the crowd Lightoiler was diminishing.

"A return to our Republican roots. I do not mean the Party. I refer to the ideal. The President and his crowd are taking our country to the end of a path begun over two hundred years ago, a Federalized system. Article 10 of the Constitution: we were founded as a Republic of States, not a Federal system. But remember this, Mr. Stillwater, the Constitution says without ambiguity: *powers not delegated to the United States by the Constitution, nor prohibited by it to the States, are reserved to the States respectively, or to the people.* Jeffersonian thinking was that the States were the core of the government. The Federal government was created by the States. And its main duty was to protect the States from external threats and to settle disputes between States.

Hamiltonian thinking had the opposite goal. It was that the States are subservient to the Federal Government. And to give you the real mindset of Hamilton, he lobbied for a king before acquiescing to a president."

Joshua gave a small, snide laugh, "And you people think you adhere to the original Constitution? I can think of ten different ways you are in violation: a currency, customs, taxes on imports and exports, free movement of your Citizens, denial of Federal authority over your National Guard, denial of Federal laws, period. And there's a lot more I could come up with."

"I agree!" Lightoiler's concurrence was almost jovial. This surprised Josh. "We are in defiance of these points. And the reason is the Federal Government has overstepped its bounds in so many other areas. In war, you do not adhere to the authority of the other side that is using that authority to crush you. You do not try foreign terrorists in courts designed for a Citizen."

"What about the courts? Couldn't you get satisfaction there?"

It was Lightoiler's time for snideness, "Which courts? It is the U.S. Supreme Court that began and accelerated our Federalization. It moved the economy, law enforcement, education and social issues under Federal purveyance. It eroded and dissolved the power of States. Today the Court is slaved to the Executive Branch; rubber stamps all of Rivera's initiatives, and sanctifies jail for Citizens that speak out. I personally have no faith in that branch. That ship sailed long ago."

"You used the word war. Is this State at war with the Federal government, Mr. Lightoiler?"

Lightoiler figidted in his chair. The question seemed to make him nervous. "We are not at war in the sense you think. We *are* at war on the political, social and economic fronts."

"So, far." General Roughton offered up this gem, casually reaching for his water glass.

# Chapter 28

## Unarmed

### Situation Room, The White House

President Rivera was underneath the White House, within the Situation Room. From here wars had been directed by past Presidents. Although the Wyoming problem could not be judged a war, it had definitely escalated past 'incident.'

It was nearing 06:00 hours Washington time, which meant that General Maxwell at Fort Collins would shortly receive the train loaded with enough heavy armor for his battalion of men to face the stolen Abrams III's. Rivera had tossed through a sleepless night and had finally risen at four AM. He had a cup of coffee and made his way to the underground command center where he now slumped in a chair. The lack of sleep was felt by all in the room.

General Declamore had stayed all night in the Sit-Room, waiting for word of Maxwell's successful deployment. He was also monitoring the progress of the supply train. On flat screens round the room could be seen the red circle indicating Ft. Collins and the blinking green dot of the approaching train, tracked by GPS. The blip was about ten minutes out. On other screens were the last known positions of the Abrams III tanks as tracked by a satellite-pass nearly eight hours prior. Revised updates would be received within another four hours.

Nearly three months earlier, Wyoming had outmaneuvered the U.S. Army with regards to the tanks. An upgrade to the tanks' electronics was designated to occur at a U.S. Army base within Wyoming. This was nothing unusual so there was no concern as it was upon Federal land. So the tanks began rolling to the State. The Abrams III was a major improvement over the II series; thirty-five percent increased mileage for the guzzling gas-turbine engines; a stronger composite armor allowing the rolling weapon to be sheathed in lighter weight material while receiving an increase in protection; electronics containing a form of artificial intelligence for determining friend from foe, along with faster firing solutions; and a new, automated loader increasing firing rates to one shell every two seconds. The world's most advanced mobile, armored killing machine was even more lethal.

Unfortunately, thirty-two of the U.S. Army's total inventory of eighty-four sat in Wyoming. The plan had been for the Wyoming facility to receive ten tanks at a time. With upgrades completed, the ten would return to operation while another ten were sent. The second part never occurred. After thirty-two arrived (another eight were halted mid transport), and battalion units complained of their upgraded tanks being long overdue, the Pentagon made inquiries. In the meantime, the political situation between Wyoming and Washington had severely deteriorated. This increased Federal suspicions. All inbound tank shipments were halted as Wyoming offered no explanation as to the disposition of the thirty-two tanks.

All questions were answered when satellite pictures showed thirty-two Abram III tanks dispersed to key defense areas along the State's borders.

The U.S. Army and the Federal government had been had.

General Declamore, the Chairman of the Joint Chiefs of Staff, was studying the deployment of the tanks, strategizing on how his field commander, General Vernon Maxwell, would counter them. An additional eighteen of the advanced tanks were now on the way via rail. This, along with other armor upon the train, would go a long way in countering the threat of the tanks Wyoming controlled.

Declamore focused upon the digital progress of the train so necessary for Maxwell's force to carry out the Presidents command.

The green dot grew closer and closer to the red circle. When the moment came that the two merged, the President slapped his knee and said, "Finally, we can get this show on the road. General Declamore, what is your thinking as to......."

The General was holding up his hand, "Sir, one moment."

Rivera looked at the screen that held the attention of the General. "What is it?"

Declamore ignored the question. Instead he turned to an aide and demanded, "Get Maxwell on the horn right now!"

Rivera was irritated at being ignored, "I asked you, General, what's going on?"

General Declamore pointed to the screen,"Mr. President, the train did not stop in Ft. Collins."

"What? How's that possible?" Rivera now focused on the green dot that was inching through and past the red circle. "What in hell is going on?"

Declamore's aide leaned over and softly spoke into the General's ear. "What line?" responded the General. "To hell with it, just put him on speaker phone." He turned to Rivera, "Sir, this is General Maxwell we will be hearing from."

A voice came clearly through speakers mounted around the room, "Is someone there? Dec, can you hear me?"

"Yes, Verne, loud and clear. What's going on out there?"

"I have Seventy-five thousand troops standing around holding their dicks while their armor is on the way north."

"Language, Verne, I'm with the President."

Rivera waved his hand, signaling it was unimportant. He leaned forward in his chair, "General, this is the President. What do you mean 'it's going north?' What is north from you?"

"Wyoming, sir. Next stop for that train is Cheyenne. Hell, it not only has our tanks, our armor, but I saw two flatbeds with DARTS launch platforms go by. What the hell was I supposed to do with those anyway? Does Wyoming have an air force I don't know about? Don't you think you should keep me in the loop?"

At the mention of 'DARTS', everyone in the room stiffened. DARTS was the acronym for Defensive Arial Resistance Termination System. It was a SAM anti-missile and anti-aircraft system that was two generations pass the Patriot. Each missile possessed the latest nano-board guidance system that provided its own radar and infrared tracking. Once it locked on to a target, there was no shaking it off. No stealth technology could hide from DARTS. Its mini rockets incorporated thrust vectoring that allowed it to nearly do U-turns in the sky. And on top of this was its speed. It could reach sixty thousand feet in less than five seconds. Once a threat from the sky was detected, DARTS eliminated it, period. It had revolutionized conventional military planning. In the past, supremacy of the air was mission number one. But with DARTS, this became virtually impossible.

Maxwell spoke, "That train came through here barreling at sixty miles per hour. Hell, it's already half way to the Wyoming border by now."

"Verne, what else was on that train? Do you know?"

"Do I know? Of course I know. I have the manifest right here."

"Give me a quick rundown, just categories, no specifics. Any tanks?" Declamore knew the answer. He just wanted to confirm the disaster.

"Let me look." The sound of rustling papers came through the speaker. "Oh, yeah, eighteen of our latest and greatest, Abrams III. Ah, let's see, Strykers, Bradleys, HumVees, Apaches, Commanches, WartHogs, NLOS platforms and other artillery. And why the hell are we transporting a plane by train? They had to have disassembled the wings. This is crazy."

"What about derailing it? Can't we shunt it off on a side rail and flip the engines, or something?

"Somebody sabotaged the switches, Dec. We've got our best electronics man on the mess right now. He says it's been all rewired and there's a virus or worm or some such damn thing in the computer system. It's going to take him an hour just to figure it out. Right now, they have green lights all the way to Cheyenne. And in about fifteen minutes, they're beyond any sidings."

"Damn! Vern, listen carefully. You must stop that train. You hear me? It is imperative!"

"What the hell you think I've been trying to do, Dec? After initial resistance I secured the assistance of the station manager. We have been calling via radio to the engineer for the last twenty minutes. But he won't answer. I don't know if they just won't answer or can't answer. I have an advance recon team up on the border as we speak. I ordered them to drive their HumVees onto the tracks, but that's about all they can do. They've only got rifles and side arms. How about air assets? Anything heavy nearby? What about Warren?"

"Good thinking, Vern. But I have a pretty good hunch Warren might not cooperate. We can get something there soon from Nellis. I'll get on it, but I have to get the Air Force up to speed real quick."

"Well, you got the man right there. Let him issue the orders. He could earn his pay for once."

Rivera glowered at Declamore who spoke at the phone, "General Maxwell, you are on a speaker phone and in the presence of the

Commander-In-Chief." Declamore was a little embarrassed, but for his friend, not the President.

"Oh, hell Harry. Right now I don't give a shit. Just handle things on your end and I'll get my boys up at the border on alert. Call me on my SAT if you have any updates."

"Okay, Vern."

The satellite phone connection was broken.

General Declamore turned to the President. "Sir I would suggest you get a call through right away to Nellis. I am sure they've got some fighter-bombers available that can take out that train. Tell them to go for the engines. Don't hit the cars. There's over twenty men in the rear car, twenty good men. And there's fifty billion NUS dollars of equipment on that train. I don't want a bunch of screaming politicians telling me that the military has to do with less than what we already have."

Rivera formed a sneer on his face, "You forget, General. I am a politician, and so is everyone else in this room."

"You're wrong, sir. I am reminded of it every day when I wake up."

# Chapter 29

## Tunnel Vision

## On Board

Another hailing interrupted his thoughts, "708, this is Central. Frank? Charlie? Anyone? Come on, guys, answer me. I have the President of the United States on the line. He wants to talk to you."

Ben looked at Hiroto who shot back a surprised look. "Impressive, Warner-san,"

Ben gave a short bow of his head. The radio crackled.

"Whoever is in charge of that train, this is President Rivera. I want to speak to you. It's for your own good. Please respond, now."

The President's voice was curt. Ben shook his head again at a now-shocked Frank. There were several moments of silence.

"Fine. Play it that way, if you want. But let me tell you what's going to happen. We have several options and the last one, which I've already authorized, is to bomb those engines you're riding in. We are not bluffing. You there?"

More silence.

"Well, you've been warned. I don't want to kill innocent civilians. You hold twenty-four hostages, unless they're already dead. But if not, let their deaths be on your head, not mine. This is President Rivera, over, ah, I mean, out."

Suddenly Frank shouted, "JESUS!" He immediately strapped himself into the chair.

Ben saw what caused the fright. Two Humvees and a troop transport truck were parked on the tracks, one after another. Ben pushed his hand on top of the engineer's and forced both forward on the controls. The train accelerated another ten miles per hour. Ben yelled to Hiroto, "HOLD ON!" and braced himself behind Frank's chair. The impact was different than Ben expected. The result of the collision was a sudden deceleration of the train, but not jarring. The heavy engine with the kinetic force of three engines and fifty-plus railcars loaded with amour merely sliced through the vehicles. Both Humvees were cut in two. The transport was turned sideways, caught for a distance on the lead engine. Then, like a bull shrugging a victim from its horns, the truck rolled onto its side, bounced and dissolved within tumultuous rolls.

Ben immediately looked for Hiroto. The Japanese had fallen to the floor and spread his arms and legs out at forty-five degree angles. The impact had spun him such that his feet were in front as he slid towards the cab nose. A metal step in front of the fireman's chair had stopped him. He now looked up at Ben and gave a thumbs-up. Ben returned the gesture with his left hand as the right pushed himself back from Frank's command chair.

He said, more to himself than anyone listening, "That was pretty feeble, especially for the Army. They're usually into overkill. I would have expected ten tanks in a row." He turned towards Hiroto, "I'm sure they have plenty more up their sleeve.

The train's radio again crackled to life. "This is General Blake. I am commander of the 302nd Tactical Air Wing at Nellis Air Force Base. I am ordering you to stop that train. I have two F 35's nearing your position. They will perform one pass over to see if you are complying with my instructions. If you do not, they are authorized to remove the engines from action. I am sure you understand. I am told you will probably not respond, so take this as our last communication."

Ben held a GPS transponder. It not only showed their position, it also gave him distance and time to destination based on their current speed. Their position was marked on the hand-held screen by a small circle. For Ben, its progress was maddeningly slow. He was mentally running time scenarios when the first bomber/fighter roared overhead. It was so low and close to the cab that Ben clearly saw the Brimstone anti-armor missiles mounted under the wings. The two bomb-bay doors were open exposing a JDAM (Joint Direct Attack Munitions) 1000 pound laser-guided bomb hanging within each bay. One of these bombs would easily destroy half of entire train, let alone a single engine. He knew the pass was meant to intimidate, and it worked. A second plane roared overhead and disappeared quickly out of the line of sight from the cabin.

Frank's face reflected pure terror and his voice raised several octaves, "They aren't kidding around. They're going to blow all of us to Kingdom Come. There's no way you can outrun them. It's twenty miles to Cheyenne. You got a death wish or what?"

Ben's response was to push the engineer's control all the way to the stops and say, "You're assuming we're going to Cheyenne, Frank." They had just crossed over into Wyoming. The distant lights of Cheyenne still shimmered in the early dawn. But that was not their destination. There were only three miles between them and safety. Every second counted.

The pilot in command notified Nellis that both planes had made their pass and the train showed no signs of slowing. He asked for permission to go "hot" and carry out his instructions. After a moment of silence a voice came through his headset, "Mission a GO. Proceed with destruction of lead engine. Do not, repeat, Do not hit troop transport car at rear of train."

The pilot toggled his wing man, "Heater, this is Bulldog. During your pass, did you see a troop transport car on the back of the train?"

Heater signed back, "Negative. Hope we got the right train."

The pilot in command nodded to himself, "I'm going to check on that." He toggled over, "Command, this is Red Leader. We understand affirmative to GO. But we saw no troop transport car on the train tail. Request permission for another pass to verify."

There was silence for an extended period. The lead pilot radioed, "Command, can you confirm our request for another pass?"

The radio shot back, "Hold your horses, Red leader. This show is being run out of D.C. and they're mulling it over......Wait a minute Red Leader.... Ok, yes Red Leader, you are GO for another pass. Troop transport definitely connected to end of train."

"Roger that, Command. Red Leader out."

Both planes again shot over the length of the train. This time they flew to the side of the train at its same level. Ben gave a short wave and smiled. Both pilots confirmed to command that there was no troop transport at the rear of the train. Again, there was a delay as Command awaited instructions from D.C. Finally it came through.

"Red Leader, we have confirmed that you have correct target. Troop transport left behind. Proceed with mission, repeat, mission a GO".

"Red Leader confirms mission a GO."

Bulldog contacted his wingman, "We have affirmative. Climb to eight thousand and set your run." The extra altitude would provide the pilots enough distance and time to steer the bombs to their targets and escape the explosion.

On board the train Ben knew how close this was going to be. He had two fears: first was being bombed from above, second was derailment when they shunted off onto the spur just ahead. They were going about thirty-miles an hour too fast. Ben saw no way past it. To slow down was certain death. He saw the spur ahead and the signal open. All Frank could muster was a soft "Jesus." Suddenly the train lurched to the left, heaving all in the cabin towards the outside, right wall. The train felt as if it were nearly leaving the tracks. Ben grabbed the control chair with his free hand while Hiroto was clutching at the frame of the open interior door. They began a rapid descent towards what appeared a tunnel. They became immersed in darkness except for the illumination of the train's head light. Frank looked at the tunnel sides and top. It had to be a reinforced concrete, especially to be this deep. But he couldn't figure out where it went. They should have been entering Cheyenne. There was no tunnel in Cheyenne. Heck, there were no mountains around Cheyenne to put a tunnel through. Frank confirmed to himself that this had been the strangest day of his life.

Ben was also looking at the tunnel concrete. Frank had no idea how reinforced this tunnel was. Began eighteen months prior, it was built for one purpose only: to receive this train. .Over five meters thick with six tons of steel within the concrete for every hundred-meters of tunnel. It surpassed even German bunkers built during WWII. Ben still worried if it was enough. He knew the explosive power of the JDAM. The only good thing was the Air Force hadn't sent bunker-busters. But Ben knew it would be a White House option once Washington figured out where their train disappeared.

The lead pilot's screen glowed red. He had acquired and was tracking the train when it veered sharply left. He spoke into his throat mic, "Change in target aspect. Revise run accordingly." Both planes banked slightly left. "Prepare to release on my count. Three..two...RELEASE!" The laser guided bombs fell away from their racks and began their descent towards the train. A night vision, real-time feed from the bombs' noses displayed on screens within each cockpit. A light flashed in front of both pilots, "Loss of Target Position." Both pilots adjusted their individual bomb's descent via a joystick. The train was literally disappearing. The pilots adjusted by pulling the bomb path further backwards along what was left of the train. "What the hell is going on?" asked the wingman. The pilot in command didn't have an answer so he didn't offer any response. The engines were gone. Was he supposed to destroy the rest of the train? His instructions had been explicit: engines only. He made a command decision.

"Heater, this is Bulldog. Aim your ordnance ahead of where you think the engines are. Maybe we can bring that tunnel on them."

The two bombs augured into the ground about a hundred meters from the tunnel opening. One fireball became visible with another shortly behind. They had managed to make a huge crater in the earth, but had no idea if it was effective in stopping the engines.

Hiroto looked at the tunnel ceiling. It blurred from a massive vibration. Chunks of concrete fell upon the rails and the engines. The cab swayed as the rail bed rippled, similar to an earthquake. Ignoring what was happening outside of the cab, Ben shouted to the engineer, "Bring this train to an immediate halt or you're literally going to run into a wall!"

Frank pulled the throttle all the way back and applied full breaks. 'Pull' tension in the cars' couplings now slammed into 'Pushing.' Hiroto shot forward as Ben compressed into the back of Frank's control chair. Squealing of metal-on-metal assaulted ears. It seemed to all in the cab as if it would go on forever. But Frank knew it was going to end very soon, one way or another. In the far distance, the tracks stopped at a concrete wall. The pitch of the squeal began to drop and the cab shook violently. Ben thought his teeth would shake loose. Just as the shuddering reached maximum Richter, all came to rest.

Ben couldn't see Hiroto and shouted, "You OK?" A response came slowly, "I am OK. Just some bruise. I will be alright." Hiroto had returned to his feet and walked back into view. Ben was rubbing his temples. His head ached terribly. His concussion was exacerbated by the noise, vibration and shaking of the emergency stop. Hiroto noted his pain, "You are the one who is not OK, Ben-san. You need a doctor."

Ben nodded, "Got one right outside."

Hiroto said, "You just happen to have a doctor on call?"

Ben said, "Yep, and a lot more besides. Take a look out this window."

Outside a large, raised concrete platform skirted the length of the train. Lights blazed. Personnel in Wyoming Army uniforms as well as civilians scurried to the train. Flatbed trucks and overhead cranes were already moving into position as men climbed aboard the rail cars and began unfastening the tarps, breaking open come-a-longs, and grinding locks off of boxcar doors.

Frank viewed the scene with amazement. "Where are we? What is this place?" Ben answered, "You're in Wyoming, Frank, and deep underground. This is probably the America's only reinforced train bunker. And even if another one exists, I'm pretty sure it doesn't beat this length. We built a spur off the main tracks. That sharp turn to the left was us pulling off and heading down into this." Then he motioned to Hiroto to follow and walked to the cab exit door.

Outside, Hiroto turned and asked Ben, "So why do you think those planes made a second pass. That was the critical moment. That is what gave us the time to make the tunnel."

Ben nodded, "I have no idea, Hiroto. I guess only the Air Force and the Gods know the answer to that. I'm just glad we made it. Would have screwed up a nice day, otherwise."

Hiroto smiled, "Very Eastern of you, Ben-san." Ben's bow was interrupted by a shout from the train cab door.

Frank said, "Hey, what am I supposed to do? Me and Charlie? Do I get my train back?"

Ben nodded, "We need you to stick around a while. It's for your own good, Frank. After our little disagreement with the Feds is resolved, you're free to go. It's prudent for you to stick around awhile until things cool off. I think there's going to be some Army types that are really pissed off. They might believe you're the ring leader. Nobody ever saw us. We got a great State here and are in serious need of tech types like you and Charlie. Look around and then decide if this State of Mine would be a good place for you and your family. Either way, you're here for the duration. I'll get someone to take care of you. Just hang in the cab for about twenty minutes until someone comes for you."

Frank removed his cap and scratched his head.

# Chapter 30

## Unwelcome Guest

## Governor's Mansion, Cheyenne

"So you think it will come to actual war, General?" Joshua was pleased the military was pulled into the conversation.

"Not my call. But I'd say seventy-five thousand army personnel sittin' across the border from Cheyenne is more than provocative."

Joshua nodded. The General shook his head, "And come daylight, I think they're gonna get real nasty."

"Why?"

"Because, they're gonna say we provoked them, that we took something of theirs."

"Did we? Ah, I mean, did you take something of theirs?"

"Don't know yet. Let ya know in about," he pulled back his uniform cuff to check his watch.

At this exact moment a distant thundering boom occurred. The floors shook. Dishes and silverware clattered, wine and water glasses overturned. The only one that panicked was Governor Fodor. He jumped from the table, overturning more glasses and shouted, "What the hell was that, a bomb? Someone trying to assassinate us?" His eyes darted back and forth along the table of guests, looking for some sort of reaction matching his.

"Sit down, Scott. I'm sure Sam will let us know what's happening once she finds out. We're all in one piece and some china got knocked around. Relax." Governor Brigham's response was casual, although she picked up a neighboring glass of white wine that had survived the trembler, raised it to her lips and slugged the remaining amber liquid down in one gulp.

Sam had excused herself and was within a knot of her top people at the other end of the tables. General Roughton was on his cell phone, nodding his head her way. Josh was watching with deep interest. Roughton had mumbled some information to the Governor and Sam was nodding. Josh watched her put on a game face as she started walking back to the head table.

"Sorry to give you all a fright, ladies and gentlemen. It appears a natural gas facility on the other side of town exploded. We really do not have all the facts, yet. It was far enough away from town that any subsidiary damage was minimal. So far there is no mention of fatalities, just burns. I hope it doesn't sound inappropriate, but let's continue our wonderful evening. I am sure I will have some updates soon and will keep you all advised."

She calmly sat down and said, "George, I think it's time for desert."

"Very good, Ms. Governor" he dipped his head and left the room.

Joshua had been mulling the incident over. He had heard and felt many explosions during his military career. And this one had all the markings. It was the same as a bombing run from overhead. He couldn't be positive, because he had never experienced a natural gas explosion.

Then his head snapped with a thought. *Ben!*

He swirled his glass casually and asked off-handedly of the General, "Would this have anything to do with a train?" he asked innocently.

The General's eye's narrowed as he stared at Josh. Lightoiler cleared his throat and said, "That's quite an assumption, Mr. Stillwater."

"I'm in the assumption business, Mr. Lightoiler."

It was now Lightoiler's turn to be circumspect, "And what business would that be, sir, exactly?"

*Touché*, thought Josh. "Anti-terrorism, exactly." He was proud to keep the veiled discussion going.

"I thought terrorism on American soil came under the purview of the FBI. How exactly does Home Land Security become involved?"

Josh smiled, "I'm sure you are aware that the Department of Homeland Security was created in response to *Nine-Eleven*. And its purview is any terrorist investigation on our soil. The FBI reports to it."

"And do you consider the people of this State terrorists, Mr. Stillwater?"

General Roughton, glass in hand, froze mid sip. He had been enjoying Lightoiler's parries and thrusts, up to this point. Now he wasn't so sure.

Josh answered, keeping up the veil, "Only if they're involved in terrorist activities."

"And do you consider our activities terrorism?"

That was it. Josh was through with the game, "OK, knock off the cow shit, Lightoiler. I wasn't invited here for your third degrees." Josh looked sideways at Sam, who was listening to his conversation intently. *Or maybe I was*, he thought.

General Roughton laughed, "Lay off Charles. Let the poor guy eat his ice cream."

Josh thought the dessert unpretentious and delicious. It was three scoops of homemade vanilla ice cream sitting on a halved banana: a banana split. There were trays placed between each three guests, filled with every conceivable topping: chocolate, strawberry, butterscotch, caramel, marshmallow, hot fudge, slivered walnuts and almonds, whole peanuts, crushed peanuts, M&M's, crushed Heath Bar, crushed Reese's Peanut Butter cups, and a myriad of other confections. The Governors were almost giddy, piling on one topping after another and laughing the entire time. Even Governor Fodor seemed to have forgotten his near death experience. Josh watched and laughed. It was good to see elected officials act like human beings. He particularly enjoyed Governor Brigham. She seemed oblivious to stares of the mountainous delight she had created. She heaped spoonful after spoonful of each offering, making sure she missed nothing. Once finished, she dug in with voraciousness.

***

The evening drifted back into another cocktail hour. Dawn was breaking. It appeared no one wanted to leave. The Governors seemed happy to let their hair down among equals. The Wyomingans were waiting for something, and this intrigued Josh. He fit into neither group, so he hung at the fringes of conversations.

Bern was giving another economics lecture, this time on why a Federal Reserve was completely unnecessary and actually harmful to an economy.

General Roughton was discussing military maneuvers for some unknown, potential battle. It was based on an offensive split of forces while, defensively, meeting two fronts at the same time.

Governor Almondo was pursuing the idea of splitting California north and south. He thought the south was a lost cause to the encroachment of illegal Latinos. He was seriously considering asking the President to present Southern California to the Mexicans in exchange for a guarantee of using the Mexican Federal Army to stop migration north of more illegals. He proposed the line be drawn at the Tehachapi Mountains. *Where ever that is*, thought Josh. Sam consoled Almondo on his State's predicament.

"There is nothing you can do Mario. Social services were designed as a net to catch the few from falling to the ground, not as a hammock for the majority to laze within. Perhaps a new start with new rules would be best. Those Citizens that suffer through this will herald your decision once the new beginning has caught hold. I only tell you, do not bend, do not yield or the north will be as lost to us as the south already is."

The Governor gave her a sad nod. It made Josh even sadder to consider the United States losing a part.

He was tired of politics and looked for an escape. He saw Jeff and Jerry over in a corner and thought; *At least their conversation might be a little lighter.* He was wrong.

As Josh walked towards them, he saw Jimmy had his arm straight out, hand lying on Jeff's shoulder. Jeff had his head bent downward and the scene looked as if Jimmy were consoling his brother. Standing next to Jimmy was his partner William. Whatever was going on between Jeff and Jimmy didn't seem to concern William. The two brothers were distracted to the point they didn't notice Joshua walking up from behind.

Josh heard Jimmy say, "Dammit, Jeff. It's not your kind of fight. You need a bar room and a pool cue to be any good. He can take care of himself. If you were there, you'd probably get both of you killed. He's trained for this kind of action and you're not. Hell, you wouldn't even have gotten your fat ass on to that train. Now lighten up before you screw-up Sam's party.

William sensed Josh's presence and broke his concentration on Jeff. He said in a voice a little too loud, "Hey there, Uncle Josh. Good to see you again."

He acted as if to signal the two brothers of Josh's approach. Jeff struggled not to spit out his drink at the announcement of a new *Uncle*.

Joshua acted as if not hearing the attribute, or noticing the reddening of Jeff, "Hey, William." He nodded towards Jeff. "What's his concern, and what's this about hopping a train? Someone I know do something stupid?" Josh said.

Jimmy fumbled his words for a moment, "Well, ah, no, nobody you know anymore. The only person doing something stupid is Jeff here. He's sucking down JD & Coke like water. Will and I are just telling him to lighten up, right Jeff?"

Jeff looked up at Jimmy, glared at William and moved on to Josh. In his alcoholic stupor he slurred, "Yeah, sure, that's it. I mean, that's all, or.something...like that."

Josh said, "Listen to Jimmy, Jeff. Cut back on the booze before you embarrass yourself and Sam."

William interjected, "Yeah, Jeff, listen to James. Warner can handle it. Stop beating yourself up."

Both Jeff and Jimmy snapped their heads towards William with anger. William was surprised by their response, especially his partner's. He had a *what-did-I-do* look on his face.

"Fag," grumbled Jeff.

"Homophobe," shot back William.

Jeff said too loudly, "Go screw yerself, Will."

William folded his arms in front and replied icily, "If I could do that, Jeff, I wouldn't need your brother."

Jeff flipped him a bird and turned away. "I'm gonna get another drink." He stumbled towards the bar.

William watched him walk away, and then turned to Jimmy, "Great party, as usual. I'll see you back at the hotel. You should stay and hold your big brother's hand, or screw top, as usual. I don't need this shit." He walked towards the front entry.

Josh tried to joke with Jimmy, "So gay guys fight over family too?"

Jimmy gave him a hard look, "Yeah, we're almost normal people. *Do we not bleed when pricked?* "

Josh bit his lip at the 'pricked' comment. It certainly wasn't the moment for any follow-on levity.

Jimmy added, "I was wondering when you'd take your shot about Will and me."

"Whoa, hold on, Jimmy. I've got no problem with you and Will. Whatever makes you happy."

"Yeah, I'm so damn deliriously happy right now."

Josh held up his hands in surrender, "I'm not the one who said *fag*. That was your dear brother."

Jimmy lazily waved his hand across his front, "Forget it. Let's just go mingle. If Jeff wants to make an ass of himself, let him. I'm tired of apologizing for him."

"Wait a minute," said Josh. "What's this about trains and a Warner? We aren't talking about Sam. I'm pretty sure of that. And Charlie's too old of a sonofabitch to try train hopping. So that leaves Ben. He in some kind of trouble? I want to know."

Jimmy took a swig from a beer bottle he had been holding by the neck while he watched Will walk away. "Nothing for you to be concerned about, Josh."

Josh felt hurt by the exclusion. "What do ya mean, nothing for me to be concerned about? Ben's one of my oldest friends, Jimmy. Tell me what's going on."

Jimmy looked at Josh and opened his mouth to speak. But he thought a moment and just shook his head.

"Come on, Jimmy, spill. You owe me." Josh said.

Jimmy was appalled, "Owe you!? Owe you what? You've been gone for fifteen years, Stillwater. Then you come waltzing back here like you're gonna get the last dance. There's been a lot of water under the bridge and it's put some good people to the test, Ben the most. You may have been his friend before you bailed, but we don't know you anymore. Who are you Josh? Who do you work for? Why did you come back here now, at this exact moment?" His eyes bored in on Joshua, "What side of the fence you on?" Jimmy took another swig and walked away.

There was the question he had avoided all night. Sam had said he was home, and these people were his family. He couldn't really be pissed at Jimmy. Everything he said was true. And Jimmy didn't feel about Josh the way Sam did. He couldn't expect these people to pat him on the back and say *Welcome home, big guy!*

There were seventy-five thousand troops that were forcing him to make up his mind. One key question dogged him. *If they invade what do I do? Do I pick up a rifle? Do I skedaddle out of here? How do I choose? And what about Sam? Do I just leave her to the invaders? Some of these people are going to hang, if Rivera has his way. And Sam would probably be at the front of the line. Do I allow it?*

He was completely confounded; his head pulled one way, his heart another. What had Sam said about that?.. Listen to your heart. But should he listen to something that would get him killed, or worse, thrown into a Federal penitentiary for the rest of his life?

These were his thoughts as he heard Lightoiler speaking with Harley Stevens, Denny Watson, and Frank Dunleavy.

"The time nears and we must steel our resolve. Think of the Minutemen. They will even the playing field."

*What's he talking about?* thought Josh, *The Minutemen from the Revolutionary War?* It didn't make sense. He drifted over to their clutch.

Lightoiler continued, "We will broadcast to the world. They will see the coming resistance as our grandest moment. They will wish us well and they will side with us, I will make sure of that. This exemplifies everything I have said about Federalism. The use of military forces against a State whose only crime is to ignore unconstitutional laws is unconscionable. We are a republic, not a federalist country. The Founding Fathers saw the wisdom of this. We are a diverse people and shall always remain so. No Federal construct can take advantage of the creativeness our diversity provides. As in Germany, it was a Federalist system which allowed Hitler to gain dictatorial power over a democracy. Concentration of power is dangerous. All you have to do is look at the march of Rivera towards his autocracy.

In opposition to Federalism, I point out that we are not only a diverse people, we are spread across an enormous and diverse landmass. The centralism of a Federal system is not only counterproductive to our nature; it is an affront to our spirit of independence and self-determination. Whether Jefferson, Paine or Thoreau said it first, I agree that, *That government is best that governs least.* And I add to this: the government that governs closest to the people reflects best the will of those same people. When I broadcast during our most dangerous moment, I will speak of this to our fellow countrymen. I will remind them that *the problem is not the Federal government, the problem is Federalism!"*

Joshua's antennae shot up at this phrase. He had heard it before. In fact, he had heard it a million times before. It was the sign-off signature of Joseph Bascomb.

*Sonofabitch*, thought Josh. He stared at the man, mentally adding fifty pounds to his girth and stripping away the beard. Then he closed his eyes and listened to the sonorous voice. *No doubt about it. And he's talking about broadcasting too. It's him, right in front of me. And I can't do a thing about it.*

*Joseph Bascomb!*

Charles Lightoiler, aka Joseph Bascomb, continued his pep talk to the group. As he spoke his eyes met Josh's. Stillwater's coal-black eyes drew in all light like a black hole. They were empty, and menacing. Joshua cracked a small, mirthless smile. And Bascomb lost his train of thought, midsentence. Stillwater's penetrating look said everything. *I know who you really are. The game is over.* Bascomb regained a look of coolness. Josh said not a word, but his face said everything. Bascomb turned to the others and ignored him.

It had definitely been an interesting evening. But what did this discovery mean? It was obvious that Bascomb was the State's spokesman. All of Josh's previous views of this man were formed from being a DDD officer, from Maxton, from the leadership in Washington D.C. But was Josh still a part of that? Was he a DDD agent anymore? Why hadn't he informed Maxton of everything he had seen, everything he had heard? Why did he always delay to call in? He now has the chance to be the hunter that bagged Joe Bascomb! It could bring him back out of the wilderness; possibly provide a path back into the military. But did he really want that? So much had changed in the last few days, so much within him. He should have never left. But it was his own fault, his own pride. Charlie Warner couldn't banish him. He had gone into self-exile, and it cost him the love of his life. But what to do about it? His thoughts were awhirl when another voice broke his concentration.

"Well, well, well, seems you're all having a grand time and forgot to invite me. I got hurt feelings."

It was delivered loud enough to override other conversations and cause most to turn towards the source…..Charlie Warner.

Across the room, Jake Dillon muttered, "Uh oh, knew this was gonna happen sometime. Just hoping it wasn't tonight."

Sam was trying to look over shoulders to see what had garnered everyone's attention. Through the throng she saw her Father. Her heart sank. Feeling all eyes upon her, she bravely put on a smile and made her way through the crowd.

"Daddy, what a surprise!"

Charlie Warner was dressed in work clothes, as if he had just come in from the back forty. "Don't give me any of your cow pies, missy. Why wasn't I invited to your little *soiree*?" He circled his long arm in a large circle. His words were slurred and his arm movement threw him off balance. He staggered a couple of steps to the right.

Josh had moved to the front of the crowd and up next to Sam. He put his arm around her waist, knowing this would infuriate Charlie. He gave the opening salvo of his own, personal battle.

"Go home, old man. You're drunk."

Sam cringed.

# Chapter 31

## Standing Tall

### Governor's Mansion, Cheyenne

The rest of the guests had, by now, formed a semi-circle. The Governors of the visiting States were asking those nearby as to the significance of the visitor and reason for the obvious confrontation underway. After hearing a brief story of past events Elizabeth Brigham was openly gleeful, and quite drunk.

"I hope Josh knocks his block off."

The other Governors were open-mouthed at her comment. It was unseemly, such a display in such surroundings. Nevin Stiles just tisked while Bern shook his head sadly. The two remaining Dillons stood at the front of the crowd, Jake stone-faced while Jeff was as jubilant as the Utah Governor. He pointed towards the confrontation with a sloshing glass and said, "Told ya, Pops! Told ya it was gonna happen sometime while Josh was here. Don't say I didn't tell ya!"

Jake barely parted his lips, "Shut up, boy. You're drunker than Charlie."

Sam had removed Josh's arm and walked over to Charlie. She was now rubbing his arm, trying to soothe the beast, "Daddy, I am truly sorry I didn't invite you. I was just introducing Josh to a few people and thought it best….."

Charlie roared, "A few people! You've got the whole damn State here, a few from outside too. What're you thinking girl? And with my boy out there risking his neck for the rest of us."

Half of the crowd understood the reference. The other half looked around for enlightenment. Josh had a pretty good idea that Ben was on some sort of dangerous mission, and that a train figured in it somewhere. His eyes were locked on Charlie. He took a few steps towards his adversary.

"Like I said, old man, you need to go."

"Not till I get you out of this State and out of my life, half-breed."

"Daddy!" exclaimed Sam. She stopped her stroking and put her hands on her hips. "Josh is right. You are making a fool out of yourself and embarrassing me. You need to go." She looked at Jake. He just shrugged. He knew he couldn't physically handle Charlie, especially when he was in this state.

"And leave you here to his animal wiles? I'd rather leave you to those troops that're on our front stoop. That's probably why he's here." Charlie's bobbing head tried to steady as he raised it to the crowd. "For those of you who don't know, this man is a DDD agent and he's probably here to arrest all of you once those troops cross our border."

"Well, that's a dog pissing on the picnic basket." Jake didn't mean to say it aloud.

Jeff roared. Elizabeth Brigham giggled. The other Governors turned white. To find out one among them was a member of the most feared, reviled agency of the Federal Government, the Department of Domestic Disturbances, put a chill on the crowd. Lightoiler glared at Josh.

Josh's face had flushed red. He didn't know if it was embarrassment, guilt or shame. All he was certain of was that he wasn't going to be stampeded by Charlie, not this time. Charlie returned his eyes to Josh's and focused. His face grew contorted. He balled his fist and took two large strides towards Josh. He cocked his arm and, when in striking distance, swung a round-house at Josh's head.

"It's on!" shouted Jeff. Ten on Josh, Dad."

"Shaddup!" answered Jake.

Sam sucked in air.

Josh didn't move. He didn't duck. He rotated his left arm with blinding speed, elbow bent, forearm straight up. The block deflected Charlie's punch. The older man, thrown off-balance, stumbled into Josh's arms. Josh grabbed him and stopped him from falling to the floor. When Josh pulled him upward to put him back on his feet, Charlie presented a crushing uppercut to Josh's chin. It rattled Josh's head and, he thought, *Probably cracked some teeth*. But Josh treated it as a slap. He pushed Charlie away from him.

"Hey, that's a cheap shot, Warner!" shouted Jeff. Jake stomped on his toe. Elizabeth Brigham nodded agreement, whirled around and unsteadily weaved towards the bar for another drink. This had the appearance of at least three rounds she surmised. And she wasn't going dry for that long.

Sam grabbed Charlie's right arm and tried to dampen further efforts to fight. Charlie flicked her off and to the floor like a gnat. This enraged Josh. He was willing to treat Charlie's attacks defensively. But Sam being thrown to the floor instantly put him into punishment mode. He took a step towards Charlie and raised his hands for battle.

"You did it now, old man!" Jeff couldn't constrain his mouth. Jake just threw up his arms in defeat.

Suddenly a loud voice barked from the back of Charlie, near the entrance to the room. "Belay that action, soldier!"

Everyone, including Josh and Charlie turned their attention to the newcomer. Ben Warner stood at attention, his cover tucked under his arm. He was in full Wyoming Army dress uniform, a single star pinned to his collars and hat, a large adhesive bandage set diagonally across his forehead.

Hiroto Ishikawa leaned against the door casing behind Ben.

Charlie was first to respond, "My Boy! You're OK, thank God!" He staggered towards Ben who put his hand out to stop the advance.

"Don't even think of hugging me, mister. Not after the disgraceful show you just put on. You could have destroyed everything we've worked for. At best, you've put a helluva dent in it. Now get your butt outside and into a CityCar before I have you hog-tied and thrown into jail."

Charlie was shocked at the rebuke, "But you don't understand, Ben." He turned and, with a shaking arm, pointed at Josh. Stillwater was bent over helping Sam up from the floor. "He's here! I've got to get rid of him. *We* have to get rid of him. You see that don't you son?" His eyes were pleading for understanding from Ben.

"The only thing we have to get rid of tonight is you, Dad. Paul!"

Paul the security man was waiting in the hallway for Ben's instructions. "Please put Mr. Warner into a CityCar and send him where ever he wants to go…except," He turned to Josh, "Where you staying, mister."

Josh answered, "The Westin."

"Except the Westin."

"Yes, General." replied Paul. He took a firm grasp on Charlie's arm and started to guide him from the room. Staggering along, Charlie turned his head over his shoulder and spoke.

"Didn't mean to hurt you, princess," he said to Sam.

"Daddy, just get out of here, now!"

Charlie Warner dropped his head. Defeated, he left quietly.

Caroline ran over, picked up Charlie's straw hat and trotted after him.

Jeff was disappointed, "Ahhhh, damn. I wanted to see Josh knock his block off."

Jake repeated, "Shaddup, boy."

***

After things had settled down and everyone reloaded their drinks, Ben huddled several minutes with Sam in a corner of the room. He broke away from the impromptu conference and asked for everyone's attention.

"Ladies and Gentlemen, on behalf of my sister and me I first wish to apologize for the rude intrusion by our father." Ben bowed his head and said in prayer form, "Forgive him Lord for he knows not what he does, particularly under the influence of a quart of Johnny Walker Black."

Everyone laughed or chuckled.

"Now, on another point, before one of our guests is assassinated," he nodded towards Josh, "I wish to set the record straight. Yes, Mr. Stillwater is a DDD agent."

A hush fell over the crowd as all eyes settled on Josh, and then moved back to Ben.

"After Josh and I managed to get him thrown out of the military, he joined the DDD as an agent working on behalf of Wyoming. His information has been invaluable. However, I think circumstances dictate that he *come in from the cold*, as they say in spy parlance, and join us openly in our forthcoming battle. Will you join us in that capacity, Colonel Stillwater?"

Josh looked like he was mule-kicked. Ben was handing him a life-line, a chance to start over with nothing to explain and nothing to be ashamed of. Those that knew him personally were shocked by the turn of events. A few grumbled that they shouldn't have been kept in the dark. Jeff was particularly pissed. Jake just knowingly smiled at Sam and mumbled to Jeff,

"I wish your Mama was here."

Josh regained his wits and slowly nodded to Ben.

"Come over here, Joshua Stillwater. Stand by me," said Ben. Josh hesitatingly complied. Sam came around Ben and held onto Josh's arm. He looked down at her, breaking a weak smile, struggling to hold back tears. From what depths sprang this generosity, this good will, this new life was unfathomable to him.

Ben spoke, "Ladies and Gentlemen, this man has endured wrongs and sacrificed a good life for all of us. Now he is back among friends. I believe he needs to be acknowledged." Ben turned sideways towards Josh and began to clap his hands together. Sam let go of Josh's arm and clapped. Others joined in until the entire room was in a cacophony of applause. Joseph Bascomb was at the front of the audience, applauding the loudest. He appeared relieved.

Josh didn't know what to do except stand there. Tears streaked down his face as he looked back and forth at Ben and Sam and, finally just shook his head in disbelief. He said to Ben, "Why?"

Ben said, "Because this State can't afford to lose a good man like you. I can't afford to lose you. I need you, Josh. And because I love you like a brother."

Josh laughed, rubbing tears into his skin, "That's what your sister's been telling me. I think I'd rather hear it from you."

Now, all three laughed.

Ben addressed the crowd again. "And now I wish to introduce someone else that has served our State well, Mr. Hiroto Ishikawa." All eyes followed Ben's over to the doorway. Hiro, always composed, merely bowed. Ben continued, "Mr. Ishikawa represents one of our strongest allies, the country of Japan."

The applause was stronger and the bow deeper.

Sam looked mildly confused, "Ishikawa? I thought it was Tanaka?"

Ben smiled while continuing to clap. He leaned near his sister's ear, "I'll explain later."

# Chapter 32

## A Federal Case

## Oval Office – The White House

All those requested for the meeting sat silent. The only one that made a sound within the Oval Office was the President. He was softly humming some song from the last century. It was a bit eerie and made everyone else more than nervous. They had expected an explosion of profanity gushing from Rivera's mouth. But he appeared calm, serene while he read a folder of briefing notes.

Dormier felt off his game. He had no idea as to what the meeting was about. Nor could he explain the relaxed mood of his boss. He expected an explosion, or at least a tantrum at the news of Wyoming's high-jacking of a train and all materiel aboard. Rivera's calmness had Dormier on edge. As no one else would presume to speak first, he felt it his duty to break the silence.

"Mr. President, is everything okay? I mean, with you, sir, this morning." It was the first time he had ever stumbled over words before this man.

"Okay? Yeah, sure, Bill. Why not?"

"Well sir, last night, or more accurate, early this morning, the train high-jacking, the stolen arms. You were quite upset a few hours ago, sir, and now, ah, you don't seem so upset. That's all."

Rivera leaned back in his chair and closed the file before him. "That's true, Bill. I was upset last night. But then, I was hit with a revelation. Like to hear it?"

Dormier glanced at the others in the room, from Manning to Pao to Fisk. He now wondered if these advisors should be here. His boss sounded like he was losing his senses. This talk about revelations might make him look like he'd gone round the bend. "Well, sir, perhaps you'd like to discuss it with me in private first and then we can share it with the group at a later time."

"Nonsense! You're all in this with me and we're all going to benefit from the outcome. Here's the revelation: they handed me the knife!" Rivera was smiling and nodding to all in the room. Dormier and Fisk dropped their eyes in embarrassment for the President. Pao coughed into her hand. Manning just maintained his stare.

"Relax, all of you. I haven't gone batty." Rivera waved his hand dismissively. "When they stole that train, they stole government property. Property, hell, it was military equipment. Don't all of you get it? They handed me the knife that I'm going to plunge right back into their hearts. They have committed, treachery, sedition, treason! And now I have all the justification I need to stop their little game of secession."

Fisk interrupted, "Sir, Wyoming has never declared secession from the Union."

"That's my real revelation, Blaine. I don't have to prove they're seceding. Their actions prove that. It was an act of insurrection. It was an act of war. And I am going to respond accordingly."

Fisk followed up, "And what is your response, Mr. President."

"It ought to be pretty damn clear. We're going to invade them. We are going to wipe them out, confiscate their gold, federalize their natural resources, federalize their companies and put an end to the WC and all their other nonsense."

"Using the military to invade a State is quite a step, Mr. President." Dormier was glad that Manning had now entered the fray.

"Alder, you're making this too big a thing. I already have the right to use the military on American soil."

Manning answered, "That may be true, sir. But that act was specific to the apprehension of terrorists within our borders. I am not sure it gives you the degree of authority we are talking of. I do not know how the other States may react to such aggressive behavior by Washington."

Rivera had now turned angry, "To hell with the other States." Dormier actually relaxed from his earlier tension. This was the Rivera he knew, hot-headed and foul-mouthed. And this was the Rivera he could control. He just had to wait for the President to paint himself into a corner. Rivera continued, "You don't get it, Alder. The other edge of the knife is that I am going to Federalize this whole damned country."

Everyone, including Dormier was stunned.

"Why keep pussy-footing around? We fund the States. We protect the States. We can take over their police forces and National Guards anytime we choose. We can close their borders. We can investigate and jail any of their elected officials. We control their relations with other nations. We control their trade laws, their customs fees. We impose Federal law onto them because Federal law trumps State law, thanks to the Supreme Court. Don't you see? We already own the States. So let's get past this entire State's Right discussion. It's archaic. Let's kill this Republic bullshit and make this truly a Federal country. Then we can solve our bigger problems quicker and with more efficiency."

"And you think the Senate will go along with your idea?" Manning asked so casually that Dormier didn't know if it were an actual question or a snide remark.

Rivera's eyes twinkled, "That's the real beauty of this idea, Alder. Currently two Senators are elected from each State, a State with borders fixed over one or two hundred years ago, right?"

Everyone nodded. Yet each wondered why Rivera was stating something so elementary.

"Yet each House of Representative's seat derives from a district whose borders can change every ten years, right?"

All nods again.

Rivera's face turned to mock seriousness, "This is patently unfair! Congressmen's boundaries change with the people, yet Senate seats do not." Now he grinned, "So, under a new Federal system, we make it fairer by making the one hundred Senate seats based on population numbers as well."

They all looked at each other in amazement. Fisk took the ball and ran, "You mean you are going to change the boundaries from which Senators come from?"

"Exactly, Blaine. Think of the advantages. These piss-ant, unpopulated States that cause us so many problems in the Senate, well their Seats are going to be balanced out over a broader spectrum. We always have to fight with these right-wing nut-job Senators on every law we want passed. They fought devaluation of the Old Dollar. They fought us on the T-Bill defaults. They fought us on National Health Care. They fought us allowing Mexican workers here to receive Social Security benefits and free medical. They fought us on halving the military budget in order to pay for health care. They fight every good idea at every turn, and I am tired of it."

STATE OF MINE – BATTLE!/M.A.Farrell

"So, you plan to gerrymander the States so that Senators more favorable to our programs win office."

"Exactly, Cecilia." Pao's response was to again cough into her hand.

Dormier, who had been taciturn during Rivera's rant, now brightened. "You know, Mr. President, that isn't all too crazy."

Rivera frowned, "I don't do crazy, Dormier."

Dormier tried to regroup, "No, sir, never. It's not what I meant. I mean that on first blush it sounds a bit too, ah, innovative. Yes, that's it, *innovative*. As I assume we are all a little overwhelmed by your *innovation*, it has taken us a bit to get up to speed with your thinking."

Everyone nodded.

"I mean, sir, transforming us into a Federal system exclusively has some very clear advantages. We could federalize the schools as well. We already provide over fifty percent of their funding. And, as has been said, control the minds of youth and you control the minds of the future."

"I like that, Bill." Rivera was enthusiastic. "So I have shown the end point. Now I need all of you to make the map on how we get there, politically, financially and legally."

"And, quite possibly, militarily as well, Mr. President. I see the possibility of more Wyomings on our hands if we take this course." It was Fisk's contribution.

"Don't worry about military, Blaine. That's now my area. And, as I have said earlier, Wyoming has given me the knife. Now it's up to me to use it. After the other States see the fate of these cowboys, I think any future, united resistance will be quite insignificant." Rivera's eyes were set on a distant dream, joined to a wicked smile.

Celia Pao shuddered.

Rivera turned to Dormier, "Get Declamore in here right now. I want to get this invasion underway the moment we resupply Maxwell. I don't want to give that State a single free moment to start revving up sympathy. Dormier, I want you on the PR front. I want everyone to understand they hijacked a train, killed over twenty soldiers plus the engineer and that other guy….."

Dormier was slightly confused, "Sir, no one died."

Rivera looked up at him with a maniacal grin, "Of course they did, Bill, because I just told you they did."

Dormier understood. But he knew it would backfire if the soldiers or engineer turned up in public. The soldiers he could quarantine through Declamore. Where the train engineer was, he had no idea.

"..and they stole Army material."

"*Materiel*, sir, not material."

"Don't correct me Blaine. I'm not one of those dumbshits outside the windows."

Fisk said calmly, "Yes, sir."

"They're terrorists, Bill. Play it up. A whole Damn State of Terrorists. And they must be punished! Got it?!"

"Got it, sir."

*There is a lot of* Sir'ing *flying around this room*, thought Alder Manning as he stirred a spoonful of sugar into his coffee.

# Chapter 33

## After-Dinner Plans

## Governor's Mansion, Cheyenne

The party dispersed with the full light of dawn. Ben waited until most had left and asked his core advisors to remain: Samantha, the four generals, Jake Dillon, Denny Watson, Harley Stevens, Hiroto Ishikawa and now, Joshua Stillwater. Normally Charlie Warner would have been in attendance. But tonight's circumstances did not allow.

"How long you estimate before they hit us, Ben?" General Roughton asked.

"I'd say forty-eight hours would be the soonest. If they pull off a miracle, they can have Maxwell resupplied by then."

"Tell us about your train trip. Anything interesting?" Denny Watson inquired.

Ben smiled, "Well, if you call almost getting fish-gutted and shot and bombed, then interesting fits the bill." He regaled them with the complete story. When he got to the part about Tex, Josh felt a little chagrined. He asked Hiroto if he could examine the Bowie knife. Hiroto handed it over and Josh knew instantly it was Tex's.

"Seen anything like it before?" Ben looked deep into Josh's eyes, sensing his friend knew something about the weapon.

"Maybe," said Josh noncommittally. He handed the blade back to Hiroto and asked, "What happened to the owner?"

Hiroto answered, "He is probably with his gods now. The last view of him disintegrating upon the fall from the train does not leave encouragement of his continued existence. If he still breathes, I am sure it is within a useless body."

Josh smiled at Hiroto, "Couldn't happen to a nicer guy, I'm sure."

Josh asked no more questions. Knowing how close Tex had come to killing Ben, he thought it best to let sleeping dogs lie.

After Ben finished, they all congratulated him on job well done. Sam effusively thanked Hiro for his part in saving Ben, throwing in a kiss on the cheek. Ben laughed. It was the first time he had seen Hiroto show emotion. He was blushing and smiling.

Then they started discussing the strategy and tactics for the upcoming battle. By the time they were finished most were yawning and begged off to get a few hours' sleep.

Ben asked Josh, Sam and Hiro to hang around after the meeting.

"Sis, I think it's a little late to safely get the Governors out of the State."

"What about the LTA craft? We could sneak them into Utah and they could return from there" suggested Sam.

Ben shook his head, "Too risky all the way around. I need every one of those craft for the upcoming engagement. And if they were downed, it would reflect badly on us that we lost four Governors. Nope, I think it best they join you and the scientists in the Energy Facility. It's a perfect bunker and Josh and I won't have to worry about you when things heat up."

Sam offered no resistance and said she'd sway the Governors to the idea.

Ben nodded and turned to Josh, "Now you get to earn your board and keep, cowboy. From today, I resign from anymore special op's. I don't think I can stand any more train rides."

Sam and Josh chuckled.

"Go ahead and laugh, big guy," said Ben sardonically. "From this day forward, you, Colonel Stillwater, are in charge of the Wyoming Intelligence Service. Congrats on your promotion."

Josh smiled, "Anything you say, General. What's my first assignment?"

"It has to do with a real nasty character. He's Russian and his name is Zhukov. I think he's going to use the upcoming battle to cause problems behind the curtain. It's up to you to track him. But it's more important you find out who he's working with. I need you to find the mole in our midst. I need you to find a traitor. Beings Hiro knows this Tex didn't try to shoot me during our huntin' trip, and we had a track on Zhukov at the time, it only makes sense it was this traitor that tried to do me in."

Josh nodded, "And what do you want me to do with him after I find him?"

"Well, even Wyoming's justice system can move a bit slow. So I leave that decision up to you. We are at war."

Josh nodded, understanding Ben's desire.

Ben added, "And take Hiro with you. He comes in real handy."

Josh looked at Hiro and smiled. Hiro just shrugged.

# Chapter 34

## Discovery

## Wyoming

The electric four-by-four pickup, powered by a hydrogen fuel-cell, silently bounced across the rugged terrain. The seat belt failed to stop Josh's six-foot-four frame from ramming his straw hat into the truck ceiling. Hiro had one hand gripped onto the overhead passenger handle. The other hand was holding a tracking device that showed a blinking green light progressing upwards.


After the earlier meeting at the mansion ended, Jake, Denny, Harley and the four generals headed out. Ben asked Sam, Hiro and Josh to remain as he needed to issue instructions along with details. Ben helped Josh with planning preparations and, afterwards, insisted Josh and Hiroto grab some shut eye. The sun was at full mast and Ben felt it best for the pursuit of Zhukov to be accomplished under cover of darkness of the coming night. Prior, Ben had advised all at the meeting his estimate as to the earliest the U.S. Army troops threatening Wyoming's border could be resupplied. They had a window of at least forty-eight hours if the minimum materiel were flown in.

Due to the lengthy dinner, Josh had pulled an all-nighter and was feeling the drag of sleep deprivation. The events and emotions from the evening had him further drained. He had no objection to hitting the rack. Ben and Hiroto were working on even less sleep. They both moved as if zombies. So Ben found them three beds within the mansion. Ben slept in his sister's bed as Sam had been successful in convincing the Governors to join her within the safety of the Energy complex. Naturally, Scott Fodor had voiced the greatest resistance. He worried about the complex being a magnet for bombs should a shooting war break out. Samantha convinced him that, to her knowledge, the Feds were unaware of the facility's existence and that it would be the safest place. Fodor, after lengthy whining, acquiesced and the group boarded the blacked-out coach for another run across Wyoming.

When Josh arose late that afternoon, he found Ben gone, already left for parts unknown. He queried Hiroto about Ben's whereabouts but received only a shrug. The Japanese man handed Josh a letter from Ben. It contained information on Zhukov with the vehicle VIN number required for tracking. As the Russian was driving a rental, there would be an anti-theft tracking device on board. Additionally, Ben had left instructions for Josh to use his pickup that Ben had earlier driven to the mansion. He had no need for it, departing with one of his military aides driving a four-wheel drive Army-issued vehicle. Inside the truck Josh would find the handheld tracker along with hand weapons and ammo.

Now speeding across pasture land in darkness, Josh hoped to miss an unseen gulley or large animal hole. A watering trough or fence line placed in his path would also cause real damage at this speed. He kept shooting his head to the left side to grab a glimpse of the far-off sedan running parallel on a country road. Stillwater opted to follow off-road, with no lights, as there was a new moon. Reflected light off patches of snow could bounce off chrome or glass. A momentary glint might attract the driver's eye in the rear-view mirror. He thought it best to make his run through the pasture at a far distance rather than follow behind on the graveled-road.

In the distance, Josh could see a pole-mounted, weak light illuminating the front yard of a small farmhouse. The sedan slowed in order to navigate a right hand turn. The pasture run would now work to Stillwater's advantage. There was a dark outline of a large structure fifty meters back of the house. This would be the hay barn and would be good cover while approaching the house. As he neared the homestead, he slowed the vehicle to a crawl. Somewhere near, he knew, would be the barbed wire fence line. Driving by Braille in the darkness, he found the wire when the dark-rusted barbs screeched across the grill.

"Oops," he said aloud. "Gonna owe Ben a re-chrome for his truck." Hiro nodded, having no idea as to what a 're-chrome' was.

He backed the crew-cab pickup five meters, turned left and ran parallel to the fence line. As his vehicle crept closer towards the barn, his appreciation for the near-silence of the electric motor grew. Where the high barn blocked any light of the moon, he parked. He snapped off the plastic cover of the interior light and pulled out the bulb. He searched the seat, looking but not finding what he needed. Then he popped open the glove compartment in front of Hiro and spied a pair of leather gloves. He knew every rancher left at least one pair in his pickup. He checked the handgun Ben had provided, a Baby Desert Eagle. He dropped the clip from the handle, made sure it had a full load of .40 S&W shells, rammed it home, chambered a round and flipped on the safety. From this maker, he would have preferred the .44 Magnum. But with an overall length of two-hundred and seventy millimeters, it was a long gun and tough to conceal. Additionally, the number of shots dropped from twelve in the Baby to eight in the Magnum. Firearms always had trade-offs.

Josh tucked the weapon back into a clip holster inside the small of his back. He shook Ben's hunting vest that he now wore, listening for the sound of additional clips and looked at Hiro. "Sure you don't want one? I've got an extra sidearm under the back seat."

Hiroto shook his head, "I prefer not to carry such a weapon. It is difficult to explain to authorities if one is searched." He raised his hands, "These are weapons enough, and they leave no ballistics to trace. Besides, I have *Baby*." He patted the Bowie knife in his belt and grinned. Josh shook his head, thinking, *I sure hope that knife doesn't have some curse that makes its owner go nuts.* He popped the door quietly and exited the dark cab.

At the wire, he slipped on the leather gloves, protecting his hands while parting the fence wire. He hunched through, turned, and held the wire open for Hiro. Then he dropped the gloves on the ground and quietly worked his way to the side of the barn. Peering from the corner, he saw past the house to the sedan parked under the pool of light. To call it a house was being generous. The small, four-room clapboard showed the neglect of years. Paint had peeled down to raw, rotting wood. The ridgeline of the roof sagged near the middle. Boards were missing from the back porch. The windows were covered by paper blinds, yellowed with age. The back screen door contained only a hanging border of screen material. If someone lived here on a regular basis, they sure weren't into maintenance.

Halfway between the house and barn was, what appeared to Josh, a small garden area. It was bordered by a short picket fence in the same shabby condition as the house. There was a tree growing in the center, probably an ash, with two dark objects on either side. In the darkness they were irregular outlines, making Josh think they were large stones. This would be good cover to approach the back of the house. He checked the windows, looking for moving shadows or profiles. Seeing none, he reached around, pulled out the weapon and, with a toggle of the barrel, signaled Hiro to follow. They scrunched over and quick-stepped to the garden. Once there, he scissor-kicked over the short fence and threw his back against the tree, gun up in hand. Hiro sat on his haunches before him. He listened for a while, checking to see if their approach had caused a reaction in the house. Hearing none, he lowered the weapon and checked to the left around the tree, plotting his next move. Then he turned round to look on the right side, but something caught his eye. The rock reflected light coming from the house. This was curious as rugged stone didn't reflect light. He squatted down, reached out and brushed accumulated dirt of the stone's front, smooth surface. There was writing chiseled into the face. Josh tilted his head left and right to catch the weak light from the house. It appeared to be a name. He put the letters together in his head. It was a woman's name. There was a birth and death date below it. It was a head stone, a grave marker. He duck-walked to the other stone. It was also engraved. *Definitely Russian*, he thought. The man's birth date was a year before the woman's, but, curiously, they had died the same year. He wished the last names had been Zhukov as it would bolster the evidence that scar-face was inside. Now he wondered about the connection between the man in the house and the grave stones. He stood up and shrugged. There was only one way to find out.

He stepped over the front gate of the garden and crept towards the house. A back porch light was on, but the glass fixture covering the bulb was so encrusted in filth, it provided little illumination. Not taking any chances, he ran crouched over to the protection of the left side of the farm house. Hiro had broken to the right. Josh rose up to check the first window and saw nothing because of the covering blind. The window covering hung about a centimeter from the casing on both sides. He studied these slots, trying to discern a change in the light if someone were moving about. There was no evidence of people in the back room. However, there were bags of powder on the floor. A table in the center of the room held an electronic scale that was still on. Glass beakers, flasks, glass tubes, a Bunsen burner and loops of glass tubing covered the table. Powder and bag material made from some type of woven plastic were scattered on the floor. It looked familiar to Josh, but he couldn't place it. A roll of wide adhesive tape sat half-used in a dispenser. *Either someone's cooking meth or explosives. I think it's the last. Naughty boy*, he thought.

Josh moved towards the next window. It was also covered by a blind, but there was a diagonal rip half up. He moved closer to focus one eye on the narrow slot. He jerked his head back when he saw Zhukov standing in the front room, looking in Stillwater's direction. *God, that sucker is big!* thought Josh.

Pressing his back against the clapboard and readying his gun, he waited for some noise or movement indicating he had been seen. When none developed, he felt secure enough to chance another look. This time he saw that the big man's eyes were looking at someone near the window, not at Stillwater. There was an argument ensuing, with scar face, as Josh had named him, flailing his hands and pointing at something to his right.

Josh slowly moved left and pushed his face as close to the glass as he dared. On an angle now, he could see another person. It was a teen-aged girl, her head held high, defiant. Her hands and feet were secured together with duct tape. *Sasha!* Josh recognized her from the party. *What the hell is she doing here? She's definitely not here out of free will. Where's Leo?*

Joshua turned his head so his ear was closest to the glass. He listened intently but couldn't make out the words. Finally he understood. They weren't speaking English. It sounded as some sort of Slavic language. Josh guessed it was Russian because of the connection with Zhukov and the Russian names on the grave markers.

The presence of the girl curtailed Josh's potential actions. *What are they doing with her, or to her?* She appeared physically okay. And her spirit seemed strong. It was probably fortunate that he had found Zhukov and Sasha together. If they had left the girl at some unknown hide out, she could be used as a bargaining chip. But rescuing a hostage was a little different from just barging through the front door and killing everyone. He wished Hiro had stayed with him. A coordinated attack might work. He wondered if his Japanese compatriot had this view, but from the other side.

Josh was strategizing his next move when the situation changed. The two men were moving around inside. He peered through the blind rip, hoping to catch a glimpse of the second man's face. Suddenly a belt came into view. It was the backside of the other person, a man. He wore a wide leather belt with scroll work. This wasn't much of an identifier to Josh, as those belts were common in Wyoming, at least for a cowboy. The man's back moved off towards the middle of the room. He looked definitely a Wyomingan with cowboy boots, hat and Western shirt. The man walked quickly to the front door, saying something to Zhukov while pointing to the girl. Scar face pulled a spring-loaded knife from inside his jacket. He thumbed the side, popping forth the long, razor-sharp blade. He used it to cut the tape from her feet. Then he yanked the girl from her seat, held her in a bear hug with the knife blade poking her neck. They were all heading out the door to Zhukov's car, post haste. When the cowboy moved for the door, Josh crouched down and made his way to the front corner of the house. He was peering around the house side when Zhukov opened the passenger door, slid the girl into the middle of the seat and followed with his large body. The cowboy opened the driver's door and entered the vehicle, squishing the girl between him and the oversized Russian. Josh quickly calculated his odds of taking two head shots. He glanced at the pistol in hand. He had never fired it had no feel for its accuracy. If he were armed with a rifle and scope, his actions would have been bolder. But with a hostage involved, he didn't like the probability of keeping Sasha alive.

The driver knocked his hat askew when entering the car and now straightened it. Josh focused on the head-ware as it rang of familiarity. To this feature he added his earlier sighting of a momentary glint off metal when the driver walked under the weak light of the yard pole. Josh put the two together and a face emerged in his mind.

"Sonnabitch," he whispered. He had found Ben's mole.

*** 

Josh and Hiro were following at such distance as to not be spotted by their quarry. He lost the taillights of the Sumitomo sedan in the kicked-up dust, but saw this as aiding their attempt to stay out of view. Josh looked at the digital speedometer and heard himself emitting a low whistle. One-hundred and thirty kilometers per hour was a helluva clip on a graveled road, at night, with no headlights. He was tempted to slow down and just use steers from Hiro using the WXM tracker. But if the driver stopped and let someone out and then kept going, Josh would never know. *Better to maintain a visual for now.*

He wasn't exactly sure where they were. But he had a pretty good idea as to where they were all headed. His hunch was confirmed when they hit Highway 789 and punched through the stop signs at full speed, shooting past Lamont and onto 73. Josh thanked the gods it was late and there was no traffic either way. When they reached Bairoil, the lead vehicle slowed a bit and slid sideways to make the turnoff at Hwy 4. Josh copied the maneuver, but almost rolled the raised-suspension four-by-four. He straightened the wheels for a second to relieve some of the centrifugal force. This action slewed the vehicle off-road, chewing up dirt. It was pitch black and he didn't know if he was going to get unfriendly with a culvert or ditch. So he slammed on the brakes, plowing up dirt and gravel. When the pick-up came to a halt, he dared turning on his headlights, as his quarry was long gone. Less than a meter from his front bumper was the beginning of a metal highway barrier. He looked at Hiro, but the man was concentrating on the tracker screen.

Josh shook his head and smiled, *Ben told me he was a cool character.* Then he looked back to the metal barrier and uttered, "That would've caused some damage." Hiro looked up a moment, nodded and resumed studying the tracker.

Josh backed up the truck a short distance, cranked the wheels left and steered back onto the road. From here on he was going to use the tracker, and his headlamps.


He stopped fifty meters short of an entrance through the chain-link fence. He had been searching for such an opening as the last ten minutes the road he was on ran parallel to the fence. This had to be the Energy Facility as it was the only paved side road out this far. The tracking signal was lost several minutes ago. He knew the WXM handheld was capable of tracking a vehicle out to thirty-five kilometers and suspected that the disappearance of signal meant the car had gone underground. This matched his strong hunch as to their ultimate destination.

Peering through darkness, Josh made out the silhouette of a small building about a kilometer down the side road. From his tour the day before, he remembered a stop after a turn off. Logic told him it was this guard post. From that stop, Josh further remembered the motor coach slanting downward to the underground garage where he disembarked. That is why he was unconcerned with the loss of a tracking signal. It was a pretty easy guess as to where tonight's quarry had run: down into the rabbit hole.

Now he was concerned for Sam. She was right at ground zero for this Russian death ballet. If Ben were looking for a mole that would help Zhukov destroy **Wystar**, why would he let his sister come here? Did Ben think he, Josh, would stop Zhukov before he got this far? Was Ben using Sam and the Governors as some kind of bait? His thoughts started to rile him. He shook away the negativity. He had a mission to think about. Ben could explain later…after Josh saved Sam.

Josh slowly drove up the highway to the side road entrance, turned and preceded cautiously towards the guard building. Reaching the small blockhouse, he knew things weren't right. The barrier posts were down, flush with the roadway, allowing anyone to pass. He thought about roaring straight through, as he had no authorization to enter. But he dismissed the idea. Any aggressive action would produce a swarm of guards down the line, delaying his pursuit as he tried to explain his mission. He pulled up to the guard post and waited. No one came out. He then spotted the red swash across the back of the booth. Leaning out the driver's window, he looked into the small building and saw the guard crumpled against the wall; a still-oozing hole in the middle of his forehead. Prior, he had removed from his pocket the Wyoming military ID Ben had provided. It was certainly better than his ALIEN card. But now, seeing the dead guard, he tossed the ID onto the seat between he and Hiro and said, "Doesn't look like I'm gonna need that." He stomped on the accelerator, shot past the guard facility and into a tunnel ramping downward.

Hiro jumped from the vehicle before Josh had brought it to a complete stop. The two then ran for the entry doors and burst into the complex looking for some clue as to where the two men and one girl had gone. Josh made his way through the complex by memory from his first visit. The carnage they found started at the reception area and, like breadcrumbs, led them from one guard posting to the next. Josh silently excoriated himself for not taking the two men down at the farm house, Sasha or no Sasha. He flexed his hands as he stepped over and around freshly killed corpses. He focused his mind on finding the bastards, remembering Ben's words: Dispose of them. *Damn right!* he thought.

Obviously the sentries weren't on guard against the sedan's driver, as he was familiar to them and had been through their stations a thousand times before. This provoked a thought, *How did the mole get past the security panels? It takes two hands a long distance apart to punch in codes. There's no way Zhukov could have gained clearance.* While Josh and walked down the corridor with Hiro a few steps behind, he pondered this and began thinking as to how *he* would defeat the hand scanners. It proved an unnecessary concern as the first hatch, and all subsequent ones, were blocked open by the bodies of dead guards. Apparently, the saboteurs were leaving a clear run to exit the complex after completing their plans. They were definitely here to blow the place up.

Josh and Hiroto passed through the portals, finally making their way to the elevator. Josh hadn't figured out this part of the puzzle yet. He knew the elevator was kept at the bottom of the shaft. And the only way to retrieve it was if someone down there sent it up. He would either have to call down and have the car sent up, or try to pry open the heavy elevator blast doors with his bare hands. Even if he succeeded with this impossible task, he would then face shinnying down a greasy, slick elevator cable that plunged seven-hundred and fifty meters straight down. Neither option was appealing.

Hiro and Josh put their heads together to come up with some plan. Their options were limited. The only idea they had would require a feat of physical prowess from Hiro, as the elevator had no trap door in the ceiling. It was designed this way for security reasons.

Josh looked at Hiro, shrugged and punched the CALL button. There were several minutes of silence. "Probably trying to figure out who in the hell comes knocking this time of night," Josh said, trying to break the tension. He punched the button again. After about a minute, a voice came through the speaker. It was low and garbled and sounded phony to Josh. It was a feeble attempt to disguise a voice.

"Sergeant Kelly."

*OK, we're going to pretend,* thought Josh.

"Top o' the evening to you, Sergeant Kelly. This is Joshua Stillwater. Governor Warner is expecting me. Would you please send up the car?"

More silence. Josh decided to push them. "Is there a problem?"

"She says for you to go away."

Josh shook his head slowly, "Look, Alex, let's stop the charade. You've got a trail of bodies up here leading to the front door."

"How the hell do you know it's me?" The voice disguising was gone.

"I know everything, Alex. Or should I call you Alexi, as in Alexi Sidorov."

"Where'd you get that name?"

Josh read genuine surprise, even shock in the response. His only play was to see how powerful Alex's curiosity was. He remained silent.

The voice came back when Josh didn't answer, "You alone?"

"Yeah, everyone else is a little busy on the borders, if you remember. And none of the guards you left up here are, what you call, stand-up guys."

"Anybody else comes down with you, or if you're armed, I'm gonna start blowing brains out, beginning with Samantha's. You got it?

"Yeah, I got it."

A few minutes later, the whir of wheels and cables told him the car was on the way.

Josh pulled the gun from his back and offered it to Hiroto. The Japanese shook his head, "I must have my hands free."

Josh sighed. He sat the gun down upon the floor, looked at it forlornly, and said goodbye to his one advantage. Hiro held up his hands, "Don't worry. We still have these."

Josh produced a faint smile and thought, *Great.*

Once the car arrived, the two stepped in. Hiroto immediately pulled Tex's knife from his belt and applied the sharp edge to the screw slots on the control panel's plate. The elevator's rear doors required insertion and turn of a security key; a key Josh didn't have. After removing the cover and reaching within, he pulled out specific wires and began stripping them with the knife. Finished, he returned the wires and cover and then punched the rear door button. It parted. He grinned as he flashed the knife blade and said, "Looks like she's *my* Baby now." Josh weakly smiled.

***

Below Leo stood with Alexi and Zhukov. He had finished helping the two adhere twelve sausage-looking bags of explosive to each reactor, using double-backed tape. Leo's assistance was coerced by the threat to his daughter. His two enemies had promised they would allow the girl to live if he helped Alex get Zhukov into the complex. Leo vacillated between anger at Alex and anger at himself for being duped into trusting the man. How could he have known? Alex had been so smooth in accepting charge of Sasha. He had even feigned resistance at the idea, not wanting the responsibility. But Leo had pressed him to take the girl and protect her. He never conceived that he was passing the light of his life over to the ones he feared most. *I am so stupid!* he thought as he taped the bags over 'X's Alexi made earlier with a black marker.

An hour before, Alex had phoned Leo and told him to meet him at the facility. He used the ruse of an emergency involving Sasha. Before Leo could garner more information, Alex had hung up. Leo was near hysteria as he sped to the Energy facility. His mind concocted numerous scenarios as to what had happened to his daughter, each worse than the one before.

Alex required Leo's palm print along with his in order to pass through the security checks. After Leo arrived and was told of his required complicity in Alex's plan, he refused. But the threat to Sasha convinced him to acquiesce. Now Leo, Alex and Zhukov looked at each other and waited for the descent of the elevator. Two of them had guns.

The explosive powder within the bags was a hybrid of BTATz and DHT. For three years Alexi had developed the product in his self-built laboratory within the back room of the old farm house. It had taken this long to conquer not only the chemistry of the nanostructure, but the manufacturing process as well. He found that these ultra-fine reactant particles dramatically increased the energy release rate of the thermite-like materials and provided twice the total energy of high explosives. As it was of his creation, he made sure it didn't register on mechanical scent detectors, such as ion mobility spectrometry or gas chromatography. Months ago, when he started bringing the three-kilo sacks through security at the Complex, he was brazen. He claimed it was a specialized desiccant required for an experiment he was running. No one questioned him. The guards rarely knew what the scientists were talking about even when they explained in detail. Infiltration of the explosive had been the easiest part, until he was bringing the last bags. That is when Zhou and the tour of governors almost stopped him with the sausage-like evidence in hand. If not for the guests, Zhou's suspicious nature might have forced further query, ruining Alex's plan.

Within each sack he packed an electronic chip about the size of a dime. It was his custom design, built with parts from an electronics store. The chip performed three functions: signal receiving, timer and detonation. It could only be activated after receiving a specific frequency from less than a meter away. The chip would then time a thirty minute delay, ending with a condenser-charged spark across a nichrome bridgewire. This was all it took to ignite the incredible explosive force within each bag. The explosion would exponentially add to the other twelve attached to the reactor. The first action would be a concussive wave that would rip the containment chambers apart. A millisecond later the thermite fireball of nearly 5,000 degrees F would melt the fission external chambers, then the outer core of the pebbles within, growing the fireball enough to melt the concrete walls and leave the entire underground a molten mass seething with radiation.

**WyStar** would suffer a similar fate with the plasma breaking through the destroyed containment chamber, combining with the fireball. In a way, the fireball would replace the magnetic and ionic fields of containment, holding the plasma yet allowing it to expand in a millisecond, to the size of the room and then turning back onto it until the heat exceeded the carbon fiber girders' melting point. With the ceiling rock crystallized, it would crack and collapse inward. The entire Energy Facilities would become nothing more than a depression within the Green River Basin.

Several minutes later, the elevator dinged, announcing its arrival. Zhukov and Alexi were standing ten meters away from the doors. Each held a hostage in front, a gun raised around the prisoner's body. Sidorov's arm clamped Sasha's neck and Zhukov held a struggling Sam up off the floor, her feet kicking furiously. Leo stood to the side, wringing his hands. When the doors parted, Josh was leaning against the back wall, arms folded, legs crossed.

"Howdy," he smiled. The two Russians didn't. Instead they tensed.

"Come out of the elevator now. And keep your hands in view." Alexi was disconcerted by Josh's easy manner.

Josh scanned the large chamber. Of the nineteen hostages, seventeen were lying prone on the concrete floor, hands and ankles duct taped. There were the scientists Josh had met at Sam's dinner plus several other scientists important enough for Alex to include in the explosion. Additionally, the four Governors were bound. Josh looked at Sam and communicated his resolve through his eyes. She stopped struggling and nodded. Sidorov circled around Josh, keeping him at a distance, Sasha between, and waving the gun for Josh to move away from the elevator. He then ducked his head into the car and gave it a quick glance. It was empty. He pushed Sasha hard towards Josh. She tripped and he grabbed her. Josh said, "Don't worry, girl. These big, bad men won't hurt us."

Sidorov sneered at the comment. A familiar voice came from one of the hostages on the floor.

It was Charlie Warner. Having a daughter's love for her father that even an alcoholic tantrum couldn't cleave, Sam had phoned Charlie and asked him to join her at the facility. She wanted his strength for the ordeal ahead. She was wore out from the pressure of running the State and Charlie could bear some of that burden while she rested.

Josh had missed Charlie's face on first scan. Warner spoke to Stillwater with disdain, "You really are a dumb-shit, Stillwater. Why didn't you just wait topside? You might have got the drop on them when they came up."

An eye was swollen shut and his lip showed of dried blood. He had obviously offered resistance to being hog-tied.

He could clearly pick out the cantankerous old man now, "Is that before or after he blows you all up? Besides, I figured all the fun was down here. Didn't want to miss the party."

Sam shook her head in a resigned manner.

Zhukov mumbled something in Russian to Alexi, who chuckled.

"Don't tell me Frankenstein-face there has a sense of humor." Josh smiled. Zhukov glared at Josh, obviously understanding the insult.

Alexi waived him off, "Yeah, he's got a sense of humor, all right. He said you're gonna to get a real blast out of this party."

Josh nodded, "Oh, yeah, the explosion. You really think it'll do any harm through those thick blast doors?"

It was Alexi's turn to smile, "We're not stupid. Every blast door is open. It's gonna be one helluva conflagration. But don't worry. It won't hurt. You'll all be vaporized in a split second."

"I ain't no scientist, but I remember from the tour all of the fission reactor rooms were filled with helium. Isn't it risky to leave those open?" asked Josh.

"Like I care," snarled Alex. "It's a safety precaution and I'm not really into safety right now. Besides, when those bags of explosives go off, the Pebble Beds Reactors will burn for months. I like that ending."

Governor Fodor yelled from the floor, "YOU SICK BASTARDS! YOU CAN'T KILL A GOVERNOR!" He struggled at his taped bonds.

Zhukov drug Samantha over to the writhing man. He kicked the Governor in the ribs. The man yelped in pain, turned on his side and tucked into a fetal position, whimpering.

Josh looked at Alexi, "That what they teach you in spy school, Sidorov? How to kick a defenseless man?"

"Yeah, and also how to shoot someone with a big mouth." Josh thought he had gotten under Alexi's skin. He just shrugged.

Alex 'Sidney' remembered something, "By the way, the price of admission was you telling me how you knew my name."

"The farm house."

"You were there?"

Josh nodded, "Followed you, Zhukov and the girl there. Saw your little lab in the back room too. That where you cooked up the explosives?"

It was Sidorov's turn to nod, "Ok, then you saw me through the window. But how'd you know my name?"

Josh shook his head, "Never saw your face, even when you got into the car. Your buckle gave you away."

Sidorov was confused, "What?"

"Your belt buckle, the bull-riding trophy. The light caught it just right outside the car. I remembered you wearing it to Sam's dinner. Then I saw that dirty, mangy straw giving you problems in the car. Put the two together and knew it was you."

"And my name?"

"The grave markers out back. Their last names were Sidorov, obviously a Russian name. Then I heard you two speaking Russian. Once I figured out who you were, it was pretty easy to put Sidney with Sidorov. Alex to Alexi was kindofa guess. They your folks, those graves? They spies too?"

Sidorov looked down and shook his head, "That wasn't my folks' graves. It was my adoptive parents. They gave me their name. I was with my folks when they died in a train wreck in Russia. I was a year old. Both my parents were high-ranking scientists: physicists. Thinking the apple doesn't fall far from the tree, the KGB couldn't let a good thing go to waste. So they delivered me to the Sidorovs. They had tried unsuccessfully for years to have a kid. I didn't know they were 'sleepers' until I was twelve. A GDU agent came for me then. Said I was gonna live in Russia for a few years. I was already Russian fluent from my family, so I guess I saw it as kind of an adventure. My adoptive parents protested until the agent reminded them of what would happen to all of us if they made trouble. I didn't know then, but the agent came back for them the night I left."

"That why their deaths are both on the same date?"

Sidorov nodded, his face screwed up with a painful memory.

Josh thought he might have a play, "You don't have to do this Alex. You're as much part of Wyoming as I am. I left, you know. But I came back and so can you. These people have created something the entire world needs. They're builders. It's not up to us, the destroyers, to deprive humanity of their gain."

The words hit Alex hard. He looked down at his feet, then raised his head. His eyes were moist. "Goddam you Stillwater, it's none of your damn business. My life was set when my parents died and that's the way it is. So just shut up."

Josh knew he had gotten to him; had pierced his personal armor. "Don't lose yourself, Alex. I was cut off from myself for fifteen years. It was a personal desert. Don't cut yourself off from everything good inside. These people will take you back. All you gotta do is a sharp U-turn. You can put it right."

Alex shook his head violently, "STOP IT! It's all been written. The die was cast when I was twelve. I've been through indoctrination classes, demolition and sabotage, small arms, martial arts....spy school, as you called it. They saw I had my parents' aptitude for math and science, so they pushed me down the physics trail and I ended up here."

"Wyoming can put all those skills to use...for the good, not the bad." Josh felt his edge slipping. But he wanted to keep trying, if for no other reason than just to buy time. His mind was screaming, trying to devise some way to open the elevator rear doors.

Alex's face hardened. He raised his gun, "It won't work Stillwater. I know what you're up to. I know what I am. I am Russian. These people may have built something, but they're way over their heads. They are screwin' with Mother Russia. And if I know one thing, she spanks when she's mad."

Leo, now bound by Zhukov and pushed down onto the floor next to a bound Sasha, shouted in Russian. Josh knew it was encouragement of his point. Zhukov turned to Leo, pointed his gun at Sasha and shouted back. Leo cringed and rolled over the other way. Then Zhukov turned to Sidorov and barked in Russian. Alexi nodded vigorously, snapping out of his thoughts.

He replied in English, "You're right. We've got no time for this. Pat him down and tie him up."

Zhukov angrily waggled the barrel of the gun at Josh. "You turn now. Put hands up." Josh complied, expecting the big man to approach him and search for weapons. Josh thought it might be his only opportunity to get everyone out of this mess. He was wrong. With Josh turned around, Zhukov tromped over, flipped the gun around so he was holding the barrel, and then slammed the handle into the back of Josh's head. Brilliant flashes shot before Josh's eyes. The next moment, he fell into blackness.

# Chapter 35

## Battle Ready

## Wyoming

The night was cold.  The moon and stars were hidden by a fall blanket of clouds.  The wind had kicked up.  The prairie grass was sparse this far east and dirt rose in upward spirals that made vision across the plains obscured.  General Benjamin Warner saw the conditions as being the best he could hope.  Certainly the invaders would be using infrared and thermal sensors, as well as ground radar.  But with what they would soon face, these technologies, hopefully, would be rendered useless.  At this thought, Ben's mouth crooked upward slightly on one side.  It could not really be called a smile.  It was more satisfaction that the pieces were in place and he could do nothing more until the enemy made their move.  The usual stoic face now wore the hard mask of a determined soldier, a face of war.  No one under his command cared who his sister or father was.  The only priority was trust: could they trust the man or woman left and right.  Could they trust the judgment of their officers?  All thoughts were focused on getting thru this night alive.

On the flank, thirty-five kilometers due east was the enemy: two divisions of infantry, nearly twenty-five thousand soldiers of the seventy-five thousand total United States Army troops sitting on Wyoming's borders.  In addition to this were fifteen Abrams M1a1 tanks, eight A-10C's Thunderbolt II (or WartHogs), one hundred helicopters (one-hundred H-92 SuperHawks for troop transport and eight AH-64D Longbows), two-hundred and fifty M2A3 Bradleys , and numerous FMTV's to transport the bulk of the manned force.  The aircraft had flown in from bases within surrounding States.  Armor and supplies were flown in on large transports.   The heaviest equipment had been trucked in convoys speeding down interstates behind blaring sirens of military police.

Ben knew commanders of such might facing a lowly State Army, or National Guard as the Feds referred to it, could be cocky and, hopefully, underestimate their opponent.  At least that's what General Roughton had preached to Ben and his troops.  But Ben didn't really hinge success, or even survival, on such hope.  His confidence stemmed from technology.  And on that they had a distinct edge.  The problem was that Wyoming's technology was designed to be non-lethal.  Sun Tzu had written that war was the failure of politics.  Ben saw this battle an extension of the political war between Wyoming and the U.S. Federal government. Even a stalemate with the U.S. Army would elevate Wyoming's cause not only in this nation, but throughout the world. But it was just as important as to *how* they won as well as *who* won. The enemy they faced was coming for bear, to kill all the terrorists, as the Federally-controlled media had trumpeted. Such a slaughter might extinguish Wyoming's revolution, but it could also boomerang as the other States, other democracies, would shudder at the abuse of raw power. Wyoming was trying to win a PR battle as well as military. This is why their front-line weapons were non-lethal. This is why the game was a bit more exciting. This is why Ben's face now twitched with the hint of a smile.

He turned around and surveyed the arsenal he had at hand. His one-deep defensive line was comprised of one battle group to the left of his mobile Command-and-Communications, and one to his right. This added up to shy of seven thousand armed men and women spread out over two miles. The remaining State's two-hundred and fifty thousand forces stretched out over one thousand, three-hundred miles of border, one-hundred thousand concentrated south of Cheyenne with Roughton. With five different States on its borders and none with the strength (even fewer with courage) to refuse Federal intrusion, the task of repelling an armed force was daunting. Some of their neighboring States were sympathetic, if not openly supportive of Wyoming's plight. These sympathetic few kept the beleaguered State aware of Federal troop movements within their borders. Utah and Idaho were the most loyal in their support of Wyoming. Colorado and Montana were schizophrenic, bordering on civil war between the right, hard-scrabble libertarian founders and the left, moneyed and liberal Aspen/Vail/Butte, Hollywood nature-lovers. Nebraska and South Dakota had even less population than Wyoming. They decided early on to take a wait-and-see approach. A successful stand by Wyoming now could tilt these and other States away from passivity towards active support of Wyoming's goals.

So now Wyoming sat and waited. To the few members of the press that were imbedded on Wyoming's side, it seemed an unfair fight. But they were unaware of the battle tactics and technologies soon to be unveiled by this upstart State. Only Lightoiler-Bascomb was in the know of what would happen shortly. Only he would be allowed a live broadcast. He was inside mobile command, behind a five-centimeter thick, bullet-proof window, electronics perched upon his head and around his waist. If he left the room and went outside to witness the battle up close, internet, satellite, shortwave and video feeds would continue his remote broadcast. He already started his broadcast with a running commentary over shortwave, satellite and internet, extolling the virtues of the beleaguered

Athenian State (Wyoming) against the barbaric Persian hordes (read, U.S. Army) readying to breach the walls. Even with Federal efforts at jamming and blocking internet routes, it would be said later that it had garnered the third largest audience in broadcast history, behind only Princess Dianna's funeral and Elvis's concert in Hawaii.

Twenty-four hours ago, all Federal troops were in Colorado, sitting south of Cheyenne. It was a logical move, for it was the shortest thrust to the State Capitol, with the endgame of capture-the-flag. But Wyoming's General of the State Army, Roughton had called it correctly. He had surmised that no route to the interior of the State would be left open by the Feds whereby State political leaders and military echelon could make good an escape. Roughton predicted a splitting of U.S. Army forces. After all, there were now forty Abram's III tanks under Wyoming control, along with one-hundred thousand State Army troops in front of the Fed's concentration. To attack head-on would result in significant casualties. However, if there were significant Federal casualties, even if the U.S. Army won, it would be a PR loss. Again, the *David vs. Goliath* syndrome. General Roughton knew General Maxwell. He was a solid soldier who followed orders as tightly as he adhered to West Point strategies. Before him was opportunity for a classic pincer movement, a frontal attack combined to a flanking maneuver, thus cutting off escape of routes. The difficulty with the strategy was that a flanking maneuver generally had more ground to cover, and therefore had to begin the frontal assault before a main assault if the vice were to close upon itself. The trick was to figure out how many troops and materiel to spare for the flanking forces. If too much were sent and the move discovered, the surprise element against the flank was lost. Additionally, if the frontal assault forces were weakened and became unable to overwhelm the center and push the enemy back in chaos, then the assault could be blunted and enemy forces would then be freed for reinforcing the flank. Roughton had deduced this would be Maxwell's strategy. Israeli and Chinese satellites confirmed the nighttime movement of men and materiel. Maxwell's gamble of moving nearly twenty percent of his resources to the eastern, Nebraska flank had proven timely. Now General Benjamin Warner was in command of a substantial force with assets that would prove a test to the U.S. Army flanking force. Although outmanned, Ben's defensive force contained a technological edge that he hoped would sow equal doses of confusion and fear, if not panic among the attackers.

All of Wyoming's officers had studied and discussed U.S. Army battle tactics under the tutelage of General Roughton for nearly a year. They knew that the U.S. military prided itself on owning the night during war. Until night and thermal vision capabilities, along with ground radar, had been perfected, it was dangerous to begin battles earlier than a few hours before dawn. In darkness, troops can become disoriented, cut-off or lost, or stumble accidentally upon enemy forces, or even fire upon their own troops. Additionally, artillery barrages and air support were difficult, if not impossible, to site and hit mobile targets. But all this changed with technological advances. Everyone in Wyoming's military command structure was convinced the battle would begin in the dark, early hours of morning, when the U.S. thought its enemies asleep, or at least nodding off. And they were not often disappointed.

At oh-one-hundred hours, the Eastern Armored Command center snapped to. He received his first SitRep, this coming between General Roughton in the South and Major James Dillon in the West, manning a DARTS launcher.

# Chapter 36

## An Explosive Situation

## Down Under, Wyoming

An angel called Josh's name. She was far away but growing nearer, incredibly beautiful, a Helen of Troy calling to him. She drifted nearer and stroked his face. Then she kicked him.

"JOSH! WAKE UP!" It wasn't an angel. It was a very loud Sam, kicking at him with bound feet. "Daddy's got a point. You certainly aren't helping us much."

He slowly raised his head. It was throbbing. "That sonnabitch cold-cocked me."

"Good deduction, Sherlock. Now, how are you getting us out of here, in one piece?" sniped Charlie.

He tugged at his wrists and ankles. He didn't have to look to know they had bound him as well. "Where are the bastards?" he asked.

Leo answered, "I tink dey are in reactor rooms."

Leo might have murdered the King's English, but Josh understood. None of them had much time.

Charlie growled, "So what are you going to do, big DDD man."

Josh flinched. He didn't know whether to protest or not. He decided to deflect it with anger, "Shut up, you old wind bag, or I'll punch your lights out, like I was gonna last night. I see you really took 'em on. Did you give them a good beating with your face?"

Charlie's growl was even louder.

But Josh wasn't being idle. He cleared his mind. If he exposed Hiro now and Sidorov and Zhukov returned, he lost any element of surprise, and probably Hiro as well. He spoke in the loudest whisper he could.

"Hiro, you okay? Still with us?"

A muffled voice came from the direction of the elevator car, "Prepared, Josh-san," came a voice. "How will you make him open the rear door?"

Josh answered perkily, "I have a plan, Hiroto. Don't worry. Just be ready when I shout 'that's a dumb thing to do.' Got it? The doors should open right after that?"

Josh could barely hear the muted response, "Okay, Josh-san. I shall be prepared."

Josh thought, *God, I need to come up with a plan, and fast.*

Sam's face sparkled with surprise, "You brought Hiro? He's in the elevator?"

"Well, not exactly *in* it," offered Josh lamely. He brought his knees to his chest and began inching his hands below his butt.

Sam was confused, "But Sidorov looked in there. How did he miss him?"

Josh had to roll up onto his shoulders to make the last few inches, but he finally got his bound wrists past his rear.

"He's outside of the car waiting on the roof for someone to open the back maintenance doors. Once they open, he'll spring into action."

"And how are you going to get the back doors opened," asked Sam enthusiastically.

"I'm workin' on that part right now."

"Oh, God," groaned Sam. "Daddy's right. We're screwed. You don't have a clue how to get those doors open, do you?"

"Woman, you are riling me. Now let me concentrate on what I'm doing or we're all going to be ashes in a dust bin."

Josh bent his knees tight to his chest, pointed his toes and stuck them into the hole created by his arms. He stopped pulling his legs down when his knees were even with his wrists. He wanted to see if he could push outward and break the tape binding his hands. Instead he suffered tape burns and cuts to his wrists. *Tough stuff,* he thought.

Sam couldn't help sounding skeptical, "You got a Plan B?"

"'B' as in 'bitching'? Cut me some slack and ease up on the slashing tongue, will ya. I'm workin' on it."

Sam's loud exhale demonstrated her frustration.

Josh groaned and grimaced as he pulled his legs downward. Finally his knees made it past his wrists and his legs stretched straight out. His hands were now in front instead of behind.

Charlie chided, "Great, he performed a Houdini trick. Too bad we don't have a tank of water to drop you in."

"I'm telling you one time, Warner. Keep your mouth shut or I'm leaving your ass here to be fried in the explosion." *Jeeze, what a tough room to play*, he thought.

"Do we really have time for this verbal sparring? I thought the bad guys were supposed to be back any minute" scorned Governor Brigham.

"I'm with her," snipped Sam

Josh stopped moving when he heard footfalls upon the cement. Zhukov had returned through the **WyStar** portal, returning to the transition hall. Josh knew if the Russian spotted his hands in front, there would be hell to pay. He quickly rolled on his side towards Sam and hoarsely whispered for her to do the same. She immediately rolled staring into Josh's eyes. The footsteps sounded as if they were getting closer. Josh couldn't see the big man because of Sam's position. And he certainly couldn't raise his head for fear of attracting the assassin's attention. All he could do was stare at Sam and wait. She winked at him. It had the desired effect, relaxing a few of his taut muscles. He smiled back. They heard no movement of Zhukov until, nearly two minutes later, heavy feet walked towards the fission door.

"That was close," whispered Sam.

"Yeah, I've got to get busy. Don't know when they're both coming back." He rolled onto his back and sat up. He reached down and tried to pull up his right pants leg. But the material was bound with duct tape. *Shit*, he thought. *Now I've got to pull the boot off*. With both legs bound he couldn't use the toe of one boot to push on the heel of the other. He brought his knees to his chest and grabbed the right boot with both hands. With hands and feet bound, it was awkward. The boot didn't move. He realized the taped jeans material held his boot on through pressure. He thought for a moment and got an idea. He spun perpendicular to Sam, his feet nearest her.

"Can you pull on my right boot while I try to push the top down?"

Sam assessed the situation and nodded. She rolled over to her other side, facing away from Josh. She then stuck her hands out and scooted back towards him until she felt the boots. She brailed with her hands until she was sure it was the right boot. Then she clasped one hand over the arch top and the other behind the heel.

"Wait a sec," said Josh. "Let me find the top." He smoothed his hand down the pants until he felt the ridge of the boot top. "Got it. Start pulling. I'm gonna push."

Both were lowly grunting. Sam was losing her grip and Josh didn't feel movement of the top. "Hold on. This isn't working. Let's try something different. Grab the heel with both hands. I'll push on the back. That way we've got all the force in one place."

"Okay," muffled Sam. "Let me get both hands back there." She positioned both hands at the heel. "Ready."

Josh twisted his torso to the left to get his hands behind his right leg. He found the boot top and said, "Go."

Both were grunting and straining. Josh wasn't feeling any progress and was about to abort when the boot top moved a centimeter. They both stopped pushing and pulling.

"It moved," he said low, but with enthusiasm. "You got another good tug in you?" He saw the back of Sam's head nod. They both repositioned and Josh said, "Go."

He felt small movements from the beginning of this effort. "It's going. Don't give up. Keep pulling!" Sam hung in there, even though her fingers were burning and the sharp edges of the heel cut her skin. Finally, the back half was beyond the tape, freed. They both stopped to let Sam rest her fingers. Josh brought his hands from under his leg back to the front of his pants. While Sam rested, he pushed hard on the top. Because the back was freed from the tape pressure, it caused some small slack that allowed him to get the boot top below the binds.

"It's free, Sam. Now I need your help one more time. You ready to pull the heel?" Sam nodded.

Pulling from the heel was about the only way to get a boot off under normal circumstances. Sam readied her hands and pulled. Josh wriggled on his back away from her. He felt his foot release the heel from the boot and start bending upwards. He kept wriggling until the foot was free.

Sam dropped the boot and massaged her hands together. Josh turned back parallel to her and scooted over. He picked up the boot.

"You did good, darlin'."

Again the back of her head nodded.

"Great. Boy genius got his boot off." Charlie's voice dripped with sarcasm. "Whaddaya gonna do now, throw it at 'em."

"Nope, but I might throw it at you after I get my knife out." Josh reached to the inside sheath and pulled out the flat blade of a thin knife. The handle was only slightly thicker than the blade, bound in a thin leather binding. The knife slid easily from an interior sheath Josh had custom-sewn into the boot. The ceramic material was chosen for its ability to evade security measures at airports.

Charlie sat up, grunting at prior injuries inflicted by Zhukov. Seeing the blade, he involuntarily smiled.

"Well shit 'n howdy. The boy's worth a plug nickel after all. But that's all."

"High praise," Josh retorted as he rolled over and cut through Sam's bindings around her hands. She yanked her arms apart, pulling the tape completely off one. "Now do me," said Josh. After she sat up, he gave her the knife and she returned the favor. Sam returned the knife to Josh. He reached down and cut through the top of the tape holding his legs and ripped it off. He handed the knife back to Sam and instructed her to cut the leg binding on only one side.

"Why?" she asked.

"We're gonna have to lay them back over to make the Russians think we're still hog-tied. After you're free, start on the others. Tell them how to put the tape back on and then remain on the floor. No talking, either. Our only hope is surprise, or a suicide charge."

Sam nodded and began cutting tape, "I prefer surprise."

The others were intensely watching this progress and started to gain hope they might get out of this predicament. Governor Fodor said in a loud and excited voice, "Me. Get me free next! I WANT OUT OF HERE NEXT!

"Shaddup!" said Charlie. "You're gonna blow our only chance if they hear ya."

Josh looked sternly at the Governor. "That's the first thing Charlie said I agree with. Now listen up, we can't just cut ourselves loose and head on out."

The Governor was shocked, "Why not! We're no heroes. You be the hero. I'm getting on that elevator and heading topside. Now cut me loose. That's an order!"

Josh glared at the panicked man. "I don't take orders from you, asshole. So get a grip or I'll leave ya tied up for when they come back."

"You wouldn't dare!"

Josh stood up and walked over to the governor. He ripped off a piece of tape from the strip that had been around his wrists. In horror, the Governor began to protest as Josh bent over and slapped the piece over his mouth.

Governor Hughes said, "Thank God. I was so tired of listening to that guy whimper like an old woman."

Josh smiled at him. "We're gonna get you out of here, John."

He said, "I have no doubt, Josh."

***

After they were all freed, Josh told them to stay on the floor and stay put. Leo asked why, and the others had the same question on their faces. "We go up in elevator before horses petuties return, Dah?" It was his best attempt at a Wyoming swear word.

Josh wanted to laugh, but shook his head and said in a strong whisper, "Nyet, Leo. We can't all fit in the elevator at the same time. It'll take two trips. That's nearly thirty minutes round trip for those not on the first ride. And they're bound to come back by then. I know you're all anxious to split. But I'm gonna have to ask you for a brave act, if all of us are going to get out of here alive."

"We're with you Josh," Sam said, trying to encourage the others.

"Now here's what we're all gonna do." Then he launched into his plan. Governor Fodor's eyes were big around as saucers. "You're all crazy," he tried to say through tape over his mouth. But it only came out as muffled gibberish.

"I'm glad you're with us, Scott." Governor Brigham smiled, looking over at him.

# Chapter 37

## Battle – Laying Out the Plan

## Situation Room, The White House

Rivera looked as if he were readied to deliver the nightly news. His hair was perfectly coifed, his face covered with makeup designed to smooth his complexion and provide a faux tanned look. A piece of tissue paper tucked round his neck ensured none of the cosmetics rubbed off onto his light blue shirt. His was prepared for a televised presentation scheduled one hour after the beginning assault on Wyoming. The White House consensus predicted an overwhelming victory in short order. Such heavy-handedness would be explained away in the President's address to the Nation as Wyoming being a run-a-way teenager brought home by the loving father. To Rivera and his advisors, this really wasn't a battle. It was a PR event and the Federal government had to appear the Good Guy. A quick victory would crush Wyoming's own projection, using Bascomb's words, of *David v. Goliath*. The majority sitting around the conference table had privately placed wagers among themselves as to the brevity of the war. Cecilia Pao was the most conservative, with the longest time of three hours. The rest jockeyed for numbers nearer two hours.

Declamore did not voice such bravado. His forces were arrayed against an unknown foe. Unpredictability was a potent weapon, and a cause for concern. His troops were essentially on foreign soil, fighting a rebel force.

Declamore addressed the assemblage with the strategy of a two-staged attack, one frontal and the other flanking. With the right flank assault already begun, he quickly described tactics. First would be the aerial bombing run of strategic targets as set by the White House. At the same time, the ground assault would step-off. Mobile heavy armor, meaning tanks, followed by light mobile infantry, the Bradley armored vehicles. Next up, the Strykers carrying the bulk of the force.

Once General Maxwell was assured the flank assault had broken through, a frontal assault with the main force would commence against the defenders of Cheyenne.

# Chapter 38

## Battle – Bringing Them Down Easy

## Wyoming

The thermometer had plunged below zero degrees centigrade from the daytime high. Yet Major James Dillon was sweating. He held a missile between his legs and was trying to pull the top, half-meter cone down onto the body. All but two of the modified warheads upon the DARTS missiles had been mounted. But now he struggled with the quarter-turn ring of the last two.

"Shit, did anybody check these out before hand?" he groused to the four State Army specialists ringing him. They all looked at each other accusingly.

A sergeant leaned out of the armored command post, "INBOUND!" he yelled excitedly. Jimmy kept trying to pull and turn the warhead while keeping the missile body stationary. He never broke concentration as he responded.

"Calm down, Franklin. Have you punched the target aspect into the DARTS tracker?"

"Yeah, Major, but there's a glitch somewhere. The tracker's tracking but the DARTS' module isn't accepting the download."

Jimmy groaned, "How far out?"

"They're just crossing over into Utah. They'll probably go supersonic here in a few minutes."

"How long till they're here?

"Five minutes, seven tops."

Jimmy barked at the specialists, "Someone grab this damn missile body and hold it tight. I'm gonna try pushing instead of pulling.

Two of the soldiers ran over and grabbed the missile from his hands. Jimmy told them to angle it towards him. He grabbed the warhead and pushed with all he had. The ring appeared flush and accepted the quarter turn with an audible click.

"Okay, you two," he pointed to the soldiers that had stood nervously by, "Grab this thing and load it." He pointed to the other two, "And you two, finish the last one the same way we did this one." Then he turned and ran up the metal steps into his Command Center.

Inside was packed an electronics jungle. Green and blue screens were the only illumination. Jimmy pulled a tech corporal up from his seat in front of a large screen. He jumped into the vacated seat and furiously began typing at, what he thought, an antiquated keyboard before him. His eyes bounced up and down the screen as code flew past his view.

"This 'C+++' language is the most archaic crap I've ever seen. I could write five hundred lines of this shit in ten lines of BLOCK." The soldiers nearby knew how tense the situation was because the Major never swore in their presence. Jimmy's fingers banged rapidly on the keys.

A lieutenant, viewing another screen shouted, "TWO MINUTES!"

Jimmy refused to be panicked. He was nodding at himself as his fingers furiously typed. "There it is. The synch command got crushed. Have it repaired in two secs." His hands were now flying over the keys. He dramatically raised his right hand and stabbed ENTER. The screen in front of him illuminated six blocks moving rapidly across a digital Utah. Figures and numbers scrolled beneath each tracked target. The two lead targets changed color, from green to red. A second later, the other four followed the same change.

Jimmy watched the screen intently. Without turning his head he ordered the Lieutenant, "Make sure those guys are well away from the launchers. They've got fifteen seconds." The Lieutenant bounded from the command post, cleared the stairs in one jump and headed towards the specialists.

Jimmy heard the tone through his NEU-Net connection, "Air-Stop One here."

"Major? General Roughton here. You boys grab that launch?"

"Yes, sir. In ten seconds we'll see if the hardware is successful. I only hope the missiles are more advanced than these electronics. Stand by General, here they come."

Jimmy ran outside. He stood there with the other soldiers, a thermo-detecting monocular to his eye, straining to catch a glimpse of the inbound targets. He knew they were too far away, too fast and too high for visual contact. But still he waited and watched. A second later, all twelve of the DARTS screamed out of their launching tubes. The battle would be at nearly thirty thousand feet. It was probably already over. Only the debris of war, or lack of, would herald success or failure.

The Lieutenant poked a pair of infra-red binoculars into Jimmy's shoulder. He took his eyes off the sky and accepted them. But before they could be raised, a flash of reflected light streaked earthward at a sharp angle. A vapor and smoke trail traced where it had come from. Jimmy 'netted' without verbalizing, "General, one on a trajectory to auger in about one-five-oh clicks from us. Wait a minute, here's number two and three, make that four, nope, now five and six. They're all heading in the same direction. Should be able to collect the scrap within a hundred square kilometers."

The General acknowledged, "We're tracking them now. Will send out recovery teams from here." His 'voice' became concerned, "What about chutes? Do you see chutes? We can't track them."

Jimmy was now holding the binoculars to his eyes, "Stand by," he replied. He positioned the glasses on where the white streaks had begun. As he scanned the skies, it seemed an hour had passed, although it had only been a few minutes. Then he saw a tiny blackish dot moving laterally against his glowing, greenish lense. He focused the glasses best he could, but his target was still too high for identification. He waited as it came closer. Then he recognized the black shape of a delta chute skidding in front of clouds.

"We've got one breaking through the cloud layer at twenty-five hundred meters."

"Only one?" came the disappointed reply.

"Hang on, sir. Two more, no make that three. Total of four so far." He paused, intently focusing on the area that had produced the first chutes. "There's five!" It was looking good, he thought. But number six was still missing and a lot hung on the recovery being a hundred percent.

"See six yet?" The General was as antsy as Jimmy.

"Not yet sir." They both knew the preferred outcome came with low odds. " Maybe we can just deny that there were six. We still have the five to parade out and …..Wait a minute sir. I might have seen something…." He refocused his glasses and willed his eyes to see any movement.

Jimmy's thought-vocal came through as a shout, "YES!"

"You see number six?! You see them all?" Fhe General asked plaintively.

Jimmy let the binoculars drop from his eyes and hang at his side. He smiled, "General, you need to send out the Welcome Wagon. We have six guests for dinner."

Jimmy mentally opened the band to his men nearby and reported the news. The men 'hollered' triumphantly and slapped their commanding officer on his back.

# Chapter 39

## Battle – Operation Buzz Kill

## Wyoming

The screens were filled with incoming bogies. They had been moved from Nellis and re-positioned at Minot Air Force base in South Dakota. Ben was aware of this from intelligence reports he'd received from General Toomey two days prior. With Jimmy's success in the West, Ben was confident his DARTS launchers could handle the air assault. On the screens he watched green boxes turn red. He could hear outside the missiles streaking into the starless night. The missiles were tracking across the same screen as the intruders. Even though the air battle was twenty kilometers away and five-thousand meters up, Ben saw the air battle in his mind, F-35's bobbing, weaving, climbing and diving in desperate attempts to escape their own country's deadly technology. The evasions were useless as one blip after another disappeared from the scopes. The air attack to destroy eastern Wyoming's Command-and-Control structure, as well as its anti-aircraft capabilities, was blunted.

It had not been done in a conventional manner as the DARTS warheads were non-explosive. Jimmy's genius had been tapped to provide a missile that attacked only the engines. It would not strike the plane tail, wings or fuselage if it could successfully match the jutes and jags or the pilot. In a remarkable bit of programming, the missiles overtook and accelerated beyond the targeted craft. Then, using directional nozzles the missiles performed an immediate one-eighty and attacked the divertless engine intakes. The missile warheads were made of a carbon-crystalline structure. Within the nano-carbon structure were industrial grade diamond particles. It was designed to fracture into a thousand particles with impact of the duct walls. The effect was to abrade and shatter the titanium turbo-fan blades within. The resulting destruction would be similar to a flame-out. At worst the destabilized and unbalanced engine would create such forces as to cause wing separation. The hope was that the pilot could bail out before the craft broke completely up and pulled him to his death. It wasn't fool-proof. But this was, after all, war.

Ben reported the initial success to General Roughton. The General was buoyed, but told Ben to remain alert and stick to the pre-determined game plan. He also reported that the Southern front was still quiet. So far the assumption that General Maxwell would await positive results of the flank assault was correct. Ben had previously asked General Roughton what would happen if the Eastern flank held the Federal Army. Would

Maxwell begin the frontal attack anyway? Roughton wouldn't even speculate. The probability of stopping the U.S. Army had been such a remote possibility it seemed pointless.

Phase two was now underway. Ground radar picked up the advancing tanks. Abrams were rolling towards them at nearly fifty kilometers-per-hour. In advance of this, Apache helicopters were scoped as they jumped up from hiding behind small hills, targeting tanks in less than ten seconds. This is all they required to get a fix on Ben's Abrams III's. Then the sophisticated tank killers could duck back down and fire anti-tank missiles from safety. Missiles streaked over Ben's head, heading ten kilometers to his rear. This is where the Abrams sat. At least it's where the Apaches thought they sat. As the missiles made contact, the deadly hunters had no idea they had targeted not tanks, but fiberglass shells filled with concrete, painted to appear as an Abrams tank. An interior void was filled with drums of gasoline and spare munitions. The turrets, incorporating steel tubing to resemble the 120mm gun, had been molded as a separate piece and filled with concrete to duplicate the effect of an explosion blowing a heavy turret straight up and askew from the tank body. The thermal signature of the rear engine was duplicated with the use of propane heaters and metal diffusers. All of this subterfuge now exploded in balls of flames, lighting up the night sky. The Apaches, infused with quick victory, begrudgingly followed orders and headed back to base. Something had to be left for the A-10's to strafe and bomb. Army personnel thought it would be good training.

The ugly, yet effective ground support planes sped towards Ben's line of troops, ready to annihilate every living sole via north-to-south runs along his line of dug-in troops. DARTS were ineffective at the near-ground level where these planes roamed. After the troops were eliminated, the 'Wart Hogs' were to take out the mobile CnC and anti-aircraft units that had been targeted originally for F-35 elimination. However, the anticipated cake walk came with some sticky icing.

Ben was standing outside the armored unit, looking towards the approaching A-10's when he heard an anticipated noise from above. He looked at his watch and was pleased with the arrival. They had made it in record time, none too soon to meet the attackers. The sound overhead was an ear-piercing buzz, as if a swarm a mile wide and a mile deep of five-foot long hornets were attacking. The dense, dark cloud dispersed outward left and right, forming a line nearly two miles wide. The throng buzzed along at one-thousand meters. It included hundreds of drone airplanes with long, metal, needle noses incorporating six, titanium, serrated and spiraled blades. Identical serrated blades, but flat, were imbedded into the leading edges the eight foot wing spans. The black, carbon fiber bodies glinted with tiny particles of diamond dust. A pusher prop at the back of the fuselage proved the source of the menacing sound. A black window above the nose covered the infra-red and thermal-vision camera. It was relaying internet images via a Chinese satellite back to a deep bunker command hidden outside of Gillette. Inside the bunker, youths aged twelve to sixteen, stared intently through dark glasses, their hands grasping a joy-stick controller. There was one exception to the age range. It was a very excited nine-year-old boy.

Ben received an excited transmission over his NEU-Net, "We see them, General! They're passing from Flight Level three and are leveling out nearly in front of us. I don't think they even see us!"

"Calm down, Bernie," ordered Ben to Jimmy and William's son. He turned and bounded up the stairs of the command unit. On multiple screens were split sections of the drones. They showed before them the greenish glow of the A-10's. Multiple images were lining up on the different turbines, using thermal imaging to hone in on engines. It appeared that Bernie was right. The large turbo-fan attack planes made no evasive action or attempted to break formation. One after another, the screen images went black as the drones disappeared, sucked into the vortex of enormous power plants. The force-of-impact combined with shredding of turbofan blades by titanium, carbon fiber and diamond dust gutted the A-10 engines. One by one the ugly war planes either crash-landed in the prairie or turned and limped back to base. As the planes disappeared from the radar screens, a cheer went up in the command room. Ben raised and lowered his hands in a quieting motion.

"People, let's focus. This is far from being over. We have troops and tanks heading this way at this exact moment. We need to be prepared."

Smiles disappeared and faces turned serious. General Warner gave a far-off look and broadcast, "Cadets, you did excellent work on the A-10's. They're either chewing dirt or are running for home." A huge yell came over through his hearing senses. Youthful hoots, hollers and whistles exploded in the Gillette bunker. Ben demanded silence over the communicator at least ten times before the sound subsided.

"Now listen up, Operation Buzz Kill is not completely over. Operation StinkBomb, get ready. You people have to deal with the helo-transports. We're gonna be busy with tanks in a few minutes. Are Bretling's Bombers ready?"

A young, female voice responded, "Loaded with stank and ready to lift off upon your command, sir."

Ben had to chuckle at this, "Okay, okay. Good luck. And if you're not a unit leader, keep off the frequencies unless it's an emergency. That includes you, Private Dillon. Am I clear?"

"Crystal, sir," Bernie said in his most serious voice. This made Ben shake his head while a grin spread across his face. He turned to study the screen in front of him. The fifteen large blips and the seventy-five smaller blips evaporated his smile. The Abrams were closing, with the Bradleys not too far behind. A voice rang out behind him.

"Sir, radar shows nearly fifty blips twenty miles out. Must be the troop helos."

Ben nodded, "The cadets have the remaining BUZZKILL in position. Major, where are we on SUNBURN?"

"Just got the Unibots off the *Gillette* for ROUNDUP, sir . *Casper, Cheyenne* and *Jackson* already off-loaded and are heading for SUNBURN positions."

"Good, Major. Keep the Unibots tracking the Bradley's flanks. The dust should obscure them enough that the helo's won't pick them up in this darkness."

A Unibot was built upon Dillon Industries' 360i Wheel technology. Josh would have recognized the weapon from his clandestine viewing at Jimmy's business. This was the product of Building Number Four.

It consisted of one wheel, about sixty percent the size of the car wheel, hence the Uni designation. Over the wheel was a half mating piece, similar to the carbon fiber wheel well utilized in Wyoming's hi-tech auto industry. Atop the well was attached a bell housing that contained multiple gimbles. The rings were not of bearing design. Instead they were rounded, made from a NASA-licensed material that was harder than diamond, smoother than any precision-machined bearing and self-lubricating. The gimble rings were of declining size, one sitting within the void of another. This gave the attached mast freedom of movement across nearly every plane. As example, the well could slide ninety – degrees to the side of the wheel and the mast could take any position from there. Around the bell housing rotated a slanted, digital camera ring. It wasn't a camera in the conventional sense. It was fifteen-thousand micro-optical sensors contiguously arrayed. The ring was fixed. But the Unibot had a three-hundred-and-sixty-degree view at all times. Any portion of the ring could provide day, night, thermal, or infrared vision simultaneously from different angles. Halfway up the mast and at its top were other gimlet-joints. The Unibot had more articulation to its mast than its model, the human shoulder, arm, elbow and wrist. At the top of the mast sat a platform for attaching various armaments or any desired appendage. A battery skin of Gaston Quick-Charge material covered the robotic soldier from top of mast to half-way down the wheel. Through the nano-structure of the frame flowed liquid nitrogen, a key element in providing directional motivation of the superconducting wheel.

With a top speed of forty kilometers per-hour, the Unibot had more acceleration, speed and agility than any NFL running back. Flexible feed-cartridges containing ammunition could be clipped along the length of the mobile arm. With liquid nitrogen flowing throughout, the Unibot ran extremely cool. It did not even register on thermal or infrared sensors. Even its fifty-caliber machine gun barrel was jacketed to run cool with nitrogen. Departing bullets and ejecting brass left a signature. But the Unibot fired on the run, making it extremely difficult to target.

Between the liquid nitrogen and electrical storage, the Unibots had a fifteen minute contact time at full speed. On the modern battlefield, this was an eternity. The core of the wheel contained gyros, microchips and uplink equipment. It maintained a constant satellite link with CnC, primarily to report hits, kills, position and condition of each unit. A Unibot communicated with other units via microwaves. For individual control, the Unibot had self-contained logic-and-learning processors that allowed instantaneous decision-making. Its mission parameters and decision templates were pre-loaded. Once the battle began, Unibots followed basic strategy but exercised its own tactics, constantly adjusting to the enemy's moves. When the Unibot ran low on power or munitions, it would automatically take itself out of battle and race for the nearest recharging/rearming station. Within four minutes a Quick-Charge would have it back in the game. It usually took longer to rearm than recharge. Initially only half the Unibot force would be committed. As one unit required recharging, it would broadcast its withdrawal from battle while another Unibot on the sideline would become its replacement. This tag-team approach allowed the Unibots continued presence on the battle field for as long as recharging stations remained functional.

Recharging stations contained tanks of liquid nitrogen along with water storage for hydrogen batteries providing electrical generation. The stations were built as compact as possible so that they could be transported by helicopter or truck to multiple locations throughout the battle theater. Placed on an all-terrain chassis and tires, the stations changed locations at irregular intervals to avoid potential sighting and targeting by enemy forces. Camouflaged, cool and independent in their operations, they required no human in attendance. The uplink gave CnC and the Unibots real-time on the station's remaining running time and number of ports available for recharge. This way the Unibot could chose the closest station or one with open ports. Additionally, CnC –Control and Command - had knowledge of when to replace a station. If a Unibot were damaged yet still mobile, it could elect to either park next to the station for pickup or make its way back to friendly lines, its decision based on self-assessment of damage.

The wheels awaited combat.

# Chapter 40

## Racing the Clock

## Down Under

When Sidorov and Zhukov returned they found all their hostages in the same place, lying on the cement floor, tape around their ankles and hands underneath their backs. Everything looked as before. At least at first glance.

Josh diverted Sidorov's eyes in his direction by barking his name, "ALEX!"

Sidorov looked at him. Josh, maintaining his prone position on the floor, had a plan, "Alex, I'll give you this last chance to surrender. You'll never make it out of here alive any other way."

The Russian agent was scornful in his response, "Yeah, right, Stillwater. You and what army are going to stop me? The cavalry isn't coming to rescue you, cowboy."

"Oh yes they are. In fact, they should be repelling down the maintenance shaft right now."

Sidorov snapped his head towards the open elevator. Seeing nothing, he slowly turned his eyes back to Josh, "Bullshit."

Josh tried to sound as confident and cool as his nerve allowed, "Don't believe me? Go take a look. They're going to blow the roof of the car. Open the back doors and see for yourself."

Sidorov wasn't buying it, "What are you up to, Stillwater?"

Josh, lying on his back to hide the cut tape, gave his best shrug. "Not much, under these circumstances. You've got me more trussed up than calf at a roping event."

Alex pondered, boring in on Josh's expressionless face and unblinking eyes. Then he spun on his heels and quick-stepped towards the elevator.

At this moment, one of the hostages in the middle row towards the back wall wriggled, trying to speak. But there was tape across his mouth. His words were inaudible. Zhukov knew he hadn't put tape over anyone's mouth. As Sidorov headed into the elevator car, Zhukov moved down the rows of hostages towards Scott Fodor. He pulled his weapon from his waist band and waggled it threateningly at those on the floor.

Josh's plan required the behemoth of man to walk by him, yet he was a row over, "HEY, UGLY!," yelled Stillwater. Zhukov reacted angrily by jerking his head towards Josh. "Why don't you pick on someone your own size, slash-face! You get satisfaction from beating up girls and wimpy Governors?"

Sam rolled her eyes, *Great, playground banter with a bully. This is so appropriate right now!* she thought.

Zhukov scowled at Josh as he stepped over Leo and into Josh's row. *Well, that worked good,* thought Josh. *He's coming over to kick the shit out of me. Now if Sidorov takes the bait, the games can commence.*

Alex pressed the button to open the back doors of the elevator. He slowly poked the barrel of the machine pistol through the opening. Then he followed with his head in order to look up the shaft, unsuspecting that a taekwondo master was atop the roof, perched upside-down upon hands gripping a safety rail.

Scar face had stopped next to Josh. He began to pull his foot back for a powerful side kick into Josh's ribs when Stillwater shouted, "THAT'S A DUMB THING TO DO!" At the same moment, Josh sat up and grabbed Zhukov's gun. In the corner of his eye he saw Charlie getting to his feet.

Josh was hoping to snatch the gun from the Russian's grasp, but the burly man stopped his kick and pulled away. Josh held on to the weapon with both hands and found himself jerked to his feet. He was now directly in front of Zhukov pushing the weapon down and away. Zhukov reflexively pulled the trigger twice, ricocheting bullets off the cement floor. Josh's hands sizzled with the heat generated by the muzzle, but there was no way he could let go. The size of the other man and the red in his eyes told him it was going to be tough fight. He had ridden bulls before, but never wrestled one.

Hiro, hearing Josh's cue, swung his body from above the roof. He shot into the elevator feet first, smashing into Sidorov. Releasing his hands, Hiroto's momentum catapulted his and the Russian mole's bodies out of the car in a tangle of rolling arms, torso and legs. Sidorov's gun skittered to one side. Hiro was having a difficult time following up on his initial attack as his arms were rubbery and his head dizzy from maintaining the handstand since Josh's first communication. His lightning speed was severely diminished. All he could do for the instant was to head butt the other man.

Sidorov absorbed the skull crack, but remained conscious. He punched Hiroto in the side rolling his body with the swing. The heap reversed as Sidorov was now on top. The Russian stretched to the side and retrieved his weapon. He was trying to bring it to bear on Hiroto when the Japanese freed a hand and jabbed a stiff hand into Sidorov's throat. The Russian mole fell backwards off Hiro, screeching a sucking sound while frantically trying to breathe through a partially crushed larynx. Again, the Japanese's body came flying at him. Instinctively, Sidorov raised the machine pistol and fired. It was on 'single-shot' but was enough to punch through Hiro with such forced that his momentum was diverted from forward off to the side of the Russian

Having put this surprise attacker out of action, Sidorov was trying to gain his feet to help Zhukov. Unexpectedly, again, he was hit from the side. Charlie Warner knew Josh only had seconds before the big man swung him into Sidorov's aim, or the Russian mole moved to a better shooting angle. Reacting, he charged the side of Sidorov, flinging both off their feet. The mole landed flat on his back, knocking the wind from him, but not his gun. One-handed, Sidorov pulled the barrel between them and fired. Blood gushed while Charlie's eyes opened wide with shock.

Josh's fight had turned into a wrestling match, not with a bull, but with a bear…a big, mean, pissed-off grizzly bear with a handgun. Zhukov had five inches height on Josh plus a hundred and fifty pounds. And it wasn't all fat. Josh caught a fleeting glimpse of Leo running away towards the safety of the experimental lab. *Glad for the support, Leo* flashed across Josh's thoughts.

A gun had gone off, twice, but Josh knew it wasn't Zhukov's as Josh still kept his hands gripped to the barrel. A woman screamed "NO!" Josh had no idea what was going on beyond his immediate predicament, as he had to remove one hand in order to counter Zhukov's massive arm squeezing his neck in a head lock. He knew he had only seconds to loosen the man's grip. It was a tossup if he was going to pass-out from lack of blood or lack of oxygen. He pushed his free hand between the Russian bear's inside crook of his elbow and his own face and felt blood start to flow back to his brain. But this didn't solve his lack of air. He was also losing the battle for the gun. Slowly Zhukov's massive hand was inching the barrel from between them and towards Josh's abdomen. In a desperate move, Josh picked up his right foot and slammed the boot heel into the top of Zhukov's foot. He felt a momentary letup on the gun and Josh used the instant to push it back towards Zhukov. Then he felt his opponent stiffen, release his grip on the gun and crumple to his knees, pulling Josh down with him.

Flat on the floor, Josh pulled at the choking arm. It had gone limp but was still pressing against his neck. He struggled out from underneath, clutching at the handgun and completely baffled as to what had transpired. Rising to his knees, he looked over Zhukov's motionless body and saw Leo standing behind, a lead ingot in his hands with blood smeared on one end. The little Russian had brought down the big Russian with a mighty blow to the head. Now it was clear to Josh why Leo had run into the experiment lab. He was in search of a weapon.

Leo was looking down at his victim, his breathing labored, "I bin wanting dis since Moscow. Pig!" He spat on Zhukov's back. Josh smiled at Leo and said as he rose to his feet, "Thanks, pardner. I'm sure glad you came to the rescue. I needed the help." Leo nodded.

The good feelings ended abruptly when Josh heard Sam sobbing. He looked away from Leo over to where Sam was kneeling by a body. Then he spotted Sidorov in the elevator, frantically pushing a button. But the doors didn't close.

"SIDOROV!" Josh yelled. He aimed Zhukov's gun at the mole. "Don't you remember? Someone has to press the button outside the cage. You'd think someone who's been here since the beginning would remember that little detail."

Sidorov was pointing his gun back at Josh. His eyes, wide with fear, were darting along the group now staring at him. He snapped his gun aim towards Sam. "Shoot me, Stillwater and I'll shoot your girlfriend. Now get someone over here to press that button. And do it damn fast!"

Josh knew it was a Mexican standoff. The big problem was that, with the explosives armed, there wasn't a lot of time for chit chat. At his feet, Zhukov moaned and began to stir. Josh moved a few steps away from the menace, along with Leo. The Goliath gained his feet slowly. He felt the back of his head and examined his hand. It was bloody. He looked at the lead ingot in Leo's hands and then up to the short man's face. His own expression contorted into a violent anger. Josh took a step between the two men and waggled the gun. "Get going Goliath before I let this gun finish what Leo started."

The big man looked toward the elevator and saw his compatriot still armed. Reflexively he stumbled towards the lift. "Hurry up, Zhukov" ordered Sidorov. We've got less than twenty-five minutes and this ride takes a while. Now one of you push that button or I'll spray the entire lot of you."

With both threats inside the elevator, Dr. Zhou, closest to the external button, looked at Josh. Josh nodded and the elevator doors closed, eliminating the first threat. Josh ran to the other side of the body that Sam tended. He assumed by her grief that it was Charlie. Now it was confirmed as he knelt down to the wounded man's side. "You shouldn't have done that, old man." Josh's words were with grudging respect to his nemesis. He inspected Charlie's condition and knew the wound was fatal. There was a hole in his chest with a spreading blossom of blood. Red liquid trickled from one corner of his lips. If there had been paramedic's on-scene at this moment, the old man might have had a twenty-percent chance of making it. But under these circumstances....

"Looks like I did it up good this time," Charlie coughed out the words along with a spray of blood.

"You'll be fine, Daddy. Won't he be fine, Josh." Sam's voice trembled with fear as she stroked his hair.

Josh reached under his shirt and began tearing strips from his T-shirt. Charlie slowly shook his head back and forth. "You got more urgent things to take care of boy. You got to save my girl from those explosives. Don't waste another second on me." His voice rattled through the blood filling his lungs.

Josh knew he was right. Sam looked up at Josh with tears streaming down her cheeks. She searched his eyes for some sign of hope. Seeing none, she looked back down at her father. "Daddy, you need to tell him, before it's too late." Charlie's eyes suddenly flashed with anger. "Tell Josh now, Daddy. You owe him that. You owe all of us."

The dying man struggled to shake his head.

"Daddy, if you don't tell him, I won't bury you next to Mama. And I'll tell him anyway."

Charlie exhaled a sigh of bloody mist.

"Tell me what?" Josh was completely confused as to what could be so important to garner a death bed confession.

Charlie dropped his head to the side, avoiding Josh's eyes. "I'm your Dad."

Josh thought Sam and Charlie were pulling some sick joke. "Yeah, right. And I wear ladies' underwear." It was all he could think to say.

"Your mom and I got together when Eleanor was pregnant with Ben. I was drunk and…." He was racked by a coughing fit. When he gained control, he turned his head to look at Josh, eyes welled with tears. "She was lonely, that's all, and I took advantage…."

His expression went slack, eyes still staring.

"Daddy, Daddy? DADDY!" Sam shook him gently. Then she dropped her head to touch foreheads with Charlie. Her shoulders shook with her sobs. Josh looked away. He was stunned.

Governor Brigham stood at Josh's side. She placed a soft hand upon his shoulder. "I feel like an ass, Mr. Stillwater, interrupting family revelations at death's door. But do you think you're able to turn your attentions to our remaining problems? Like how we can avoid joining your new-found father there."

Josh looked at Liz, then to Charlie's body, with Sam kneeling beside and finally, to the sea of fear-filled faces staring back. He pushed Charlie's confession to the back of his mind in order to focus on the problem at hand. He checked his watch, rose to his feet and nodded to Liz. "Okay, we've got less than fifteen minutes left. Leo, what did the explosives look like? Were they square or what?"

Leo shook his head, "Nyet, like sausages. Big, long sausages. In cloth bag."

Josh nodded, "Like what Alexi had in his arms when we first saw him down here."

Dr. Zhou was incensed, "I should have caught that. I was suspicious but did not follow on. How stupid of me."

"Don't beat yourself up, Doc. The guy was a mole with a helluva cover. I doubt he would have registered on the FBI's radar," assuaged Josh. "Now, Sausages it is. You all saw what they brought in. Go find 'em, rip 'em off and bring 'em back. Be quick, but be thorough. If those bags contain what I think they do, you leave one behind and we're all goin' to be toxic waste, if we survive the explosion."

Governor Fodor, who had finally been cut loose, was appalled. "What?!! Bring them back here. Why on God's green earth would we do that? We clear out a chamber, get behind the door and let the others go off. You're proposing we put it all together here in one massive explosion. I don't think that's very bright, Stillwater."

"Until this is over, asshole, I'm Colonel Stillwater to you. And let me tell you about those explosives. They are two-in-one. That means there's a primary explosion with massive concussion and then an explosive fireball. They will tear this place apart no matter which door you choose to hide behind. Then you will be enveloped in more radiation than Chernobyl. Sound about right to you, Dr. Zhou."

The Chinese doctor-of-physics didn't even bother to agree, "Let's go, now." He turned and started running. They stampeded towards the fission door while Dr. Zhou shouted instructions for two members to go to the fusion chamber. Josh shouted after them, "Leo, you and Governor Hughes stay here and help me." They both stopped their gait and turned back. Josh was tending to Hiro. He had first flipped the man over to check for an exit wound, and found it. *At least it's a through and through*, he thought. This meant the bullet had passed through Hiro's body completely, not leaving any lead or fragments within to advance lead poisoning. Josh tore strips from his T-shirt and began stuffing them internally into the wounds as well as bandaging Hiro's exterior. Josh barked instructions to Leo and the Governor while tending to Hiro. The two acknowledged they understood Josh's instructions, turned and ran towards the maintenance room next to the experiment lab.

Inside the maintenance room, the two scoured through metal shelves, cabinets and shop boxes, looking for Josh's requests.

"Found them!" shouted Leo excitedly. He pulled out two pry bars and a crow bar from within a metal bin.

Governor Hughes was looking through a cabinet, "And I've got the tape."

They ran back to Josh, supplies in hand.

"Perfect!" said Josh, as if they had just found buried treasure.

Josh took the roll of duct tape from Hughes, pulled out a long length and wrapped it tightly around Hiro's shoulder, overlapping the tape ends. "That should hold down his bleeding for a while." He stood and reached out to Leo.

Josh grabbed the pry bar and moved to in front of the split between the doors. He jammed his bar into the almost-seamless slot. It bounced off.

"Shit! Give me that crow bar, Leo. It has a narrower point." Leo handed it over. Josh speared the beveled point into the slot and found some purchase. He leveraged the bar some small degree to one side. The doors hardly moved.

"If you don't remember, fearless Leader, these are blast doors two feet thick. You really think you can overcome the springs that close them? Is this the best plan?" The Governor was losing faith.

Josh explained, "Just 'cause these doors are thick doesn't mean they put in massive springs to close them as well. Explosions push. They don't open doors. It's their dead weight we have to overcome. Now let's put our tug where our mouths our and we'll get 'em open. Alright?!"

Governor Hughes acquiesced.

Josh checked his watch, "I'm gonna spear the slot with the crowbar. The second I get it in a little ways, you two start jimmying the pry pars in. John, you go above me, Leo below. Ready?" They both nodded.

Stillwater took the crow bar back as far as his shoulders rotated in a straight line, and then, with a grunt, rammed it into the slot. He again leveraged the bar aside. The veins in his arms and neck popped. Movement was visible. The two other men thrust their pry bars into the slot. Josh removed his bar. He grabbed Leo's pry bar and told the Russian to go back to the lab and find the biggest hammer he could. Leo nodded and took off running. During his absence, individual runners were coming back from the vaults. They deposited bags near the elevator and ran back for more. Josh was heartened by the furious activity. He checked his watch, again.

*It's gonna be a horse race*, he thought.

Leo came huffing back. Out of breath, he said nothing as he handed the tool to Josh. He had done better than expected. It was a small 5lb sledge hammer.

"Good job, Leo." Josh patted him on the shoulder and turned to his pry bar. He held it with one hand while he wielded the hammer with the other. He drove the five centimeter diameter rod into the slot until the Governor's bar loosened and began sliding downward.

"Take it out," instructed Josh. The Governor obliged. With the weight of the doors holding Josh's bar in place, he grabbed the Governor's bar from his hands. "Now watch me or we lose what we gained. I'm taking yours and putting it against the front of the door on an angle and as far back in the door thickness as it will go without slipping. Got it?

The Governor nodded.

"Then I'll start prying, you grab your bar and go opposite of me."

Again a nod.

Josh started prying. The lower bar was loose. The Governor jammed it in almost to the end of the door and began prying opposite to Josh. To the Governor's credit, he was straining as hard as Josh. Both were groaning and grunting. The doors parted to about a third of a meter. Still straining, Josh shouted to Leo, "Put something nearly this width in the door way to hold them open. It's got to be strong or the doors will crush it. And hurry, Leo."

The short Russian man looked around frantically. He was about to run to the lab when he spotted something. "Dis?" he asked?

Josh wanted to smile, "Perfect, Leo."

Leo picked up the lead ingot he had smashed Zhukov with. He place it the opening, length wise. There was less than a half centimeter clearance on both sides. Josh and the Governor let the bars go slack. The doors slammed against the brick. It held them open with no problem. The Governor placed his hands on his knees to catch his breath. Josh knew there was no time for recovery.

He told Leo, "Grab these bags and start throwing them in the shaft.

"Where isk timer for explosion?" Leo asked as he tossed bags between the doors.

"Probably inside the bags. Some chip with an ignition on it, if I had to guess." They both talked as they threw.

"Den how we know when time up?"

Josh laughed, "Oh, you'll know, Leo. When you're standing in front of Saint Peter, it'll be a pretty good clue."

Governor Hughes glared. He did not appreciate the humor. Instead he was in a flurry of throwing bags into the elevator shaft. "If the doors and walls in this place couldn't hold back this explosion, then how do you think these blast doors on the elevator shaft will do?

Josh didn't pause between throws, "Because that shaft goes up nearly a mile and is nearly thirty meters square. Remember, it's a utility shaft as well as an elevator shaft. They run pipes and electricity inside it. That's a lot of space, volume, to dissipate the explosion. Hell, maybe it'll blow the dome off the top and relieve all the pressure." More runners arrived with bags. Josh knew everyone was well motivated.

Leo added his assessment, "Do not tink explosion will remove dome. Blow these doors before. That my calculation, if you correct with power of exploding."

"Can't argue with a math whiz. Probably so, but we're gonna be behind those doors over there. How does that calculate, Leo?"

Leo ran it through his head while continuing to toss. "Maybe so. Isk possible, I tink. Odds better now."

The Governor perked up at Leo's authentication. Josh thought, *Politicians always believe anyone with a title in front or behind their name.*

The herd was returning now, standing a distance from the diminishing pile they had made. Sam returned, dropped her bags and said to a tossing Josh, "That's all of it. Doctors Zhou and Bharat are going chamber by chamber to make sure and to close all doors. They've turned on the helium to force the oxygen out of the chambers. What do we do now?"

Josh kept tossing, "Get everyone through one of those doors. Personally, I'd pick the Fusion door. From what I've learned there's a bit less radiation if this whole thing goes south. But what do I know? I don't have Doctor before my name."

Leo said, "He is correct. Go behind Fusion door. We be there one minute."

Governor Fodor overheard the discussion. He turned and broke into a sprint for the Fusion-side portal."

The rest of the group followed at a quick walk. Governor Brigham said towards her front, "Always the hero, Scott. Always the hero."

Dr. Zhou and Bharat came running through the fission door. Their hands were empty.

"We didn't find any more bags. It's clean."

Josh nodded and asked if they had closed all the doors behind. They said yes. Then he instructed them, Governor Hughes and Leo, to get behind the fusion door. Hughes asked with concern, "What about you?"

"Don't worry, John. Just keep it open to the last second. I'll be there."

"This didn't salve Leo's conscience. "I stay and helps you."

"Really Leo, I've got it. Now move! That's an order."

Leo slumped his shoulders and shuffled in his slippers behind Zhou and Bharat. Governor Hughes was a step behind him. Governor Fodor had his head sticking out the narrow opening. "Hurry up. You heard the man. He's got it."

Josh grinned as he sat down on the floor in front of the elevator. *A born leader, Scott.* He braced his arms behind him and leaned back. He felt Charlie's body behind and used it for an anchor. *You're still useful, old man. Thanks.* Then he started kicking at the lead ingot, trying to dislodge it from between the doors. It didn't move. It was wedged with the weight of the both doors. He checked his watch. It was below a minute. There was no more time. He jumped to his feet, picked up Hiro in a fireman's lift and began running for the door, *the closed door!*. Governor Fodor made sure there was going to be no breach at the last minute. It didn't surprise Josh. He expected as much. He kept running but altered his path to the experiment lab.

# Chapter 41

## Battle -Operations Sunburn and Rolling Thunder

## Wyoming

"Tell ROLLING THUNDER to attack. Tell them to turn off their night scopes in two minutes, and be ready for daylight. And make sure SUNBURN is dropping down to effective altitude."

"Yes sir!" The Major turned and started barking orders. Ben had been working another twenty-four hours on adrenaline and little food. His legs were twitching and beginning to wobble. He grabbed a chair and sat down casually enough so as not to attract undue attention. It didn't bother him that he was a having a momentary body crash. It came with battle. He just wanted to make sure his mind stayed clear.

"Major Rawlings, we have any 24 Rush left?" The drink was a mega-dose of caffeine, amino acids and sugar. Ben had been living on it all day.

"Cases, sir. I'll get you a couple of cans."

Ben nodded his appreciation.

***

As the U.S. Army tanks neared to within ten kilometers of the Wyoming front lines, the flat plains on both sides became a little less flat. Operation ROLLING THUNDER burst into action. Camouflaged panels flipped over backwards and gas turbine engines fired up. In less than a minute four Wyoming Abrams III tanks on each side - eight total- clawed up ten-meter deep gully banks, pushing straight into air for half their length and slamming back to a horizontal plane, level with the sides of invading tanks. Immediately the Wyoming tanks, designated North One through Four and South Five through Eight, sighted and fired. Shells burst from cannon's end, followed by an attached cable. They screamed for nearly a thousand meters. It was a perfect firing. Eight of the fifteen tanks were hit. But there was no explosion. Instead, an arching, chaotic lightning storm engulfed each target. The U.S. Army tanks died in place. Engines shut down, electronics failed, lighting disappeared. They had been hit with an REMPS - Remote Electro-Magnetic Pulse Shell. The cable that was attached to the shell and uncoiled as it flew the distance-to-target was similarly attached to a connection in the cannon breech. Another cable, attached to the backside connection of the breech, led through the tank, outward a back port and downward into the gully where an enormous truck loaded with hydrogen fuel cells generated the pulse charge.

"RELOAD!" shouted each tank commander.

At this moment on the north flank, behind the Wyoming tanks, Operation SUNBURN appeared in full brilliance and intensity. It wasn't quite the sun, but it was a brilliant lightshow emanating from the side of two LTA ships. The Gillette and Casper were pouring all their wattage onto one side of each craft, creating a wall of light that blinded the night scopes of the Army tanks. The Cheyenne and Jackson were performing similarly to the south. Like a flash-bang grenade, it was designed to cause a momentary paralysis of the onlooker. This was to give time for reloading of the REMPS as it was not a quick task. One tank crewman had to jump out the forward hatch, shiny out to the end of the hot cannon barrel, break the cable-breech connection with a sharp tug and pull the spent cable out the six meter long tube. Then he would swing over the cannon, drop to the ground and scramble back into the tank. A new shell was loaded by then and its cable plugged into the breech connection. Then the crew could site, range and fire. It was a slow process compared to standard shell loading. It also forced the tank to be stationary while the man was outside pulling cable. And there were still seven U.S. tanks, mobile with live ordinance ready to fire.

One U.S. tank commander was so enraged by the blinding light; he popped the cupola hatch and fumbled for the fifty-caliber handle. Grabbing it, he lifted his body upright and started wildly firing upward. He had no idea what was generating the light. He just wanted to kill it. If it had been God displaying his brilliance, the Deity would have been stitched with fifty-caliber bullets. It was probably too risky for Operation SUNBURN to last for any time. But everything Wyoming deployed tonight was risky. The Gillette and Casper were now leaking helium at an alarming rate, fortunate that none of the stored hydrogen had been hit. Their engines wound up to hurricane force as they climbed up and backed away from the battle field. It was iffy if they could reach base.

Once the Army commander regained his sight he ordered the turret gun rotated north, directly at North One. On this flank, only North Three and Four had finished reloading the REMPS. They had already sited on two tanks, neither one of them the U.S. tank with his gun pointing north. The commanders of Three and Four gave their firing command almost simultaneously. Two Army tanks webbed with electrical charges and died. Their crews jumped from hatches, thinking they were sitting ducks for a follow-on shot.

North Two was having problems with the cable connection to the breech. Valiantly, the commander calmly told his crew to work the problem.

North One knew he was targeted. Instead of firing, he ordered their armor into reverse and backed up at nearly fifty kilometers per hour towards the gully. The tank's rear dropped off the edge, raising the tank's front upwards and exposing its underside. At that moment, a shell slammed into the tank's belly, flipping the metal beast straight up, back and down the ravine's side. It crunched, rear deck first, into the gully bottom. The rear-positioned gasoline tanks ruptured and were ignited by electrical arcing from the splintered cable. The crew was incinerated. The blazing inferno surged over the EMP generator truck, expanding hydrogen gas stored within tanks. The support crew, knowing the danger, ran in different directions. Two that made it up the gully walls and over the top actually survived the gas explosion. But they were machine-gunned by the U.S. tank that had initially fired. The explosion and resulting fireball swept up and over the gully bank and engulfed North Two. No crew escaped.

The remaining tanks, Three and Four, had no way to fire another round, even if they could reload quickly. The EMP generator was destroyed, making their shells useless. The commander of North Three barked to commander Four to high-tail it west, back towards their lines. It was obvious that both tanks would not escape. The Army tank that had done so much damage had rotated cannon and turret in hunt of new prey. Three and Four maneuvered in different directions. Four headed due west at full speed. North Three set a collision course south for the Army tank. The Army tank began to range and site North Four's escape, but a warning yell from a crewman deflected attention to Three's suicide charge. The U.S. commander ordered the turret to swing and site North Three. As the charging Wyoming tank closed within twenty meters of their adversary, the U.S. Army commander shouted with urgency, 'FIRE'!'' The range was so close that the gunner was able to target the Wyoming tank exactly where the top turret met the chassis deck. The explosion lifted the turret of North Three straight up. When it came back down, its broken 120mm gun drooped downward, like a knight's lance at rest. But the Wyoming tank kept coming. The driver of the burning tank was dead, his hands melted to the motorcycle-type T-bar handles, throttle opened full-wide. North Three slammed into the U.S. tank at an acute angle, the sagging gun barrel able to hit the front skirt and deflect sideways into the forward notch. This snapped the track retaining ring, and buckled the track off the front drive sprocket. The U.S. crew was alive, but their tank was dead.

On the south flank, all four Wyoming tanks were having better luck. Operation SUNBURN with the *Cheyenne* and *Jackson* had sowed the required confusion to allow all four tanks to reload and fire. The remaining four enemy tanks fell silent after suffering individual lightning storms. The Wyoming tanks had finished their mission. They and their EMT charging unit headed west as fast as possible. Phase three was about to begin.

Ben ran his hands through his hair. The loss of three tank crews was a crushing weight. He had been an officer his entire military tour. But he had been in Intelligence, where missions had put only himself in harm's way. He had never ordered other men into battle nor had to watch them die under his command. The full weight of being a commanding officer fell hard upon him with the first reported deaths. He had no fantasies that they would get through this scot-free. But he had hoped. Now reality set in. He knew all three crews. They had practiced and discussed the plan a hundred times. All of the crews were experienced in tanks. None of them were wild about using non-lethal weapons, especially ones that put them in jeopardy. The idea of flashing bright lights to delay the enemy firing was considered loony. Tank three Commander, Major Cummings was its strongest opponent. And he and his men paid the ultimate price for Ben's decision. It was only lack of a better solution that finally forced Cummings to go along. And now he was dead.

Major Rawlings laid a hand on Ben's soldier. "You have to forget it, at least for now. You'll have plenty of nights to remember this one. There are a lot more men and women depending on you than just twelve. Those tank crews probably won't be the last. You're doing good at a tough job, General. Keep it together and most of us will make it. That's what you have to focus on. Anything else means a whole lot more death."

Ben recognized that Rawlings knew of what he spoke. The officer had been in Georgia. He had commanded men that didn't come back alive. He was definitely right about this being a time to focus. He nodded to the Major and walked towards the bank of screens.

"What's the situation, Corporal?"

"Bradley's racing towards us. They stopped for a while at the tanks. Probably picking up stranded crews, or else wanted to know what the hell happened. Maybe both. Anyway, they're back on their horses and should come galloping our way in about fifteen minutes. We sent the Unibots to do some trail blazing, keeping them out of site. The helo's are sleeping in the saddle at four hundred meters above. Guess they don't want to do insertion until the troops crash into us with their shock and awe."

Corporal Donovan had a unique way of boiling down every situation to its simplest form, usually with several cowboy metaphors.

"When they hit the minefield, you reckon they'll dismount, cowboy?" Ben liked the cowboy talk. It took the edge off the seriousness.

"Oh, I'd say they're gonna take a break, have a sneaky-peek and then decide. Some of them green-brokes will charge ahead to prove they're bulls. Then, after a few of those mines turn 'em into steers, they'll stampede back, holding their balls in their hats. Least, that's how I see it."

Ben nodded. Donovan was another of his battle-hardened vets, twelve years a Marine. He was also a real cowboy. The catcher's mitt face and calloused hands spoke to years of punching cows. At forty-five, he was the oldest Corporal in Wyoming's State Army. He had turned down promotions three times, explaining that he always rode alone and didn't want to tell other men what to do. Ben finally convinced him to take the Corporal promotion over remaining a private by pointing out sergeants picked on privates and relied on Corporals. He would be left alone a lot more as Corporal than Private. This made some sense to Donovan, so he begrudgingly accepted the pay raise. Regardless of rank, though, his experience and wisdom commanded the respect due a Master Sergeant, even from other sergeants. Ben had come to appreciate and trust this man's military assessments.

"Major Rawlings, as planned, have those Unibots positioned when the advancing enemy arrives in front of the minefield. Also, tell the tanks that made it back to retreat to the furthest point behind our lines. Their of no use without conventional firing systems, so there's no reason to make them targets. Bring the conventional Abrams up and position them forward of the troops, between the lines-of-fire for the rear artillery units." Ben started to turn away, but stopped, "And Major,…."

"Yes General?"

"Tell all officers to remind their people that anything gets through that minefield,…. kill it dead, with real bullets and real shells. Non-lethal ends at that line in the dirt."

"Yes, General." Rawlings saluted, turned and issued commands to the staff.

# Chapter 42

## A Shocking End

### Above and Below

For Sidorov, the elevator ride was excruciatingly slow. He kept glancing at his watch, hoping it was accurate. Zhukov stood propped in the corner. His moans told the other that he had probably suffered a serious concussion. He was lucky to be alive. The blow from Leo would have killed anyone else. He was also lucky that Sidorov hadn't left him down there. Alexi just hoped that his generosity towards this ape hadn't killed them both.

Fifty-eight seconds left. *Maybe the elevator doors will buy me some time*, he thought. The whine of gears continued. Then there was silence. The car stopped. The doors opened. He was relieved to see the portal still open. He banked on being able to quickly exit the building. He ran from the elevator, through the door and was about to close it after himself, but was stopped by the view of Zhukov. The man had raised his head and was looking at him. There was no discernible expression. He just stared, a miserable creature in a miserable state. Sidorov sighed. He stepped back through the portal and started towards the wounded man.

Halfway to the elevator, the floor quaked. There was no loud sound, more muffled. But the jarring had been strong enough to knock him off his feet. Then pressure began to build in the ante room. Air rushed through the space around the car, a screaming whistle arriving like a train wreck. Sidorov turned round and, on hands and knees, scurried back towards the hatch door. He dove across the threshold, stood and began to pull the hatch closed. A spray of water pellets and steam shot at him like shot gun pellets. It knocked him backwards before he could close the door. He looked outward as a water column the width of the shaft shot the elevator car upwards beyond the opening. His last view of Zhukov was the huge man compressed against the cabin floor. He looked thinner.

The geyser diverted Siderov's way as he pulled at the hatch. He was fortunate to have the water pressure pushing against the door, helping him close it. He spun the wheel and collapsed to the floor sitting in six inches of water, leaning against the steel door. He was alive. He didn't feel lucky, he felt vindicated. He had pulled it off. The loss of Zhukov would not concern Moscow. They would probably be glad to be rid of the psychopath. With everyone dead, he was the only one to tell the story, to Moscow, and Cheyenne. Maybe he didn't have to defect after all.

The explosion was accompanied by the fire of Hades. It had roiled into the chamber with such a flash temperature that the lead ingot holding the elevator doors open was vaporized.

Instantly the doors slammed shut.

Finding no escape at the bottom, the fury found an easier path upward. But the explosion had also torn water pipes and valves apart. Millions of gallons of lake water poured into the utility shaft. Outgoing electrical transmission lines were rent from the walls. The water didn't extinguish the fireball that rode atop. The water closest to the fire became expanding steam, driving the column even faster. When it reached the elevator, it slammed into the car's bottom and shot it upwards like a bullet. Reaching the shafts top, the car broke through steel struts and the winch cables at top. Then it continued on into the concrete dome. Here the column compressed the car, crushing it flat. Somewhere inside, the crushed remains of Zhukov leaked. This was short lived as the arriving steam penetrated the smallest fissures and scoured the metal cube of any human remains.

Riding along with the current was a million kilowatts of electrical energy. The arcing waters searched out any grounding mechanisms, including the metal door that Sidorov leaned against. With his feet and bottom side completing the connection to the water on the floor, thousands of volts passed through him. His flesh burned, his skull and body burst and then he vaporized.

Moscow wouldn't be concerned at his loss either.

# Chapter 43

## Battle – Operation Roundup

## Wyoming

As the Bradleys neared the fifteen hundred meter mark, a booming voice reverberated from the dark sky. It sounded as if coming from the heavens. In reality it emanated from the *Cheyenne* and *Jackson*, both moving invisibly at two-hundred meters altitude; one a kilometer to the north; the other a kilometer to the south. The message had been repeating for the last five hundred meters of the Bradley's advance and, as well, was being broadcast to known Army com frequencies.

"HALT! YOU ARE ENTERING A MINE FIELD. TO AVOID HUMAN CASULATIES. HALT!"

This repeated over and over. Six-foot, reflective signs were posted every ten meters along the two mile front. A white line made from lime ran straight between the signs for an unseen distance both left and right. All signs delivered the same message, "MINE FIELD! DO NOT CROSS LINE! "

Ben was outside the command center. He had night vision binoculars pressed to his eyes. He saw that the Bradleys had stopped. He surmised they were probably getting a visual on the situation while contacting command for orders. Darting brilliances of light flared as Bradley twenty-millimeter cannons tore up the ground in front of them. Ben shook his head. There were nearly one million mines in the two-mile long by half-mile deep zone. The odds of taking out enough mines to clear a path was non-existent.

The day before this night, Wyoming Black Hawk helicopters, sporting multiple tubes from both side doors, had seeded the zone with pressure-plate screw-mines. 25cm's long, the mines had a tapered point with an auger thread shaped into the body. The mines were only 8cm in diameter at the upper end of the cone containing the point, and tapered inward to 6cm's at the top of its cylindrical shape. They were made from composite materials and, therefore, did not register on magnetometers designed as locators. Only two small components of the firing system were metal, too small for detection.

The mines were spewed from the helicopters via an automatic feed-tube with rifling to match the auger thread. They were fired towards the ground with compressed air from five-hundred feet up. Vertical stabilizing wings popped from the mines during their high-velocity descent towards the ground, snapping off with final impact, the mini-missile burrowing nearly 18cm's below the surface. The spinning auger thread was able to pass dirt up into the void of the tapered sides. Although nearly buried by its own dirt, the top of the mines still left visible depressions. After seeding, the zone looked like a prairie dog village. The final step was to run small ATV's over the mine field. Steel drag-mats trailing behind the vehicle filled the voids and erased visual evidence of the mines. A bar the width of the ATV and set upon wheels was attached by cable to the vehicle. It rolled behind the mat and emitted a radio frequency that activated the mine. Once 'ON', the mine could not be deactivated by the same method. It required a special key inserted into the top and turned a specific number of times and direction. Even with the mines activated, the ATV drivers had little worry of triggering one. The pressure plates required several tons to set them off. A division of men could walk across the mine field without detonation. This was as close as Ben could get to non-lethal and still provide some last-ditch protection for his own people.

Viewing the Bradley's attempts to set off the mines, Ben could only hope they would discover the futility of their actions before blowing themselves up. A few mines did explode, but it was insignificant to the total number that lay before the enemy.

At that moment four Bradley's, in unison revved engines. Ignoring all warnings, they plowed forward into the zone. One track-layer failed to have its entire length across the line before a mine blew off the left track. One by one, each vehicle was disabled, with the winner reaching an impressive thirty meters. The explosives were enough to disable treads, yet insufficient to penetrate belly armor. Slowly doors to the wounded Bradleys opened at the rear. First rifle barrels, then heads of soldiers peered round the sides of the vehicles. The twenty millimeter cannons fired to the front, with their commanders providing cover as troops ran back to their lines, paying attention to stay on the path the tracks had lain during the failed intrusion. When all troops were accounted for, the commanders made their way back from the individual wrecks.

One Bradley commander that had not participated in the initial folly became frustrated. He ordered his vehicle forward, careful to stay in the tracks of the disabled armor that had made the deepest penetration. Upon reaching the dead vehicle, he had his own Bradley creep slowly forward until the front of his vehicle made contact with the back of the other. Then he revved his engine and began pushing the dead weight in front. One, two, three mines detonated. The rear armored vehicle kept pushing.

Ben vacillated between admiration for this ingenuity and being pissed at the commander's obstinacy. Pissed won. He mentally barked and order through his NEU-Net connection. A minute later one of Wyoming's Abrams massive 120mm cannon recoiled after firing. The disabled and empty Bradley exploded upward, flipping backwards onto the pushing vehicle. Pinned in place, the creative commander gave up the hunt and ordered his men to make their way back to the others. Ben chuckled, but it wasn't a friendly laugh. It was obvious these troopers needed encouragement to turn around and go home. At this moment he heard the SuperHawks fly overhead. *Show time*, he thought.

"Captain Rawlings, send in ROUNDUP. Get STINKBOMB airborn now!"

The command for ROUNDUP sent the Unibots into the fray. From both flanks and rear, a thousand round wheels rolled silently into the Bradley group. They sliced between the Army vehicles. Some were upright while others wheeled round turns with their masts angled nearly perpendicular to the ground. The first wave was all-black. Atop their masts a twenty-millimeter cannon spewed depleted uranium rounds. Their aim was precise, directing shells into the turbo-diesel engine compartment as they sped by. Confused gunners within the transports tried to draw a bead with either the M242 25mm Bushmaster machine gun or the smaller 7.62mm M240C machine gun, mounted to the right of the Bushmaster. Neither armament could be brought to bear as the Unibots were less than a meter-and-a-half tall and kept close proximity to the Bradleys. The constant skittering, leaning, side shifting, and dodging wheels made targeting impossible. When a gunner let go with a burst, the Unibot was gone and, most often, another nearby Bradley would receive the brunt of the firing. Internal shouts of men combined with screams of 'CEASE FIRE!' over the radios caused guns to fall silent. Troops began the breakout from their disabled vehicles. Rear doors were thrown open and soldiers began spraying automatic fire as they disembarked. Rarely would a round hit one of the Unibots as they sped around a corner and weaved round another Bradley. The black-colored Unibots began retreating, but were soon replaced with white ones, a different specialized armament mounted upon its mast. The White Unit fired directly at the soldiers. Many thought they were dead, but most soon wished it so. All Unibot shots were aimed at soldiers' upper legs. The specialized bullets were hard and hollow, formed from a thermoplastic. The ends were rounded in a ballistic form, not sharp for penetration. A small amount of gel resided within the hollow. Upon impact, the rounded point penetrated clothing but not skin. The soldier's thighs were subjected to massive contusions with the added assault of a chemical spewing from the hollow of the burst projectile. The gel was a Wyoming-designed skin irritant that slowly spread 10cm's in diameter from point of impact. It burned to all-mighty, sometimes leaving a first or second degree burn. Then the wound morphed into a powerful itch. It was most debilitating. It had the added charm of scaring the wits out of the victim. The source and affect were completely unknown to Army medicine. So the sufferer thought he had fallen prey to a horrid plague. Instructions for effective salves would be eventually forwarded to Army medical personnel by the Wyoming government if the battle ended favorable to the State. But only after weeks of misery.

The State Army of Wyoming allowed the tormented troops to stagger the thirty-five kilometers east to their starting point. There was no reason to take prisoners. Streaming videos from the Unibots and Bascomb's running commentary was proof enough to the world of the U.S. Army's humiliation.

When the first wave of replacement troops in truck transports met their fellow G.I.'s staggering from the front in agony, a halt was ordered. Communications buzzed both ways between Central Command and commanders in the field. It was finally decided to halt in position until doctors, rushed from the rear, could make an assessment of the wounds. The medical professionals were stymied and recommended to General Maxwell not to incur further casualties until the victims could be studied.

The final phase, number four was now in full swing. With the loss of ground forces, the airborne assault forces felt honor-bound to snatch victory from the jaws of defeat. Without awaiting orders, the SuperHawks, loaded with Army Rangers, buzzed across the line, over the heads of dug-in Wyoming troops. As the helo's dove towards the ground, the troops readied to exit. Both sides of the helo's doors were opened. When the crafts hovered and dropped repelling line, surprise awaited. Operation STINK BOMB was underway.

# Chapter 44

## Angry Attacks

### Situation Room – The White House

The main body of the Army's force was now dependent on the Strykers breaking through. All at the conference table watched streaming video of the crews from the Bradley limping back towards the mechanized infantry division, vehicles abandoned. Cecilia Pao's wager of three hours appeared a winner. Unfortunately, the winner was the wrong side. The scenes projected along the walls dampened the President's hope of a quick and decisive win over the rebels. He was dismayed. On one of the several mounted screens surrounding the room, the play-by-play from Bascomb's internet feed was muted. Watching the whirling dervishes of attack robots demolish an entire force, Rivera's dismay congealed into anger.

"How in the hell can the most advanced military in the world be defeated by this rag-tag band of rebels?"

Cecilia Pao allowed a sense of history to overwhelm her mental filter, "I think King George asked the same question of Lord North after Burgoyne's army surrendered at Saratoga." Those who knew the details of the American Revolution admonished her quip with glares.

"I don't need your damn history lessons, Cecilia." She noted how Rivera had become increasingly profane as this Wyoming affair deteriorated.

"No, sir."

Rivera pulled his glare of Pao loose and deposited it on General Declamore. "I hope, for your sake, General, the Stryker assault is more successful. Either way, I want you to order Maxwell to stop pussy-footing and turn his main force loose on Cheyenne."

"I trust the judgment of my people on the ground, sir."

Rivera barked back at the General, "I don't. You order it or I will. Don't forget, Dec, I'm the Commander-In-Chief of the Army. You and Maxwell do what I say or I'll fire you both and find people that will."

# Chapter 45

## Baptism by Fire

## Down Under

The massive vault door on the Fusion side slowly came open. Leo peeked out and sniffed the air. Grey ash still swirled.

"I tink is OK," he said to the group. They pushed the door open further and began filing out. Leo looked at the elevator doors. They were bowed outward, but had held. Josh had been correct about the blast within the shaft directing its power upwards. The others followed, but stayed near the door. Leo and Samantha walked towards the elevator. High pressure water was spraying from between the bent blast doors.

Leo bent down and looked at some shiny material washed along the floor. He flaked a piece off and verified it was lead. It had to be from the lead ingot, he surmised. But he was trying to figure out why it was melted this side of the door. He held the flake up and turned to show it to Sam. But she was looking for another stain. It was the black smudge that had been her father. The water spraying forth had scoured the charred remains of Charles Warner from the floor.

"Oh, Daddy," was all she could say. Then she raised her head. Where was Josh? Had he survived this? Or was he wet ash, co-mingled with her Father for eternity?

"Didn't have time to drag his body away, Sam."

She spun around to the voice. Her heart jumped. Joshua Stillwater stood there, alive and in one piece. He was covered by some sort of ash. His head was bald and his eyebrows were missing. His face, scalp, neck and hands looked like he had suffered massive sunburn. He looked like a ghost. She ran to him and threw her arms around him.

"Thank God, you're alive!"

He winced at her embrace. His skin was burnt all over. She saw he was in pain so she released her arms and stepped back. Josh looked at the water spray and said, "I saw an acetylene torch in the maintenance room. I'll weld that thing shut. Should hold out the water till they can rescue us."

By now, the rest of the group encircled him. Fodor spoke first, "What the hell happened to you, Stillwater?"

"Glad for your concern Scott," Josh said sarcastically. He turned his eyes to Sam. "I knew I was out of time, so I picked up Hiro and scurried into the lab. I threw him into that space within the lead ingots, joined him and pulled some nonflammable  blankets over the top. When the explosion occurred, I felt the air pressure. Damn near blew my ears out. They're still ringing. Then the heat hit. God, it was hot and getting hotter. I literally felt like I was gonna cook. Then it started to let up, things started settling down and I decided to look around. Heard you guys talking out here. Still have no idea why the fireball stopped and why I didn't get fried."

Leo now understood the series of events. "You not able to removes the lead brick, Dah?"

"Dah, Leo," replied Josh.

"It melt in instant, look." Leo showed him the lead streak along the floor. "First heat melt it, den doors close. Save you from worst."

Josh was still looking at the floor. "Well, I'll be a monkey's uncle. Guess I'm the luckiest guy in the room." He tried to smile, but the crinkling of skin hurt.

Sam said, "I think I'd look in a mirror before you pass final judgment on that one, mister." She wanted to chuckle but thought it was completely inappropriate. She pulled out a small compact from her pants suit and held up the mirror for Josh to see.

That didn't stop Governor Fodor, "Yeah, you look like a hairless baboon that's been boiled."

Liz Brigham spoke up, "Thank you, Scott.  Your sensitivity shines through. How the hell did you ever get elected?

The Colorado Governor frowned.

Josh was also frowning. But it was at his image in the mirror. He said, "Could some of you go tend to Hiro. He's probably fried like me, not to mention the bullet hole in his shoulder. Might want to handle him easy. This hurts."

Dr. Zhou and two other scientists turned towards the experiment lab. Josh added a comment, "And if he's conscious, don't give him a mirror for a while. The bullet wound's enough to contend with."

Josh looked down at the smudge that was Charlie Warner. Sam's eyes followed. Josh said, "Sorry I couldn't save your Dad's body, Sam."

She looked up at him, "It's more important that you're alive, Josh, and Hiro. And remember, it's *our* Dad."

Josh nodded slowly, "Yeah, guess so. Kinda weird to think about it. Wish we could have had more time, ya know, to talk. Or to beat his brains out."

Sam weakly smiled, "It seems there's never enough time, Josh. We have to make the best........." She stopped midsentence.

"OH MY GOD!" she shouted.

Everyone jumped, including Josh, "What??"

"What time is it, quick, Josh?" He looked at his watch. But the crystal was cracked and the digital readout was black. Sam turned to Elizabeth Brigham. She quickly looked at hers and advised Sam of the time.

"I have to make a phone call right now! The fate of Wyoming rides on it. And maybe our lives!"

Scott Fodor groaned, "Again?"

She looked urgently at Josh. He shrugged, "I don't know this place. Ask one of them. Why don't you use your NEU-Net thingee?"

"Doesn't work down here. Too deep and shielded." She turned to Leo, "How do I make a call?" Liz Brigham had pulled out her cell phone. Sam shook her head, "Doesn't work down here, either. We need a land line. Quick, Leo."

"In da office. Over der."

The two took off running. Josh, Liz and the others followed quick step.


***

Sam slammed down the receiver in frustration. "Dead as a door nail."

Dr. Gleispach had an idea, "Please vait a minute." He ran out of the office and returned shortly with a laptop computer. "Ve should still have internet. Ve ran fiber opticz zown here at zee very beginning. A zeparate hole vas drilled directly down from zee offices on zee east zide. It vas an emergenzy backup. If zis place vent radioactive, our plan vas to back fill zee main shaft mit concrete. Ve vanted metering and meazuring zystems down zere to zee vat vas happening. So ve drilled a zeparate accezz und made zure it vas zealed."

"Great, Franz, now translate that into English and a phone call and you're a hero."

"I need a real long Eternet cable and zomething to get me up to zee ceiling."

"The ceiling? Like in this cavern? It's twenty meters high!"

Dr. Gleispach shrugged, "Bezt I can offer."

Josh sighed, "OK, get me the cable and tell me what to do. I'll figure how to get up there."

Sam looked at him, "You up to this Josh? We have less than fifteen minutes."

"Who the hell else is going to do it, Sam? Scott?" He snorted and began to walk out. "Come on Franz, tell me where to look and what's involved."

In the open vestibule, Dr. Gleispach pointed upward at three instruments fastened to the ceiling at the end run of a metal conduit. Josh studied the set up for a minute. There was a sprinkler line about a half-meter from the instruments. It was hung about the same distance away from the ceiling. Concrete anchors secured the run.

"Think that pipe would hold me?" Josh asked the Austrian scientist. He shrugged. Josh sighed.

He ran into the maintenance room that had saved his life. He looked down into the lead fortress and found what he was looking for, the

Markov he had taken off Zhukov. He snatched it up, looked quickly around the room and found what he needed.

He came running back with a coil of rope over his shoulder, a ball of twine in one hand and the gun in the other. He dropped the rope and twine on the floor, then ejected the magazine out of the gun. He thumbed out a bullet and held it up for the scientists to see.

"Can any of you drill a one millimeter hole across this bullet's diameter?"

They all looked at each other. No one volunteered. Gleispach said, "Zis zort of ting either a tech or Alex, eh, Alexi vould do for uz."

Leo spoke up, "Gives it to me. If bad Russian can do, good Russian can do."

Josh handed him the bullet and Leo ran back to the machining room. A few minutes later he emerged and proudly handed the bullet back to Josh. It had a clean hole right through its diameter. "I check with micrometer. Exactly one millimeters," said Leo. Josh had to smile at this, even though it hurt.

Josh grabbed the twine and cut off a lengthy piece. He fed the twine down the front of the barrel and out the opened breech. He grabbed the end, pulled it through the breech, and threaded it into the bullet hole. This took a few tries. He kept wetting the end with his saliva to get the fibers together. Finally he was able to feed it through. He pulled half of the twine through the bullet and fed the end back through the barrel. He popped the bullet into the chamber and closed it. He grabbed the two ends of twine sticking out of the barrel and secured both to the rope. Then he told everyone to stand back. There was going to be a ricochet and he didn't want anyone getting hit by shrapnel.

All were intrigued what he was up to. Some were sharing theories. Josh ignored them, raised his left arm sideways and rested the barrel of the gun in his right hand, steading the gun upon his left arm. He aimed carefully, knowing he was going to have to make it through the space between the ceiling and pipe. Then he slowly squeezed the trigger. The resulting bang made everyone jump. It was not only the loud sound, but frayed nerves from the recent battle with Sidorov and Zhukov.

The bullet raced towards the pipe and ceiling, twine being pulled upwards. The bullet went through the middle of the void, hit the ceiling and ricocheted downward. Josh, pleased with his aim, turned to the people around him and said, "Now go find me that bullet and twine."

Within two minutes Leo shouted from atop the dormitory roof. "I have twine, but bullet is buried into metal."

"Cut it, Leo. I just need the twine."

Leo said, "Someone gifs me a knife." Scott Fodor tossed one up to him. It was completely flat and a grey color.

"Hey, that's my knife! Wondered where it went to." He looked at the Governor. "Should have known."

Leo raced back to Josh, twine end and knife in hand. Josh put the knife back in his boot and, gently, began pulling the twine. The rope attached to the other end rose towards the pipe. Josh was able to get it over the pipe with little problem, and then pulled it down to the floor.

"Pretty slick, Josh. Just like James Bond." Josh smiled at Elizabeth Brigham's comment.

He tied knots in the rope and a large bowline at the end. He stepped into the loop, secured it under his rump, and turned to the group. "Now comes the death defying part. All of you get on the other end of the rope and slowly pull me up. You let go or slip and I will find you after I get out of the hospital." No one thought he was joking. "Now hand me that Ethernet cord and start pulling, smoothly. Each of you find a space on the rope and just start walking away. Shortest people on the end and tallest near me. Strongest man at each end."

Scott Fodor grabbed the farthest end. Josh grumbled "I said *man* Scott." Elizabeth Brigham chuckled. Leo grabbed the end away from Fodor and tied it around his body. He said, "If everyone let go, I must be lifted to pipe before you fall hard."

"Thank you, Leo." Said Josh.

They lined up, Leo at one end and John Hughes at the other with the balance in between. John had also tied the rope around his waist. This gave Josh comfort. The line started walking away. *Just like a line of boatmen on the Volga*, thought Leo. Josh smoothly rose towards the ceiling. When he was at the pipe he called a halt. He grabbed the pipe and pushed himself near one of the instrument covers. He ripped it off, found its connection, unplugged the cord and inserted the Ethernet end, listening for the distinctive click that meant it was secured. Then he instructed them to start lowering him. When his feet touched down, he generously thanked all.

Franz Gleispach had already plugged the cord into his laptop. After a few taps on the mouse pad, he turned to Sam, "Zee phone number pleaze." She smiled, looked at her cell phone and read it off.

# Chapter 46

## Battle – Operation StinkBomb

## Wyoming

Out of the darkness, large, black drones dove toward the helo's open cabins. Bretling's Bomber Squadron had been circling at a higher altitude than the helicopters' approach. The incoming choppers was being tracked on Wyoming radar. Now, several pairs of Wyoming night vision binoculars were trained on the descent. When the helo's cabin doors slid open, Senior Cadet Bretling was notified to begin the attack.

The bombers weren't of the small drone design. They were large, giant scale, RC - remote controlled - jets with delta wings nearly two meters in span. The nose of each RC was made of a clear crystalline. The planes angled downward and adjusted descents perfectly, shattering planes and nosecones onto the metal floors of the SuperHawks while knocking Rangers back into the cabins. Immediately a stench wafted through the entire craft. It was of such a potent, vial nature, most of the Rangers vomited immediately. Some soldiers were successful in pulling gas masks from kits. But even the smallest amount already inhaled produced waves of nausea, blurred vision and disorientation. Those that donned masks quickly regretted the action as their masks filled with vomit. Soldiers trying to escape the stench either jumped or rolled out of the crafts, falling nearly five meters. But escape was not possible as more stink-nosed bombers crashed nearby.

Even the pilots weren't immune, projectile vomiting onto their instrument panels as they struggled to land their crafts. After every helicopter was down, controls were abandoned, engines still running. Soldiers wearing Wyoming uniforms and full-face respirators calmly walked among the retching men, removing weapons and other ordinance. A few of the masks wore the blue of Wyoming's Air Defense. These trained pilots jumped into the helos and, where the few Army pilots had remained at controls, removed them at gun point. The blue-suits manned the pilot's vacant seat and flew the prized copters southwest to bolster Cheyenne's defenders. Of course the crafts would need a good hosing down before they were put back into service.

After the vomiting subsided, the Rangers were rounded up by Wyoming Army personnel, and led through the minefield via a contorted path, this to keep the illusion that even foot soldiers were susceptible to mine detonation. At the end of the zone, a hundred white Unibots took over escort duty.

General Warner had been watching the engagement outside of his command post. With exhilaration over the results, he bounded up the stairs and barked, "Reports!"

Major Rawlings turned from a screen, "They have the Apaches in reserve. And a division is still parked ten clicks away. I can't tell if this thing is over or we're just sitting through a lull."

Ben was chewing on this, "Donovan! Give me your take."

Donovan leaned his lanky body backwards, tilting the metal chair on two legs. He looked at the ceiling for a moment and then spoke, "Well, sir, I see it this way. They've been trying to rope a heifer and found out they've lassoed a bull. Right now they're trying to figure if they should uncinch from the horn and drop the rope or have the saddle yanked out from underneath 'em. I figure we ought to let them puking Rangers stumble back to the convoy. Should help with their decision making. Then we need to give them a parting gift to push 'em over the edge."

Ben stared at Donovan while he rubbed his chin, "The NLOS cannons?"

When Donovan grinned, the weathered face looked a mass of crevices, "That should end the cattle rustlin' with a necktie party."

Ben nodded, "Captain Rawlings, have the Unibots drop the pukes a click from the convoy. Recall all the wheels 'cept two to signal GPS coordinates and give us a video feed. Keep them to the sides of the shelling. Ten minutes after, order the NLOS cannons to start a creeping barrage from one click back from their formation. Ground impact only. I don't want any airbursts shredding their people. And throw in an illumination every third shell. Initially, four shells per gun, then keep moving it up ten meters per interval. I want the shelling coordinated so they are simultaneous. Should be one helluva show. Hopefully, that convoy slams it into reverse before we get too close."

"And if they don't, sir?"

Ben had a hard look on his face, "Keep creeping. We aren't playing chicken anymore."

***

At oh-four-thirty exactly, all eyes from the convoy snapped westward. Miles away thunder and lightning shattered the night. The soldiers thought it to be a massive thunderstorm. But the screaming of artillery shells dispelled the notion.

"INCOMING!" shouted several troops and officers in unison. A scramble for space underneath the trucks ensued. When the 155mm shells hit a kilometer away, the earth underneath jolted them for nine seconds. To those from the West Coast, it equated to what they thought an 8.0 on the Richter would feel. Before anyone fully recovered, another shell hit. Then a burst overhead illuminated the battle field like a strobe light. The pattern repeated itself four times. It was deafening, and horrifying. Then silence. A few troops braved a look with raised heads. But reprieve was short. Another barrage ten meters closer shook even harder. The explosions were of such power that showers of dirt and rock fell over the convoy. Twelve shells and four illuminations, then, again, silence. When it resumed another ten meters closer, a few soldiers jumped to their feet and ran east. Officers yelled threats after them to no avail. When the barrage continued closer, stationary soldiers began to think the deserters had chosen wisely. The Colonel in command began to question his own stoicism. Perhaps caution was required.

When the explosions closed to half the distance from their start, the sky was raining debris. It was becoming more than annoying. It was dangerous. Officers exchanged soft cover for hard helmets. Some of the troops had moved to the sides of the convoy and began to dig-in. The few battle vets reasoned that the trucks would be targeted first. Many of the greener troops agreed with this thinking. Officers were looking to the Colonel for orders. Their leader was shouting into his communicator, trying to convey the danger inching towards them. The full-bird Colonel bypassed his one-star commander back at the jump-off point. Instead he established direct communication with General Maxwell. At first, the battle-veteran had little sympathy for the whining of his field commander. War was hell and a good shelling made men from boys. Besides, the Wyomingans hadn't been lethal to this point. It was obvious they were avoiding U.S. casualties. It was for good press, the same reason his force sat idle south of Cheyenne, awaiting the flanking assault outcome.

*Pussies*, he thought.

His mind began to shift when an explosion heard over an open communicator nearly blew out his eardrum.

"Jeese, Colonel, how close is it?" The General's voice now contained some sense of urgency.

"Fifty meters, General. I don't think they're going to stop. If you want blood to justify your push in the south, I think you're going to have buckets full in about ten minutes! What's your order, SIR!" The last word was spit with disdain into the mike.

General Maxwell pursed his lips. Some fear and insubordination from his subordinates during battle was to be expected. It was up to him to decide if it was justified. Retreat wasn't in his vocabulary. But offering troops up as sacrifice in an untenable situation was anathema. He had been ordered to do this in Georgia, all for adding to his Commander's fruit salad, the metals worn proudly at White House receptions. He had sworn afterwards, never again.

Another ear-shattering explosion in his ear broke the thought.

"You think they're bluffing, Colonel?"

"NO I DO NOT, SIR!" The response was nearly a scream, yet barely discernible over the sound of shelling.

The General was under orders to follow White House directives in event of "major battle field developments". He raised his shoulders, puffed out his chest and said out loud, "Guess I'm just gonna have to convince the politicos this isn't 'major.' His subordinates stared quizzically at the outburst.

"Colonel, get your men out of there, post haste."

"YES SIR!"

\*\*\*

"They're bugging out, sir." Donovan pushed himself back from the screen. He crossed his arms over his chest in a self-satisfied look.

362

A holler went up in the crowded command car. Rawlings slapped Ben on the back. It was only one, but it was a hard, sharp slap. Ben winced.

"OK, people. Settle down. Nothing's for sure, yet. Let's be vigilant and keep an eye on the screens." Ben didn't take joy in dampening the celebration. But he was only cautiously optimistic. He wondered if Sam had made her call yet. Now was definitely the time.

# Chapter 47

## Make the Call

### Situation Room, The White House

Rivera's blood pressure climbed and his forehead sprouted in perspiration. The theatrical makeup covering his face heated his entire body. He mopped his brow with a handkerchief offered by Manning. The resulting mixture of sweat, makeup and swirling cloth gave his face a blotched look. He appeared demented as he spoke.

"I have never seen such incompetence in my entire life! You assured me, General, we would go through these forces like corn through a goose. I was supposed to address the nation thirty minutes ago. What the hell am I to say, 'Sorry for the U.S. Army invading one of our States. But we got the hell kicked out of us, so don't be mad. No harm, no foul.'"

He disgustingly threw the used handkerchief back to Manning. The Director of Homeland Security gingerly picked up the brown-stained linen with two fingers and discretely deposited it in a waste basket.

General Declamore sat through the hysteria with no comment. He was surely disappointed with his commanders' lack of adaptability to a changing battlefield. But in the recesses of his mind, he begrudgingly acknowledged respect for a resourceful foe. He actually felt sad for the Wyomingans. Because their flank had resisted brilliantly, now their Capital and its defending force would be laid waste. Regardless the loss, he knew defeat was not an option. The President's political survival depended on a victory. Declamore would not be surprised if the irrational leader ordered the use of tactical nuclear weapons. He was ruminating on this point when one of the President's aids walked past, towards the end of the table and whispered in his boss's ear.

Rivera instantly sat straighter. An evil smile tugged at the corners of his mouth. He scanned the faces surrounding the table with a fire in his eyes that all present thought had been extinguished permanently.

"I was just informed that we have the Governor of Wyoming on the phone. We must have bloodied their noses more than we thought, General."

Declamore thought, *Now it's We?* However, he wasn't buoyed like the President. The only bloodied noses were theirs.

Rivera turned to his aide, "Put him on speaker. I want everyone to hear him grovel."

"Her," said Secretary of State Pao.

"What are you babbling, Cecelia?"

"He is a she, sir. The Governor of Wyoming is Samantha Warner, a woman."

"Whatever," Rivera looked at his aide, punching the air with his finger, "Put her on."

There was a momentary hiss through the overhead speakers. Then a woman's voice spoke. It was clear, strong and confident. Declamore did not take this as a good sign.

"Good evening, Mr. President. Or should I say Good Morning?"

"Either works for me, ah...." He looked at Pao who mouthed a whispered 'Samantha Warner.'

"Sam," he said insolently. Pao, Fisk and Manning cringed at the insulting familiarity. This resulted in a momentary pause over the speakers.

"Yes, well George," Declamore struggled not to smile. He instantly liked this woman. "As our State has demonstrated a resistance to your invasion, I was hopeful that you might see the futility of further military action."

Rivera's creeping smile of evil had consumed his entire face, "Futility? Hardly, missy. Maybe a few nukes dropped on Cheyenne will demonstrate that our resistance against being dictated to by a piss-ant State is damn serious." He sharply dipped his head towards Declamore, emphasizing his resolve. Declamore just stared.

"I am truly sorry to hear you say that." Her voiced expressed sadness, not concern. This further bothered Declamore. He knew the nuke threat was not idle. This President was backing himself into a corner.

Samantha continued, "Then you have left us little option but to top your threat."

Rivera laughed scornfully, "And how do you top nukes woman?"

"With our nukes. In the slang words of men, George, ours are bigger than yours."

Declamore's placid expression showed cracks. The President scoffed, "I think the time for bluffing has passed, Governor."

Manning thought Rivera's use of the woman's title showed lack of certainty. He sensed the man's confidence had been breached.

"We are not bluffing. I assume I am on speaker and that General Declamore is present."

Rivera pointed a finger at the General. Declamore spoke, "I am, ma'am."

"General, would you please inform your President as to the significance of these two military bases: Warren and Minot."

Declamore's face paled. Rivera said in a clipped tone, "Well, inform me, General."

The General's posture relaxed. He knew they had just been checkmated. In one sense, he was relieved. No one was going to be throwing nukes around any time soon. At least not under his orders, "Sir, Warren and Minot are Air Force bases that control our Minute Men III launch sites. Combined they are responsible for approximately three hundred nuclear missiles."

"That is correct, General." Samantha continued, "And if you check with General Statler, I am sure he will verify that General Toomey, a Wyomingan by birth, is in command of Minot and General Thomas Grant, also a Wyomingan by birth, is in command of Warren. Additionally, the crews manning the actual bunkers are all Wyomingans as well."

Declamore spun in his seat and snapped his fingers at an aide. The Colonel dipped his head in acknowledgment and quickly paced to a back office. The General spun back to face the President, "I will have that verified quickly, sir."

Rivera's eyes were wild, "Are you kidding me, General? How could you let this happen? It's a conspiracy, a damn conspiracy. And you're part of it, aren't you?" His arm was straight out pointing at the General.

The calm voice continued over the speakers, "He had nothing to do with it, Mr. President. We have been inserting our people into key positions for years, ever since you reneged on every campaign promise you made to right the ship of our Nation. General Declamore did not become the military's Chief-of-Staff until two years ago."

Rivera's arm and finger was still quivering before him. General Declamore ignored the accusation. Instead he tried to gain the advantage, "And to what use are those missiles to you, Ms. Governor. Your people must realize that Central Command has control over them. You may launch, but the warheads would be cold, unarmed."

President Rivera dropped his arm. He began to relax back into his chair. He knew what the General was correct. He felt embarrassment at his outburst, but surely was not about to apologize.

"Like I said, Governor, nice bluff. But I'm tired of your games. Now here's how things are going to play out. First, your so-called army stands down and everyone goes home. That is, everyone except your officers. I want anyone higher than Sergeant to surrender themselves to the nearest U.S. Army personnel. Then,......" He was cut off by the speakers.

"Before you start dictating terms, perhaps you should hear some details of our control over the missiles. General?"

Declamore looked at the President for permission to speak. All he saw was Rivera's wild eyes returning. He spoke, "Go ahead, ma'am."

"We have interrupted your computer link to the bunkers. What your Command Center believes is a status response is actually a continuous loop that we programmed. Secondly, we have removed your warheads from the missiles, replaced and rewired them with ours."

Declamore was floored. When he found his voice he asked, "May I inquire where you came by three hundred MIRV'd – Multiple Independently-targetable Reentry Vehicles - nuclear warheads?"

Samantha knew that in order for her words to ring true, she would have to divulge some sensitive information, "I can only tell you, General, that we purchased the warheads from a foreign government, a government that supports our efforts and joins in our prosperity. I must, however, be truthful on one item. This government was not willing to part with their MIRV'd product. They did though, provide quite a deal on their older inventory of obsolete warheads. Being a thrifty people, we Wyomingans are always on the lookout for a deal."

General Declamore didn't know if to laugh or cry at this quip. Everything the woman said was not only possible, but plausible. His aide quick-marched back into the conference room, bent down and whispered into the General's ear. Declamore looked at the President and nodded.

Rivera was a cauldron of boiling frustration. He had to do something, say something. "Fine, Warner, you want to play it that way, we can play hardball too. I'll have the General here order an immediate bombing of those silos, followed-up with an assault from Special Forces. We'll have those missiles back under our control, or destroyed, before your people can even get them warmed up. That's a promise."

Declamore was trying to wave off the President's comment with one hand. He was not successful.

The Governor answered, "And here is my promise to you, Mr. President. The hatches on those silos are open. The birds are *warming up* as we speak. If we see one blip on a radar screen coming our way, we launch. And I guarantee you, that is no bluff. We have programmed our own targets, some domestic, some international. It might cause consternation within the nation's capital to know it is targeted. Also, you might want to ask Cecilia Pao what the Russians, Chinese, Iranians, North Koreans, Israelis, French and Brits might think about all this activity. I am sure they are reaching for their phones right now. Those most unfriendly to us will probably not even wait for us to launch. I hope the Situation Room doubles as a bomb shelter, Mr. President. I personally am about a thousand meters underground in a hardened cavern."

An aide to the President listened to his earpiece. He walked quickly to his boss's side and mumbled. Rivera listened and then looked at his aide for a long moment. "Jesus, put him on, right now!"

The aide spoke into his bone mic and then nodded to the President. Rivera grabbed up the phone receiver and tried not to sound harried, "President Win, good to hear from you."

"Win-Shi" mumbled Pao.

Rivera ignored her, "How is everything in China? Ah, no, I mean, yes, I , ah, well sir, you have my word those missiles are not preparing to launch." There was silence as he listened, "Yes, I understand your concern, sir, but it's just an, an exercise, like a training exercise."

Declamore shook his head and thought, *The Chinese President is not a stupid man. Countries don't open silo hatches and fire up ballistic nuclear missiles unless they're going to launch. What would Rivera's response be if the shoe were on the other foot? Immediate prep for retaliation?* At least he hoped it so. With this President, there was certainty of nothing.

Rivera kept up the stumbling dialog, "I understand. Yes, Mr. President, immediately. They will all be shut down and the hatches closed right now. Yes, I know the consequences." He held the phone for a few moments, stunned. Obviously the Chinese President had hung up earlier.

Samantha's voice came through the overhead speakers, "Seems you have a small conundrum, George. Care to discuss terms."

*Christ!* thought Rivera. *That woman is listening to every word I say. Am I completely surrounded by incompetents?* He glared at his aide.

"What do you people want? If you think you are going to secede, forget it. I'll risk your nukes against mine. Then you can explain why entire cities were destroyed along with the millions of people in them."

"We're not seceding, Mr. President. Now here are our terms."

***

The conversation with Governor Warner lasted another five minutes.

"That's all we want, Mr. President. We will know your acceptance or rejection by your first response."

Then the voice was gone.

The President's aide listened to his ear piece, "She hung up, Sir."

Rivera was a lump in his chair. He felt completely defeated. Declamore was first to speak, "Shall I order the stand-down, sir?"

Rivera didn't respond at first. He had spun his chair around backwards, not wanting to make eye contact with anyone. One arm flailed a loose wrist from the side of the chair, "Whatever," was all he said.

Declamore again snapped his fingers at the Colonel. The officer took off quickly for the back office.

Suddenly, Rivera spun his chair around. His eyes had gone beyond wild to maniacal. "What did she say?"

Fisk asked, "What, Sir?"

Pao flinched.

"That bitch Governor. What did she say about a bunker?" The President looked at Declamore. Rivera appeared unhinged. "Don't you get it, General? We know where she is. She's in a bunker. She's not in Cheyenne. She wouldn't be that stupid!"

No one in the room liked the tone of Rivera's voice. He sounded crazy.

Rivera had a look as if he had found the Holy Grail, "She's in that damn military facility, the one built with the mountains and lake. That's what it is, a bunker for all the leaders to survive a nuclear strike."

"We can't be sure of that, Sir." Declamore was talking low and calm, the way one would speak to a deranged person holding a weapon.

Rivera chopped him off, "Dammit, it's pretty obvious. That's where I would be." He slapped both hands on the table and grasped the edge as if he were going to fall off the earth. "I want it bombed the minute she shuts down those missiles and closes those hatches."

"What bombed?" Declamore was just stalling until someone helped the President collect his sea legs.

"The damn bunker, you moron. What? Are you stupid? Order it now."

The General surveyed the room, looking for someone else to start talking the President down from the ledge before he jumped. All eyes were either downcast or looking at him.

"Sir, that would be a direct violation of the terms you just agreed to with the Governor."

"To hell with her! I want that facility bombed and now! Use one of those bunker busting things your people are always bragging about. But order it right now, from this room."

Declamore looked down at the table and slowly shook his head, "I can't do that, Sir." He still kept his voice low while speaking to this mental patient.

"Then you're fired. Get out, NOW! I'll call Statler myself and order it. Get out of my sight, you worthless piece of Army shit."

General Declamore slowly rose from his chair. The Colonel aide pulled it back for him. Declamore snapped the ends of his tunic straight and came to attention. Then he slowly raised his right hand. Everyone thought he was going to give a final salute. In a way, they were correct. He stopped his hand half-way up and extended a middle finger to the President of The United States.

Cecilia Pao gasped and said, "Oh my."

# Chapter 48

## The President's Bomb Run

## Over Wyoming

Colonel Halverson ran the throttles of the F-117 to max as he crossed over the Colorado-Wyoming western border. He squelched the mike. As this was a NOCOM mission, meaning radio silence, he had worked out a system of squelches to communicate with his wing man, Lt. Colonel Brian White. The first squelch marked crossing into enemy territory.

The route of their Southwest entry to the State had been decided after the results of the other Air Force planes that had been lost during the night to enemy fire while entering Wyoming on East/West runs. The plane was nearly thirty years old and there had been advances in radar detection since its hey days early in the millennium. But its stealth design was still a potent weapon, except to a DARTS system. He had been briefed that Wyoming had hijacked four of the launchers. This caused him great concern as no one had tested the DARTS against an F-117. But with the targets being in the southwest part of the State, he felt confident they could make a quick, successful drop and beat it out before any SAM crews could react. This brought up another problem, the plane's speed, or more accurately, lack of speed. Flying at less than Mach 1, it was certainly not the fastest plane in the U.S. arsenal. No, mailing the package wasn't going to be the problem, he thought. It was the return postage that concerned him.

His Nav screen blipped that the target was nearing. He looked out the left side of his canopy as the target flashed by. As they were escaping the way they came, he would have to fly beyond the target some fifty kilometers before banking aileron left and pushing rudder right. This would reverse his direction and set him up for a north-to-south bomb run. Now abreast the target, White banked right, flew out fifty kilometers, U-turned and headed back for his east-to-west run. White's was actually the most difficult. He would fly across the two mountains, dropping two five-hundred pound JDAM's, one each into the center of the mountains. A military command structure was suspected of being housed within the mountains.

Halverson's run was not as technically difficult, but was deemed most important. He was to drop a bunker-buster into the lake in hopes that it hit some sort of concrete plug submerged beneath the water. The existence of the plug was theoretical and unconfirmed. But the President personally ordered this run, so he wasn't going to argue. He hoped the coordinates provided were correct. Apparently they had built the lake over a mine shaft some years past. The shaft had been plugged with tons of steel and concrete.

All he had to work from were photos from a second-rate eye-in-the-sky. He would make sure the drop was on the money. It was someone else's problem as to where they said the money was. Halverston maintained his course. He programmed in the coordinates. At twenty kilometers from target, he opened the bomb bay, flicked the cover from the arming switch and toggled it. At nine kilometers from target, he pressed the release button and the armed GBU-28 Bunker Buster sailed away. Immediately the plane jumped altitude, free from the 2000 kilogram weight of an ordinance packed with over 300 kilograms of explosives. He watched the screen as the laser-guided munitions fell towards its end. He made slight adjustments to its flight path until it was directly in the crosshairs on screen. He saw no immediate detonation when the bomb hit the lake water. Its fuse was set for the greater resistance of busting through six meters of reinforced concrete prior to detonation. A momentary whiteout on his screen indicated it had found the mark.

As he passed over the lake, Halverston saw White screaming towards the mountains. There was a strange beauty of precision to the two runs, one crossing over the other. Of course, beauty was probably the last adjective those on the ground thought. White released his bombs, a second after the first. Each hit their intended mountain. As Halverson banked left he saw the mountains heave upward and then sink back down. It was similar to a volcano exploding, except the top of these mountains remained. They created a valley down the middle of what, a moment before, had been the crest line. It was obvious to Halverson that, prior, there had been some void within the mountain. But now it was filled solid. He thanked whoever was in charge of the universe that he wasn't inside there. *Poor bastards*, he thought.

A stranger sight was the lake splitting in half and collapsing at one end. It appeared that a waterfall had been created. There had been no huge upward column of exploding water. *That's weird*, he thought. But his attention was immediately switched to a bigger concern.

An urgent beeping, than a horn blaring within the cockpit forced his attention.

"Son-of-a-bitch," was all he could say to the blip on his screen. A missile was streaking towards him. He turned west and began evasive action.

The F-117 could roll and dive with the best, but its climb rate was right there with its top speed: poor. He bobbed and weaved the craft, but the missile followed his jukes without hesitation. He knew he was toast. The only question was if he could eject before the toaster popped.

# Chapter 49

## Battle – Aftermath

## Wyoming

All were slow to return to their duties. They were tired and most had bloodshot eyes from staring at red and green blips for hours. Their adrenaline disappeared and lack of sleep was a weight, pulling them down. But they understood the commander's reticence to consider the battle over.

"Reports," Ben requested in a tired and unenthusiastic voice.

"Apaches left five minutes ago, heading south to the border."

"Convoy nearly to the primary staging area. Support units already on the move south."

Ben nodded, "When the convoy breaks south and is ten clicks away, then we can break the news to the troops, OK?"

Everyone nodded.

After the convoy passed the set demarcation, a cheer went up along the Wyoming line. Obviously someone in the command center had leaked the word. It didn't bother Ben. It was time for a quick celebration, self-congratulations and a lot of relief.

Now they had to pack-up and hustle south to be of aid to the Cheyenne defenders.

Ben walked out of the command center. He wanted to report in, but knew it would be difficult to concentrate over his staff's hoots and hollers. "General Roughton? Warner here."

"Yes, Ben. We were waiting for you to report in."

"I can report, sir, that it is all over here."

General Roughton chuckled, "Sorry to steal your thunder, Ben. We've been watching Bascomb's broadcast all along. Also, the Chinese bird overhead kept us posted on their troop movements. We're watching them stream south right now."

Ben replied, "That shouldn't make you too happy. You know they're gonna join up with the main force facing you."

"I'd agree with you, except I think your sister made her call. Ben, the whole damn force is pulling out! Loading railcars and heading south to Denver. We're having our own little celebration right now."

Ben cracked a large grin. *She did it!* he thought

"Ben?" the General continued.

"Yes, sir?"

"You were going to halt that bombing before you got too close, weren't you?"

Ben fell silent.

"Ben?"

Warner's voice was serious, "General, we'll never know the answer to that one."

Now General Roughton fell silent.

***

It was discovered later that the White House had been watching Bascomb's live feed and listening to his running commentary. One of Ben's staff had linked the Unibots' and drones' cameras as well as Chinese satellite images directly to the broadcaster. At first, Ben was angered by such security breaches. But then he remembered that this was as much a political battle as military, so he let the issue die. If the battle had gone the other way, all the American public would have seen would be Washington's sanitized version of a rouge State being spanked by the Federal government.

Bascomb's visual and auditory live record could not be refuted. There were no press releases or press conferences from the White House for over a week. When their silence was broken, all questions about The Wyoming Affair were met with "No comment." Bascomb's broadcast of the entire battle had the world deriding Washington's impotency and cheering Wyoming's cheek.

# Chapter 50

## Rescue

## Down Under and Above

After channels were dug within the valley to channel out the lake water, the debris of the metal lake bottom and supports were hauled away. Then the first step to rescuing those trapped could begin. This required the scientists below scrambling the reactors and shutting down turbines, thereby ending the electrical flow that made the water-filled shaft impossible for human contact.

President Rivera would have been incensed if he had known his bombing of the facility, though killing many workers within the mountain facilities, actually aided the leadership trapped. The bunker-buster had penetrated to one side of the dome, creating a five meter access hole directly into the flood chamber that Sidorov thought his haven. It blew apart the closed hatch, allowing tons of lake water to spill in and continue on into the elevator/maintenance shaft. Through the opening, crews immediately set to pumping out water. The largest pumps from mining and drilling operations throughout Wyoming were brought to bear. In less than twenty-four hours, one million gallons of water had been evacuated.

Next, the top, twisted wreckage of the elevator, elevator rails, pulleys and winch had to be cut away and new installed. As the extra-large elevator car was originally a special order from Shanghai, and had been installed prior to the dome, the smallest standard car was found that could fit through the hole and placed within the shaft. The original elevator system worked with a counter-weight that traveled the opposite direction as the car. Although a winch wound up cable at the top of the shaft, it was only a smaller-diameter safety cable. No winch system could have spooled the enormous-diameter primary cable over seven-hundred meters in length. The smaller elevator car did not reach the width of the pre-existing rails and was of insufficient weight for the counter balance. To compensate, steel was welded top and bottom of the car to span the distance to the rails and add the correct weight.

Once installed, the first car trip was with workers equipped to cut open the bottom blast doors that Josh had welded shut.

The last of those rescued arrived at the top and stepped out into the ante-room. The car held only Samantha Warner and Joshua Stillwater. They had spent three days below until rescue was possible.

Ben Warner and Jeff Dillon had been directing the operation. They were also the first to greet the survivors within the small room cramped with a cheering crowd. Ben walked forward, hugged his sister and then shook Josh's hand.

"Good job, soldier," he said grinning. "From what Sis has said over the IP, congratulations are in order for some fast thinking and a lot of bravery. Sorry we haven't stamped our own medals yet. Maybe you can help design one."

At first Josh laughed, then turned serious, "I think if anybody should get a medal, it should be your dad. Sidorov would have killed me if Charlie hadn't knocked him down."

"You mean *our* Dad, don't ya?" Ben had one arm around Sam's waist. He threw the other around Josh's shoulder and said solemnly, "Let's go home, Brother."

# Chapter 51

## Press Conference

## Cheyenne, Wyoming

From the U.S. were the six puppet networks and, internationally, three wire lip-services. Additionally there were news organizations from twenty-six countries, nine government-controlled services and over a hundred underground blogs.

Samantha Warner slowly mounted the stage, walked to a podium and tapped a microphone. She raised her fist to mouth, clearing her throat. Her fixed eyes speared the audience, jaw firmly set. The room full of reporters, camera men, lighting and sound engineers fell silent. She had no notes as she needed none. It was for their Citizens, for their allies, for other States, for the Citizens of the Nation. But, most, it was for Statesmen, wherever they survived. All the intrigue had ended. It was for her fellow Statesmen, wherever they stirred. Those that had purchase of shared ideals. She felt as Salisbury in *Henry V*, "God's arm strike with us! 'tis a fearful odds

"I am Samantha Warner, Governor of Wyoming. I am proud to be before you today. It is only by the efforts of hundreds of thousands of our Citizens that I stand here. I am sorry there has been a three-day delay from the recent, armed conflict to my appearance today. For those of you unaware, I was indisposed, nearly a thousand meters below ground with a million gallons of water overhead. I personally thank President Rivera for the isolation. It was his bombs that sealed me, and others, within. The resulting solitude allowed time to ponder my words today."

Her words, accompanied with a relaxed smile caused Ben and Joshua, both standing to the sides, to chuckle.

"I first wish to speak to my fellow Citizens of Wyoming. We are engaged in a war of which we did not instigate. We have been attacked by a corrupt government with no concern for its people, grasping at its last visages of power. The United States Federal government is a crumbling monolith that is the maker of its own demise. It has failed in every promise to its citizens. It has debased its currency. It has trampled human rights without regard to our common history that demands otherwise. It has failed to protect our borders. It has turned a blind eye to the Monroe Doctrine by allowing our enemies hegemony within this hemisphere, all the while executing wars far from our soil and further from our national interests. It has destroyed the once, greatest economy that our former enemies now strive to emulate. Where freedom and free enterprise once breathed opportunity for all, it has been usurped with the Socialist State's promise of *equality*. They achieved this one goal, for now all our countrymen share the same misery, equally. It has replaced hope with despair, freedom with despotism, safety with fear, learning with obedience, achievement with failure, culture with colloquialisms. It has turned countryman against countryman and has set families against themselves. Like the Roman destruction of Carthage, it has dismantled the shining city on a hill and salted the earth to bear no future harvest."

"Many have bemoaned the results of this betrayal, yet few have acted against it. One State, this *State of Mine*, Wyoming, decided many years ago not to suffer the agony any further. We acted. We were alone, but we acted. We fused our meager resources with our resourceful Citizens into an economic dynamo. We asked nothing of the Federal government, nothing from other States, except to be left alone to follow our dream. And when the dream became reality, Washington D.C. felt threatened. If one State could produce such a miracle against overwhelming odds and against an antagonistic government that worked towards its downfall, what would other States think? What if they chose to follow Wyoming's path? It would mean loss of Federal control, loss of Federal hegemony. And this was too threatening for them. Big ideas always frighten small men. And in Washington D.C. only small men are found.

So the locusts lording over the ant hill decided we could not exist in our present form one more day. At first they tried embargo. This failed. Then intimidation from the courts. This failed. Then terrorizing with Federal armies. This failed. Finally armed conflict. And this failed, but at a cost. Many innocent people died from this Federal invasion. They will be mourned by all of us left to finish what they began. I know what the survivors are feeling, for I too have lost. My Father was killed defending this State from enemies. He was a strength that buoyed us all, a driving force behind the creation of the new Wyoming,

We also mourn the loss of nearly one-hundred of the world's best scientists in the field of energy. Defenseless, unarmed, innocent to their pending doom, they were destroyed in a bombing mission at our Energy Development Complex. One of those killed was the nephew of the Chinese President, Win-Shi. Another was the daughter of the Israeli Defense Minister. To all of the relatives of our fallen comrades, we share your sadness, your loss. Nearly eighty percent of those killed were representative of our international partners. To all of these countries, you have our greatest appreciation for the ultimate sacrifice of your sons and daughters. We hope you have opportunity to express your deepest feelings with the man that ordered the bombing, President Rivera."

Josh and Ben glanced at each other sternly, appreciating her political acumen.

"These wonderful people's loss is of even greater sadness to us because it was so senseless, so unnecessary. After I personally negotiated with President Rivera an end to hostilities, he immediately broke the pact and ordered the bombing. It was his ultimate act of frustration. It was a temper tantrum wrapped in a lie. None of us should be a surprised, for Washington has lied and broken promises with the American people for decades. The blood of these good people is on the hands of President Rivera. Like Pontius, I can only hope he spends his end of days trying to wash it off. But he will never be clean."

When you realize that everything that emanates from our Nation's Capital is a lie, then, maybe, we will not be forced to present evidence in the world court of opinion. But for now let us provide some proof to dispel their lies.

First, the engineer, fireman and two soldiers in the front cab of the train we borrowed from the Federal Army were not killed as Washington claims. They stand before you today.

Sam turned sideways and introduced a group that was led onto the stage. It was Frank the engineer, Charlie the fireman, and the two soldiers Ben and Hiro had subdued. Camera strobes were set off like a lightning storm. Television spot lights blinded those on stage. Frank cupped his hand over his brow in order to shade his eyes.

"As to the twenty-four men within the accompanying troop transport car, they were disconnected and left to find their way on foot. I am sure with a little investigation you, the press, can find out where the Army is holding them in isolation.

To the pilots we supposedly killed,….well, I let you draw your own conclusions."

Twelve pilots, including Colonel Halverson were paraded forth. Their heads hung in embarrassment.

"We killed no one, in battle or peace, though we lost our own: three tank crews of brave men."

Ben nodded crisply, punctuating the point.

"All of these men are free to go."

"You are all probably wondering why a conflict between our State and the Federal Government exists. It is simple, really. We are tired of Washington's failures. We are tired of Washington's lies and we are tired of their intrusion into our daily lives. I would rather be a free Citizen of a lone State than an oppressed subject of the America that exists today. If a union of States will secure our liberties, then it shall be welcome. However, in its current form, such a union has proved contrary to the interests and freedom of our Citizens. It has become despotic.

Despotism takes many forms. It is not only the control of individual movements. It is control of our thoughts, our hopes. It is control of our economy. It is control of our future.

We founded this nation on the principle that such control is inherently evil. Our forefathers knew that our strength derived from the individual. And for the individual to contribute, he or she must be free. This means freedom of thought, expression and action. This means freedom to dream and to make those dreams a reality. This means freedom to reap the benefit of our labor and our capital. Conversely, it also means the freedom to hazard the loss of ill-venture.

Only when a people are free can their full power serve the advancement of society. It is soundly reasoned that seven billion people freely making decisions can surmount the problems of today with the solutions of tomorrow. The handful protecting their supremacy, cloistered within a citadel of power, issuing *diktats* that bring forth the destruction of our society, our culture, our economy; these are the enemy and surely need to be swept aside if we are to regain our destiny.

Our nation has been deemed the shining city on the hill, the great hope of democracy, the last, best chance for mankind. We *were* the standard to which those in bondage held their own governments. We *were* pointed to as the flame of hope that burned in the hearts of millions shackled within tyranny. Can we make claim today of these adulations? Sadly, no. The city on the hill no longer shines. It cannot even keep the lights on.

Montesquieu said *that the construction of the government should be suitable to the genius and disposition of its people.* It is our disposition to be free to build. Not to take from another without consent. Not to squander our seed-grain on immediate gratification. Not to place those who disagree with us into shackles. We *were* a people of genius. Look at what our ancestors brought forth upon this continent. We can be a people of genius again. All that is required is freedom.

Our Founders established an order of hierarchy nearly three hundred years ago. It placed the individual atop, the States second, and the Federal government last. This pyramid of power has today been inverted, usurped, destroyed.

How did this occur? Was there a coup, a thief in the night unaware to us, stealing our liberties? No. It was a slow process, incrementally stripping us of rights, gradually eroding our beliefs, our freedoms, our economy, and our national security.

But who allowed this? *They must be held accountable!"* Sam pounded the podium at this last statement, raising her voice, contorting her face with anger. But just as quickly, she returned to her prosaic self, voice lower, calm and steady while continuing.

"I agree. Perhaps we should inquire of our elected leaders. They must be the responsible party. They are the ones who passed the laws. But I ask every countryman; who put them into a position of power without demanding a reckoning? The answer is, *You.* It was *Me.* It was *all of us.* We may have been lied to. We may have been manipulated. But the truth is we wanted such. We wanted to receive something for nothing. We wanted solutions without pain or sacrifice. We wanted to be told that there would be a return to our former greatness through a continuation, if not acceleration, of the same policies that brought on the start of our decline: irrational spending, accumulation of increasing debt, burgeoning growth of an already massive Federal government.

And we believed it because we *wanted* to believe it. There were several elected officials, Statesmen that warned us time and again ours was a ruinous path. They shouted while standing atop their desks. But their voices were drowned out by our indifference. We found them annoying, out-of-sync, anachronistic, old fashioned, irritating. So we dispensed with them and replaced them with those that told us what we wanted to hear, those more appealing: adept speakers of lies packaged within heart-tugging emotions. They *appeared* competent for they were trained in hyperbole and scripted rhetoric, ready for any sound bite. We were enamored with the delivery, not the content of their message. It was style over substance, a problem pervasive in American society. They didn't govern because they didn't *know* how to govern. To govern on behalf of the people, one must be a Statesman. And a Statesman knows there are important times in a nation's history that political concerns must be cast to the wind in order effect the right decision. Instead, the politicians in Washington D.C. have chosen to cast our liberties, our future to the wind.

I may heap scorn on the leaders in Washington. But I remind all out there that it is up to each individual to be diligent in safeguarding one's own freedom. For if a nation of a people are not armed with constant vigilance, then the thief will come in the night. My countrymen, we were not vigilant. We allowed our Federal government, using force we approved, to relinquish our natural rights. And we did it for crumbs, literally. We traded freedom for a scrap of bread and a promise of a better tomorrow that never came.

Therefore, I ask everyone listening to now to look within. We allowed photo ops to replace town hall meetings, political machines to subvert participatory elections, puppet news organizations to handle our inquiries. Yes, we can blame elected officials, for this is the easier path. Introspection requires strength and, in this we have demonstrated a lacking. Remember, a people receive the government they deserve.

We in Wyoming have built a government we deserve, and one in which we are prideful. It has served us well. We invite those attending this press conference to stay and study our miracle. Visit our towns. Talk to our Citizens. Attend our State government assemblies. Participate in our Town Hall meetings. We are a State led by strong people with good ideas. And it is watched over, carefully, by a strong Citizenry. Our Citizens participate in this government in the knowledge that their voices will be heard at the highest levels. We are rich in more than that derived from a successful economy. We are rich in liberties. Even the few liberties we have truncated for survival as a united people was done so willingly and overwhelmingly. No one is forced to participate, yet the great majority does. No one is forced to help other Citizens, but the great majority does. It is our belief that, in time of common need, when our most unselfish gifts of time and treasure are called upon, we willingly provide. If the goal is clear, the cause just, and those first in authority are first in sacrifice, then Citizens respond. They demand one condition, however: ask; do not *order*.

This Federal government has not only ordered, not only demanded, it has threatened. It has imprisoned our Citizens. It has engaged us in armed conflict. The pyramid of our founders has been inverted. The Federal government occupies the top ninety percent, the States the bottom ten percent, and the individual excluded entirely, beneath the pyramid, shouldering the entire burden without opportunity of comment or freedom of action.

Acquiescence to tyranny means loss of our souls. And for us, this is intolerable. At the founding of this nation, another people of another time also found the situation intolerable. And they spoke eloquently. We hear the echoes of their anguish and the timber of their resolve through their own words, *The Declaration of Independence*. I read part of it to you now:

*That to secure these rights, Governments are instituted among Men, deriving their just powers from the consent of the governed, — That whenever any Form of Government becomes destructive of these ends, it is the Right of the People to alter or to abolish it, and to institute new Government, laying its foundation on such principles and organizing its powers in such form, as to them shall seem most likely to effect their Safety and Happiness. Prudence, indeed, will dictate that Governments long established should not be changed for light and transient causes; and accordingly all experience hath shewn that mankind are more disposed to suffer, while evils are sufferable than to right themselves by abolishing the forms to which they are accustomed. But when a long train of abuses and usurpations, pursuing invariably the same Object evinces a design to reduce them under absolute Despotism, it is their right, it is their duty, to throw off such Government, and to provide new Guards for their future security. — Such has been the patient sufferance of these Colonies; and such is now the necessity which constrains them to alter their former Systems of Government. The history of the present King of Great Britain is a history of repeated injuries and usurpations, all having in direct object the establishment of an absolute Tyranny over these States.*

All of the persons of the United States of America have long suffered these abuses. Wyoming decided nearly fifteen years past to suffer them no more. We have taken a path separate from the rest of the country and we stand today as a testament to this decision. Our Citizens are the most free, most prosperous, most educated, most fulfilled, most safe and most happy on this Continent. We are not mired in the despair, suffering and tedium of daily existence as are our fellow countrymen. We view each day with renewed excitement and challenge, ready to see what that day's test can be wrought. We say to our fellow countrymen, join us.

We have not made our stand for *light and transient causes*. We have made it for liberty.

We and you have *suffered a long train of abuses and usurpations that have envince[d] a design to reduce them under absolute Despotism.*

"As varied and wide ranging our grievances against the Federal government may be, I am sure each State could produce its own list. But if we catalogued our grievances, what to do with such a list? Deliver it to Congress and the President requesting immediate resolution?

Even though the subject is serious, I am sure many of you chuckle at such action. But I know it is a sardonic laugh, one inspired by the thought of such folly. Yet again, I ask, what should we do? And again, I turn to the Declaration of Independence, with amendment, for inspiration:

*It is [our] right, it is [our] duty, to throw off such Government, and to provide new Guards for [our] future security. — Such has been the patient sufferance of these States; and such is now the necessity which constrains them to alter [our] former Systems of Government. The history of the present [President and Congress] is a history of repeated injuries and usurpations, all having in direct object the establishment of an absolute Tyranny over these States.*

I remind all persons in this once-great country of the Tenth Amendment from our Constitution. I quote:

*The powers not delegated to the United States by the Constitution, nor prohibited by it to the States, are reserved to the States respectively, or to the people.*

Can anyone with a straight face actually agree that the Federal government has stayed within Constitutional bounds? Has adhered to this Amendment in, not only word but spirit of the law? Congress and the Executive have used the U.S. Supreme Court to nullify this Amendment.

There are those that argue some of our State's actions violate the U.S. Constitution. But can they truly expect us to abide to the letter of this legal instrument when the Federal government has so abused and ignored its words, its spirit? We base our responsibilities to our Citizens upon another significant Article of this same Amendment:

*We were founded as a Republic of States, not as a Federal system.*

This, more than any other part of the Constitution does Wyoming derive legitimacy of its actions. The Republic has been destroyed; replaced with a centralized, Federal system of no legitimacy. We therefore ignore it.

We say to you now that it is time for action, to throw off such a Government, to restore our a system of government that our Forefathers intended. I know such a view will initially cause consternation if not trepidation. But courage is called for, demanded. Our document, our history speaks to us about this moment, *accordingly all experience [has shown] that mankind are more disposed to suffer, while evils are sufferable than to right themselves by abolishing the forms to which they are accustomed.*

There is no need to suffer further. Remember this; individuals created our State governments and the States created the Federal government. Anything we make, we can unmake. Hence individuals and States can unmake the Federal government.

Of what do I speak? Secession? A Balkanization of the American continent? No. Nor do I envision new elections as solving our problems. We need to fix what has gone horribly wrong. What I am calling for, here, today, is a new Constitutional Convention. Every State can send two representatives. How they are selected is between you and your State government. Every State will be on an equal footing, Rhode Island with New York, Maryland with Virginia. And from this we will fashion a new Constitution, one pairing back an overreaching Federal government. And the first place I recommend is to severely restrict how the Federal government raises money and how it can spend it. But I will promise you one thing, I will never approve a system that allows the Federal government to print money or issue bonds. If you cut off the power of money, you have defanged the beast.

Now this may sound like a radical idea. We of Wyoming do not view it as such, for we have already transformed ourselves from a Federalized State to an Independent State, ready to stand with our brother States in equality. There is no need for radicalism. We have already taken that leap for you. All left now is discussion and consensus.

It may surprise most of you, but I have here a document calling for a new Constitutional Convention and signed by thirty-six of your Governors, odds are a Governor of the State in which you reside. Each one of these signatures is an act of courage. I have copies to give each press member today, so that shortly all will know who has signed. Do not besiege your Governor if he has not signed it for we have not made it available to all States until today. However, every missing Governor will be afforded the opportunity to sign within the next seventy-two hours. If your Governor is already a signee, please give him, or her, your greatest outpouring of support. After the Federal government makes contact, he or she will need it.

The next step will be for your State Legislatures to approve. We do not accept a requirement of the Federal Congress' approval, as corrupt institutions rarely call for their own demise.

Here I must provide a warning. Wyoming has gone a different direction than that which currently exists for the rest of the nation. If the sufficient number of States approve, then we will have a Constitutional Convention including all States. If States less than the amount specified approve, then we shall create a new Union with these. We prefer the former, but that is for you to decide.

I have taken a great deal of your time this evening, and I thank you for your attention. Everything from here on out will seem different to you. The sunrises will be dazzling, the sunsets calming, the day exciting, the night safe and warm. For tonight, we Citizens of Wyoming have shared our greatest possession with you, hope.

And so, I leave you now with the final words of The Declaration of Independence:

*And for the support of this Declaration, with a firm reliance on the protection of Divine Providence, we mutually pledge to each other our Lives, our Fortunes, and our sacred Honor.*

## Epilogue

The endless roofline of the Warner estate house on Five Fingers Ranch wore a thin blanket of snow. It was November and it was going to be a cold Thanksgiving. Inside the massive great room, the logs had burned down within the large, river rock fireplace to a pile of glowing embers. Of the three near the fireplace, none presently spoke. They were looking into the dying coals, lost in thought. Josh Stillwater sat in the overstuffed, leather chair that was, once, the domain of Charlie Warner. He slouched down with his legs straight out, one crossed over the other. His long arm was draped over the side of the chair. Near the floor, his hand held a highball glass of bourbon and branch water, slowly being stirred by wrist action.

Samantha Warner was sitting in a winged back chair, her feet propped up on an ottoman. She sipped a dry white wine. The chair had been her mother's favorite when she was alive.

Ben Warner stood to the right of the firebox, leaning against the thick mantel that ran the length of the rock wall. He was sipping Jack Daniels, Black Label and was first to break the silence.

"So, Josh, have you thought things over yet, as regards the family?"

"Still mullin'. Look, Ben, I'm really touched by yours and Sam's attitude towards me. I just feel like I'm a freeloader, that's all. It ain't my style."

Ben shook his head strongly, "You have as much right to Five Fingers as Sam and I. Probably more because of all the horse puckie you had to put up with along the way. And there's a lot more than just the ranch. Heck, Warner Inc. is energy reserves, energy generation, transportation and over a dozen other companies. We have a piece of Dillon & Dillon and Dillon Enterprises as well. Dad,...ah, Charlie, had his finger in a lot of things. And you are due one-third of all of it, period. If you don't take it, I'll be putting WC's into your account every month anyway. The least you could do is help out."

Josh sighed dramatically, "Okay, Okay, the way you say it, I'm a freeloader if I don't accept."

"Yep, so get used to it. And I want you to run the ranch along with your intelligence duties. Perky Fessler is an old man and he's been wantin' to retire for the last five years. With the money Charlie left him, he needs the time off to spend it before he's worm dirt. You always were the best cowboy among us. Even Charlie wouldn't refute it."

393

Josh nodded. This appealed to him. His first love had always been ranching. "Okay, that part I buy. Heck, I buy the whole package. You guys are too much." Josh's eyes began moistening.

"Oh, crap, don't start that again. We've all been drinking an' we'll be in our cups." Ben said, playing at being disgusted. "How about the name change? Josh Warner has a nice ring to it. Buys a lot of sashay in this State."

"No, that one I've given a lot of thought to. I am Joshua Stillwater. I can deal with half-breed better than bastard son. And knowin' it ain't so makes it an inside joke. 'Sides, Ben, the Warner name is Charlie's legacy to you. Whether he was a sonofabitch or not, he deserves that memorial. I'm already sleeping under his roof…." Josh took a sip from his glass, "….and drinkin' his booze. That'll give him pause enough to turn over in his grave."

Ben chuckled and nodded. Wanting to change the subject away from him, Josh turned to Sam.

"How's the States' votes coming along, Sam."

"We accomplished the mission today at 16:42 hours."

"And, what exactly was the mission again?" asked Josh, coyly.

"You know, smarty. Giving this Nation a new Constitutional Convention. And we did it with three-fourths of the State Legislatures. And I think we'll have 45 States before the Convention begins."

"Who's the hold-outs?" asked Ben.

"Well, New York and California are two. We sort of expected that. I am a little disappointed that Massachusetts voted nay. Maybe they'll change their minds once things get started. It would have been nice to have the original State that started the first revolution. Their loss."

Josh asked, "So what do you think Rivera's got up his sleeve. He's got to be seething by now."

"Russell Colter says he spends his days walking around the Oval Office either mumbling to himself or dictating new laws to Dormier."

"Get any of them passed?" Josh was concerned.

"Naw," chimed in Ben. "Forty-six of the States have recalled their Senators and Congressmen. There's no quorum. Every one's getting ready for the Convention first of next year."

"What about him using the military to create more mischief?"

Ben answered this one, "Declamore told Rivera he wouldn't resign and that it was illegal and unconstitutional for any President to use the military as a police force on domestic soil. The General is basically ignoring any direct orders from the White House until we get things sorted out during the Convention. Dec turned out to be okay after all."

"They settle on the Convention location?" asked Josh. "I know you declined it here. And, boy, am I glad." He was addressing Samantha.

"It's going to be in Missouri, actually just outside of K.C. in Independence. We thought it had a lot of symbolism. And we want our brethren States from the two Coasts to discover the other America, the one that gives them so much consternation." She looked at Josh, "So, what makes you happy about it not being here?"

"Security. I would have been responsible for all those politicians."

"Josh, I can truthfully say these people are going to be Statesmen. I have seen the list from most States. Debate should be spirited, lively and intelligent. Look at *our* selection: Milton Bern and Nevin Stiles."

Josh nodded and asked, "So, you just gonna throw out the Constitution and start over?"

"Heavens, no. We are going through the existing Constitution, line-by-line. Each line will either be left alone, amended or thrown out completely. Until, we've done that, there will be no new amendments."

Josh thought about this a moment, "Makes sense. At least you're keeping a frame work to start from instead of just anarchy."

"However, the absolute first thing that's going to happen is to negate Rivera's FCC rulings regarding broadcasters, repeal the Sedition Acts, disband the DDD, name a new Director of DHS, and throw out that law about U.S. troops operating on American soil. I'm already working behind the scenes and am nearing the two-thirds required before the gavel even slams down."

Josh laughed, "I'm sure you are. But if you get rid of all the bad guys, you're gonna end up putting a dent in Bascomb's ratings."

Ben spoke up, "Oh, I think Joe's going to be popular for a long time. We already have our people set to push the *Freedom Award* for him at the Convention."

Josh nodded his assent. "I still think you should have the Convention try Rivera for treason and hang him."

Ben disagreed, "We're all trying to keep this process on a high note. A trial like that would just pull things into the muck. Best off letting him serve out his term. He'll be toothless by the time Sam gets through with the States' business."

"Yeah, but he repealed the term limits for the Presidency. What if he runs again?"

Sam spoke, "I should have included that on my First list. That will also be nullified right out of the shoot. Besides, we probably won't elect Presidents anymore the way we used to. It certainly hasn't served this Nation well."

"Really? What would you replace it with?"

"Well, our plan is to have the States be the top dogs, again. There are a lot of options. We could have the Senators elect a President from their body, the way the country started. Or the President could be one of the Governors. Being President will not be the job it is today if we strip from the Federal government ninety percent of its power."

"How would it work? I mean would the Governors vote for one of themselves? Would you throw names in a hat? Would you each take turns at it?"

Sam casually said, "I think serving by reverse alphabetical order of the States has merit." She took a sip of wine and conspiratorially looked at her two brothers.

Ben and Josh looked at each other, thought a moment, and then roared with                                                                                         laughter.

**LOOK FOR THE EXCITING CONCLUSION TO**

# STATE OF MINE

# A POLITICAL THRILLER TRILOGY

## ARRIVING 2012